SAVING GRACE

SAVING GRACE

A NOVEL OF SUSPENSE

DEBBIE BABITT

SCARLET
NEW YORK

SAVING GRACE

Scarlet
An Imprint of Penzler Publishers
58 Warren Street
New York, N.Y. 10007

First edition

Interior design by Maria Fernandez

Library of Congress Control Number: 2020923824

ISBN: 978-1-61316-206-4

10 9 8 7 6 5 4 3 2 1

Printed in the United States of America
Distributed by W. W. Norton & Company

PART I

I was coming up on the anniversary of my parents' death when the girls began disappearing.

That summer twenty-four years ago, right before it all started, I was the one who wanted to disappear.

I nearly got my wish.

But three months later, I wasn't the reason for the panic tearing through town. I wasn't the one search parties went combing the woods to find, while folks prayed they wouldn't come home with a body to bury. It wasn't my face staring out from the missing children posters tacked to every tree.

That was when I really wanted to disappear, just vanish without a trace. A girl who was really and truly gone.

Because I knew that nothing I did would change what I'd done. I could repent for a thousand Sundays and it wouldn't bring back those girls.

Was I sorry?

I wish I could say I was. I know that I suffered. There were some in town who would say I didn't suffer enough. That I needed to confess, confession being the only true path to salvation. And they might be right, but I was too afraid to travel down that road.

That's what I remember most. Being scared. Scared I'd be found out. Scared of what I'd see in everyone's eyes if I told the truth. Scared of the evil that felt like it was part of my blood, something I could feel shifting and growing and pulsing like a second heartbeat.

I was terrified I'd burn in hell.

And I wouldn't ever be saved.

Church only confirmed my worst fears. I started to count how many times the pastor mentioned my name in a sermon. *Amazing Grace. The grace of god. God by his grace. The exalted state of grace. His eternal grace. Grace through faith. Fallen from grace. Grace as the only pathway to salvation. We are guilty and sinners without the grace of God in our lives.* And my personal favorite: *By how much greater the grace is, by so much is the punishment more for those who sin.*

One Sunday, he mentioned it thirty times.

By then I'd already decided I wasn't deserving of my name anymore. I told people they were no longer to call me Mary Grace. It was just Mary now, even if she was the mother of Jesus and pure in all things. But folks kept right on calling me by my two Christian names as if I hadn't uttered a word.

You have to understand, I was still a child. On the cusp of adolescence, but a child nevertheless, with a child's tunnel vision and black and white view of the world. You were either good or evil. The one elevated you to an exalted status; the other damned you forever. Your soul belonged either to God or the Devil. There was no middle ground. And our Baptist faith didn't give the lie to any of that. In fact, the Scriptures were most emphatic on that particular issue.

So there I was, a kid weighed down by guilt, terrifyingly aware that the wages of sin lead to death. I believed absolutely that I was going to hell in a handbasket. In other words, I was doomed.

What I didn't, couldn't, reckon on was the toll keeping everything bottled up would take on me. The years of wildness and acting out before I finally calmed down, surprising no one more than myself when I devoted myself—unconscious penance for what happened decades earlier?—to protecting my town and the lives with which I'd been entrusted. One life most precious of all.

Back then, when the wounds were still raw, I was also blessed with something else: a child's resilience. The ability to bounce back from tragedy. If anything was going to save me, it was my youth. I gradually began seeing the past not as an enemy out to destroy me, but as something finite and controllable, something that no longer had power over me and therefore couldn't hurt me.

The future, on the other hand, I saw as infinite. There I agreed with our pastor, although his take on it had more to do with the eternal and our ultimate redemption. For me, the future was laid out like a magic carpet that could take you anywhere. A place where hope lived and you could become anything or anyone you wanted. As the years went by, I began to believe, cautiously at first, and then with increasing velocity and faith, that I had a future.

Later, as I took on the responsibilities of adulthood and looked back from the vantage point of decades, I dared to believe I could find redemption. That I'd even be forgiven.

I should have known better.

Wickedness never goes unpunished. Sooner or later, the piper must be paid.

And I still didn't have the answers to the questions that had haunted me for twenty-four years.

Was it of my own free will that I journeyed down that sinful path?

Was there any point along the way I could have stopped it? Or was it already too late? Even before those girls vanished. Before my parents died.

Did evil choose me?

Or did I choose evil?

NOW

ONE

The summer of 2019 was sure to go down as one of the wettest on record.

It had been raining almost nonstop for more than two weeks across most of northwest Arkansas. The rivers and lakes had risen to dangerously high levels, and flooding caused the closing of dozens of roads. As is always the case, the smaller villages and towns suffered the most because there were fewer safeguards in place to protect them. The Repentance fire department had to evacuate one family from their home near a creek that overflowed, while felled trees and a small mudslide caused the partial closure of one of the town's busiest roadways. So far, no weather-related injuries had been reported, but motorists were urged to avoid driving through areas of high water. If it kept up, the governor would have to declare a state of emergency.

Those looking for signs and doomsday portents could always find it in the weather. As the winds blew and the rain poured down, some feared their town would be swept away on a rising tide of evil, the extreme weather signifying God's displeasure and his plague on humankind. They reasoned that evil could only gain a foothold because they relaxed their vigilance, a result of not praying hard enough. Others said it was a modern-day version of the trials of Job, a test of their fortitude and faith.

One thing all were agreed on: seventeen days of unrelenting wet weather had put a serious crimp in tourism, Arkansas's biggest industry, second only to the business generated by the Walmart empire in Bentonville. Every year folks traveled to this part of northwest Arkansas to avail themselves of the awe-inspiring wonders the Natural State had to offer.

And one unnatural wonder.

Strangers flocked to Repentance in record numbers. They eagerly lined up for the guided tours that many townsfolk were dead set against, unwavering in their belief that it was a sin to exploit the tragedies that had torn their community apart. But not even the most God-fearing among them could turn their backs on something that put sorely needed cash into the town coffers.

People came from as far south as Louisiana. They'd stand in that field and snap away with their cameras and later with their phones (even though by then there was nothing to see), their minds filled with what they read in the papers and online. In this case, it was the age of the girls that made what happened here all the more titillating and newsworthy.

The next stop was the cabin in the woods.

They'd also heard the stories about the wreck of a house at the northernmost edge of those woods. They'd stare at the sagging front porch with its rotting wood boards for signs of life as they passed, before continuing on to the cabin where they didn't even bother wiping their shoes on the welcome mat.

As the years passed, the numbers of thrill-seeking tourists dwindled as other, more sensational events took place. In the fall of 2002, there was a series of hate crimes in scenic Devil's Den State Park just outside Fayetteville, where gangs of roving tenth graders beat two boys to death for being gay. In Eureka Springs in 2010, the thirteen-year-old victim of an internet bully turned the tables on her tormentor, fatally stabbing her in the schoolyard as her stunned classmates recorded the bloodletting and carnage on their phones. And in 2013, a fifteen-year-old killed nine students and three teachers and wounded five others at a Little Rock high school before turning his assault weapon on himself, making it the worst mass shooting in Arkansas since the Jonesboro massacre of '98.

Not that Repentance hadn't seen its share of sorrow over the years. But there was nothing of man's hand in it. Those tragedies were more in keeping with the natural order of things. Though for folks looking for someone to point their fingers at, it was cold comfort. They couldn't very well blame the God they prayed to every Sunday at their local church. So when seventy-nine-year-old First Baptist congregant Abigail Gould, who suffered from Parkinson's along with failing eyesight, tripped while heading down her basement steps with the wash and broke her neck, they said it was *God's will.* When eighty-seven-year-old, dementia-addled Ethan Bilbrey sneaked out of the house one frigid February night and ended up freezing to death, they said it was *his time.*

But the death of Timmy Ray Clark on a warm, dazzlingly sunny April afternoon left a lot of folks scratching their heads because it went against the natural order. He'd just celebrated his eighth birthday, his parents would later tell anyone who would listen, between wrenching sobs. Some said it was the sun in his eyes, or the wind—especially strong that day—or a rock in the road that made Timmy Ray and his shiny new red bicycle go careening into the middle of the highway. They couldn't even fault the driver who hit Timmy Ray, killing him instantly after being unable to stop in time. And nobody was about to lay the blame at young, dead Timmy Ray's door. But his despairing parents needed someone to rail at, so they chose the Almighty, having lost their faith in a God who'd seen fit to take their only child. They moved away from Repentance a few months after the funeral.

The big news this July is the death of Parnell Vaughan II. His auto body and repair shop has been a fixture in town for decades, with the first shop started by his great-great-grandfather. Over the years, Vaughan followed a natural expansion into parking garages. He'd opened several in Arkansas towns, including Repentance, and was closing on one in Mississippi, the first out of state, when he keeled over in his usual booth at the Repentance Diner, landing face down in the sunny-side-up eggs he'd been having every morning for thirty years. Cause of death was a massive coronary and, because he was only sixty-three, folks were divided as to who was responsible. Was it really Vaughan's time? Or his own fault for clogging up his arteries by consuming too much cholesterol? But all were agreed that he deserved one hell of a send-off.

Parnell Vaughan II was the closest thing to royalty in Repentance, so a funeral procession has been planned down Main Street. As if ordained by God himself, the weather miraculously clears up, which is just confirmation for the folks who take the weather as a sign and proves what a towering paragon the deceased was. The whole town has turned out for the spectacle, with everyone craning their necks for the first glimpse of the expensive pine coffin that some already viewed at the First Baptist Church the evening before.

The pallbearers finally appear, led by Jackson Briggs, who has held the position of head pallbearer for decades. And he's not about to end that tradition now, despite the bad blood between Vaughans and Briggses.

Briggs's family goes back even further than the Vaughans. For decades, the two men have been locked in a dead heat as to who could get his name on more buildings in town. That terrible business back in '95 just added fuel to their decades-long feud. But ever since the new prison was erected last year, Jackson Briggs has had the edge. Briggs (no one is quite sure how he came by his fortune) may have most of the town in his pocket, according to the town wags.

But Owen Kanady will never be one of them. Tall and unbowed, he bears Parnell Vaughan II's casket easily on his shoulders. Sheriff Kanady is the law in Repentance, has been for over a quarter of a century, and that counts for a lot. He's not, as folks well know, a man who can be bought or sold. To the everlasting fury of Jackson Briggs.

Directly behind Kanady is Repentance's longtime pastor, Josiah Mills. Older and less fire-and-brimstone these days, he shoulders the casket that holds his old friend with a solemnity befitting the occasion. Across from Mills is his longtime ally Samuel Mathews. Uncle to Mary Grace Dobbs, he has been selling Bibles across most of northwest Arkansas since long before his niece was born. Behind Mathews is Landon Willcockson, Vaughan's nephew on his sister's side.

Standing next to her daughter, Mary Grace has eyes only for the last pallbearer. She stares at the familiar, beloved face as if she didn't just see him at church yesterday.

At thirty-eight, Parnell Vaughan III is as achingly beautiful as ever. The sight of him now, in his dark mourning clothes that are a counterpoint to his fair beauty, with the gray at his temples just adding to his allure, once again fills Mary Grace with a rush of emotions. She ignores the whispers in the crowd, already knows the rumors that Vaughan and his son were at odds, which has only given rise to more rumors about whether Parnell Vaughan III will take over his father's business. He's been managing the Vaughan Garage ever since he came back from college fifteen years ago.

The procession is nearing now, Parnell almost close enough for Mary Grace to reach out and touch. He's the reason she stood in front of her mirror for hours yesterday, something she rarely does. She has never been comfortable with her looks, which she always found average at best. Yet there she stood, already late for the wake, trying to decide between the only two dresses she owns, finally settling on the one that showcased her long legs—her best asset.

She even went so far as to apply a touch of blush and lipstick, something she does even more seldom than wearing a dress, which opened up a whole other can of worms when her daughter asked if she could wear makeup too. Mary Grace might be more lenient than is wise when it comes to her only child, but on this she stood firm. Twelve was too young to be thinking about such things, even though Felicity pointed out that she'd been a woman for the past three months and had the agonizing monthly pain to show for it.

From there on, it only got worse. On the receiving line last night, Mary Grace approached Parnell, thinking this was the time to finally put all the bad blood behind them. As she stood in front of the man she'd loved most of her life, she repeated the condolences she'd just said to his stricken mother and sister. Mary Grace knew how it felt to lose a parent, even if her folks had been gone a long time. You never get over that kind of loss.

"Thank you, Mary Grace."

The four words—the first Parnell had spoken to her in two decades—were a death knell in her ears. He didn't call her "Gracie," the longtime nickname she allowed only him to ever call her. Instead, he uttered her two Christian names with no emotion, his face stony, hands stiffly at his sides. So different from the last time they met, that terrible encounter in the woods twenty-four years ago. Yet in spite of everything, she still hoped that with time they could get past the tragic events of that long-ago November and begin to move forward. But there are some wounds that won't heal, some sins that can never be forgiven. No one knows that better than Mary Grace.

The procession is passing by now, Parnell's blue gaze fixed straight ahead. His features could be carved from stone.

Then he's gone, and Mary Grace feels the loss in the very marrow of her bones. It's as if something precious has been taken from her, something she can never get back. She feels numb as the procession winds down to the end of Main Street, turning onto the village green. There, the casket is placed into the waiting hearse for transport to Repentance Cemetery.

Mary Grace would rather skip this part. But given her position in town, her absence would be conspicuous and sure to be the subject of the evening gossip session. So twenty minutes later, there she is in front of the open grave, standing next to Owen Kanady, mind wandering as Pastor Mills drones on about what a wonderful husband, father, and pillar of the community Parnell Vaughan II was.

Despite the light drizzle that begins as the service ends, Mary Grace decides to check on her parents' graves on the other side of the cemetery, where the regular folks are buried. Sure enough, when she and Felicity get there, twigs and small branches from fallen trees nearly obscure their headstones. As she clears away the debris, Mary Grace pictures the headstones that will one day be placed next to her parents'. The two plots Mary Grace bought for herself and her daughter lie empty now. God willing, it will be years before her body is lowered into the earth, next to her daddy. And Felicity's decades later, if she has anything to say about it.

The natural order of things.

As she straightens, Mary Grace hears the reedy whistle of the wind blowing through the trees. Means a heavy rain isn't far behind. During the funeral procession, the sun seemed to actually peek out for a few seconds. God showing His face, Mary Grace can imagine the believers among them saying, their faith steady and unwavering. A part of her admires that, the kind of faith that comes from a clear conscience.

That's when she feels it. A shuddery chill down her back that has nothing to do with the weather. If she believed in signs, she'd say it feels like a ghost walking over her grave. Her skin erupts in gooseflesh, dampness pooling under her arms and behind her bare knees. She experienced something similar about a week ago. Bolting up in bed in a cold sweat, heart racing like a runaway horse, her body wracked by a nightmare she couldn't remember. She feels it now, only stronger and more insistent.

Something stirring.

She can smell it on the rising wind as it lifts the fallen leaves and creates swirling eddies of fog that blanket the cemetery like a shroud.

Things starting up again.

She looks over at Felicity, who's texting on her phone as usual, oblivious to matters of life and death. Which is as it should be. Mary Grace feels a fierce, protective love for her daughter at that moment, almost violent in its intensity. Felicity looks up. Her eyes—the same hazel-specked-with-gold as her mother's—fix on her, as if sensing what Mary Grace is thinking. It's always been this way between them, her daughter attuned to her every mood. As if they share some preternatural bond.

Felicity is frowning now. Mary Grace smiles to ease her anxiety. Her young life has been untouched by tragedy, unlike Mary Grace's at her age, and she intends to keep it that way.

The wind has picked up and the rain is really starting to come down. Mary Grace curses herself for leaving her umbrella in the car as she hurries her daughter out of this place that holds Repentance's dead.

But death isn't done with their town.

On a gloomy, overcast day in early August, an aneurysm in Owen Kanady's brain ruptures while he's fishing on a rare day off. This time, there's no procession down Main Street. But twenty-four hours after Kanady is laid to rest beside his wife Sheila, his chief deputy Mary Grace Dobbs is sworn in as the first female sheriff of Repentance.

Mary Grace is still grieving the loss of her friend and mentor when the Devil comes back to town. He shows up just ahead of a storm front that lights up the skies with the most spectacular display of God's fireworks anyone ever saw, and folks are sure to be talking about it for months to come. His arrival sets tongues furiously wagging, some wondering how he managed to slither back in without their knowing. Others insist the Devil's been here all along, which makes still others question why he would be here all this time without making his presence known. But all agree it's a sign. And everyone knows that bad news always travels in packs of three.

True to his name, the reappearance of Darryl Stokes in their midst ignites anger and outrage. Mary Grace feels just as outraged as everyone else, but it's mixed in with another emotion.

The guilt that's been dogging her heels for twenty-four years.

THEN

TWO

All Alone in the World

The summer of 1995 was one of the hottest anyone could remember. The heat wave stretched across the entire state, setting a record for the longest number of days of ninety-plus temperatures since Arkansas started keeping records. We hadn't had a good rain since late June, which was weird because we usually got hit with a number of thunderstorms being that we were smack in the middle of Tornado Alley. But this summer, the land was parched and the fireball of a sun was stripping everything of its natural color. We'd already had two wildfires and everyone was afraid the next one—unlucky number three—would do permanent damage.

It didn't stop the tourists from descending on our corner of the world by the car and bus loads.

Hot or not, it was high season in our tiny town of Repentance. Blink and you might miss it.

Summer was when we got the most visitors because kids were out of school.

And it was usually pretty damn spectacular, too, when we weren't in the middle of a dry spell. Then the grass was laid out like the greenest carpet you ever saw and the lakes and creeks overflowed with water so crystal clear you could drink it.

When it was like that, there was no other place on earth you'd want to be.

At eleven, I was still in the throes of a passionate love affair with my town. The only talk of evil was in church on Sundays when Pastor Mills railed about how it was the root cause of all human suffering because we were born in sin and you had to repent if you wanted to be saved. I didn't understand how repenting was going to help if you were already doomed from birth.

When I had asked my daddy about it, he smiled and told me not to take the pastor's sermons too seriously. I started to ask if that was the case why did we have to go to church every week, but just then my mama walked in and my daddy clammed right up. Still, I thought about what he said, and decided he was right. When Pastor Mills went on about hellfire and eternal damnation, it felt like he was trying to scare religion into us.

But for the past eight and half months, I'd started to take those words to heart. My folks were dead and nothing would ever be the same.

The place I was headed for that scorching summer afternoon wasn't on any guided tour. You had to squint to see, what with the haze covering everything and the exhaust from the cars turning the land into one giant dustbowl. It didn't stop the tourists from snapping pictures and oohing and ahhing over every little thing. I just trudged along, thinking my private thoughts. A couple of times in the last few months, I'd feel the weight of my sorrow starting to roll off my shoulders. Then all of a sudden I'd remember, and my heart would sink like a stone.

That day, I was feeling pretty good, not minding the hot sun and thinking how soon I'd be settled in that cave eating the sandwich waiting in my backpack. Until a family stopped me to ask directions.

It was a mother, father, and a girl who looked about my age. Then I saw a boy running up. I always wanted a younger brother to hike and climb trees with, but my folks said I was enough for them. I didn't believe it and remember thinking in the ways kids do sometimes when they sense someone's lying to them that it was because my mama couldn't have any more children. That would explain the way I used to catch her looking at me sometimes, like she was sad she couldn't give me a little brother.

The sight of that family really tore me up inside.

After I gave them directions, I continued on my way and felt that hard knot in my chest harden a little more. Then a prickling behind my eyes, which could have been the heat or the dust. I blinked a couple of times, but my eyes stayed bone dry.

I never was one for crying and didn't shed a tear at the funeral. It was a few days after Thanksgiving and freezing outside. But most of the town turned out because of who my daddy was. I could feel them all staring like there was something wrong with me. Just because I couldn't turn on and off the waterworks like Chloe Ann Briggs. But I knew what was keeping those tears from flowing out of me. It made me want to jump into those frozen graves next to my parents. Only my uncle's hand pressing down on my shoulder stopped me.

There were other times when the grief was a living thing inside me, like a wild animal trying to claw its way out. It would get so unbearable I'd run off, but I never got farther than the town limits. One time I tried hitching a ride, but someone must have seen me because the next thing I knew, the sheriff's cruiser was pulling up next to me. Sheriff Kanady said I shouldn't be upsetting my aunt, especially with her condition. I wouldn't get into his car and started kicking up a fuss like a regular hellion, yelling that he shouldn't be messing with me but catching the one who killed my mama and daddy. It took the sheriff and his deputy both to get me into the cruiser.

I'd calmed down some by the time they drove me back to my aunt and uncle's. It was while Chief Deputy Wood walked me to the house that he told me running away never solved your troubles because you carried them with you wherever you went. I knew he was talking from experience because everyone knew that as a kid he was always running away from the children's home in Fayetteville.

As we neared the front porch, he told me he knew what it was like being an orphan, feeling you didn't belong anyplace and nobody caring if you lived or died. I didn't feel like that exactly because I knew my aunt and uncle cared in their way, but I wasn't their child and never would be. Deputy Wood said I was lucky because at least I knew my parents and got to be with them on earth for a time. That was when the guilt caught me by the throat and wouldn't let go.

Because it was my fault they were dead.

That August day, my destination was a small cave tucked into the side of the mountain. It wasn't closed to the public like some of the other caves that try to preserve the wildlife inside them. But it wasn't big or interesting enough for tourists. There wasn't any story attached, either. If anyone came up this far, they'd pass it right by.

It was the perfect place to be invisible.

My stomach growled as I approached the mouth of the cave. I was short enough that I didn't have to duck to get inside. It was much cooler here. I sat where I always did: on a limestone ledge under a stalactite hanging from the ceiling that reminded me of the icicles around my heart.

I reached into my backpack and pulled out my sandwich. The bread was soggy and the peanut butter and jelly had run off into the saran wrap, but I was famished by now so I wolfed it down in a couple of bites. Then I leaned back against the limestone wall and closed my eyes. Maybe it was wishful thinking, or seeing that family, but I could swear my daddy was right here with me. Something stole over me then. Not peace exactly, but the closest thing I'd felt to it in a long time.

With the cave throwing off distorted echoes of my voice, I told him I missed him and was sorry for what happened and could he ever forgive me and what was it like where he was. When I stopped to catch my breath, I swear I heard him answering. I strained my ears so I could listen better, but his words were getting swallowed up by the sound of rushing water from somewhere deep inside the cave.

That's when it hit me that it wasn't my daddy's voice I was hearing. But it was familiar, all right.

I got up and poked out my head.

". . . know you're in there, Mary Grace," came Tyler Lee Hibbard's whiny voice as he stepped out from behind a tall outcropping of rock dressed in the dirty gray coveralls he wore no matter what the season. "Who you talking to?"

I should have known. The little runt was always tagging after me. Now he'd found my secret place and it was spoiled forever. "Don't come any closer!"

"Whatcha gonna do? You don't own this cave. You don't own nothin'. You don't even got a house of your own to live in no more."

"Get out of here!" I was so mad I was shaking.

He kept kicking small rocks out of his way as he ambled toward me. "I don't see no sign that says this here cave is the property of Mary Grace Dobbs."

"I'm warning you, Tyler Lee!" I took a menacing step toward him, wondering how he managed to follow me all this way without my knowing.

He tried to look past me, into the cave. "Hope you got camping gear in that there backpack 'cause your aunt and uncle ain't taking you back this time."

"Shut up!"

"I heard tell they're washing their hands of you and hauling you off to that children's home in Fayetteville."

My heart felt ready to burst right out of my chest. "You're a fibber, Tyler Lee, and God's going to punish you."

"No he ain't. Cuz I saw it for myself. I saw your suitcase, setting right there on your front porch."

"You're making it up!"

"I ain't neither. I swear on my mammy's life. And I saw your uncle's car idlin' in the driveway just waitin' to take you there."

"You filthy little liar!" Then, before I knew what was happening, I was flying through the air. I landed on top of Tyler Lee and tackled him to the ground. Then we were both rolling down the mountain. Sharp rocks and pebbles cut my skin, but I didn't notice. All I could think about was how I wanted to kill him. When we got to the bottom, he tried to scoot away, but he wasn't any match for my superior size. I caught him by his skinny shoulders and threw him down on the ground. Then I straddled him and put my hands around his scrawny neck.

He flailed around some, tried grabbing at my hands. But he couldn't budge me.

"Take it back, you hear? Take it back!"

He tried to talk, but his words came out all garbled because of how tight I was squeezing. Then his face turned red, his eyes practically bugging out of his head.

After a few seconds, he stopped struggling. That was when I finally let him go.

Tyler Lee coughed a blue streak as he sat up, staring at me like I was the Devil. "You're crazy," he choked out. "I'm gonna tell Sheriff Kanady how you tried to kill me and he'll come and lock you up and you won't never get out."

"You do that and I'll kill you for sure!"

"No, you won't neither. You got a mean streak, Mary Grace. Everyone knows you're just evil through and through. That's why your folks up and left you. Cuz they didn't want to be raising no little monster."

"You shut your mouth, Tyler Lee!" I shot to my feet. His eyes got really big again, then he turned tail and ran as fast as his little legs would carry him. I took off after him and only stopped when I got a stitch in my side and had to lean over to get a proper breath. When I looked up, Tyler Lee was just a tiny gray speck in the distance.

THREE

Sticks and Stones

Long after he was gone, I was still standing there.

Then I felt that prickling behind my eyes again and tried to tell myself sticks and stones and all that.

I knew I shouldn't let him get to me. He was an ignorant cuss like his daddy. People said Tyler Lee Hibbard Sr. was lucky to have landed a job over at Parnell Vaughan II's auto shop when he didn't even graduate from high school and drank too much. I probably should feel sorry for his son, but Tyler Lee's words had hurt. My daddy told me there was a grain of truth in everything people said. He taught me that words were important so you had to be careful how you used them. Once they flew out of your mouth, they could never be taken back. But what about the words you didn't say out loud?

In the eyes of God, did the words nobody else heard count as just as terrible a sin?

Which got me thinking again about what Tyler Lee said. Did my daddy and mama know about the evil inside me? Was it my fault I did the things I did? I knew I wasn't like other kids. But most of them couldn't pitch a fastball to save their lives. Did that make me a bad person? Or just different?

I wished my daddy was here right now to set me straight about things.

One thing I was sure of. God wasn't going to skip over me. If I sinned, I'd be punished. And not just for trying to strangle Tyler Lee.

There wasn't any sign of him now. I'd scared him off, I hoped for good this time.

I watched a blue grosbeak alight on a high branch, warbling his sweet tune to his little heart's content. The temperature had cooled off some. The sun was a lot lower in the sky.

Panic skittered through me. I should have been home by now. Now I was going to get it. I started to run, then remembered my backpack was still in the cave. There was nothing for it but to traipse back up the mountain. That took a good ten minutes. After I got it, I ran back down the mountain and kept going, picturing my suitcase sitting on the front porch and my uncle's car idling in the driveway.

Or maybe my uncle got sick of waiting and called Sheriff Kanady and at this very minute they were organizing a search party. Or they really had washed their hands of me like Tyler Lee said, and no one was out looking for me. That got me feeling sorry for myself again, but I tried to ignore it and concentrate on getting home. When I got within spitting distance of the town proper, I stopped, now faced with a dilemma. I could walk the usual way to my uncle's house—

Or I could bypass the town entirely and take a shortcut, which would shave fifteen minutes off my trip, easy.

It meant going into the woods.

Where I was forbidden ever to go.

I lost another precious couple of minutes trying to make up my mind. My feet must have known before my brain did because I was in the woods before I even knew I'd decided.

FOUR

A Frightening Encounter

I hadn't been here in a long time, not since my dad took me hiking along one of the dozen trails that wind through the forests of Repentance and its environs. It was a lot darker than I remembered. And I wasn't used to all the little animals I couldn't see but could hear chittering away. Maybe they were annoyed I was intruding on their private place.

I heard a couple of birdsongs, so that made me feel better.

As I trudged through, hoping I was headed in the right direction, I thought of the stories I'd heard growing up. How no kids made it out of the woods alive after being eaten by big black bears. What I couldn't remember was if the bears lived here in the summer. You'd think it'd be too hot then, with all that fur.

I tromped along, making my usual bargain with God about how if I made it out of here I'd go to church on Sundays with an open heart instead of being all closed up the way I was now.

The forest sounds were getting louder. I broke into a run, trying to avoid getting swiped by low branches, which was hard when you could barely see where you were going. My heart nearly exploded out of my chest when something flew right in front of me. But it was just a bat swooping down from a branch. I continued on my way, hoping I'd come to the clearing soon. That was when I heard it.

Footsteps behind me.

I stopped dead. The footsteps did, too. "That you, Tyler Lee?" I called out.

The woods threw back eerie echoes of his name. But I knew it wasn't him. He was too chicken to ever set foot here and besides, his mama would give him a good hiding if he did. And he had been wearing those torn moccasins he always had on and was too small to make those sounds.

Was a bear smart enough to stop when I stopped? I didn't think so. But I wasn't sticking around to find out. I took off like the Devil. I just wanted to get the hell out of there. The pounding started up again, so loud it felt like it was coming right through the forest floor. The animals were cheeping louder, scurrying this way and that as if they knew danger was coming. Now I could hear heavy breathing behind me.

No bear sounded like that.

I was panting so hard I thought I'd keel over. When I saw the cabin half-hidden in a stand of pine trees, I thought it was my eyes playing tricks. I knew there were a bunch of abandoned cabins in the woods that stretched from Repentance to other towns, but I'd never seen one.

I ran for that cabin as if my life depended on it, grabbing the door so hard it almost fell off its hinges. Then I darted inside as if it was the last place on earth. I slammed the door, praying the hinges would hold. The old wood floor creaked under my feet and I almost slipped a couple times on some missing planks. I could still hear it or him or whatever it was outside so I looked around to see what I could use.

I blinked a couple of time to adjust my eyes to the gloom. I made out a wood-burning stove in one corner. A few feet away were a low table and chair. Still breathing hard, I grabbed up the chair, which was made of wood and lighter than I would have liked, and shoved it against the door. I did the same with the table. It wasn't enough. But no way I could move that stove. There were two kerosene lamps in the other corner, the light in them down to a tiny flicker. What I needed was a weapon.

A wooden hutch sat against the back wall. From here I could see china and plates and such. Maybe there were some utensils or sharp cutlery in the drawers. My heart still beating triple time, I headed over in that direction. I almost tripped on something on the floor. A backpack was sitting there next to a musty-smelling sofa with paisley slipcovers that were coming apart at the seams.

Was someone here? I went quiet, but didn't hear a sound. Whoever it was had to have heard me what with all the racket I made. I looked at the backpack again. It was bigger than mine. Khaki, with two straps across the front and lots of zippered compartments with khaki-colored zippers. In the middle was a square with the company name inside in loopy capital letters. Instead of the purple-and-white butterflies on mine, it had the neatest scenes of mountains and lakes, with trees reflected in the water.

I listened again. Nothing. Did some tourist leave it behind? Maybe he went for a hike in the woods and got lost. But you can bet he was the one who lit those kerosene lamps. Unless—was somebody squatting here? That made more sense. This cabin was too far off the beaten track for a tourist.

Which meant he could be coming back any minute. Time to make my exit, sorely tempted though I was to unzip one of those compartments. I was finally starting to calm down. I figured whoever was chasing me had given up. I made my way back across the floor, this time keeping an eye out for missing planks.

As I passed the window, I saw a shadowy face. I let out a scream. That wasn't any bear. Now an arm was lifting up the sash. I didn't wait for him to get that window open. I raced for the door. I shoved the chair and table away and ran from that cabin like a bat out of hell. I had no idea which direction I was going and didn't care. I heard the footsteps start up again and ran faster. I was concentrating so hard on getting away, I didn't see the outcropping of rock. I stumbled and went sprawling into a bed of pine needles.

Out of my mind with terror, I shot to my feet. Pain ripped through my right knee. Pine needles stuck to my face and hands. He was gaining on me. My skin was stinging from the needles and my knee was hurting something fierce. Up ahead was an enormous tree. I ducked behind it, hoping he couldn't see in the dark. My breath whooshed out of me when I heard his footsteps thundering past. I waited till I couldn't hear them anymore, then poked my head out to see if the coast was clear.

So far, so good.

I crept out, putting most of my weight on the other leg. It was dark and I had no idea which way the clearing was that would take me out of the woods. Then I saw it. The stone chimney rising up from the sloping roofline of the ramshackle house at the northernmost edge of the woods. If you ever got lost or somehow turned around, you could get your bearings by looking for that chimney where fat plumes of smoke curled out even in the dead of summer.

Lord only knows what was being burned up in there.

I had to keep going in this direction because my uncle's house was closer to this part of the woods, a couple blocks from the house where I used to live with my folks. I kept creeping along, my eye on that chimney. I was getting closer, and in another few minutes I'd be upon it. Kids who sneaked into the woods didn't like to go past that house, knowing who lived there. But I didn't see as I had any choice. It was brighter now, which meant I was getting closer to the clearing. I could see bits of sunlight peeping through the thick trees. Then I heard something behind me and started running again in spite of the pain—

—and ran right into him!

It was like smashing into the side of a mountain.

I let out a yelp. He grabbed me before I could get away. I struggled like the dickens, but he held me fast. His eyes stared down at me from his long moon face, like two black holes waiting to swallow me up. His filthy hair hung in thick clumps past his shoulders.

It was him.

The Boogeyman of Repentance.

He lived in that old house with his mama until she died and he smelled like he hadn't had a bath in months.

"Let me go!"

I struggled some more, but he just held on tighter, his fingers like claws as they dug into my arms.

Then he opened his mouth and I could see the spaces in his gums where his teeth were missing. His breath stank as he leaned his big head closer, those eyes staring me up and down in a way that creeped me out and made me feel ashamed at the same time. Like he was going to do something a lot worse than eat me.

Then he shook his head and out came a torrent of words.

I couldn't understand what he was saying. All I knew was his name was Meurice and he had a last name no one could pronounce. Legend had it that his family was descended from the French. But whatever he was saying in that other language, I knew it couldn't be nice by the way those black eyes were fixed on me.

Then I felt my feet leaving the ground. I yelled and kicked my legs like crazy but he paid me no mind, just lifting me higher like he was getting ready to carry me off. Just when I thought it was all over and I was going to be joining my folks in heaven after all, the ground started to shake again.

Meurice swiveled his big moon head. He heard the footsteps, too.

Someone else was here.

I wanted to scream, but no sound came out. The footsteps stopped, then started up again, like somebody was taking stock of the situation.

Then they got fainter and fainter. Like whoever it was had made up his mind about coming any closer and took off in the other direction.

Maybe Meurice scared him off.

That was when I finally found my voice again and started yelling at the top of my lungs.

The footsteps had all but died out, and my chance of being saved was dying right along with them when Meurice started cussing in French again. Then he dropped me so fast I fell hard right on my backside. Meurice was already disappearing through the trees as I picked myself up off the ground, picturing a big black bear just waiting to grab me. I wasn't sticking around to find out.

Ignoring the pain in my knee, I raced through those miserable woods just as fast as my short, stumpy legs would carry me.

FIVE

A Narrow Escape

My heart was batting around in my chest like a trapped finch after that narrow escape. I counted myself lucky to be alive when I finally made it out of the thicket of pines where my uncle's land sloped down and made it feel like the woods were coming into our backyard. Uncle Samuel never got around to clearing those pines because no one was sure if they belonged to him or not. But it wasn't where his property line ended and the woods began that concerned me. That feud had been going on between my uncle and the town for years and would no doubt continue for decades to come.

I was picturing the front porch and what might or might not be sitting there.

I finally forced my feet to climb up past the pines. After I crossed the field and came around to the front of the house, my breath whooshed out of me.

Tyler Lee had fibbed.

My suitcase wasn't on the porch and my uncle's car wasn't waiting in the driveway to take me to that children's home in Fayetteville.

Unless he really was out looking for me.

I went up the steps and pulled open the screen door. The front door was never locked because of the zero crime rate in Repentance. The house was so quiet you could hear the old wood settling.

The big black case with the Bibles my uncle sold wasn't in its usual spot on the round table under the mirror in the hall. Maybe he was still on the road. Which meant he wasn't out looking for me. Then I heard it: the telltale squeak of wheels rolling across linoleum.

"That you, Mary Grace?"

I froze in my tracks. I was headed for my bedroom at the back of the house to change out of my filthy shorts and t-shirt, which got torn rolling down that mountain with Tyler Lee. My arms and legs were all cut up and I had dozens of crisscrossing scrapes from the pine needles in the woods. There was dried blood on my knee and it still hurt something fierce.

My aunt called my name again.

"Yes, it's me," I shouted out as I trudged toward the kitchen in defeat, pulling out the twigs and leaves that nested in my hair and shoving them in the pocket of my shorts. Now there was nothing for it but to own up to what I did and take my punishment.

When I came in, my aunt was by the stove. Two big pots were sitting on burners with steam coming out. Guilt pinged through me. Simmering the soup and setting the water boiling for the potatoes was my job.

Saying I was sorry was on the tip of my tongue, but the look on her face froze the words in my mouth. It wasn't a mean look, exactly. But it didn't have much of a welcome in it, either.

She kept staring at me with those eyes that always set me on edge because they were the same color as my daddy's. When I first came to live here, back in December, I kept looking for him in my aunt's face. They had the same high foreheads, long noses, and dimples in their chins. But my daddy's features looked different on his sister's face, like God had plopped down her features without much thought or care. They both had the same thick dark hair, but my aunt's had a lot of gray because she was older.

I was told I took after the Dobbs side of the family, that I was all my daddy except his eyes were brown where mine were hazel with specks of gold. Maybe because I was always outside playing ball, my hair seemed to be getting this lighter shade of squirrel brown. I always wished I took after my mama in the looks department, with her bright blue eyes like Parnell and dark blond hair that waved around her heart-shaped face like waves of grain.

The seconds crawled by. Then my aunt pulled up on the brake of her wheelchair and started rolling toward me. I was already working the lies in my head about how I was tree climbing and lost track of time. Except the caked mud on the bottoms of my sneakers didn't come from climbing trees. She came closer, and I could see the muscles bunching in her arms that were strong from wheeling herself around all the time.

She stopped right in front of me and she lifted her arm. My aunt had never once hit me, but there was always a first time. She reached for my head and I thought she was going to box my ears, but her hand came away with a leaf I must have missed.

"Go get yourself cleaned up. Then you can help me get supper on the table."

Then she wheeled away. I ran out of that kitchen, thinking I'd had another close call.

I put out four place settings, but it was just the three of us when I set down three bowls of the butternut-squash soup Aunt Hester had cooked and frozen the week before.

Uncle Samuel was at his usual place at the head of the table. He'd come home while I was adding the milk to the potatoes, which was the secret of making them come out soft and sweet. We joined hands and said grace, which always used to perk me up because Daddy said it made him feel twice blessed. It was how I got my name. He wanted to call me Grace Mary, but my mama wanted me to carry her mama's name, which was Mary Rose, so Mary Grace it was.

After we finished thanking the Lord, Uncle Samuel unfolded his napkin and put it on his lap. When we were done with the soup, I got up and started clearing the bowls away.

"Where's the boy this time?" My uncle's light brown eyes had turned the color of the mud on my sneakers as he stared at the empty chair.

"Samuel."

I heard the warning in my aunt's voice even if he didn't.

"I asked you a question, Hester." Now Uncle Samuel was tapping the fingers of one hand on the table, which he always did when he was trying to get ahold of his temper. I didn't hear what my aunt said next because I was carrying the bowls into the kitchen. When I came back out through the swinging door with the peas and potatoes, my uncle's voice was louder. ". . . disrespects me in my own house. I won't tolerate it!"

"Leave him be," my aunt said. "Let him enjoy his last few weeks of freedom."

"Freedom? He's sixteen! He should be working, not out gallivanting till all hours. I'm telling you, this is the last time—"

My uncle never finished what he was saying, because at that moment the front door opened and a few seconds later in walked my cousin Noah.

"Where have you been?"

My aunt put a hand on my uncle's arm, but he shook it off.

"Out," Noah said as he lowered his long, gangly body into the chair.

"Out where? Do you know how hard your mother worked to put your supper on the table?"

He didn't include me in that, but it was all right. They were still talking when I went back through the swinging door for the meat. It was the same story every night. Noah always ambled in in the middle of supper. Sometimes I think he did it on purpose so he wouldn't have to say grace. In church he always acted like he was being forced there against his will.

"You hungry, son?" Aunt Hester asked my cousin as I was laying the plate with the meat and carving knife in front of my uncle. She always perked up whenever Noah was around. It was like a light went on somewhere inside her. My mama never looked at me like that, unless it was when I didn't notice. But I couldn't understand why my aunt acted like the sun rose and set in Noah. He was the reason she was stuck in that wheelchair. Daddy told me she got the MS when she was carrying him.

I stole a look at my cousin, who was busy loading potatoes onto his plate. He was lucky even if he didn't deserve it. He was tall for his age, and looked like my uncle. But Uncle Samuel had more meat on his bones, especially around his belly. And Noah's face was pockmarked from the acne he had when he was younger. He had skinny arms with the longest fingers. My aunt called them piano fingers, but I never once saw him sit down at the piano in the living room my uncle bought for her back when money wasn't tight.

I never could warm up to Noah. He had a cruel streak.

"I'm taking you on the road with me," Uncle Samuel said after he'd piled thick slabs of meat on our plates. "It's high time you learned my trade."

"What do I want to do that for? Nobody reads the Bible anymore."

"How dare you blaspheme!" My uncle's face was getting as red as the wine in his glass.

"Stop it, Samuel. Let him eat his supper."

My aunt's voice was sharp. My uncle opened his mouth again, but nothing came out. He chugged down the rest of his wine and poured himself another glass. This was usually the time when I started chattering away, anything to ease all the sore feelings. But I was afraid if I started talking, I'd mention the woods and Meurice and then I'd be in real trouble. So I kept myself to myself.

"That raccoon got into the garage again," my aunt said, changing the subject. "Exterminator's coming in the morning."

I knew all about that. The pesky critters used to get into our chimney over the winter until my daddy finally put in a raccoon-proof chimney cap. This particular one had found a way to untie the garbage ties. Most mornings this summer, we'd find trash strewn all over the yard.

"That'll cost a pretty penny," my uncle was saying.

"I keep telling you, we don't need an exterminator," Noah said. "We got to set a trap."

Uncle Samuel stabbed the piece of meat with his fork like he was trying to kill it. "What we need is to put in metal fencing, but you're never around to help me do it."

The rest of the meal went on like that, with my uncle and cousin going at each other and my aunt trying to keep the peace. When supper was finally finished, Noah threw his napkin on the table and shoved back his chair.

"I didn't hear you ask to be excused. Where you in such a hurry to get to?"

"I got things to do."

My uncle opened his mouth again, but Aunt Hester gave him one of her looks. Like the way I imagined a mama bear would look if somebody tried to get between her and her cub.

"You be back before eleven, you hear?"

But my cousin was already halfway across the dining room. A few seconds later, the front door slammed.

My uncle and aunt sat there, neither saying a word. I started clearing the dishes. They didn't pay me any mind, which suited me fine. When I was done cleaning the kitchen, I stood there trying to figure out what to do. There was still enough light outside to practice my pitching, but tonight I didn't feel like playing by myself.

So I said goodnight and went off to my room.

SIX

Did I Belong Anywhere?

It was hotter here, at the other end of the house where my bedroom was. I peeled off the clean blouse I'd put on for supper. It still felt steamy with my undershirt, so that came off, too. I had a training bra in the drawer, but didn't need to wear it as I had no breasts yet to speak of.

I wasn't tired, but decided to get ready for bed anyway. I'd finished brushing my teeth and was back in my room when I heard the elevator door in the hall creak open. My uncle put that in for my aunt a couple of years ago when she couldn't get up the stairs anymore.

Uncle Samuel was wheeling my aunt into the elevator. They must have thought I was asleep, but I had my door open a crack to let in some air. Aunt Hester was saying it was a good thing that come the fall, I wouldn't be going to Baptist Day School because the little bit of money my folks left wasn't going to last much longer.

Hearing the name of that school got the guilt going full steam again, making the hard knot turn into a landslide of rocks in my chest.

". . . take in boarders if Mary Grace wasn't in the spare bedroom," my aunt was saying.

Then my Uncle Samuel said something I couldn't make out. The elevator door closed and a couple of minutes later I heard it open upstairs. Then my aunt's wheelchair was rolling across the wood on the landing over my head.

I wished I didn't hear what they said when they didn't think I was listening. Now I didn't just feel guilty, I felt like a burden. The truth was, I hadn't been officially adopted by my aunt and uncle even though I'd been living in their house all these months. I wondered what they were waiting for. Maybe they weren't sure yet if they were going to keep me. That's why they were thinking of renting out my room.

But even if they decided to adopt me, I already made up my mind I wasn't going to take their name. Aunt Hester was a Dobbs like my daddy until she married Uncle Samuel. Now she was a Mathews, and so was Noah. My daddy's name was the only thing I had left of him and I wasn't about to part with it so easily. So, it was all probably just as well. But my heart was heavy as I got into bed. I'd give my pitching arm to do it all over if I only got the chance. I'd go to Baptist Day and you'd never hear a complaining peep out of me.

Except I couldn't change what happened. And now I might end up someplace a lot worse, like that children's home in Fayetteville where Chief Deputy Wood grew up.

Then where would I belong?

The chief deputy was right. Ever since my folks passed, I didn't feel like I belonged anywhere. I wasn't officially born in Repentance, but in a town over in the next county, because my mama had complications while she was carrying me. Why she and my daddy thought a big-city doctor knew more than the doctor in their hometown, I have no idea.

Seven years later, I came home crying one day after softball practice. Our second-grade team called ourselves the Mockingbirds, after the name of our state bird that we share with Florida, Mississippi, Tennessee, and Texas. But Chloe Ann Briggs said I couldn't call myself a Mockingbird because I wasn't born in Repentance.

Mama was in her room as usual. Daddy was grading papers for his fifth-grade class. But that afternoon he took one look at my face and knew it was serious.

"What have I told you about listening to Chloe Ann Briggs? She's just jealous because she doesn't have your talents. You can't let what other kids say change how you feel about yourself."

Then he said it didn't make a whit of difference where I was born. It was where I lived my life that mattered. He said I was luckier than Chloe Ann and him and my mama as well. When I asked why that was, he said my mama and he were born and raised in Repentance. But I was from two places so that made me special.

I thought on that for a good long time. I wondered if Chief Deputy Wood was born in the children's home or someplace else. I suspected my daddy said that to make me feel better. But he looked so unhappy I ended up trying to make him feel better because I said then I guess that made it okay. But in my heart I wasn't too sure. I had to belong to someplace.

I had a lot of sleepless nights trying to figure it out. I guess if I had to pick a place, it would be Repentance. I really did love my town. But then my folks died and since then nothing felt the same.

I must have dozed off because the next thing I knew I was in the passenger seat of a car, swaddled in a blanket because I was only six weeks old. We were driving home to Repentance. Only all of a sudden, the way it goes sometimes in dreams, I wasn't in the car anymore. I was outside, up in the heavens somewhere looking down on my mama and daddy who were still in the car. Snow and ice were swirling all around and they didn't see that big rig coming at them until it was too late.

I woke up in a sweat, my heart thumping like a runaway horse in my chest, the blanket and sheets in a tangled ball on the floor.

Moonlight was shining in through my window.

SEVEN

A Bullfrog, a Raccoon . . .

There was somebody out there.

I crept closer to the windowsill to see. Someone was at the edge of the property, where the field dropped down into the stand of pines. Just then another cloud scuttled in front of the moon, pitching everything into blackness.

I shivered in spite of the heat. Did Meurice follow me? I could still feel his sour breath on my cheeks and his fingers digging into my flesh. Just then the cloud moved, and I saw him better.

It was my cousin. My curiosity getting the better of me, I grabbed my shorts and T-shirt and clambered out the window. When I jumped down, the grass felt damp under my bare feet.

I scurried across the field. Now I couldn't see him at all. At the top of the field, I looked down. Noah was standing with his back to me, holding the shovel from the garage. He was digging a hole. Something told me not to make a sound, so I slithered down the slope and hid behind a tree. After he was done digging, he leaned down and picked up a brown paper bag. When he opened it and I saw what was inside, I couldn't help myself. I let out a gasp.

Without turning around my cousin said, "I know you're there, Mary Grace."

I couldn't talk if I wanted to. I just stared at what was dangling from his hand.

"Come on out. I got something to show you."

And still I stayed frozen to the spot, like I'd turned into a tree and grown roots. That was when Noah turned around, grinning like the jack-o'-lanterns we carved up every Halloween.

He looked exactly like that the time my folks and I came over here one Thanksgiving. I was around six. He cornered me in the hall and made me guess what was in his fist. When I couldn't, he opened his hand. He was holding a bullfrog. But it didn't look right. Its eyes were bulging and its skin was all shriveled.

"What'd you do to him?" I asked.

"I didn't do anything. How long you think he can live out of water before his little heart gives out?"

"I have no idea." I was so shocked I couldn't think straight.

"That's what I'm fixing to find out."

"You going to just wait for him to die?"

I never heard his answer because just then my uncle announced that supper was being served. My cousin stuffed the frog in his pocket and we all went into the dining room. I sat between my folks at the table, but I couldn't eat a bite even though turkey with all the trimmings was my favorite holiday meal. I kept picturing that poor frog in Noah's pocket fighting for its life.

I stared at the critter now dangling from my cousin's hand by its striped tail and knew it was the raccoon that had been giving us so much trouble. He smiled as he waved it back and forth like he was trying to hypnotize me or something. At first I thought he strangled it, but then I saw the blood.

Its throat was cut.

I thought of that bullfrog. Noah might not have done it with his own two hands, but he killed it just the same.

"Why'd you have to slit its throat?" My voice came out all whispery.

"Why do you think? Want to know how I trapped him? I dug a hole under the porch and threw some scraps on top. When he came sniffing around, the dumb critter dropped right into that hole. Then I hit him with the shovel. He was still alive when I pulled him out. I got my hands around his neck and started squeezing."

I shut my eyes, seeing my fingers pressing into Tyler Lee's throat, his eyes bulging out of his head like that poor bullfrog.

"You know the best part? The moment that raccoon realized he was going to die. I could see it in its eyes. Knowing that no one was going to save him. I could feel the surrender in his writhing little body. That's when I took out my knife and finished the job."

My eyes flew open. The sound of Noah's voice had been washing over me, lulling me like Mama's voice used to when she read to me when I was little and too young to understand the words. I started backing away.

"What's the matter, Mary Grace? You telling me you don't have fantasies about killing something weaker than you?"

I felt Tyler Lee's scrawny neck between my hands again.

"It's a high like you can't believe. Like having more power than God."

"The Bible says it's a sin to kill." But I had trouble getting the words out.

"The Bible says everything's a sin! If you believe what the Old Testament says, you're even dumber than I thought."

"You better not let your father hear you talk like that."

"I'm not scared of him. Acting like a God-fearing man in church every Sunday when he's drinking and doing the Lord only knows what all those nights on the road. He's the biggest sinner of them all."

I pictured my uncle at the supper table, his face getting as red as the wine he was drinking. Were two glasses of wine a blasphemy against God?

"Selling Bibles to stupid folks who don't know any better isn't going to get him salvation. But he'll spend the rest of his life waiting to be saved. Who's going to save you, Mary Grace?"

Noah took a step closer. I could smell that dead raccoon.

"You're the one who's going to hell for what you did," I said.

Noah just threw back his head and laughed.

"I'm going to tell."

"No, you're not."

"Yes, I am. And Sheriff Kanady will lock you up," I said, echoing Tyler Lee's words to me. "It's a crime murdering that raccoon like you did."

My cousin took another menacing step toward me. "You tell, and I'll say it was all your doing. Who do you think my ma's gonna believe? Her son or a little orphan ingrate?"

I started hopping from one foot to the other. I was so mad I couldn't get any words out.

"Now you're gonna help me give him a proper burial."

"I won't!"

"Is that the way you treat the family who puts food in your mouth? You better start earning your keep, Mary Grace. Or I'll tell my folks I saw you in the woods today."

"What were you doing there?"

"Never you mind."

I watched Noah drop the raccoon into the hole he'd dug. Was it his face I saw at the window of that cabin? His footsteps when I was fighting to get away from Meurice? That would be just like my cousin, to run off and leave me to fend for myself.

Noah was holding out the shovel.

I was shaking so bad, I couldn't get a proper grip on it. I tried not to look as I shoveled dirt, faster and faster until the raccoon was totally covered by the earth and I didn't have to see its dead eyes staring up at me.

After it was done, Noah took the shovel from me, laughing as he headed back across the field. I watched him untangle the long green hose and wash off the shovel. Then he put it in the garage and disappeared around the side of the house.

I don't know how long I stood there staring down at that grave. My head was pounding something awful. I felt sick to my stomach. My cousin had done something horrible and I couldn't ever tell my aunt and uncle.

It wasn't the only secret I'd be keeping that year. But right then it was just one more to add to the growing heap of others.

EIGHT

. . . a Field Mouse, and Him

When I climbed back through my window, I couldn't fall back to sleep worth a damn. I was afraid if I closed my eyes I'd see Noah slashing that raccoon's throat.

I must have dropped off at some point because I was having a nightmare about being chased through the woods. My legs felt like rubber, like I was stuck in molasses. I could hear him laughing. But when I looked over my shoulder, it was Meurice. The dead raccoon was dangling from his hand.

When we sat down to supper that night, my aunt went on about how the trap Noah laid must have worked because they hadn't been bothered by the raccoon. I stole a look at my cousin, wondering if he was feeling guilty. But he just smirked and I knew he wasn't a bit sorry for what he did.

A couple days later, my aunt got a bee in her bonnet about the field mice that were getting into the cellar. And I just knew those mice would end up in the woods.

Sure enough, I looked out my window that night and saw Noah walking toward the edge of the field. He wouldn't need to dig a big hole because mice are a lot smaller than raccoons. That got me wondering how many other animals were buried out there. For all I knew, my cousin had been killing for years, ever since that Thanksgiving he showed me the dying bullfrog.

I was down in the cellar one morning after my aunt stopped complaining about the mice. I was putting the sheets in the dryer when I saw something out of the corner of my eye.

It was a baby field mouse my cousin must have missed. He was darting this way and that, sniffing around for food. Silent as the grave, making sure to keep an eye on him, I padded over to the refrigerator we kept down there and pulled out a hunk of cheese. It wasn't Swiss, but it should do the trick. Then I got out a paring knife from a drawer, all the while thinking about my cousin slashing the throats of the field mouse's relatives.

He was over by the washing machine now. In another second, he'd find a hiding place behind it. Quick as a lick, I got out the dustpan. Then I laid my trap.

I put the tiny chunk of cheese I'd just sliced on the dustpan and set it down in front of the dryer. Then I backed up a few steps.

And waited.

Sure enough, the mouse's whiskers started twitching. It changed direction and scampered closer. Once its tiny feet were on the dustpan, I scooped it up and went out the door of the cellar and up the steps. By now the mouse had forgotten all about the cheese and was frozen to the spot, its eyes darting crazily around. I carried that dustpan with the mouse on it clear across the field. When I got to the part of the property where it slopes down to the woods, I laid the dustpan on the ground.

I told him that his brothers and sisters were buried here and he should count himself lucky that he had a narrow escape. As I talked, I swear I could see the mounds that held their tiny bodies. The stupid mouse didn't move. He was up on his hind legs now, his tail twitching and his little eyes full of terror.

I heard my cousin's voice in my head, asking if I had fantasies about killing something weaker than me. I stared at that quivering mouse and now I was the one who couldn't move. Like someone had put a spell on me.

My head was pounding again. I leaned down. The mouse must have smelled me or something because he scampered off that dustpan with lightning speed. I watched him dart off through the pines. Then he was gone.

I was breathing hard as I picked up that dustpan with the cheese on it and started back up the slope. I thought about how I'd saved that mouse.

But who did I save him from? That was when I started shaking and couldn't stop.

∞

The rest of the summer turtled by.

Finally, it was the last week of August, and really hot. My uncle was on the road again and my aunt was having a lie-down. I was just finishing my kitchen chores when the screen door banged open.

It was Noah. But it was who was with him that stole the breath right out of my body.

"Hi, Gracie."

My heart started a stampede in my chest, which was the effect Parnell Vaughan III always had on me. With his blond hair and blue eyes, he looked like some god straight out of the Greek myths my daddy used to tell me about. He was so beautiful it hurt just to look at him. Like trying to fix your eyes on the sun.

His voice was as beautiful as the rest of him.

"Hey, Parnell," I managed to mumble while all the time my cousin smirked like he knew what was going on inside me. I hated Noah so much right then.

"How's that pitching arm?" Parnell asked while my cousin got two beers out of the fridge. Noah only did that when my uncle wasn't around. He was sixteen. The legal drinking age in Arkansas was twenty-one. That never stopped my cousin. He gave one beer to Parnell, who was still waiting on my answer.

"Okay, I guess." I didn't want to tell him I'd been falling down a little in my practicing. It's no fun when there's no one to hit the ball back to you.

"Want to hit a few?"

I stared like I couldn't be hearing him right. I couldn't believe he was even asking.

"Aw, come on, Parnell," Noah whined. I swear he sounded more like Tyler Lee every day. "You said we could take that new baby out for a spin. See how she handles the back roads."

That was all my cousin cared about. Tooling around in a convertible from Parnell's daddy's shop. My uncle wasn't buying him one even though he recently got his intermediate driver's license.

That was why Noah had cozied up to Parnell.

But what Parnell was doing with my cousin I couldn't figure out.

"She handles those roads like a dream," Parnell was saying as he twisted the cap off his bottle. "Darryl fixed her up real good."

"Who's Darryl?" I asked.

"Darryl Stokes. My daddy's new hire." Parnell took a swig of his beer.

"You mean the drifter I heard tell about?"

"He isn't a drifter."

"So where's he staying then?"

"Over to Miss Lillian's boarding house."

"Where's he from? Did he have to give your daddy references?"

"Don't pay her no mind," Noah said. "She's always asking a million questions. Don't you have chores to do, Mary Grace?"

He fixed me with a look like he was trying to scare me. But I wasn't letting him get between me and Parnell even if he was an animal killer.

I wondered what Parnell would say if he knew.

"For your information, I'm all done." I turned my back on Noah and perched on the edge of the kitchen table. "Is it true he's black as sin?"

"The color of his skin doesn't make him a sinner."

Parnell's beautiful eyes got the color of the river that runs through town just when night's about to fall. I didn't know why he was reacting like that. "I was just asking. What's he like?"

"Same as you and me, what do you think?"

I shrugged. Truth was, I hadn't seen a whole lot of black people in my short life.

You have to understand how it was in our town back then. We had a real small population, barely three hundred people. And almost every last one of them was white. I wasn't one to pass judgment, but a black drifter really got tongues wagging. Probably started by Julia Allred, the old crone who lived at the top of town in one of the oldest houses in Repentance. She'd always be sitting on her front porch whenever I rode by on my bike. I pictured her ancestors rocking away on that same porch waiting for the Pony Express to come up the hill. She'd call my name as I passed, but I pretended not to hear. My daddy said gossiping was like spreading poison through the town. So, I gave a wide berth to Julia Allred and her friends.

Parnell still looked mad.

"I'm sorry," I said, though in truth I wasn't sure what I was sorry for. "He's probably nice," I said when Parnell still didn't answer, more to get him to stop being mad at me than anything else.

He finished off his beer, then took a napkin from the holder on the table to wipe his mouth. Not like Noah, who used his shirtsleeve. When he looked at me, he was Parnell again. "Want to play some ball?"

"Sure thing."

I forgot everything else as I raced out of the kitchen to get my mitt and bat.

We played for almost an hour. While Noah groused in the part of the property we turned into the outfield, I pitched a couple of winners to Parnell, underhanded, the major difference between softball and baseball aside from the size of the ball, which is bigger in softball and, to my way of thinking, easier to handle. I had a sneaky suspicion Parnell was purposely messing up. He was one of Briggs High's star athletes. But it sure felt good to strike him out. When it was my turn at bat, I hit every one of the balls he pitched to me, low and fast the way I liked it. I didn't even feel the cut on my knee open up after I made it past all the bases and was sliding into home. Then, too fast, it was over and Parnell and Noah were getting ready to go. Parnell invited me to come along, but I wouldn't have even if my cousin wasn't looking at me like he wanted to put me in the ground next to those murdered animals.

Before he left, Parnell leaned down and told me I was developing a heck of a pitching arm. Then he smiled a smile that felt like it was just for me. When he walked away, it was like he took the sun right along with him. I looked up and saw clouds scudding across the sky like big gray wings. I heard a far-off clap of thunder right before lightning lit up everything. That was when the heavens opened and down fell the biggest, fattest drops you ever saw.

The rains had finally come.

NOW

NINE

"Think this rain'll ever let up?"

Mary Grace looks up from her desk, but it's a rhetorical question. The better one is if it continues much longer, will the governor make good on his promise (or threat, depending how you look at it) and declare a state of emergency?

Between the weather and her new duties as sheriff, Mary Grace's workdays have been bordering on close to an unholy twelve hours. Almost three weeks on the job, and she's barely made a dent in the paperwork Owen Kanady never got around to filing, which truth to tell isn't her strong suit, either. And with him dying so suddenly, she has no one to show her the ropes. It wasn't the strong suit of Isaac Wood, either, Kanady's longtime chief deputy who was fired this past spring. Mary Grace had been assistant sheriff and got his position by default.

Kanady said letting Wood go was one of the hardest things he ever had to do, but his personal life had begun affecting his job. Right now Wood was in the middle of a bitter custody battle with his second ex-wife. To Mary Grace, he'd never been anything but kind. Maybe because they were both orphans; it was as if they shared a secret.

"Maybe this God-awful weather really is a sign."

Mary Grace sits back and massages a crick in her neck as she watches Conner Mitchell hang up his wet slicker on the coatrack by the door that's been there since she was a kid and head for the coffeemaker that also dates back decades. She lets herself be momentarily distracted by the sight of his long, lean frame in uniform.

She still finds it hard to believe that her smoking-hot deputy and the skinny ninth grader with big ears and braces are one and the same person. Back then, she was in danger of failing science because she couldn't bring herself to dissect a mouse without thinking about that field mouse she let loose in the woods behind her uncle's house. This was decades before cruelty to animals became an issue and individual states (not Arkansas) upheld a student's right to choose humane alternatives without fear of punishment. Conner, a geek one year ahead of her whom she barely noticed in elementary school, was the one who came to her rescue. He helped her see things differently, even though she still threw up in the girls' room after cutting open that embalmed rodent.

Not that she fared much better in her other subjects at Briggs High. Things were never the same after the winter of '95.

Conner's walking toward her with two steaming mugs. As he gives her her coffee—black with two lumps just the way she likes it—his hand lingers on hers, which Mary Grace chooses to ignore.

It was when they were working together, he as assistant sheriff, she as chief deputy, that Mary Grace realized that his ninth-grade crush had blossomed into a full-blown infatuation.

"Tell me you're not buying into that superstitious claptrap." She doesn't quite meet his eyes as she takes the coffee, knowing what she'll see there. The same expression she imagines shining out of her own every time she's near Parnell.

Conner shrugs, then ambles over to his own desk to nurse his hurt feelings.

It's her fault. She let things go too far. Although there's nothing in the town bylaws explicitly forbidding it, a romantic relationship between a sheriff and her second-in-command is generally frowned upon. And their attraction is getting perilously close to blossoming into a sexual affair. Does she really want to sneak around, lying to everyone, including her daughter? Didn't she promise herself after Felicity was born that she was done with secrets?

It's that wild side of me, Mary Grace thinks. The part of her she has never been able to eradicate completely.

It's like there have always been two Mary Graces. The good Mary Grace, sworn to keep her town safe and raise her daughter the best way she knows how. And the wicked Mary Grace, who's always pushing the envelope. Seeing how far she can go until she's caught. Shamelessly leading on her chief deputy.

She really should stop things before they progress any further. She can never give Conner what he wants because Parnell will always own her heart, even if he stomped all over it the last time they met.

Mary Grace would be the first to admit that her feelings for Parnell are complicated. But the truth is, she has belonged to him ever since she was nine and watched from the bleachers as he led the Briggs High football team to victory. Loving Parnell is part of her DNA; she's just wired that way.

The door opens again and her assistant sheriff stomps in, shaking the rainwater off his boots.

"I just saw Stokes," Lucas Smith announces as he tosses his wet umbrella into the stand by the door.

"Where?" Mary Grace and Conner echo in unison.

"He was coming into the diner as I was paying my bill. You should have heard the silence that came over the place. Stokes paid it no mind. He sat himself down at the soda fountain and ordered up a cheeseburger medium rare as if he's been doing it for years."

"A man's got a right to eat where he chooses." Mary Grace can't believe the words coming out of her mouth.

"Really? And here I thought you'd be leading the pack to run him out of town." Lucas fixes her with his clear, blue-eyed gaze. He's the youngest of four brothers, all married now, leaving the twenty-one-year old whom Mary Grace hired fresh out of police academy to play the field. But Lucas is as devout a churchgoer as you're likely to find and believes in the inherent goodness of people.

"Can't fault someone for setting down roots where he likes. It's a free country, last time I checked." Now both Conner and Lucas are looking at Mary Grace as if she'd grown two heads.

The truth is, she has her reasons for wanting Stokes gone, too. But the law's the law and she's sworn to uphold it.

"What I don't get is why he'd come back at all," Lucas says. "Knowing how everyone feels."

"My money's on a woman."

Of course Conner would say that. It's what people have been talking about for the past five days. Just like they did in '95, though nothing was ever proven. It didn't stop the rumors.

"Maybe he and his lady love are secretly rendezvousing in that cabin in the woods," Conner goes on. "Though you have to wonder why nobody saw fit to tear the place down in all these years. Just on principle."

That cabin was what got things snowballing. Mary Grace goes back to her paperwork. This isn't a conversation she wants to have.

"Lots of folks feel that justice wasn't done," Lucas says, all het up now that he's had his first sighting of Stokes. But he's just parroting the stories he heard growing up; he wasn't even born back then. "Must stick in your craw that he got away after what you did. How old were you? Twelve?"

"Eleven." With less than six weeks to go before her birthday.

"Mary Grace was a real hero back then."

She looks up sharply. She can't tell whether Conner really believes that or is mocking her. Of all the names she could call herself, hero isn't one of them.

Lucas gets up to pour himself coffee. "Where do you suppose Stokes is getting the money to eat and pay for his room and board? I haven't heard any noises about Parnell Vaughan III giving him his old job back now that he's running the show."

"Doubt most folks in Repentance would take kindly to that." Conner splays his hands behind his head and puts his feet up on his desk, ready to settle in for a long gossip session.

As if it were yesterday, Mary Grace sees her younger self perched on the edge of the kitchen table swinging her legs as she peppered Parnell with questions about his daddy's new hire. When he all but accused her of being racist.

Back then, she had no clue what racism really was. Not truly comprehending the whole *us versus them* mentality. But over the years she has given it a lot of thought, remembering the day she saw Darryl Stokes for the first time. When their paths unexpectedly crossed.

"That's enough lollygagging," she says now. "There's work to be done. Starting with emptying that bucket."

Lucas responds in his usual good-natured way, pushing back from his desk and whistling as he heads for the almost-full bucket sitting in the middle of the room. In the few weeks since she hired him, Mary Grace can't recall him ever losing his temper.

As low man on the totem pole, he's relegated to the more menial tasks Mary Grace herself was doing only a couple of months ago. When she graduated from the police academy, she already had two strikes against her. She was female and a single mother. Although she knew there was little chance for advancement, she'd always be grateful to Owen Kanady for bucking the status quo and hiring the first woman to ever serve in the Repentance sheriff's office. He used to joke that what was wrong with this town was there weren't enough women in power to balance out the weaknesses of its men.

What he didn't know was that Mary Grace had been training for the job since she was eleven, although she had a different reason for making a nuisance of herself back when Kanady was the one behind this desk.

Lucas is on his second trip to empty the bucket when the phone rings, Mary Grace thinking, not for the first time, how the town had enough money to build a brand-new prison last year but not enough to put a new roof on the ancient building that houses their office and holding cells. When she ends the call, her expression is grim. "Another tree's down. A big elm sitting in the middle of the eastbound side of the highway."

Conner looks at his phone as he swings his legs down from his desk. "It's almost rush hour, too."

"It's still coming down pretty hard," Mary Grace says, looking out the window. "Take the SUV."

"Maybe someone's trying to tell us something," Conner says.

"Like what?" Lucas says, taking the bait as he places the now-empty bucket back on the floor under the leaky roof.

"Hell if I know." Conner lets out a low belly laugh. Lucas rolls his eyes, then heads for the men's room. Conner waits until he's out of earshot, then walks over to Mary Grace's desk. "Can we get together tonight?"

"Can't. I promised Felicity I'd take her to the movies."

Fibs still fall easily from her lips. The truth is, Felicity would much rather be home texting on her phone. Or tweeting or posting on Instagram. Mary Grace regularly gives thanks that social media wasn't around when she was her daughter's age. She doesn't care how fast you can connect with the world, it can't be a good thing for kids to always have the Internet at their fingertips. Especially in this age of cyber-bullying.

"We good?" Conner's asking now.

"Sure." The lies just keep coming.

"Ready?" Lucas is back and watching them as he slides his slicker off the hook. Did Mary Grace really think they could fool everyone?

After Conner and Lucas leave, the office feels too quiet, the silence seeping into Mary Grace's bones. Except for the occasional, maddening *plop plop* of rainwater hitting the bucket.

Her thoughts circle back to Darryl Stokes.

She can't help but take his reappearance personally. The first thing she did when she heard he was back in town was Google him. Then she made some calls. But if she thought she'd find an easily verifiable explanation of where he's been for the last twenty-four years, she was doomed to disappointment. She discovered precious little except that he was born in Alabama and spent his boyhood shuttling between foster homes.

Which meant he was speaking the truth that day; the only time they ever talked.

And now he'd turned up again like a bad penny.

She feels edgy, like she's about to crawl out of her skin. At the same time, she feels her younger self closer than ever, as if the years are erasing themselves and she's eleven again. Memories of that time as close as a lover's kiss.

"Damn you, Darryl Stokes!" Her voice echoes through the empty room. "Why did you have to come back?"

He's still in Repentance the Tuesday after Labor Day.

It's raining again. Over Felicity's objections, Mary Grace insists on driving her to school. Her daughter's starting the sixth grade, her last year of elementary school. Unlike most other northwest Arkansas towns, Repentance doesn't have a middle school, an always controversial subject at town halls where the devout among them argue against change that will bring in more teachers (read: outsiders) with looser morals and therefore more opportunities for their offspring to be corrupted. When in fact this doesn't represent change at all, as middle schools have been around for decades.

As she pulls into the parking lot that's already wall-to-wall cars, Mary Grace imagines that overhauling the school system is the last thing on everyone's minds this morning. She pictures mothers inside their rain-spattered cars holding their daughters a little closer, as spooked as she is by the presence of Darryl Stokes after an absence of more than two decades.

She shifts into park, assailed by a totally irrational impulse to keep her daughter from leaving the car. She knows she's overprotective; Felicity has complained often enough. Maybe it's because she almost wasn't born, a decision Mary Grace is grateful every day that she didn't make. And then, when Felicity was finally ready to make her grand entrance—two weeks late—she came into the world red-faced and squalling, raising up such a ruckus Mary Grace thought she was dying. She'll never forget the feeling when her baby was placed in her arms for the first time, unable to believe this miraculous creature had emerged from her body. From then on, she felt something sacred had come into her life, and vowed to protect her child with her dying breath. But like all parents, she knows she can't keep her safe forever. Eventually she has to let her loose into the world.

But oh how she wishes she didn't have to this wet, Devil-shadowed morning.

"Call me if it's still raining later," Mary Grace says now. "I'll come get you."

"Mo—om." Felicity turns to give her a look, always managing to drag out the one syllable into two whenever she thinks Mary Grace is babying her.

"You don't want to ruin your new dress." The one that cost Mary Grace almost half a week's overtime, along with the new smartphone with the pink, glitter-covered case Felicity had to have because all her friends did.

Not that Mary Grace begrudges her daughter anything, though she does wonder where Felicity gets her love of material things, especially dressing up—certainly not from Mary Grace, who's always happiest in T-shirts, shorts, and sneakers.

"Call me," she tells her daughter again, her tone brooking no opposition.

"Okay, Mom. Jesus."

"What did I tell you about swearing?"

"Okay, okay. Can I go now?" Felicity pulls her backpack over the pretty blue slicker she also cajoled her mother into buying, her umbrella opening effortlessly as she gets out of the car. Mary Grace watches her side-step a huge puddle, graceful as a gazelle with those long legs that make her such a superb athlete. (One thing she and her mother have in common.). A car pulls out just then, speeding past Mary Grace and sending a wave of water scudding across her windshield.

She can't see Felicity. She can't see anything. Frantic, she sets the windshield wipers going full blast. She still can't see her daughter. She finally spots her in a group of kids hurrying through the open doors of the school. Only then does she start breathing again. She watches until Felicity is safely inside, her heart pounding painfully against her ribs.

Shaken, she takes several deep breaths to calm herself down. After a few minutes, she shifts into reverse. Everyone is wrong, she thinks as she backs out of the lot, rain lashing her from all sides. It's not the Devil they should fear.

It's something worse.

God's wrath.

THEN

TEN

God's X-Ray Vision

It rained almost every day that last week of August as if it was making up for the whole summer.

I kept looking out for Parnell, but Noah never brought him around again. Then, before I knew it, it was the first day of school.

It was raining too hard to wait for the bus, but even with my yellow slicker on, the rain pelted me and sloshed into the tops of my boots as I ran from the porch to the driveway. I know it wasn't nice, but as I got into the front seat of my uncle's car I couldn't help but measure his beat-up old station wagon against the shiny red convertible Parnell tooled around town in, mostly with his girlfriend Anna Mae Burns. Which didn't sit too well with my cousin. Not because of Noah being jealous that Parnell was dating the most popular girl at Briggs High. He wanted to be the one tooling around in that sports car.

I twisted in my seat to get away from the heat pouring out of the vents. My uncle's dusty black case was sitting in the back seat. "You going back on the road, Uncle Samuel?"

He nodded. "Just overnight."

I thought about Noah killing those animals while my uncle was out there trying to sell folks salvation. It was on the tip of my tongue to tell him what his son was doing while he and my aunt were asleep, but the words stuck in my throat. I didn't believe what my cousin said about the sinful things my uncle was doing on the road, even if he did like his wine with supper. It was just a mean lie Noah made up out of wickedness and spite.

I was also smart enough to know that even though Uncle Samuel had a temper when it came to Noah, he might not believe me. My uncle cared for me in his own way, but Noah was his son. His only child. Blood was blood, and that had to count for more.

My uncle made a right-hand turn and even with the rain hitting us sideways, I knew we were on School Street. I always wondered which came first, the schools or the name of the street. Now we were passing Briggs High, where I'd be a seventh grader next year. Noah and Parnell were starting there as juniors today. Thinking about Parnell eased up my nerves a little.

My uncle was pulling up in front of Vaughan Elementary. "Want me to wait until you get inside?"

"That's okay." Through the rain, I could see the cars lining up. The biggest belonged to Chloe Ann Briggs. It wasn't even her daddy behind the wheel. He was too important for that. His driver took her to school every day and when he picked her up, she made sure that everyone saw.

Right now he was getting out of the car and opening the biggest umbrella I ever saw. Then he went around to the passenger side and opened the door like Chloe Ann couldn't do it herself. He held that umbrella over her as they walked to the front steps to make sure not a drop of water got on her. She wasn't wearing an old hand-me-down slicker like me. She had on this long red raincoat with a hood so not a strand of her hair got wet.

My uncle shifted into park. I had my hand on the door, but I didn't get out.

"Umm. Uncle Samuel?"

"Yes?" He must have figured I had something important to say because he twisted in his seat so he could look at me.

"Thanks for not sending me to Baptist Day." The words came out in a rush. I wasn't used to thanking anyone for anything, but figured I owed it to my aunt and uncle for taking me in when no one else wanted me.

He didn't answer right away. He always thought something through before he opened his mouth. Except when it came to Noah. He couldn't seem to hold on to his temper then. "Your folks had their reasons for wanting to send you there," he finally said.

I knew why. My mama thought I was wild, so wild she was ready to pluck me out of elementary school the year I was supposed to graduate so the Bible teachers at Baptist Day could set me straight. Then I remembered what Tyler Lee said about me being evil after I almost strangled him to death back in August.

I couldn't look at my uncle, for fear he'd see my wickedness glowing inside me like the Devil's light. "You're going to work hard, aren't you?" he said. "Make your aunt and me proud like your folks would have wanted?" I nodded but couldn't talk past the giant lump that had suddenly formed in my throat. "You know your daddy set a great store by education. He'd want to know you're getting on with your learning."

I nodded some more, but my eyes were stinging again.

"Better get along now," my uncle said. "If it stops raining when school's out, you walk home with Noah? You hear?"

"Okay," I said even though I knew my cousin wouldn't do that in a million years. I pushed open the door, trying to clear my mind of bad thoughts. The minute I opened my umbrella, the wind turned it inside out, so I just threw the broken thing on the ground. Rain slashed my face as I slid my backpack onto my shoulders and ran for the steps so I wasn't looking where I was going, and wouldn't you know it I stepped in a huge puddle. Water splashed up over my boots and soaked my knee highs and the hem of the skirt Aunt Hester spent the better part of the summer sewing for me. When I started shooting up this spring, none of my clothes fit and there wasn't enough money to buy new ones.

Chloe Ann was already inside so at least I didn't have to see her snickering behind her hand.

After I made it to the top step under the overhang, I turned and watched my uncle drive away. I felt bad thinking it, but I hoped no one saw me pulling up in his old car. I would have never lived that one down.

Everyone was crowding the steps, trying to get out of the rain. Umbrellas were closing and kids pushing past me through the open door.

It hit me the second I got inside. That smell that tells you you're in school and nowhere else. I wanted to turn and run back out, but I'd never have made it past all the kids swarming into the building. So I just stood there, feeling lost and invisible as the place filled with the sound of kids shouting and greeting other kids they hadn't seen all summer.

It was bad enough coming back to school last winter after my folks passed. But seeing somebody else's name on the door to the principal's office gave me the weirdest feeling and just made me feel even emptier inside. I knew then that my daddy was really gone and nothing I did was going to bring him back.

Kids were jostling me, racing to get to their lockers. I was pulling off my hood and shaking the raindrops off my slicker when I spied Chloe Ann down the hall. She was in front of her locker, taking off that red raincoat like she knew everyone was watching. Underneath she was wearing the skirt, blouse, and blazer that had been the Vaughan Elementary dress code since forever. Only her skirt was this really pretty shade of blue and had a neat little flare that came to just above her knees. Her knee socks were a creamy shade of white and even from here I could see the shiny gold buttons on her brand-new-looking navy blazer.

I was piling my stuff into my locker when Madison Driver came down the hall.

Madison was Chloe Ann's best friend. Chloe Ann didn't go anywhere without her constant shadow. Madison's daddy wasn't as rich as Chloe Ann's, but they had a live-in maid and took vacations. The two of them were always bragging about their trips and all the shopping they did while they were away.

Madison opened the locker on the other side of Chloe Ann. She had a pretty face, but outweighed Chloe Ann by at least ten pounds. I always suspected Chloe Ann picked Madison for her best friend because when they stood side by side she made Chloe Ann look skinnier. Right now they were whispering and letting out their usual shrieks and giggles like they were still in fifth grade. Then Chloe Ann stopped giggling, and turned to look down the hall.

I knew without turning around that the popular girls had arrived.

Skylar Hardisty and Paige Trimble were the prettiest girls at Vaughan Elementary and looked like clones of each other with their midnight-blue blazers, short skirts and black patent-leather shoes. I always wondered if there was some law about popular girls having to have long blond hair and matching red headbands.

Skylar and Paige glided by with these secret smiles. Their feet never seemed to touch the scuffed linoleum floors. It was like they breathed different air from the rest of us. The look on Chloe Ann's face almost made me feel sorry for her.

Every year, Skylar and Paige would select one girl to initiate into their club. Chloe Ann was never chosen. I guess not even having the richest daddy in town automatically gives you a free pass to popularity.

I didn't much care one way or the other, and it wasn't sour grapes because they didn't pick me. Skylar and Paige were too cool to go out for sports, which I never understood. What good were they if they couldn't throw a ball? Maybe they thought it would mess up their perfect hair they wasted hours on with the curling iron when they could have been practicing their pitching.

Down the hall, Chloe Ann had a whispered conference with Madison as Skylar and Paige got closer, their almost identical backpacks bobbing on their backs.

"Hey." Chloe Ann threw out the word like she'd just noticed the popular girls approaching, and it wasn't a big deal.

Skylar and Paige looked at Chloe Ann, then at each other. Then they glided past Madison and Chloe Ann like they didn't exist, like they weren't worth the dirt under their shiny new Mary Janes.

Chloe Ann got all red in the face. Even from down the hall I could see how upset she was, even if she tried to act like she wasn't, tossing her mousy hair back over her shoulders, which didn't work because it wasn't long and silky like Skylar and Paige's. It didn't even reach the top of her canary-yellow flowered backpack that I'd been secretly admiring. After she slammed her locker, so loud the sound echoed down the hall, she started walking so fast Madison had to run to keep up.

In the locker next to mine, Cadence Mills was hanging up her raincoat.

Cadence was the only child of Pastor Mills. She wore high-necked blouses and her skirts were longer than anybody else's and she was always trying to convert the rest of us to her fanatical religious beliefs. Like she had her own personal pipeline to God. She was even worse than her daddy because rumor had it she secretly followed a primitive sect of foot-washing Baptists. According to my daddy, the whole thing started as a Christian ritual where Jesus washed the feet of his twelve disciples after the Last Supper. Foot-washers believe pleasure is a sin and females are the most sinful because of Eve tempting Adam to eat that apple in the Garden of Eden.

The other kids made fun of Cadence behind her back and never invited her to their parties, but it didn't seem to bother her any. She acted like we were all sinners, not just the girls, and the sooner we accepted Christ into our lives and prayed for forgiveness, the sooner our souls would be saved. That was probably why her daddy didn't send her to Baptist Day: nobody to convert over there. Though I guess it was a good thing most of us needed saving, or my uncle would be out of business.

Cadence had closed her locker and was staring at me.

Ever since my folks passed, I felt she was singling me out in particular. Like she'd made me her personal mission. I could have told her it wasn't going to work, but the words refused to come out of my mouth. It always seemed to happen when I was around her, like she had this power over me that turned me into a mute.

She kept right on staring at me in that creepy way of hers. I was finding it hard to breathe. I stood rooted to the spot, like I'd been turned to stone.

Even after I finally got my feet to move, I could feel her eyes boring into my back like she could pry out every last one of my secrets.

ELEVEN

Basking in Her Approval

Everyone was really raucous as they piled into the classroom. It was the first day of our last year at Vaughan Elementary. Except for the ones who got left back, most of us would graduate come June.

Our teacher's back was to us as she wrote something on the blackboard. Maybe it was the sun coming in the window that made it look like she had a halo around her head, almost like she was being lit up from the inside.

Then she turned around.

The first thing I thought was that she was even prettier in person. I'd seen her around school and in town sometimes, but never up close. She had wavy brown hair that she wore parted in the middle and came down to just past her neck. Behind her tortoiseshell glasses, her eyes were green. Like the color of grass after a hard rain.

That's what stuck with me: the color of her eyes.

Althea Vale had been teaching sixth grade at Vaughan Elementary for years and years. Like me, she wasn't born in Repentance. She wasn't a Baptist either, which the town wags counted as another mark against her and was why I never saw her at Sunday services. Somebody did see her once at a Lutheran church in the next town over. Leastways, that was how the gossip went. I didn't see what her religion had to with teaching sixth grade.

I'd never heard a bad word said against her, except by my cousin. But a teacher would have to be a miracle worker to make a student out of Noah. Parnell liked Althea Vale, so that ended the subject for me. And I figured she had to be better than our fifth grade teacher.

After my daddy was promoted to assistant principal when I was in third grade, Millicent Beard took his place as fifth-grade teacher. She hailed from one of the oldest families in Repentance, and everyone had to address her as Miss Millie because we still followed the Deep South tradition of calling unmarried females by their first names.

Miss Millie was tall and skinny and looked like Olive Oyl from the Popeye comic strips. She was real strict and one time rapped a kid's knuckles with her ruler. She didn't have a beard or anything like it, but she had a mole in the middle of her chin from which my cousin Noah and his friends swore one time they saw several long hairs sprouting. They probably started the nickname everyone got to calling Miss Millie behind her back: Miss Hairy Mole.

Miss Althea smiled as she waited for us to settle down. She looked my way, and I swear her smile got bigger. Then she stepped away from the blackboard, and we could see what she'd written: *Welcome*, in all capital letters. We all looked at each other. No teacher had ever done that before.

I let out a sigh as we headed for our desks, in alphabetical order like we'd been doing since kindergarten. Mine was in the third row, where as usual I'd have to stare at the back of Chloe Ann Briggs's head all year.

Next to Chloe Ann were Dylan Bryant and Nicholas Buck, the class cut-ups who were always getting called to my daddy's office for one prank or another and who Chloe Ann ignored like they didn't exist.

Although there were scores of Cobbs, Coopers, and Cumptons buried in the cemetery, their issue must have ended with them because we had only one Cooper, first name Austin, whose grandparents hailed from South Carolina and was no relation to our Repentance dead. He was a quiet kid who didn't have any friends and always sat at the second to last desk in Chloe Ann's row. At the end of the row was Brandon Cowan, who hardly ever spoke up in class, and when he did you had to lean forward to hear him because he was born with a cleft palate.

Then came my row—the Ds. Wyatt Dake was a serious-minded student whose daddy sat on the town council, which was probably why Wyatt never let anyone cheat off of him during tests. Next to him was Olivia Davis, a pretty brunette who surprised everyone when she turned out to be one of our fifth-grade softball team's Most Valuable Players, hitting almost as many home runs as me in last season's spring league. But over the summer, rumors spread that she'd been seen with Skylar and Paige and was a shoo-in to be the new popular girl. Which would be a darned shame and a real loss to our softball team, especially with the special fall league that was started a couple years ago kicking into gear again in a few weeks. This was a really important season because it would be our first as a sixth-grade team.

Timothy Dickson sat on the other side of Olivia. He was on the freak rung of the ladder because he tried to live his life according to the Scriptures. He was always talking doom and gloom like it was already too late and there was no hope for Repentance. I usually got the brunt of it being stuck sitting on the other side of him. But he couldn't be any worse than Madison, who sat on my right like she'd been doing since kindergarten.

I'd no sooner got settled at my desk and was thinking it was going to be a long year when Chloe Ann twisted around in her seat. "Well, if isn't Little Orphan Mary."

She'd taken to calling me that ever since my folks passed. Under my desk, my hands balled into fists.

Next to me, Madison started chanting "Little Orphan Mary" in a sing-song whisper. The kids sitting around us watched to see what I would do. Probably remembering what happened in fifth grade last year when Alexis Hamilton, whose family moved away over the summer, said I purposely hit her with the ball when I was pitching. The truth was she was in the wrong batting position and got in the way of the ball, so how on earth was that my fault?

But Chloe Ann wasn't finished. "You still a Dobbs?" she sneered under her breath. "Guess your aunt and uncle haven't made up their minds if they're going to keep you or not. Why would they want to adopt a loser?"

You know how they say you see red when you get really mad? Well, I didn't just see red, I saw a swirling kaleidoscope of colors doing a dizzying whirligig behind my eyes. My head was pounding so loud it blocked out everything else. Chloe Ann was still talking because I could see her lips moving.

If I could have murdered her right then and there I would have.

The whole business between Chloe Ann and me started in the second grade when I was appointed captain of our softball team, the Mockingbirds. I didn't pick her because she couldn't run to save her life. Ever since then she'd been out to get me.

Everyone had settled down and Miss Althea was looking at Chloe Ann and me like she knew something was up. Chloe Ann must have had eyes in the back of her head, because she turned around and gave Miss Althea the biggest, fakest grin you ever saw. She did that with all the teachers, brownnosing them so she could be class pet.

I had a hard time concentrating while Miss Althea talked about the subjects we'd be studying. Until she got to social studies. That was my favorite. My daddy would tell me to put my finger on the big round globe in his study and pick a place I had a hankering to visit. My mama told him not to put ideas in my head, like she knew I'd never travel to those places. As if I wasn't going to live and die right here in Repentance like everyone else.

Miss Althea asked if any of us knew who the first settlers were in our part of northwest Arkansas.

My pitching arm shot up like it had a mind of its own. Something about Miss Althea made me want to give the right answer, if only to see that smile light up her face.

"Mary Grace?" Miss Althea had the tiniest trace of an accent, even though her name didn't sound French. I thought of Meurice, who spewed out all those foreign words in the woods and was supposed to be descended from the French. I didn't know where Miss Althea came from, but maybe she also carried the blood of those early settlers.

"The French explorers came here first," I said, my voice loud and clear. Which surprised me because I didn't like speaking in class.

"That's correct," Miss Althea said. "Thank you, Mary Grace."

I sat back in my seat. In the row in front of me. Chloe Ann looked fit to be tied.

For once it didn't bother me. I was too busy basking in the approval of my sixth-grade teacher.

TWELVE

Most Valuable Player

The last class of the day was physical education, my favorite subject. But the only thing anyone wanted to talk about was Hunter Fewell, the new PE teacher.

He moved to Repentance over the summer and the gossip mill had been churning overtime ever since. For one thing, he was single and all the teachers at Vaughan Elementary were married with the exceptions of Miss Millie and Miss Althea. He was young—some said the same age as our fourth-grade teacher Emily King—which was another mark against him.

Half the boys in our fourth-grade class had crushes on Mrs. King, who moved here with her husband six years ago and was the youngest teacher at Vaughan Elementary. I liked her because she was always nice to me and looked a little like my mama with her big blue eyes and honey-blond hair that curled at the bottom.

The big mystery was why Mr. Fewell would come to Repentance, which was the tiniest speck on the map you had to squint to see.

But it was his looks that the girls wouldn't stop talking about. I'd only caught a glimpse of him once or twice over the summer, but always from a distance and never in church. All I cared about was: Did he have what it took to coach our softball team?

This was also an important season for our softball team, because it was the first time in Repentance's history that sixth graders would be allowed to compete in extramural games. Which meant we could play against schools in other towns. It took a lot of going back and forth before the board gave their permission. A bunch of fiery town halls where Pastor Mills said sixth graders were too young to be engaged in competitive sports. My uncle sided with the pastor. I tried not to hold it against him. At one meeting, I heard it was my uncle who said our time would be better spent studying the Bible. Personally, I didn't see what was so sinful about throwing a softball, not counting the time I hit Alexis Hamilton and, like I said, that wasn't on purpose.

As we piled into the gymnasium, I got my first good look at Mr. Fewell and honestly didn't see what the fuss was about. He was dark and looked like a pirate and couldn't hold a candle to Parnell, who was fair and how I imagined God might look in human form.

After we got assigned our lockers, we changed into our gym clothes and Mr. Fewell took our height and weight. I'd shot up over the summer, but didn't have a lot more pounds to go with the nearly half-inch I'd grown. I could feel more muscles in my arms and legs though, and I sailed through the calisthenics Mr. Fewell assigned, using his whistle to time us. I noticed with glee how Chloe Ann barely made it through a set of sit-ups and push-ups. I was sure that by tomorrow she'd have a note from her mama excusing her from gym.

When school let out, all I could think about was the softball tryouts next week. I'd been looking forward to them all through the long, hot summer, which was an added bonus of having a fall league. And the weather usually cooperated.

If I got my chores done quick enough, I might get in some practice before supper.

I aced the tryouts and was named captain again. This didn't surprise me. And I was still a Mockingbird, ever since we stole the name from the second graders. Even without Olivia, our team was shaping up to be pretty awesome.

I revised my opinion of Mr. Fewell, who was a fair coach and made me feel like I was the team's Most Valuable Player. The only fly in the ointment was Chloe Ann, who was still as mean as ever. And in class Madison still whispered "Little Orphan Mary" in my ear. One morning, I'd had enough and told her she'd better stop if she knew what was good for her. I fixed her with a look that showed I meant business. Madison glared right back, which showed she had more backbone than I gave her credit for. But she quit her whispering, which was all I cared about.

All in all, I was feeling pretty good. The weather had turned summer-like again as if to make up for all that rain in August. With a string of sunny days, it looked like Indian summer was here to stay. Then it was the third week in September and the next day was our first game against the Pinetree Pirates.

THIRTEEN

Kids Can Be Cruel

I woke up that morning with a terrible pain in my stomach. I suspected the culprit was my second helping of freshly churned vanilla ice cream my uncle brought home last night as a surprise.

My tummy ache came and went during the day. In class, I caught Miss Althea looking at me once or twice like she knew my mind was someplace else. But even if I weren't feeling poorly, I was too excited to concentrate on schoolwork.

The minute the bell rang, I was up like a shot. I raced down the hall, shoved my books into my locker, and took off for the gymnasium. Once we were all in uniform—my number was lucky seven—Coach Fewell gave the pep talk he'd been giving the past few weeks. He ended by saying how important this game was and he knew we had the right stuff to cream the competition. Those were his exact words: cream the competition. Then we all gave each other high-fives.

A few minutes before we set out for the field, Coach Fewell took me aside and whispered that I was our team's secret weapon and he knew I could win it for them. He said I was the best pitcher he'd ever coached and he was depending on me not to let him or the Mockingbirds down. This should have made me nervous but for some reason didn't. Maybe it was because he was smiling that smile I was starting to like more and more. My stomach wasn't hurting anymore, and I figured that for another sign.

Outside, the stands were full. My aunt wasn't there, of course; she rarely ever left the house these days unless my uncle lifted her out of the wheelchair and put her in the car. But that happened only when they had somewhere important to go, like my folks' funeral back in November. My aunt didn't even come to church anymore. And my uncle went back on the road this morning. As for my cousin, Noah had never once come to watch me play and I didn't expect him to start now. Some of the teachers were here, though. I spotted Miss Althea sitting next to Miss Sydney, our longtime school librarian.

The game lasted over two hours. At bat, we hit a few doubles in the first inning, but the other team came back at the bottom of the third when our rightfielder caught a fly ball, knocking out their batter. But then the runner on third tagged up and scored. I got us back on track in the next inning with the changeup I'd been practicing. My slower, off-speed pitch worked, confusing the first Pirates batter, who I struck out easily. After Jasmine Kirby, who was the second-best pitcher on the fifth-grade team, threw some nice curve balls in the bottom of the fifth, causing batters to foul, then strike out, we figured we had it clinched. But she'd given up a hit and we'd made an error, and a little dribbler past the mound loaded the bases. When their cleanup hitter earned a walk, it sent the player on third home, tying the score.

Then came the critical inning—the bottom of the sixth. It was our turn at bat. The Pirates pitcher used my changeup technique, causing our leadoff hitter to swing and miss at the first two pitches. But she got the hang of it and on the next pitch—another changeup—she hit a long fly ball that bounced in fair territory and went over the outfield fence for a ground rule double, so she had to stop at second base. One down, one on. Our next batter swung and missed at the first pitch, but she hit a grounder to second on the next pitch, getting thrown at first. The runner on second then broke for third, but the Pirates' first baseman made a great throw and their third baseman made a perfect tag to get her out. Double play! It was the kind of a play that no one makes in sixth-grade softball . . . until I saw the Pirates pull it off.

Then I was up. The pressure was enormous. With no one on base and two down, I needed a hit or it was all over. I focused like I always did, erasing everything else from my mind. I followed the trajectory of the ball as it came at me and swung.

I missed. I couldn't believe it. I swung a second time. Another miss. I bent down to grab a handful of dirt to dry my sweaty palms, and I saw the Pirates' pitcher smile. With two strikes against me, I had only one chance left. I felt my hands stiffening on the bat, which was the absolute worst thing that could happen to a batter. Panic closed up my throat. I could hear sounds coming from the stands and thought of my daddy. He was the one who taught me how to hit a softball. Wherever he was, maybe he was watching.

I couldn't let him down. I took a deep breath to try to relax.

The Pirates' pitcher reared back. Her face scrunched in concentration, she finally tossed the ball, low and fast the way Parnell had pitched it to me over the summer. I was ready. I swung. The crack of the bat as it hit the ball was the most beautiful sound I'd ever heard. I threw down my bat and ran as if my life depended on it. As the ball sailed into the gap between center and right, I hit the first base bag and kept on going. The right fielder raced to retrieve the ball, but by then I was already around second and heading for third. My helmet flew off, and my hair was blowing back in the breeze. I glanced over my shoulder . . . the right fielder had the ball now and threw it in, missing the cutoff. The ball skipped off the grass to the third baseman, who fumbled it. It bounced off her foot and then dribbled behind her. I rounded third and kept on going, the third base coach waving me around. The third baseman retrieved the ball and tossed it to the plate. The on-deck batter motioned for me to slide. It was going to be close. But the throw was too late. I was safe at home.

The crowd went wild.

We held the Pirates scoreless in the top of the sixth and that was the game. We had won.

Flush with victory, I felt light as a feather as my feet left the ground and the team lifted me into the air. Then we walked back to the dugout where Coach Fewell was waiting. He congratulated us and clapped me on the back as the team broke out in an off-key chorus of "For She's a Jolly Good Fellow." I'd never been happier. All I could think was I hadn't let Coach down.

Back in the locker room, we couldn't stop high-fiving each other and crowing about our victory. It was our first win against an away team, and we went back over the game, play by play. Everyone was spellbound listening, with so many of us piled into the locker room and nobody in any hurry to change out of our sweaty uniforms. It felt like most of the sixth grade was here.

I was so busy feeling proud of myself that I didn't notice how quiet the place had suddenly gotten. Everyone was staring at me. Maybe they were expecting a speech. I cleared my throat, and that was when I heard it.

A snicker.

It was coming from Chloe Ann. I hadn't seen her or Madison on the bleachers or noticed them in the locker room. But there they were front and center. Now they were both snickering and pointing at the lower half of my body.

I looked down and was shocked to see a big red stain on my white shorts. At first I thought I must have injured myself sliding into home. But I didn't feel pain or see any open cuts. Then something warm gushed out between my legs. Had I peed myself? I was beyond mortified.

Then I remembered the stomachache that had been ailing me all day, and I knew. It had finally happened. I'd started my monthlies.

"Someone get that girl a tampon." Skylar's voice sounded like a cannon as it thundered across the locker room.

"If she even knows what it is!"

That set off more snickers that turned into gales of laughter, Chloe Ann laughing loudest of all.

I was sure my face was as red as my blood-stained shorts. I wanted to crawl under a rock. I stood frozen in the middle of the locker room thinking that now I was officially a woman and had never been more miserable in my life.

It was the hardest thing I ever had to do, but I finally made myself start moving. I turned my back on those girls and headed for my locker. It was the longest walk ever. Finally, the laughter died out. It seemed like forever until they all left. Only then did I turn around.

The locker room still echoed with their laughter. Tomorrow it would be all over town. I'd never hear the end of it. But right now all I could think was how my sweet victory had turned to ashes, trampled like dirt under the feet of those awful girls.

A sharp cramp fisted in my belly. I felt stickiness between my thighs. I marched into the girls' room, my mind on getting the blood out of my shorts. I barely registered the sound of a coin clinking in one of the dispensers on the wall.

I wasn't alone.

Paige was walking toward me. She handed me something long and rectangular covered in light-pink wrapping. "Here. This should help."

My face was still flaming hot. I managed to mumble "thank you." Paige nodded, then hurried out of the bathroom. Skylar was probably wondering where she was. I thought that that was the second nice thing Paige had done. Telling me she was sorry about my folks, then giving me this.

I looked down at what was in my hand. A sanitary napkin. I put it down and went over to the sink. I took off my shorts and turned on the water full blast. But the bloodstains wouldn't go away, no matter how hard I scrubbed. I'd have to use some bleach when I got home. I was glad for once that I was in charge of doing the laundry so my aunt wouldn't see my shame. She hadn't talked to me about what to expect, and my mama never told me. She probably figured there was still time.

I read the directions on the sanitary napkin package, but the problem was my panties were soaked through with blood. I had to wear something under my skirt on the walk home or I'd leak all over the place. I checked the stalls to make sure another girl wasn't hiding inside one, ready to humiliate me all over again. Then I darted into one and unwrapped the napkin, which felt thick, like a pad. I put the sticky side in my panties, hoping it would hold. Then, just to be on the safe side, I stuffed wads of toilet paper on top of that.

As I left the bathroom, I saw a tampon dispenser on the wall next to the sanitary napkin dispenser. My face got red again when I remembered what Skylar had said in the locker room. I wouldn't be in their club now even if she got on her hands and knees.

After I'd put on my blouse, skirt, and knee-highs, I sat on the bench and buckled my shoes, thinking that this was only the first day of my period. Which meant I had six more days of horrible pain to get through.

As I walked through the empty halls, another cramp knifed through my lower belly. As I passed the big hall clock, I saw that it was already gone on five. I should have been home by now, helping to get supper ready. My mind was occupied with all these thoughts so I didn't notice the light on in my sixth-grade classroom.

I tried to tiptoe past, but it was too late.

Miss Althea had seen me.

FOURTEEN

Good and Evil

"Mary Grace?"

What was she doing here this late? And what was I supposed to do now? I couldn't pretend I didn't hear her.

"Congratulations." Miss Althea had come out from behind her desk. "You did great today. I'm proud of you."

I mumbled "Thanks" with my head down, hoping she'd get the message that I wasn't in a talking frame of mind. "Mary Grace?" she said again as she stepped into the hall. "Are you all right?"

I started to nod. My throat welled up. Tears stung my eyes.

"Whatever has happened, child?" Miss Althea took me by the hand into the classroom and closed the door.

Maybe it was her touch. Or her familiar perfume. Or the sound of her voice, like she really cared.

Suddenly I was telling her about the locker room. Between sobs, I said it was because of what was inside me. That I made it happen.

Even blinded by tears, I could see how upset Miss Althea was. Like she was taking my troubles to heart. "Why ever would you say that?"

"Because it's true! I'm wicked and I deserved what those girls did." Then, before I knew it, I was blurting out the terrible secret I'd kept bottled up all these months.

It was Thanksgiving night, and all anybody could talk about was the ice storm that had just started. Everyone had been warned to stay inside. After we got home from my uncle's house, my folks called me into the living room. They sat me down, which right away set off warning bells. I tried to think what I'd done this time. I knew it was bad because my mama usually took to her room right after supper. Because of her heart, my daddy told me when I was five and asked why she could never come and watch me play.

My daddy said, "Your mother and I have come to a decision. We've decided to send you to Baptist Day. We think the change will be good for you." My daddy did all the talking, my mama just sitting there and nodding as if the whole thing wasn't her idea.

"I'll never go there!" I jumped up and stamped my feet so hard the lamp on the glass table shook.

"I told you she'd react like this," Mama said as if I wasn't in the room.

"It's all your doing!" I yelled at her. A pained look came over her face and she clutched her chest. But I didn't care if she had a heart attack right there on the living room floor. I ran out of the room. My mama shouted for my daddy to go after me, but I already had my coat on and was out the front door.

The wind hit my face the second I got outside. Everything was covered in ice. I stumbled a couple of times as I ran into the backyard, where branches that had broken off trees littered the white ground. But the huge elm in the middle of the yard was still standing. I clambered up even though it was slippery going and hid in the shelter of the secret tree house I'd built that fall.

Down below, I heard my daddy calling for me, but the wind kept throwing back my name so after awhile I wasn't sure if he was still out here or it was just echoes of his voice. I couldn't see him. My fingers and toes were numb by now and it wouldn't be long before I froze to death. Then my folks would be sorry. Defeated, I climbed back down. As the wind slashed my face, I thought how I'd run away tomorrow once the storm cleared out.

I went back into the house through the kitchen door, which was always unlocked. I called out for my mama and daddy, but silence was my only answer. I walked through every room in the house, but they weren't there. Then I went to the garage.

The car was gone. I ran back outside, but now I couldn't see anything because the storm had picked up. I thought of calling Sheriff Kanady, but then he'd know I was the reason my folks went out in that storm. When I went back inside, the lights started flickering, then went out. The storm must have knocked out the power lines. By now my head was pounding something fierce and I lay down on the sofa to try to ease it some. The next thing I knew, sunlight was pouring in through the blinds and someone was knocking on the front door.

It was Sheriff Kanady. There'd been an accident the night before. A trucker's rig slid on the ice and crashed into my parents' car.

"It's my fault, don't you see?" I sobbed. "If I hadn't run out in that storm, my folks would still be alive!"

"Oh, my dear child. This terrible thing has been festering inside you all these months? There, there."

Miss Althea's soothing voice only made it worse, opening a bottomless wellspring of guilt and grief. Then I was in her arms and the painful hurt in my chest gave way to a rockslide of tears. It felt like mini-explosions going off inside me. As I wept and Miss Althea rocked me in her arms, a strange feeling came over me. I could almost imagine the wetness on my face was holy water, like a baptism. Cleansing me of sin. Did immersion in one's own tears count?

But I already knew the answer. It only made me cry harder.

Between sobs, I told Miss Althea how lonely I felt. How nothing I did would bring back my folks. How scared I was that my aunt and uncle would pack me off to that children's home in Fayetteville. But most of all, I was afraid I'd never be forgiven. Especially by my mama, who never loved me the way my daddy did.

"Hush, now," Miss Althea said. "Your mama loved you very much or she wouldn't have gone out in that storm to find you. What happened isn't your fault. You couldn't have known that truck would hit them."

I shook my head as I pulled away, swiping at my wet face. "I made it happen," I insisted.

"You did nothing of the kind! The accident was God's will. It was your folks' time and nothing you did could have changed that."

I wanted so badly to believe her, but the guilt was making it hard to breathe. "How do you know when it's your time?"

"You don't. That's why in the short spell you have on earth you must try to be the best person you can. Your parents have forgiven you, Mary Grace. Now it's time to forgive yourself."

How could she be so sure my folks had forgiven me? And how could I forgive myself? I thought about those times I ran away. Remembered my hands around Tyler Lee's throat. "Sometimes these feelings come over me," I heard myself saying. "Like I want to hurt someone real bad."

She didn't say anything for so long I figured it was because she knew I was wicked. Just like Tyler Lee said.

"We all have evil inside us," Miss Althea finally said.

"Because we're born in sin?"

Again, she was slow to answer. Then she took off her glasses, so I had a real good look at her pretty green eyes. Even if I couldn't read what was in them.

"Some of us," she finally said. "But there's also good in us."

I was quiet, trying to take that in. "You saying good and evil can live together in one person?"

"Yes. You can't have one without the other. They're both in us. No matter how wicked you think you are."

I was still stuck on how good and evil could both be inside us at the same time. I thought of my cousin Noah and how I never once saw the good in him unless he was hiding it pretty good.

"The trick is to find a way to balance them," Miss Althea said, "and keep the evil from killing off the good."

It sounded almost like a sacrilege. In church, Pastor Mills said you could only be one or the other. But his sermons sure made it sound like evil had the upper hand. And he didn't tell us what we were supposed to do when we felt it rising up in us. I couldn't see how praying would stop me from getting mad at Chloe Ann as if she was put on earth just to torment me.

"We have to be vigilant and work hard to cast out the evil," Miss Althea said like she was reading my mind. "Harder than you've ever worked at anything in your life."

I still wasn't convinced. "If I do that, Chloe Ann won't pick on me anymore?"

"Chloe Ann is jealous of you. She hasn't tried to fight the evil inside her. But you can do it. You can be the bigger person."

I heard my daddy's voice in her words, the same words he'd once said to me.

"You had a great victory today." Miss Althea was smiling her pretty smile. "Never forget that. And remember, the things that come hard are what test us and show what we're made of. But if you choose good, you can never go wrong. You are good, Mary Grace. Never stop believing that."

I wasn't so sure about the good part. Or if I'd ever find the right path, the one that led to salvation. But that adult part of me could see Miss Althea was trying to ease my burden, and I loved her for it.

My eyes slid to the clock on the wall. I told Miss Althea I had to go. She said she hoped she'd helped and was here anytime I wanted to talk. I found it hard to look at her now that I'd spilled my innermost feelings.

I just thanked her and left.

As I trudged along, I thought about what Miss Althea had said. The trouble was, I hadn't told her everything. There was something else about the night my folks died that could keep me out of heaven for sure. I didn't tell her because if she knew she might not believe that I wasn't pure evil. The last thing I wanted was for her to turn her back on me like God probably had. That was what made it so hard to sit in church every Sunday, knowing the other terrible thing I'd done.

Was there really no hope for me? My uncle gave people hope, even if business was slow right now because folks didn't have enough money to pay for their souls to be saved. Miss Althea believed there was good in me, even if she didn't know the whole story. If we could only be saved by the grace of God, there had to be a chance for me, right? Or why would my parents have named me Grace?

That had to mean I had good inside me, but how much? What percent was good and what percent was evil? I knew it wasn't anywhere near fifty-fifty.

I stopped walking. I was sure I'd been planning to take the long way home because the good part of me wouldn't take the shortcut through the woods where I was forbidden to go. And truth to tell, I wasn't keen on running into the Boogeyman again.

Yet here I was, at the entrance to the woods.

Shadows were everywhere.

And the sound of footsteps stomping through the underbrush.

FIFTEEN

A Shot at Salvation?

It wasn't the Boogeyman.

Who never came this close to the edge of the woods, leastways not as long as I'd been living.

He looked tall, though not nearly as tall as Meurice.

But he was darker. He blended right in with the vegetation around him.

He stopped next to a tree. I couldn't tell if he'd seen me. I saw a red spark darting here and there as he brought a cigarette to his mouth. He took a few puffs, then put it out under the heel of his boot.

I must have made some kind of sound, because his head shot up.

I backed up, ready to turn tail and run.

Too late. He started walking, came all the way out of the woods. He was even bigger up close. But his eyes weren't what I imagined. They were a bright blue-green that put me in mind of photographs I'd seen of the ocean.

He took another step toward me. I stood my ground, but I'd started to shake and my heart was thumping around my chest like crazy.

He stopped a few feet away. Something in the way he looked at me told me he knew I'd been here the whole time.

Then he reached into his pocket.

And pulled out a bag.

I forgot everything else as I stared at the long strands of red licorice inside, trying to remember the last time I'd eaten. It must have been breakfast, which was hard to get down what with the cramps. My mouth watered, and I was mortified to hear my stomach grumbling. I wondered if he heard it, too.

He opened the bag. "Want a piece?" His voice was deep and he dragged out his words in the drawl I'd been hearing all my life. But then, most of the drifters who blew into our town hailed from somewhere in the South.

I still hadn't said anything. He cocked his head like he was taking the measure of me. "Or maybe your parents told you not to take candy from strangers."

"My parents are dead." The words just tumbled out. Tears pricked my eyes and I was afraid I'd start bawling again, like I did with Miss Althea. "Where are your parents?" I asked, more to keep him from seeing me cry than anything else.

"Gone away."

"Gone away where?"

"Beats me." He shrugged, but his face changed and his ocean eyes got dark, like a storm cloud was passing through them. "Sure you don't want some?"

He was holding out the bag of licorice. I shook my head, then remembered my manners. "No, thank you."

He nodded like it was what he thought I'd say. Then he took out a long red twist and stuck it in his mouth. After he put the bag back in his pocket, he turned and walked away. I stood staring after him, my mind buzzing with questions. Such as what would make his folks leave on their own steam without God having had some hand in it, like Miss Althea said.

I wondered if that was why he drifted around the South. Because he didn't have a home anymore.

If he ever got lonely living in a room by himself at Miss Lillian's.

And what he was doing in the woods.

When I woke up the next day, I was still thinking about my encounter with the drifter. I kept it to myself, knowing if I told it'd just land me in hot water. I thought of how he offered to to share his food, which was more than my cousin ever did. Then I heard Miss Althea's voice, saying we all had good and evil in us.

Maybe this was Darryl Stokes's way of squaring things with God.

As for me, even if I was ninety-nine-percent evil, the other one percent had to be good, right? At least my cramps were gone, which I took as a sign. I started helping more around the house and took to doing the laundry before it piled up. I said my prayers every night and in church looked Pastor Mills right in the eye as I repeated the Scriptures. Maybe God wouldn't judge me so harshly now and He'd put me over on the side of the angels.

School was harder going because everyone heard what happened in the locker room and for a few days didn't let up with the taunts. I tried to follow Miss Althea's advice and be the bigger person, but it wasn't easy with Chloe Ann giving me no peace. Still, I managed to hold on to my temper and let what she said roll right off of me. Even Miss Althea noticed and would smile at me sometimes, like we shared a secret. I started whistling again, a habit I'd gotten out of after my folks passed.

I felt more like myself than I had in a long time. What I didn't, couldn't, know was that this was the beginning of my coming out of the cocoon of grief that had gripped me for the past ten months.

As the days passed, I could feel the evil starting to seep out of me like the sap from the pines in winter. I thought maybe I had this thing licked.

Then one morning near the end of September, the door to our classroom opened.

And my life changed again.

NOW

SIXTEEN

At eight forty-five in the morning of the third Sunday in September, the faithful and devout of Repentance make their way to the local church.

Built in 1900 and rebuilt in 1946 after a tornado ripped through most of the weatherboard and novelty siding and decimated the gable-roofed bell tower, the First Baptist Church has always been a haven for those seeking solace and direction. The sermons in this tiny House of God have seen them through hard times, illness, and grievous loss, including that winter twenty-four years back when everyone packed the place in hopes of receiving divine enlightenment.

Now, all this time later, they're once again looking for answers. And not only because of recent attacks on churches, notably the 2017 massacre at another First Baptist Church in Sutherland Springs, to date the largest mass shooting in the Lone Star state's history. That explains why the past several Sundays have seen a significant swelling in their ranks. Though Mary Grace suspects this has less to do with the sermons themselves than folks believing there's safety and strength in numbers. That the collective power of their faith could go a long way toward shielding them from the next enraged gunman.

Or eradicating the Devil from their midst.

So far this has proved as ineffective as the weekly town halls that have grown more vociferous, with folks who normally keep a low profile speaking out, bonding with others they wouldn't give the time of day to if they met on the street. But conditions are far from ordinary and being joined in common purpose is a powerful unifier.

From her vantage point in the second to last pew on the left, Mary Grace watches everyone file in. As if by unwritten law, the rows closest to the pulpit are reserved for the rich and powerful. It's been that way for over a century. Parnell has taken over the aisle seat from his dead daddy in the first pew on the left. His mother and sister are next to him. As befits the family that's the closest thing to royalty in Repentance, folks nod at the Vaughans as they pass. Across the aisle, Jackson Briggs sits alone in the first pew on the right as he's done every Sunday for seven years, ever since his wife Charlotte died from early-onset Alzheimer's.

Briggs is leading the movement to run Stokes out of town, but as Mary Grace has pointed out at every meeting, this isn't the wild west and the law isn't on their side. But she can't stop him from speaking his mind, which is only setting the town more on edge than it already is, especially with each day that brings the calendar closer to November. It's as though everyone's holding their breath waiting for the other shoe to drop.

Darryl Stokes has been in Repentance five weeks and two days. The circumstances under which he departed two decades ago paved the way for all sorts of interpretations of the events of that long-ago November. It caused a rift between Owen Kanady and Jackson Briggs that never healed.

More congregants are coming through the double doors. All observed by the sharp eyes of Alma Allred, who took over her mama's rumor-mongering business and always sits in the last pew on the right, her knitting needles clickety-clacketing as if she were on her front porch and not in God's house. Mary Grace earns a nod as congregants pass her row because she's the law now and whatever else folks might say, her position commands respect. A tall, slender woman with shoulder-length brown hair turns a few heads as she enters with her daughter.

Mary Grace watches Madison Driver make her way across the church, never failing to marvel at how her childhood adversary has changed. As she passes her row, Madison glares at Emily King, who's sitting a few seats down from Mary Grace with her husband and two sons.

After high school, Madison went to college in Little Rock and came back with a husband, a new figure, and a shortened version of her name—the trendier-sounding Maddie. Without those extra pounds, she was a stunning woman. It didn't stop her husband from running off with their former Vaughan Elementary fourth-grade teacher, which caused a huge scandal and made Madison the subject of gossip for months.

When Madison's husband dumped her for someone else, Emily King slunk back to Repentance, where's she's been persona non grata ever since. Mostly for leaving her children, a more unforgivable sin in the eyes of the town than being an adulterer. Which is why no one could believe it when her husband took her back.

After Madison and her daughter find seats in a pew a few rows up, Madison shifts around. Her gaze falls (whether by accident or design) on Mary Grace. Something in Madison's expression throws her back in time. Not that it takes much these days. She's remembering that last Friday in September. How relieved she was when she didn't have to sit next to Madison in class anymore.

Five weeks later, she and Madison were in the same seats waiting their turn to be questioned by Sheriff Kanady. Both trying to ignore what was between them. Because Dobbs came before Driver, Mary Grace had to go first. Even though it was cold out, she was sweating under her school uniform.

She wonders if the reappearance of Darryl Stokes has brought back memories for Madison, too.

Madison's daughter is looking her way now. Allison Driver is the spitting image of her mother at that age, something Mary Grace always finds unsettling. The way she's looking—not at her as Mary Grace initially thought, but at the girls next to her—Allison could be Madison all over again, that same yearning expression on her face as she stood next to her locker with Chloe Ann Briggs, watching the popular girls pass by.

Loud squeals erupt in Mary Grace's pew. Felicity and her friends are giggling at something they're watching on Felicity's phone. Over their heads—Felicity's long dark hair a striking contrast to the two blond girls next to her—Paige Trimble Reeves rolls her eyes at Mary Grace, two mothers of preteen girls bonded in their common purpose. But Mary Grace remembers all the years when they shared nothing in common, Paige gliding through junior high and high school with nary a bump along the way. After being crowned homecoming queen in their senior year, she married Aiden Reeves, her longtime boyfriend. Aiden's home sick today with a stomach flu. As far as Mary Grace knows, the Reeves family has never missed a Sunday sermon.

Although they aren't friends or anywhere near, Mary Grace never forgot Paige's act of kindness that afternoon in the girls' room after she suffered the worst humiliation of her young life. Even all these years later, just the sweaty smell of a locker room brings it all back.

Madison, who laughed at her that long-ago day, has a protective arm around her daughter and is whispering to her. Probably telling her those girls aren't worth getting upset over; that being one of the popular girls doesn't matter. Except it does. Because being popular means being accepted.

As she watches her daughter now, Mary Grace can't help but feel a surge of maternal pride. Felicity isn't just a star athlete and straight-A student. She was chosen by Haley and Lauren Reeves, who have taken up the cudgels of their mother and Skylar Hardisty before them and head up the popular crowd. Except that unlike Paige and Skylar, who weren't really twins even if they dressed and acted alike, Haley and Lauren were born minutes apart and are identical in almost every way.

That includes the sound of their laughter, which is getting louder.

"Hush now," Paige admonishes her daughters.

"Put your phone away. What have I told you about smartphones in church?" Mary Grace scolds Felicity, who rarely disobeys (except when it comes to her electronic gadgets or when she's with her friends). The three instantly quiet down, but none of them looks the slightest bit remorseful.

Mary Grace wonders if Felicity ever thinks about the fact that she's in a house of worship. Her daughter has never been full of the questions that have plagued Mary Grace as long as she can remember. Questions that only got worse after her parents died.

She can see herself in the fifth row from the back on the right, sandwiched between her uncle and cousin, who always sat with his long legs out in the aisle like he was hoping to trip someone. Then, over her uncle's head Noah would stare at her, as if to remind her of the unholy secrets they shared.

Over the years, she has given a lot of thought to the afternoon Althea Vale talked about evil and good, informed though it was by Mary Grace's own black and white view of the world. As if the two could really be weighed in percentages. And yet, for a brief time, she truly believed she had a shot at salvation.

The heavy oak doors are starting to close.

Tyler Lee Hibbard hurries in, his daughter at his side. In the attractive, sandy-haired man, Mary Grace can barely see the pesky boy who used to trail her everywhere. Until the hot August day when he showed up outside her secret cave, where she stopped going after that.

Everyone thought Tyler Lee would follow his daddy (God rest his soul) into Parnell Vaughan II's garage, even if many in town felt Tyler Lee Sr. was partially to blame for justice not being served. Instead Tyler Lee Jr. took himself off to college in Fayetteville and when he came back he opened his own accounting office. After cancer killed his wife four years ago, he took over the sole raising of their daughter Cherie Leigh who, like Felicity, is a straight-A student and top softball player.

Back in the day, Mary Grace was the sole possessor of the number-one softball spot, something she might not have pulled off if it weren't for Hunter Fewell. His encouragement and support made her feel like a champion even if she never got to win the ultimate prize and at one point risked losing it all.

At the organ, Caroline Womack smiles as she sways in rhythm to the music. In her high-necked white dress and wide-brimmed hat, she could have stepped out of an earlier century. Miss Caroline, who also teaches piano (though Mary Grace never had a lesson), has devoted her whole life to music and has been a fixture in church since before Mary Grace was born. In all her years attending Sunday services and despite recent rumors of Miss Caroline being afflicted with dementia, she's never heard her hit a wrong note.

Just as the music reaches a crescendo, Isaac Wood pushes through the half-closed doors. Loud murmurs fill the church as he walks up the aisle, hesitating when he reaches the row where his ex-wife Adalynn and their daughter Annabelle are seated.

"This isn't going to help him win custody." Paige shakes her head as Wood stumbles into the row, almost falling over some of the congregants. "Making a spectacle of himself in front of the whole town."

Mary Grace's opinion of the former popular girl just went down a notch. She thought Paige was better than those who viewed life through the narrow lens of their own prejudice and ignorance that, in spite of some advancements, still runs rampant in Repentance.

Lauren Reeves nods in agreement with her mother. "He's always drunk. I heard he fell down in the street the other night."

"He's such a loser."

Just hearing that hateful word come out of her daughter's mouth instantly catapults Mary Grace back twenty-four years, when another sixth grader called her the same thing; she remembers that long-ago afternoon when the schoolyard echoed with it, the other kids picking up the chant.

"Felicity, that's a terrible thing to say. You know better than that. We don't label people."

"I'm not labeling anyone. He *is* a loser. And everyone knows it." Felicity turns her back on her, whispers something to Lauren. Mary Grace tries to rein in her anger at her daughter for passing judgment on a man she's never met. In her way, Felicity is as bad as Paige. Or is it this town?

"At the rate he's going, he'll be lucky if the judge lets him see Annabelle at all," Paige says, censure in every word.

Or whether his daughter will want to see him. Mary Grace watches the fifth grader turn away from her father, her face red with shame. But Mary Grace remembers the man who showed her compassion when she was an angry kid running away and acting out after her parents died. She looks at her daughter, giggling with her friends, oblivious to Wood's pain. Felicity has no idea how it feels to be all alone in the world, and Mary Grace hopes she never does.

Wood has finally settled down when a door at the side of the church opens and Cadence Mills sweeps in. More murmurs go up in the congregation. It's common knowledge that she was recently ordained. But no one actually thought she'd take over from Pastor Mills, who's been feeling poorly of late. As his daughter ascends to the pulpit, the murmurs grow louder. While some in Repentance frown upon a woman serving as pastor (or sheriff, for that matter), other churchgoers have accepted the younger Mills into their fold. No doubt because she has devoted her life to their Baptist faith, the proof of the pudding that she never married, claiming the church as her only lover. But her radical beliefs have alienated at least half the town, who will never embrace her as their religious leader.

With her dark hair and funereal clothes, Cadence is an older version of a black-tailed hawk that Mary Grace both derided and feared as a child. As her eyes light on her row, Mary Grace is thrown back to that first day of sixth grade, Cadence staring at her outside their lockers as if she knew a lost soul when she saw her.

When did she give up on her?

But Mary Grace knows the answer, has always known. It was after those girls disappeared.

Girls who weren't so lily-white themselves.

"From a woman, sin had its beginning . . ."

Cadence's voice thunders across the tiny church as she looks out over the congregation. As she talks, Mary Grace recognizes the rhetoric of the sect of Footwashers Cadence has followed since childhood that holds females as the source of sinful pleasure and direct cause of mankind's fall from grace. Never mind that it was Satan in the form of a serpent who seduced the virginal Eve in the first place.

To Mary Grace's way of thinking, Cadence's view of young girls as irredeemable sinners isn't all that different from demonizing some as losers (Mary Grace then and Isaac Wood now) and others as outcasts, or freaks (Cadence herself.).

A few rows up, Allison Driver looks nervous as Cadence fixes her fiery gaze on her, then moves past her to the last row on the right, where Cherie Leigh sits between Alma Allred and Tyler Lee. Some of the other girls in Felicity's class—the daughters of kids Mary Grace went to school with—cast down their heads, as if in shame. *"Eve deceived Adam, tempting him to eat of the forbidden fruit . . ."*

As Cadence intones her version of the Scriptures, a male voice joins in with hers. In his seat at the end of the last row on the left, Timothy Dickson stares up at Cadence, his eyes shining with religious fervor.

One of Cadence's most devoted converts, he's a far cry from the boy who sat next to Mary Grace all through elementary school. (She was grateful every day that the more enlightened Briggs High teachers didn't seat them alphabetically.) It was during the winter of '95 that Timothy stopped spouting his doomsday beliefs and started championing Cadence's view of young females as the sole source of sinfulness. It didn't help that decades later his wife left him amid rumors of her being barren.

Back then, Timothy had his own ideas about what happened to those girls. Because of one girl in particular.

They were sixth graders, too.

Like Eve, on the verge of becoming women.

Cadence's relentless gaze circles back to their row, lighting on Haley and Lauren Reeves before coming to rest on Felicity. But even as Mary Grace feels an overwhelming urge to shield her daughter from the force of the other woman's righteous fury, she's flooded by memories of another young Eve. Once again remembering that Friday morning in late September when the door to her sixth-grade classroom opened and the assistant principal walked in with a girl with long, dark hair and the biggest, brownest eyes Mary Grace had ever seen.

A girl who would become her first—and last—best friend.

The girl she would come to love and hate in equal measure.

THEN

SEVENTEEN

New Girl in Town

She stood next to Miss Althea in front of the whole class.

Everyone gawped at her, me included. Truth be told, we didn't get a lot of strangers here. You couldn't count the drifters, who were always gone by summer's end. With the exception of Darryl Stokes, who was still staying over to Miss Lillian's Boarding House, still working at Parnell's daddy's garage. I hadn't seen him since that September afternoon I saw him walking out of the woods.

"This is Nadia Doshenko," Miss Althea said. "She and her daddy just moved here all the way from California." We knew that already. Just like we knew the Doshenkos were Russian.

While Miss Althea talked, the new girl stared straight ahead. I'd hate to be the new kid in a place where I didn't know another living soul, which would have happened if I'd gone to Baptist Day.

She looked different, too, and not just because she was a foreigner. Her daddy probably didn't have time to get her fitted for a school uniform because her white blouse was tucked into a red skirt that flared out at her calves. She had on white kneesocks, but instead of Mary Janes or buckle shoes she was wearing brown boots. And a suede vest with fringes that matched her boots. The big gold hoops in her ears made her look like a gypsy.

"Let's introduce ourselves to Nadia," Miss Althea was saying now, like she didn't hear the whispering coming from a few rows behind me that I knew without turning around was Skylar. "Please remember to speak slowly and clearly. It's a lot of names for Nadia to remember."

When Miss Althea got to Chloe Ann, she said her name real loud so the new girl would know she was someone important. Olivia, who'd passed her initiation in the woods that was still a secret and was now officially a Popular Girl, said her name just loud enough to be heard. Next to Olivia, Timothy stared at the new girl like he'd been doing ever since she walked in. Not the way you'd think, for all his railing about the end of the world and us all being beyond saving. More the way I recently caught Coach Fewell looking at our fourth-grade teacher Mrs. King in church the other week. And the new girl was pretty, with those big dark eyes half-hidden under thick bangs that I wasn't allowed to wear.

When it came my turn, I looked right at her as I said my name and even threw in a smile that I wasn't sure was to put her at her ease or to score points with Miss Althea.

After that was done, Miss Althea said that next we'd be rearranging our desks to make room for her. There were some extra desks in the back of the classroom, so Miss Althea asked two of the boys to bring one to the end of my row. Then she told each kid to move over one desk.

"Not you, Mary Grace." I stopped in the middle of gathering up my books. Miss Althea was walking the new girl over to the desk Madison had just vacated. All I could think was now I didn't have to sit next to her anymore. I thanked God the new girl's last name was Doshenko, wondering if He'd decided I was worth saving after all because of how hard I'd been trying to be good.

Miss Althea waited until we settled down again. "Now, because Nadia has missed a few weeks of school, she needs someone to help her catch up on the homework assignments. Any volunteers?" My arm shot up. "Thank you, Mary Grace."

The new girl shifted in her chair to look at me. She didn't smile exactly. But there was something in those dark eyes that made me think she was keeping secrets, too.

That was how it started with Nadia and me.

∞

It was after school on a Friday again, the one day our softball team didn't have practice. We'd won another game, so I was feeling pretty good. From where we sat, on the top bleacher, you could see the whole Briggs High track field. While I was explaining our last assignment for dividing fractions, I craned my neck for a glimpse of Parnell, who was star of his tenth-grade track team and practiced all year round to keep himself in fighting shape. But I didn't see him.

Nadia was picking at something on her vest. She had her uniform by now, but the minute school was out she took off her blazer and put on that fringe vest. She still wore the brown boots and so far no one, not even Miss Althea, had anything to say about it.

Now that we were done with schoolwork, I started in on my questions. "What was it like living in California?"

Nadia shrugged her shoulders. "No different from all the other places."

"What places?"

"Any place you could think of."

"Name one."

"Pennsylvania. That was the worst. I hated being stuck in that dirt-poor town way out in the boondocks. It was like this place that time forgot. A lot like here."

Looking back on it later, I had to admit there was truth to what she said. While 1995 wasn't exactly an unenlightened time, this was rural Arkansas. Bible Belt country. I didn't realize until I met Nadia how naïve I was to the ways of the world.

"How come you don't have an accent?"

"We moved to America when I was a baby."

Like me being born in another town and coming to Repentance when I was six weeks old. "Just you and your daddy? What happened to your mama?"

"She died."

"You don't have brothers or sisters?"

She fiddled with a charm on her bracelet as she shook her head. It was a miniature silver frame with a photo of a lady with dark hair I figured must be her dead mother. "I heard your parents died in an ice storm," she said. "Were you scared?"

"I don't know. I was asleep." It was the same fib I'd told Sheriff Kanady, but for some reason I hated lying to her even though we were still new to one other.

"Why'd you move here?" I asked, more to get the conversation off me and the secrets I was keeping.

"My papi got a job."

I'd never heard anyone call their daddy "papi." Maybe it was a Russian thing. "What kind of job?"

"He goes into companies and fixes them."

"What happens after they're fixed?"

"He goes on to the next one."

"Is that why you move so much?"

"Yeah."

I felt sorry for her, always having to start over in a new school with new kids.

"Why'd you come to our town?"

"You have to swear not to tell another living soul." Nadia had lowered her voice to a whisper even though we were the only ones out here.

"I swear."

"He thought coming here would cure me."

"Of what?"

"Wickedness."

"Are you wicked?"

"What do you think?"

I stared at her, wondering if I'd see what everyone saw when they looked at me. But all I saw were eyes dark as pitch with yellow irises, like a cat's. "What'd you do?"

"Lots of stuff."

"Name one."

"I ran away a bunch of times. Once I was gone almost a week."

She had to be making that up. "You swear on your mama's grave?"

That seemed to pain her some, but she swore.

"Where'd you go?"

"I hitched a ride out of town while my papi was at work. I laid low for a while at a motor inn, then took a bus to the airport. I had fake ID and everything."

"Where'd you get the money?"

"From my allowance. The rest I stole from my papi."

I tried to hide my shock. "How'd they catch you?"

"They didn't. I didn't have enough for the bus ticket so I had to come back. But next time I'll make sure I have enough money and go somewhere they'll never find me." She fixed those big dark eyes on me again. "Bet you never ran away."

"Did too." I told her about the time I ran off after my folks died, but embellished a bit and left out the part about Sheriff Kanady catching up with me at the town limits. To hear me tell it, I was gone all night and only came back for the funeral. I knew I was fibbing to impress her, hoping God wasn't listening after I'd been trying so hard to be good.

Nadia shook her head. "I can't believe you came back. How do you stand it here? I've been in this town a week and I'm going crazy!"

For once I was without words. I didn't want to tell her it was my own unhappiness I was running from, not Repentance.

"Would you do it again? For real?"

She was waiting for my answer, like it was a test I had to pass.

"Shit!"

I stared at her. Except for Noah and my uncle when Noah got him really mad, I'd hardly ever heard anyone swear.

I looked where Nadia was looking. Timothy was standing at the bottom of the bleachers staring up at us. Nadia started climbing down the bleachers, so fast I had to move pretty quick to keep up with her. When she got to the bottom, she told Timothy to quit stalking her or she'd tell the sheriff. He just stood there, looking pathetic.

On the walk home, Nadia told me about the boys who used to follow her in the other places she lived. Part of me believed her because she was tall and pretty and I could see her breasts jutting out from under the vest. But another part of me thought she could say a hundred boys were stuck on her because who could prove they weren't?

After Nadia and I parted ways at my uncle's house and she continued north to the house she and her papi were renting, I heaved a sigh of relief.

Good thing Timothy showed up when he did.

Because I had no idea what my answer to her question would have been.

EIGHTEEN

Our Secret Place

"Those bitches think they're God's gift."

In the two weeks since she got here, Nadia had really stepped up her swearing. Today she'd used a cuss word and God in the same sentence. I wondered if that broke some kind of commandment.

School had just let out and she was watching Skylar and Paige walk to the bus. "Are they as rich as Chloe Ann and Madison?"

"Beats me," I said.

Nadia was obsessed with money. She couldn't believe I didn't get an allowance. Said it wasn't fair my cousin Noah got one and not me, which I couldn't disagree with.

The following Monday during recess, Skylar and Paige came over to us in the schoolyard. Ignoring me, Skylar asked Nadia if she could bum a cigarette.

"That'll cost you," Nadia said. I was shocked, not just because she was asking for money but because nobody talked to Skylar like that. I figured Skylar would flounce off in a huff. Instead, she asked how much. When she pulled out a pretty snakeskin wallet and paid the dollar Nadia asked for, I got jealous thinking everyone had money but me.

Three days later, Skylar and Paige changed into fringed vests after school. Nadia just laughed when I told her the popular girls imitating what she wore was the highest compliment they could pay her. In the cafeteria at lunchtime, Skylar came over to the table where I was sitting with Nadia and asked Nadia to meet her and Paige after school.

We all knew what that meant: Nadia was going to be initiated into their club.

All I could think was she was my first real friend. And now she was going to disappear from my life.

I went to softball practice with a heavy heart. Nadia had zero interest in sports, but she always waited for me after. I was surprised to see her outside the dugout that afternoon.

"How come you're not with Skylar and Paige?" I asked.

"Why would I be with them?"

"Because you're going to be a popular girl." I hoped Nadia couldn't see how jealous I felt.

"No, I'm not," she said.

"Why not?"

"Because I don't want to be in their stupid club, that's why. Come on."

"Where we going?"

"You'll see."

"I'm not supposed to go in there."

"You are so boring."

We were at the southern entrance to the woods. I hadn't been here since that time back in August, not even for the shortcut home. "I mean it," I said.

"Who's going to know?"

God, I thought. But Nadia grabbed my arm.

I forgot how dark it was in here. "Where does the Boogeyman live?" She'd unzipped her backpack and was taking out a flashlight.

I pointed. "At the northern edge of the woods. He lives in a rotting old house."

"You saw it?"

"No, but I saw him."

Her dark eyes lit up with excitement, and it wasn't even a fib. "Tell, tell."

So I told her about my encounter with Meurice back in August, leaving out the part about how scared I was and embellishing like I did about the time I ran off after my folks died.

". . . but you can't tell a soul." If it got around school I was in the woods, my aunt and uncle would send me off to that children's home for sure.

"Cross my heart."

I noticed she didn't say on her mama's grave. She'd started walking again. "Where you going?" I asked even though I knew.

Nadia was bound and determined and I would soon learn she usually got her way.

We trudged along in silence, Nadia shining the flashlight through the trees. Soon we were passing the cabin I ducked into when I was running from those footsteps that might or might not have belonged to my cousin. Then I saw it, rising above the trees. I nudged Nadia and told her it was the Boogeyman's chimney and smoke curled out of it no matter what the time of year.

She leaned down and picked up a big stick. I remembered how big Meurice was and doubted that stick would be any kind of defense. We kept walking. My heart was trip-hammering in my chest as we neared his house. A rocking chair and swing seemed out of place on the ramshackle porch. All the windows were dark. Except for the smoke rising out of the chimney, I didn't see any signs of life. Maybe he was having a lie-down, like my aunt.

"What's that?" Nadia pointed at a covered casserole dish sitting in a corner of the porch, next to a stone urn filled with fresh flowers.

"It's probably from the good Samaritan who brings Meurice food and clothes and stuff."

"Who is it?"

"Nobody knows. But they've been doing it for years. Before I was born. What are you doing?"

Nadia had run past me up the steps. She dropped into the rocking chair, setting it shaking like crazy.

"Come back here! What if he sees you?"

But Nadia just laughed. She kicked out her foot and nudged the casserole dish. "It smells good. What do you suppose is in it?"

"I don't know and I'm not waiting around to find out. Let's get out of here."

Nadia ignored me as she leaned down and lifted off the aluminum foil. "Shepherd's pie. Yummy." She stuck her finger in and put some in her mouth. "It's pretty good."

I couldn't believe she was sitting there on the Boogeyman's porch eating his food. "I'm leaving. With or without you."

"You are so lame. I don't know why I hang out with you." She clambered off the porch and scooped up some big rocks.

"That's a bad idea," I said.

She gave me one of her superior looks. "You scared? You made up that story, didn't you?"

"No. He grabbed me just like I said. I swear on my daddy's grave," I added to give it extra weight.

Nadia pointed to a tall pine a few feet away. "Skylar and Paige were hiding behind that tree when Olivia threw the rocks at his house. Skylar said he came out looking like some giant freak. That's when they all ran."

So that was Olivia's top-secret initiation.

"Don't you dare say a word. Skylar told me I couldn't tell anyone."

"I swear." But Nadia told me. Did that mean she wasn't going to ditch me for the popular girls?

Nadia took aim. The rocks landed on Meurice's porch with a loud thud. The last one hit the screen door. "Come on out, you ugly old monster!" she yelled. Then she picked up more rocks and handed them to me like it was a test. I took a really big one and swung my arm back like I was about to pitch one out of the ballpark.

Meurice came out as I threw the last one. It hit him in his right leg and bounced off his patched-up pants. Nadia made a strangled sound in her throat and started running. But I stood rooted to the spot, Meurice staring like he remembered me from that time in the woods. He took one step, then another. That was when I ran for my life.

We were still panting when we got to the thicket of pines. Nadia kept looking over her shoulder like she expected to see Meurice chasing us. I was glad she was just as scared as I was. "My uncle's house is up in that field," I said when I could catch a breath.

"How much land does he have?"

"I don't know the exact amount." I never thought about it, but if you counted the pines he and the town were feuding over, it was probably a lot.

"Is he rich?"

"I guess so." Which was probably a lie or he wouldn't be thinking about renting out my room. And he wasn't on the road nearly as much now.

Nadia got that look I'd seen before, and I knew she was calculating how much money my uncle had.

"You can come up and see for yourself, then cut across our field to your house." It was getting on and I had chores to do. But Nadia was taking something out of her backpack.

I watched her slide two cigarettes from the half-empty pack. I thought about the one Skylar bought for a dollar and hoped she wasn't going to ask me to pay for it now that she thought I was rich. But Nadia just held the cigarette out to me, which meant I had to accept it even though I had no interest in taking up smoking.

Sure enough, we'd no sooner lit up than I started coughing and Nadia laughed and said how lame I was. I said I didn't see what the big deal was, which just made her give me that superior look.

"Your papi lets you smoke at home?" I wondered if it was something they did in one of those big cities in California.

She shook her head. "Not that he'd notice."

"Why not?"

"He couldn't care less what I do. He'd be glad if I ran away and didn't come back."

"What about your mama? Did she care what you did?"

Nadia shrugged as she stomped out the cigarette under her boot. I was starting to notice that when she did that it was usually to hide what she was really feeling.

"You never said how she died."

She fiddled with that charm bracelet again. "She had a heart attack."

"How old were you?"

"Eight."

"Was she sick?" I thought of my mama in her room with the blinds closed, and the way she clutched her heart when I said I wasn't going to Baptist Day.

"She was never sick a day in her life," Nadia said. "My papi said it was because of me. I made her die."

My heart started to race as I thought about my folks and that last night. "How'd you do that?"

"I ran away and she died from worry."

Which wasn't the same thing. Not at all. "Were you sad when she died?"

She shrugged again, which meant she was.

"Was your papi?"

"He cried every night. Bet he won't shed one tear when I'm gone for good."

I thought about that. Wondered if my daddy would have blamed me if my mama had had a heart attack that night and that maybe I was lucky they were both gone.

Nadia was smoking another cigarette and pacing the woods like she had this big hurt inside her that wouldn't let her keep still.

"I'm gonna leave this town and he'll never see me again. Then he'll be sorry."

I didn't know what to say. Ever since that day on the bleachers when she asked if I'd run away for real, I'd been holding my breath hoping she wouldn't bring it up again. But she was already onto something else, putting me in mind of the bees that flit from flower to flower on the hunt for nectar.

She stood in front of a huge pine and was inspecting the trunk. "This is so perfect!" She let out a shriek that sent a bunch of birds flapping their wings.

I went over to see what the fuss was about. "It's just a hole some woodpecker made. They do that all the time, especially the sapsuckers." My uncle was always going on about them ruining the pines.

She reached her hand inside and sure enough it came out full of the sticky stuff. She didn't seem to care. "It's pretty big. We can use it to stash stuff."

"Like what?"

"Lots of things. And the cool part is nobody'll ever know." She started to put the pack of cigarettes into the hole, then stopped. "Do sapsuckers eat anything beside sap?"

I laughed because she had no idea how things in nature worked. "Mostly insects."

"That's gross." But she still looked worried, like she was picturing the long slithering tongue of the sapsucker sucking our secret stash right out. "Does your cousin know about it?"

"I don't think so."

"This can be our secret place. But you've got to swear not to tell anyone."

I didn't see the big deal, but I swore anyhow.

Nadia put the pack of cigarettes inside the tree, then turned to me.

"You ever had a best friend?"

You could have knocked me over when Nadia asked me that.

First I had to swear like it was some kind of test. Then Nadia pulled a Swiss Army knife from her backpack and said we had to take a blood oath. When she pricked my thumb with that knife it hurt something fierce. Then she said it wasn't official until we carved our initials in the tree.

NINETEEN

Best Friends Forever

At school we mostly ignored the other girls, especially Chloe Ann and Madison, who always tried to listen to Nadia whispering to me when Miss Althea wasn't looking. I couldn't stand it if Nadia talked to anyone else, afraid she'd change her mind and drop me for the popular girls.

But I was soon to learn it wasn't the girls Nadia was interested in. It was the boys. And the men.

❧

We got in the habit of going into the woods on weekends. We'd already stashed a few things inside our pine, mostly stuff we didn't want our families to find, like the cigarettes, Nadia's army knife, and makeup we weren't allowed to wear yet: lipstick, eyeliner, and black-as-sin nail polish.

One Sunday afternoon, I was waiting in our usual place. She arrived out of breath like she'd been running. I was disappointed when she opened her backpack and pulled out a pack of cigarettes. Only it wasn't cigarettes, it was marijuana. I didn't know anyone who'd tried it, not even my cousin.

The first few puffs, which she told me were called drags, made me cough. Then I got the hang of it. After we finished, Nadia took a box of Cap'n Crunch cereal out of her backpack and we ate almost the whole thing. Then she spread out a blanket and we lay there staring at the top of the pine that I swear had started moving.

"How many boys have you kissed?"

How could I tell her I hadn't kissed a single, solitary one? I waved my arm airily around like I'd seen her do and said, "I never counted."

Nadia looked at me out of the corner of her eye like she knew I was lying. "Who'd you like kissing the most?"

"Parnell Vaughan." I couldn't believe I'd just said that.

"No! Really?"

I gave her a mysterious smile. It wasn't really a lie because I thought about kissing Parnell a lot lately, even if everyone knew he was going to marry Anna Mae Burns.

"Did you go all the way with him?" I shook my head, sorry I'd said anything. Like now Parnell didn't belong to me anymore.

"I did," Nadia said. "And he was lots older than me. Now you have to tell another secret."

I was sick of this stupid game, but then I thought of something that nobody else knew. Not even Miss Althea, though I came pretty close that day after the locker room fiasco. But what if she stopped being my best friend? Or worse, told someone else. That was the thing about secrets. How did you know you could trust someone with them, even your best friend?

I looked around as I thought about what to tell her. Then I got an idea. I pointed to a spot a few feet away. "See that mound?" In truth it wasn't much more than an area where the earth rose slightly, but Nadia got up and went over to look.

"What is it?"

"The grave of a raccoon."

"Who cares about a dead rodent?"

"This one was murdered." Along with a bullfrog and a bunch of field mice, but I wasn't sure where they were buried.

"How do you know?"

"Because I dug its grave."

"Did you murder it?" I had her interest now.

I thought about taking credit, but decided I didn't want the raccoon's death on my conscience, too. "My cousin did. He strangled it, then cut its throat."

"Do your aunt and uncle know?" I shook my head. She kicked the earth a little as she inspected the mound. I thought she might ask me to dig it up to prove I wasn't lying. The last thing I wanted to see was that dead raccoon's staring eyes.

But Nadia had other ideas. The next night, I had to sneak out of the house when I was supposed to be in bed so we could hide behind the pine tree and try to catch my cousin in the act. After a few nights, we called it quits. I wondered if Noah figured out what we were up to.

Or maybe he just stopped killing.

❧

Before we knew it, it was almost the end of October. It was a weekend again, and freezing out. Nadia said we should go to her house since her papi was working.

"On a Saturday?" Even my uncle was usually back by the weekend.

Nadia shrugged. "He works all the time."

It sounded like a sin against God. I knew from church that He created man and all the creatures that live on dry land on a Saturday and that was why He rested on Sunday. But maybe after all the hard work of creating the world he took off Saturdays, too.

Then I had a thought. If God could create the world in six days, how long could it take Nadia's daddy to fix that company? "What was the longest you ever stayed in one place?"

"LA. For a whole year. That was the coolest place."

On the walk to her house, I calculated how long she'd been in Repentance already. Almost a month. Which meant even if her daddy worked slow that left only eleven months to be best friends before she moved again.

The house they were renting was two streets over from my uncle's. We smoked dope in the bathroom with the exhaust fan on in case her father came home early. After we got high, we raided the fridge. In her papi's room later, she went straight to his dresser and opened the middle drawer. There, under a bunch of socks, were a whole lot of bills. I'd never seen so much money in one place. "Did your papi find out you took the money the time you ran away?" She nodded. "Did you get punished?"

"No. But I had to promise I'd never do it again. He didn't even change his hiding place. The day I leave for good, I'll take it all. He's also got a money clip. It's fourteen-karat gold. Bet I could get a lot for that." She'd taken out the money and was counting it. "Where does your uncle keep his money?"

"Not in his sock drawer, that's for sure. It's the first place a thief would look."

"Who's going to steal it? I heard folks don't lock their doors in this stupid town. Bet he doesn't have this much." Nadia held out the money. I could see a few hundred- and fifty-dollar bills mixed in with the twenties, tens, and fives.

"I don't know." I shrugged. "He might have more."

Her eyes went wide. "You never counted it?" I shook my head. "Never took any? Not even a dollar?"

"That would be stealing."

"You are such a goody two-shoes."

That got me mad. If she only knew.

"It's not stealing if you take what belongs to you," Nadia said. "We're gonna need more money than this to last till we get jobs."

"What kind of jobs?"

"Cleaning motel rooms. They pay in cash and don't ask for paperwork."

"Is that legal?"

"No. That's why they hire illegals. I swear, sometimes I think you were born under a rock, Mary Grace. But I have to get new fake IDs anyway. And those'll cost, too." She put the money back under the socks and shut the drawer. "What about your cousin? I bet he could get his hands on some of your uncle's cash. How much allowance does he get?"

"Beats me. But it's probably not enough because he's always asking my uncle for an advance on it."

"Does your uncle give it to him?"

"He did the other week."

"How much?"

"I couldn't see. My uncle was sitting at his desk with his back to me." My aunt probably put him up to it even though it was the money they kept for emergencies.

"That's not fair. Your cousin shouldn't be getting it all. You should tell your uncle you have to have an allowance, too. We need all the money we can get or we'll die in this boring town."

She said it like it'd already been decided. But ever since she came to Repentance, I hadn't thought about running away once. It would mean never seeing Parnell again. And our softball team was on a winning streak. The championship game was less than a month away.

Nadia was looking at me like she knew what I was thinking. "You didn't change your mind, did you?"

I hadn't made it up yet, so how could I change it? The way she looked at me, it felt like our whole friendship depended on my answer. Maybe I could get her to wait until after the big game. It was only a few weeks away.

I shook my head. "No."

"Best friends forever." Nadia made a fist and touched it to mine.

TWENTY

Hell to Pay

Soon after that, Nadia asked why I didn't invite her to my house.

I had my reasons, but she wouldn't let up. So, I picked a Saturday when my aunt was having a lie-down and my cousin was helping my uncle restock the tools in the garage.

She wore her boots and fringed vest, and black eyeliner even though I told her no makeup. She also brought pot. I told her no way we could smoke here, but before I knew it we were in the bathroom near my room with the window open. I told her to keep her voice down or we'd wake up my aunt, who had to rest a lot because of her infirmity. Nadia asked how my uncle had sex with her in that wheelchair, which sent us into fits of giggles.

When we were in the kitchen scrounging around for something to eat, a voice called down the stairs. "Is that you, Mary Grace?"

"I told you to keep quiet!" I hissed at Nadia. "Yes, Aunt Hester," I shouted.

"Is someone with you?"

"Yes," I answered while Nadia made faces that sent me into another laughing fit. I jabbed her hard in the ribs.

"I'd like to meet your friend."

There was nothing for it but to go upstairs. Now that I was bigger and stronger, I was able to help my aunt in and out of her chair. As I lifted her up, her useless legs dangling off the edge of the bed, I pictured my uncle trying to have sex with her and had to bite my tongue to keep from going off again. I kept my head down so she wouldn't smell the marijuana on my breath. After I got her into the chair, huffing and puffing a bit because it was like hauling a dead weight, I wheeled her into the elevator.

When I introduced Nadia, my aunt smiled and asked how she and her daddy were getting on in Repentance. Nadia answered in this high-pitched voice I'd never heard, like she was being polite and making fun at the same time. My aunt didn't seem to notice. Nadia was telling my aunt how much she liked living here while kicking my leg under the table, when the screen door banged open and, wouldn't you know it, in walked my cousin. He trailed dirt on his sneakers that didn't escape my aunt's notice and groused how cold it was in the garage. Then he went to the fridge and pulled out a soda that I knew would be a beer if my aunt wasn't sitting there. While my aunt introduced them, Nadia gave him a flirty smile I'd seen her try out on some of the boys in our class and, lately, Coach Fewell.

Noah didn't say much, just stared at her with a look on his face that made me squirm in my seat. Nadia's dark eyes followed him as he went back out again.

When the screen door banged open again, this time my uncle was with my cousin.

Nadia gave my uncle an even bigger smile than she gave Noah. He didn't smile back.

Noah lounged by the sink as he lifted the tab off another soda can. Uncle Samuel stood behind my aunt, gripping the sides of her chair like he was trying to hold in his anger. I thought now was a good time for Nadia to leave and started to get up. But then Nadia asked my aunt where the bathroom was.

After Nadia left the kitchen, my uncle right away started in. "Is that the girl you've been spending so much time with?"

"Yes, Uncle Samuel."

"She flirts with all the boys at Briggs High." Noah threw in his two cents, which made me mad but at least solved the mystery of where Nadia got off to while I was at softball practice.

"I haven't seen her and her father at church," my uncle said.

Now wasn't the time to tell him how Nadia made fun of our religion along with school and PE, which made me wonder what she did believe in. While he went on about the sinfulness of those who didn't pray regularly, my cousin rolled his eyes.

When Nadia came back, I said I'd walk her home, knowing there wasn't a snowball's chance in hell she'd be asked to stay to supper.

~

The next night I was helping my aunt with the dishes when my uncle stomped into the kitchen, his face like a storm cloud.

"Where's the boy?"

"Up in his room. What is it?" My aunt stopped in the middle of handing me a dish to dry and wheeled around to face him.

"Tell him I want to see him in my study."

"But Samuel—"

"Now."

Then he stomped back out. I'd never seen him so mad. My aunt looked worried as she wheeled herself out of the kitchen. At the foot of the stairs, she called up to my cousin. She had to shout because as usual he had his music blaring. When he finally came clomping down the stairs, my aunt said my uncle wanted to see him.

Noah squared his shoulders, like he was fixing for a fight. When he went into the study, I could see my uncle at his desk. His back was to us, but he turned and told Noah to close the door.

My uncle's angry voice carried out into the hall, soon joined by my cousin's. The wood paneled walls muffled sound, so it was hard to hear what they were saying. My uncle was accusing my cousin of something, and he kept denying he did it. Then the door to the den opened again and Noah stormed out. Then my uncle came out, his face almost purple with rage. "Don't you dare walk out when I'm talking to you!" But Noah was gone; the sound of the front door slamming echoed through the house.

"Samuel! What's going on?" My aunt touched his arm as he stood next to her wheelchair, panting like he'd run a race.

"That boy's a thief. And he had the nerve to lie in front of me and God. Saying he didn't take it."

"Didn't take what?"

"The cash I keep in my desk drawer for emergencies. It's gone."

"All of it?"

"Do you know how long it took to save that money?"

"When did you notice it was missing?"

"Right after supper. I checked on it Friday night and it was there. I've had it with that boy, Hester. I won't live under the same roof with a thief and a liar."

"Why do you think Noah stole it?" My aunt had gone white as a sheet. I wasn't sure if it was because the money was missing or because her son was the culprit.

"He's always asking for money, that's why! Last week he asked for another advance on his allowance. And this is how he repays me. By stealing my hard-earned money! You tell him, Hester. If he wants to go on living in my house, he'd better give it back. And if he spent it, I can promise you there will be hell to pay!" With that, my uncle strode back into his den, slamming the door so hard the rafters shook.

My aunt just sat there with her shoulders slumped over, as close to weeping as I'd ever seen her.

I was in my room at the other end of the house when I heard the back door open. It was pretty late, going on eleven, and my aunt and uncle were already asleep upstairs. Which was probably why Noah waited until now to come home.

I wondered if my cousin would dare show his face at breakfast tomorrow while I turned the pages of a catalog showcasing bras. The other day in PE, Nadia said she couldn't believe I was still wearing a training bra. My breasts were still small compared to the other girls, but maybe it was time I had a proper bra. Maybe Parnell would notice.

I'd been thinking about him more and more lately. Ever since Nadia asked how many boys I'd kissed, my fantasies had graduated from holding hands to kissing. Nadia said you opened your mouth and the boy stuck his tongue down your throat, which I thought was disgusting and couldn't imagine Parnell doing that. Still, maybe I needed him to start seeing me as a woman and not as a girl anymore, the way the boys saw Nadia even if Cadence Mills called her a harlot behind her back. But the bras in the catalog cost a lot and I didn't see as how I could convince my aunt to buy me one what with the Bible business slow and my uncle's emergency money gone.

I heard the refrigerator open and close. A few minutes later I heard Noah leave the kitchen, only he didn't go upstairs. His footsteps got closer and I saw his long shadow cross my open doorway. I couldn't recall him ever coming into my room, not in all the months I'd been living here.

He walked right in as if I'd invited him, wiping the telltale beer foam off his mouth with his shirtsleeve.

"You took it."

"What?" He was accusing me of stealing the money! "Don't go pinning this on me. You're the one who took it and now you're going to get it."

"You little bitch!"

He stepped closer to the bed. I forgot how tall he was, his head almost hitting the sloping ceiling. "It's your fault for spending all your allowance." I wasn't about to let him think he could scare me. "I don't even get one."

"That's why you stole the money."

"No, I didn't. I'm no thief!"

"Neither am I."

We stared at each other, then his eyes shifted to the open catalog on my bed. He grabbed it before I could stop him. "What do you want with these for? You don't even have any tits."

"Shut up!"

"These bras cost a pretty penny."

"Give it back!"

"Not till you give back the money."

"I told you, I didn't take it."

"Yes, you did. You and your friend. If you don't return it, I'll tell my father."

Then he threw the catalog on the floor and stormed out.

My head was buzzing. I was back in Nadia's papi's bedroom, watching her count his money. Asking about my uncle's secret stash.

If Noah had the money, why would he tell me to give it back? Was it because he didn't take it?

My uncle said the money was in his desk drawer when he checked Friday night. Which meant it was pilfered sometime between yesterday and today.

I saw Nadia in the kitchen yesterday, excusing herself to go to the bathroom.

She didn't steal his money. She couldn't have. She wouldn't do that to me.

There was only one way to know for sure.

TWENTY-ONE

Nothing but a Common Thief

"Hey."

"Hey." Nadia didn't look at me as she fiddled with the lock on her locker.

"You won't believe what happened," I said. "Someone stole my uncle's secret stash."

"Really?" She opened her locker. "Bet it was your cousin."

"He said he didn't take it."

"And you believe him?"

"He said if I don't give it back, he'll tell my uncle I'm the one who stole it."

"Did you?"

I stared at her. "You know I didn't."

"How would I know that?"

"Because I'd never steal my uncle's money."

"Then it was your cousin. You said he was always asking your uncle for an advance on his allowance."

"But if he took it, why would he tell me to give it back?"

Nadia shrugged. "Beats me."

"The only way to clear my name is to find it."

"How you gonna do that?" Her tongue had slid out and was worrying her lower lip.

"I thought you could help me figure out where someone could hide all that money."

"It's not so much. My papi's stash is bigger."

"How do you know?"

"What?"

"How do you know it's not so much?"

"You told me."

"No, I didn't. I had no idea how much was there. You did it, didn't you? When you lied to my aunt about having to go to the bathroom."

"I did not! I didn't even know where your uncle hid it."

"Yes, you did. You took it and you have to give it back!"

"I didn't and you can't prove I did!"

I grabbed her arm. By now a small crowd had gathered in the hall. "This isn't over," I whispered.

"Yes, it is," she whispered back, as usual getting the last word as she locked her locker and walked away.

We ignored each other the rest of the day.

At home, supper was a silent affair. My uncle hadn't yet made good on his threat to kick Noah out unless he returned the money, which was probably my aunt's doing. I kept waiting for my cousin to say I was the culprit. But he couldn't without the money to prove it. And no way was Nadia giving it back.

I couldn't prove she took it, either.

A few days later, I was walking home after softball practice when somebody grabbed my arm. I turned around and stared into the furious eyes of my cousin.

"You think you're so smart, don't you?"

"I don't know what you're talking about." I tried to shake loose, but he held me in a death grip.

"Stop the innocent act. You won't get away with it!"

"Let me go! You're hurting me."

"I'll hurt you a lot worse if you don't give back the money."

I pictured that mound down by the pines, and I believed him. Panic choked me. "I told you I didn't steal it."

"Then you put your friend up to it! Do you know what that whore had the nerve to say? If I didn't hand over my allowance, she'd tell my father about the raccoon." Noah's voice dropped to a menacing whisper. "You told her, didn't you?"

I shouldn't have been surprised that Nadia had broken our sacred trust, but I felt hurt all the same. "What if I did? It's a free country."

Noah's eyes flashed and I thought he was going to hit me. "You tell that bitch. You tell her she better give it back."

"Or what are you gonna do?"

"You just wait and see." Then he stalked away.

TWENTY-TWO

Total Eclipse of the Heart

The next day, I couldn't concentrate worth a damn. Nadia didn't come to school and all I could think was my cousin made good on his threat. After the bell rang, Miss Althea called my name. "Can you stay a few minutes? I want to talk to you."

I knew by her tone that whatever she wanted to say, it wasn't good. I thought about telling her I didn't want to be late for softball practice, but she'd already dragged one of the extra chairs from the back and put it in front of her desk. It didn't look as if I had any choice in the matter.

"How's your aunt?" Miss Althea asked after I sat down.

"Okay." I shifted in my seat. I hadn't been alone with her since the time I cried in her arms after the locker room humiliation. I was sorry now I told her about the night my folks died, even if she didn't know the whole story. It meant she knew a secret about me. Maybe she'd use it against me like Nadia was trying to do to Noah.

"Have you been taking on more chores at home?" Miss Althea was asking.

I shook my head, then shrugged. "Maybe a few." I really had tried harder to be good after our talk. But since Nadia moved here, I'd been falling down in my domestic responsibilities.

Miss Althea took some papers out of a folder and put them on the desk. They were my last three tests: English, social studies, and the math exam. Two Cs and one C minus. Then she opened another folder.

"I'm sure you're as disappointed with these results as I am," she said. "But while I know you can do much better, this has me really worried." She put another paper in front of me. It was the science test we took the other day. "I haven't finished marking it yet, but you can see all the answers you left blank. I don't want to do it, but I'm going to have to give you an F."

My face got hot as I looked at the empty boxes next to the multiple-choice questions. The truth was, I hadn't studied at all. I was too upset over being in a fight with Nadia.

"This is very serious, Mary Grace. I may have to talk to your aunt and uncle."

"No! You can't do that."

"I don't see that I have a choice." Miss Althea didn't look happy, as if the very idea pained her.

"Please, Miss Althea. I'll try harder, I swear."

"I want to believe you. But I'm also concerned about the company you're keeping."

She could only be talking about one person. I could have told her we weren't friends anymore. "Please," I begged again. "Can't you just give me a makeup test?"

"I'd like to, but that wouldn't be fair to the other students. It's not as if you missed the test because you were absent. And there's something else. If your grades continue to slip, you could lose your place on the softball team."

"What?" Thursday was our playoff game against the Pinetree Pirates. The championship was next week.

"You know the rules. If a student performs poorly in school, it could mean suspension from all sports."

It just got worse and worse. My vision blurred.

Miss Althea came out from behind her desk and put a hand on my shoulder. Tears filled my eyes now, but no way I was going to cry in front of her again. I angrily blinked them back. "I'm so sorry. I wish there were something I could do." Her voice washed over me, lulling me like it always did.

"You could give me another chance."

"It's up to Coach Fewell. He makes the final decision." Her hand was still on my shoulder. "I'm on your side. I hope you know that."

I wanted to believe her, but lately I felt like nobody was in my corner. So I just thanked her and got the hell out of there.

After softball practice, I gathered my courage and asked the coach if I could talk to him. Nobody was in the dugout by then, but he led me to his office in Vaughan Elementary behind the gym. I'd never been in here before. Trophies and plaques lined one whole bookshelf. Coach Fewell pulled out a chair for me, then sat on the edge of his desk.

"What's on your mind, Mary Grace?"

I kept my head down and watched his legs in the gray sweats he always wore swinging back and forth. I could smell his cologne, which I never noticed before. And still I didn't open my mouth.

"Is it about the championship next week? I'm expecting to see your trophy on that shelf. You know you're our Most Valuable Player." Not a word about getting my grades up. Maybe Miss Althea was wrong, or Coach thought I was too valuable, like he said. His sneakered feet hit the floor as he got off the desk. "Are you okay?" Then he cupped his hand under my chin, forcing me to look up at him. His eyes were so dark they looked almost black. Something in the air changed then; I was having trouble breathing.

Coach Fewell kept those eyes on me and never blinked once. I got this weird tingling all over that made me feel dirty and wanting at the same time. I had to get out of here. That was when I bolted up, so fast I nearly head-butted him, and ran out of his office.

Outside Vaughan Elementary I bent over double, trying to catch my breath. It felt like I had just run a marathon. Then Coach Fewell came out, and I took off in the opposite direction. I knew I should get home and start on my homework and chores. But what if Miss Althea already called my aunt and uncle about the science test I failed? What if I ended up blamed for Nadia stealing the money because I was the one who brought her to my uncle's house in the first place?

Running away was looking better and better.

The wind was picking up. I pulled up the hood of my team jacket. If I ran away, I'd miss out on winning the MVP trophy. But I might not get to play the championship if Coach Fewell kicked me off the team after all. As for Parnell, he belonged to Anna Mae, so what did it matter?

I had to get away from Repentance, and the sooner the better.

But how far could I go without any money?

That made me think about Nadia's plan for us to run away together, and how she was always going on about the cash we needed. I blinked, thinking my thoughts must have conjured her because suddenly there she was walking across Briggs High's deserted track field. All day I was imagining the terrible things my cousin could have done to her, and she was just playing hooky.

What was she doing there?

Then I remembered one time a few weeks ago when she wasn't waiting for me in the dugout as usual after softball practice. She said it was because she was buying marijuana from a Briggs High senior who lived down by the abandoned railroad tracks with his divorced mama and was always getting in trouble with the law. She told me they always met behind the bleachers, which was where she was heading now, getting ready to fork over whatever was left of my uncle's stash. I had to stop her, had to make her give me the money before she spent every last nickel.

When she disappeared behind the bleachers, I started walking faster. My sneakers crunching across gravel sounded really loud in my ears. As I got closer, I could hear voices. I crept closer, then took a peek. I stopped dead, all the wind knocked out of me.

I knew I should go before they saw me, but it took forever to get my feet to move. Then I turned and sped away like Satan himself was nipping at my heels. But it didn't matter how fast or how far I ran. For the rest of my life I'd see them, the image burned forever in my brain.

Never changing with time.

TWENTY-THREE

Gone Girl

If I hated Nadia before, I really hated her now.

At school the next day we ignored each other, though she had no idea that I saw her behind the bleachers yesterday. When the bell rang, I dawdled at my desk so I wouldn't run into her at the lockers. There wasn't any softball practice because we were supposed to rest up before Thursday's game. I waited until Miss Althea was busy at her desk to make my exit, praying she wouldn't stop me again. But I felt her eyes boring into my back as I walked to the door. Probably waiting for me to leave so she could call my aunt and uncle.

Outside, I saw Chloe Ann heading down the street to her daddy's car, which was as usual waiting at the curb. I looked around for Madison. It had to be the first time since kindergarten they weren't together. Then I saw why. My mouth dropped open at the sight of Madison arm in arm with Nadia. Why should I care? Nadia was dead to me. I walked right past them as if they were no more than dirt under my shoes. When I got beyond the school limits, I ran the rest of the way home.

I was out in the field behind my uncle's house, practicing my pitching even though it wasn't much fun and it meant going after the ball every single time. I was about as low as I'd ever been, even worse than when my folks died. Which got me thinking about that night and that maybe I deserved all the bad things happening to me. That got me feeling sorry for myself and before I knew it I was crying. I swiped angrily at my eyes, then grasped the softball in my right hand and swung back my arm. What I saw yesterday behind the bleachers came into my mind. The ball went flying through the air as my anger at Nadia came roaring back.

The softball landed at the edge of the field where my uncle's property sloped down into the woods. If I had a dollar for every time a ball rolled down into that thicket of pines, I'd have enough to run away for sure.

There was nothing for it but to go down there. When I got to the thicket of pines, my breath whooshed out of me. Nadia was standing there.

"Get off my property."

"It's not your property."

"Says who?"

"Even if it's your uncle's, it doesn't belong to you. He just lets you live here."

"You've got until the count of three."

"Mary Grace, you have to listen! I have something to tell you!" The charms on her bracelet jangled as she took a step toward me.

"I don't want to hear it." I was sick of her and her secrets. Then I thought how she didn't know that I knew a secret about her. It didn't make me feel better.

"You'll want to hear this one," Nadia said. "You'll never guess who it's about."

"I told you—"

I never finished my sentence. Nadia had a finger to her lips and her head cocked like she was listening to something. Then I heard it: the sound of twigs snapping.

Nadia swore under her breath. "That bitch must have followed me. Get lost, Madison!"

Madison Driver? "I thought she was your new best friend." The words were out before I could stop myself.

"Her? No way. I told you to get lost!" she yelled. The twigs snapped again. But instead of Madison, a large raccoon darted out from the pines. Nadia and I looked at each other, then burst into laughter. Until I remembered the raccoon's murdered brother was buried near that tree, almost exactly where Nadia was standing. And how she tried to get my cousin to pay for what I told her in secret.

"You have to come with me," she said.

"I don't have to do anything." If she thought that now I'd be her best friend again, she had another think coming.

"What's wrong with you, Mary Grace? Forget about your uncle's stupid stash. I'm talking about big money. Enough for us to run away just like we planned. We can leave tonight."

"Where you getting it? By making someone else pay to keep their secret?"

"I'm telling you, it's gonna be the biggest payout ever." Her eyes glittered in the dark. "Aren't you dying to know?"

"If you don't get off my property, I'm calling Sheriff Kanady. One . . ."

"This is your last chance."

"Two . . ."

Nadia's face changed. "You'll be sorry," she snarled.

"Three!"

We stared at each other. Then she turned and walked deeper into the woods, her backpack bobbing behind her. She was almost out of sight when she turned to look over her shoulder, as if daring me to follow her.

The phone rang in the middle of supper, which was later than usual because my uncle had just gotten back from the road.

I didn't look up as the phone kept ringing. Then I heard the squeak of my aunt's wheelchair on the linoleum as she left the dining room to go out into the hall.

"That was Nadia Doshenko's father," she said when she came back. "She didn't come home for supper. He wanted to know if she was over here today."

I still didn't look up, just shook my head and kept moving the food around on my plate. "I haven't seen her since school let out," I lied as the blood pounded in my ears, feeling my cousin's eyes on me the whole time.

That night I lay in bed with the covers pulled up to my chin, listening for the sound of footsteps and Noah's long shadow to cross the doorway.

The next morning, it was all over town.

Nadia never came home last night.

NOW

TWENTY-FOUR

From her seat at the top of the bleachers, Mary Grace watches the softball teams take their places. It's unusually warm for the first Saturday of November, ideal weather for this important game, the last one before the championship next week. The Repentance Mockingbirds are up against the Pinetree Pirates, the same team Mary Grace's sixth-grade team was scheduled to play that long-ago November.

She's trying to stay focused, she really is. But she can't seem to stop her mind from slipping back. The memories catch up with her everywhere. In the middle of the night, when she wakes up drenched in sweat, her mind recoiling from images that don't fade with the sun. At work, remembering when it was Owen Kanady sitting behind her desk trying to keep the town from descending into full-blown panic after those girls disappeared.

Those girls had names.

For twenty-four years, Mary Grace has tried to put distance between herself and what happened. But lately, especially with Darryl Stokes back, it feels like she's fighting a losing battle.

It always begins—and ends—with Nadia.

The first time she saw her, standing in front of their sixth-grade class, so exotic and different from any girl Mary Grace had ever seen. Nadia waiting for her in the dugout, too restless to sit through a softball game. Too busy flirting with the boys at Briggs High.

One boy in particular?

Mary Grace's gaze slides to the right. She has the same unobstructed view of the Briggs High track field where all those years ago she hoped for a glimpse of the star of his tenth-grade track team.

She can still feel the emotions that raged through her that afternoon, the day before Nadia disappeared. The shame when Althea Vale told her she'd flunked her science exam. The fear mingled with sexual attraction she felt in Hunter Fewell's office. The despair as she raced out of school, an unworldly eleven-year-old who thought running away would solve all her problems. The guilt would come later, the feelings of loss and yearning years after that, long after the damage was done and she could do anything about it. Except implore God to save her soul. But as she well knows, prayer can take you only so far.

She never did tell Nadia what she saw.

Another secret she'll take to her grave.

When she heard voices behind the Briggs High bleachers, she immediately recognized Nadia's. But the other person wasn't the boy Nadia bought her pot from. Although his back was to her, she'd know that golden hair and those quarterback shoulders anywhere. Because he was nearly a foot taller, Nadia stood on tiptoe. Her eyes were closed, a rapturous look on her face as she kissed Parnell. That was when Mary Grace ran, shock quickly turning to rage.

As if it were yesterday, she remembers the first time she and Nadia got high together. Telling her best friend that Parnell was the boy she liked kissing the most. Even though it was a lie, Nadia didn't know that. Was that when she made up her mind to get him for herself because she had to seduce every male in Repentance, even if one of them was the boy Mary Grace loved?

And how could Parnell not have known how she felt? She remembered that August afternoon Noah brought him home; how flushed she got when he walked through the kitchen screen door. She thought she'd died and gone to heaven when they practiced softball in her uncle's backyard and he told her she was developing a heck of a pitching arm. Smiling the smile that felt like it was meant just for her.

She often wondered whether Nadia was the reason Parnell and Anna Mae Burns broke up. He never got serious about any woman after Anna Mae. He's still single, still the town's most eligible bachelor. And Mary Grace still fantasizes that someday they'll get together in spite of the nightmare that sometimes wakes her in the dead of night, the thunder of footsteps echoing in her head. Only when she turns around, it isn't the Boogeyman chasing her.

Over the years, she tried to block out what happened in the woods that early November day. It was the only way they'd ever be able to put the past behind them. Then, at his daddy's wake, Parnell made it clear that he'd never forgive her.

But forgiveness is a two-way street, isn't it?

A cheer goes up from the stands. Her first time at bat, Cherie Leigh Hibbard just hit a double, her long legs taking her to first base, then sliding safely to second when the second baseman misses the tag. Tyler Lee is on his feet, screaming for his daughter.

Then Felicity's up. Lucky Eleven. (She keeps her mother's old uniform, with the number seven on the back, next to her regular uniform in the closet for good luck.) As Felicity picks up the bat, Mary Grace tries to clear everything else from her mind and focus her attention on her daughter. With the sun glancing off the visor of Felicity's Mockingbirds cap, she can't tell if she's nervous, which she knows from experience can make your hands stiffen around the bat. But she's the one tensing up as Felicity swings. And misses.

Mary Grace's heart is in her throat as Felicity swings again. This time the ball explodes in the air. Felicity drops the bat and runs. The center-fielder fields the line drive on one hop and throws it to the first baseman seconds after Felicity rounds the base and races to second. Cherie Leigh scores on the play, sliding into home.

The crowd goes wild.

In the bottom of the second, the Pirates take the lead. Until the top of the third, when the Mockingbirds take it back again. They keep their lead through the next three innings, with Cherie Leigh and Felicity each earning their MVP status, Cherie Leigh blasting a homerun in the fifth inning and Felicity a close second with a long triple into the left field corner at the top of the sixth.

Then it's the bottom of the sixth with the bases loaded. Felicity is on the pitcher's mound.

Mary Grace is right there with her, hoping Felicity remembers everything from all their sessions in the backyard, vowing long ago that her child would never have to practice alone. Felicity tosses the ball low and fast, exactly the way her mother taught her. She strikes out the Pirates' star batter for the last out. The crowd goes crazy.

The Mockingbirds win, which means they'll be progressing to the championship next Saturday against the Highpoint Hawks.

Mary Grace is beyond proud. She hurries from the stands and into the dugout, where Vera Gould, Vaughan Elementary's first female coach, is congratulating the team. Mary Grace smiles as Vera and the team high-five one another. As they lift Felicity and Cherie Leigh into the air, Mary Grace sees herself at eleven, flush with victory after her team's first game against the Pinetree Pirates. She can still hear the roar of the crowd, Hunter Fewell clapping her on the back as the team broke out in a rowdy chorus of "For She's a Jolly Good Fellow."

No one was celebrating seven weeks later when the town held a vote as to whether the playoff game before the championship would take place. Some were dead set against it, believing it sinful to partake in a worldly activity, let alone a competitive sport, with a young girl missing. Even if Nadia and her father weren't practicing Baptists from Repentance or from Arkansas at all. Even if folks had their own ideas about what happened.

Three days after Nadia disappeared, no one needed a town hall to decide. This time the edict came from the sheriff himself. All extracurricular activities at Vaughan Elementary, including softball, were suspended until further notice.

"Mom?"

Her daughter's voice drags Mary Grace back.

"Lauren and Haley are going to Nick's for pizza. Is it okay if I go with them?"

Felicity stands there, flanked by the Reeves twins who have become like her second (and third) appendages. All three girls are looking at her now, Mary Grace noticing for the first time how Felicity towers over the other two. Her growth spurt started when she got her period a month after her twelfth birthday back in April. If she gets any taller, she'll need another softball uniform, not to mention a whole new set of clothes.

"Today doesn't count, right?" A troubled frown mars Felicity's face.

Then Mary Grace gets it.

Four days ago she grounded her, something she had never had to do before. On Halloween, a large rock shattered the front window of the wreck of the house that sits at the northernmost edge of the woods. No one knew who did it.

That night when she went to kiss her daughters goodnight, Paige caught Lauren threatening Haley that she better not tell anyone what they'd done. Paige confronted them, and Haley tearfully confessed that the three of them had been in the woods throwing rocks at the Boogeyman's house. But she wouldn't say who broke the window.

After Paige called and told her what happened, Mary Grace questioned Felicity. At first her daughter refused to admit she was even in the woods on Halloween, where she and the Reeves twins were forbidden to go. Not that that ever stopped anyone, Mary Grace included; for most Repentance kids, sneaking into the woods was a rite of passage.

Under her relentless interrogation, Felicity finally confessed to going to the Boogeyman's house that night, but refused to say which one of them shattered the window. Eventually she broke down and said she did it, but it was obvious to Mary Grace that she was lying. She told Felicity that covering for someone else was almost as bad as committing the actual crime. That was when her daughter finally admitted who the perpetrator was. She begged her mother not to say anything, that Lauren would stop being her best friend and throw her out of the popular club if she found out she'd ratted.

Mary Grace felt like the worst kind of hypocrite when she reamed her out for disobeying and lying, remembering her own lies as a child that were a lot worse than anything Felicity had done.

Mary Grace kept her word and didn't tell Paige the truth, which made her feel complicit and reminded her of the time she and Nadia threw rocks at Meurice's window; another rite of passage. Although Paige never knew what her four-minutes-older twin daughter had done, she and Mary Grace agreed that all three of them should be punished. Mary Grace suspended Felicity's internet and social media privileges for a week. After she assessed the damage, she and Paige also agreed that the money to repair the window would come out of all the girls' allowances.

Paige is obviously letting up on her daughters' punishment today, probably because it's Felicity's special day. Haley and Lauren don't go out for sports, the way their mother and Skylar didn't. In fact, the twins could be clones of the earlier popular girls, with their blond hair and matching red headbands that makes it almost impossible to tell them apart. But they never miss one of Felicity's games.

"So I can go, right?" Her daughter's still waiting for her answer.

Mary Grace never thought of herself as a strict disciplinarian—the Lord knows, she was wild back in the day—but her daughter needs to learn that when you do something wrong, you have to pay. No one escapes punishment. Least of all me, Mary Grace thinks, unwelcome memories crowding her. But the look on her child's face is enough to melt the hardest heart. And if Paige is relenting (if only for today), then who is Mary Grace to throw a monkey wrench into the works?

"Okay." She's rewarded by her daughter's dazzling smile that makes her feel all her sacrifices were worth it.

"Don't worry," Paige says, coming up to them, car keys in her hand. "I'll drive Felicity home later."

"Great. Thanks, Paige." Swallowing her disappointment that she and Felicity won't be celebrating her softball victory together, Mary Grace pulls out her own keys and trails them to the parking lot. Two cars over from hers, Tyler Lee is unlocking his driver's side. Cherie Leigh stands next to him, watching Felicity, Lauren, and Haley Reeves, arms linked as they chatter away while waiting for Paige to unlock the rear door of her SUV.

Mary Grace knows that look. She saw it on Allison Driver's face in church, and on the face of every girl who yearns to be popular. Even if it means doing things that are against the law, like breaking someone's window?

Olivia Davis had to throw rocks at Meurice's house for her initiation back in '95, Nadia telling Mary Grace how Skylar and Paige watched from behind a tree. After graduation from Vaughan Elementary (a somber occasion to be sure, with Mary Grace barely making it out of the sixth grade) the popular girls' club was disbanded for a couple of years. At Briggs High the following fall, everyone had other things on their minds. Like boys. Or maybe it just wasn't the same after what happened.

Mary Grace waves as Paige and the girls drive off. Being the mothers of adolescent daughters isn't all she and Paige have in common. Like Mary Grace and Nadia, Paige never had another best friend after Skylar.

Mary Grace walks to her car, thinking she should use the time to file the paperwork that's sitting on her desk. But it's almost three, and she hasn't eaten since breakfast.

Main Street is busy on a weekend. She parks her cruiser in front of the Repentance Diner, in the center of the town square.

The bell over the door tinkles as Mary Grace goes inside. She doesn't come here often. She snags a stool at the thirty-foot-long soda fountain that boasts seventeen flavors of ice cream.

Gabriel Clark, who inherited the place from his grandfather, comes over. He's wearing an apron and just served a customer a heaping plate of flapjacks.

"What can I get for you, Sheriff?"

Mary Grace still hasn't gotten used to being called that. For the first few weeks, she kept looking around for Owen Kanady. She greets him and picks up the menu, which is printed on newspaper. She orders the Excalibur, the diner's specialty: a two-pound burger stuffed between two grilled cheese sandwiches. Maybe she'll surprise Felicity and bring home a hand-dipped milkshake, her favorite.

After he pours her coffee, Gabriel seems in no hurry to leave. "You just missed all the excitement."

"Oh?"

"They were right there." He points to the last booth in the back.

"Who?"

"Sitting just as cozy as you please. Shoulders practically touching, that's how close I'm talking. Burger for him, hot chocolate for her. Totally into their conversation, like no one else existed."

"You planning to keep me in suspense?"

He scowls like she's spoiling his fun. "The guy was Darryl Stokes. Only today instead of sitting by his lonesome at the fountain, he asks for a booth."

"Who was the woman?"

A bell pings at that moment, wouldn't you guess, and he goes off to fetch her burger. After he puts it down in front her, he waits as she slathers on some ketchup. "So who was it, Gabriel?"

"You'll never guess." He lowers his voice to a conspiratorial whisper. "Maddie Driver."

She stops with the mammoth sandwich halfway to her mouth. "You're kidding."

"Scout's honor. It's got to be all over town by now."

Mary Grace has no doubt. Gabriel leaves to take another customer's order and she puts down the burger, having lost her appetite.

Is Madison the woman Stokes came back for?

Which is strange when you think of it, being that it was Madison who came forward in November of '95.

Four days after Nadia disappeared.

By then the town had another missing girl on their hands.

THEN

TWENTY-FIVE

Secrets and Lies

Everyone watched me as I walked to my desk.

The whispering got louder as I sat down, but I wasn't listening. I was too busy trying not to look at the empty desk next to me. On the other side, Madison was trying to ignore it, too. Was she thinking how it used to be her desk before Nadia moved here? I was barely settled at my desk when Chloe Ann turned around.

"Poor Madison. Nadia's gone and now you don't have a best friend." Then she looked at me. "Neither does Little Orphan Mary. Oh, I forgot. You and Nadia weren't best friends anymore, were you? Not after she dropped you for Madison. Maybe you two losers can be best friends now."

I started to see red again.

"Shut up, you bitch!"

But the words didn't shoot out of my mouth. I was so shocked I forgot how mad I was. In all the years I knew her, I'd never heard Madison utter a cuss word. Then I remembered the times I caught her glaring at Chloe Ann when she didn't think she was looking. That was the thing about Chloe Ann. She could make you crazy. Because she didn't let up.

Miss Althea was looking our way. Now we were in for it. Timothy leaned over and whispered in my ear. "Soon everyone will know what Nadia did. She's going to get her comeuppance for being a Jezebel and a thief."

That last part got to me. How did he know Nadia stole my uncle's money? Did everyone know?

Miss Althea rapped her ruler on the blackboard for quiet. When everyone settled down she said, "I know there are a lot of rumors circulating around town. But they're only rumors. Remember that when you talk to Sheriff Kanady. He's here now and wants to ask you all some questions."

The room broke out in loud noise. Miss Althea rapped the ruler again. While she organized us alphabetically, I sat frozen like a statue, my mind going a million miles a minute. After the first kid left, accompanied by Gavin Moore, the class monitor, Miss Althea told us to read the next chapter of our book for an English test next week. But I couldn't see a word on the page. The clock on the wall sounded like the minutes ticking down to my execution.

When Chloe Ann came back from her turn, she acted like the cat who'd licked up all the cream. She looked at Madison, then at me, which meant she probably told Sheriff Kanady how mad I was at Nadia in class yesterday and about Nadia leaving school with Madison. The other kids must have noticed too, but Chloe Ann probably embellished to get me and Madison in trouble.

Timothy had a weird light in his eyes when he came back, like he just had a private communion with God. I thought of him saying Nadia was sleeping with the Devil, which made me think of her kissing Parnell behind the bleachers. No matter how I tried, I couldn't rip that picture from my mind.

After Olivia, it was my turn. As I got to my feet to go to the principal's office, my heart was beating so loud I was sure everyone could hear.

∞

I tried not to squirm in the hot seat, but seeing the sheriff behind the desk where my daddy used to sit really threw me.

"There's no reason to be nervous." His voice was slow and hushed like he was trying to make me feel better. Or trick me into saying something I'd be sorry for. It was the same when he told me my folks were dead. Asking if I knew why they took the car out in that ice storm and me saying I had no idea because I was asleep the whole time. Miss Althea was the only one who knew that was a lie. And I didn't even tell her the whole story.

"I hear you and Nadia Doshenko are good friends," Sheriff Kanady said.

The whole sixth grade knew that. It wasn't a secret. I stared at my hands twisting and untwisting in my lap and waited for him to ask why I was mad at Nadia yesterday.

"Did she ever talk about running away?"

I looked up. Was that what everyone thought? Nadia ran off?

"This is serious, Mary Grace. Her father's money is missing. So are some of her things. He says she stole money from him before. She used it to run away. That time, she was gone almost a week."

Like it was yesterday, I watched Nadia counting the bills in her daddy's sock drawer.

Then I saw her eyes glittering in the darkness of the woods yesterday.

"Forget your uncle's stupid money. I'm talking about big money. Enough for us to run away just like we planned."

I never did find out the secret she came to tell me. But I knew she wasn't talking about her daddy's money. She was going to make someone else pay to keep quiet.

"Did she tell you she was planning to run away?" He put his elbows on the table, the better for me to see the letters that spelled out *Sheriff* on his sleeve. Just so I'd be clear who was the law around here. Deputy Wood stood right behind him, like they were ganging up to scare me into confessing.

"Her daddy's worried sick," Sheriff Kanady said. "We checked the bus station, but nobody's seen her. If she told you anything, anything at all, it could help us find her." He lowered his voice some more. "I understand how you feel. You don't want to tell on her. Or reveal a secret she may have told you in confidence. But think what her father's going through. And she's only twelve. What if something bad happens to her?"

I couldn't look at him. Because something bad already did.

"Mary Grace?"

"She talked about going back to LA where she used to live. She missed it there." The words rolled out of my mouth smooth as silk. Because it was the truth talking.

The sheriff and deputy passed looks. "When did she tell you that?"

"A couple weeks ago."

"Do you know if she has friends or family in LA?"

"Nobody she told me about."

Sheriff Kanady turned around to say something to Deputy Wood that I couldn't hear. Then he looked at me again. "Did she say how she planned to get to LA?"

"She was going to buy a plane ticket." I nearly said *tickets*, but stopped in the nick of time. "She had fake ID and everything."

Sheriff Kanady pushed back his chair and said he'd be right back. Outside the office I heard him ask Principal Sartin's secretary, Hazel, for an outside line. After he left, Deputy Wood leaned over the desk.

"Did you want to go to LA with Nadia?"

He smiled at me, his brown eyes warm and gentle. I remembered overhearing Paige telling Skylar how handsome she thought he was. Then I remembered how nice he was the time he and the sheriff caught me at the town limits. "No," I said, "I didn't want to go to LA," and it was the truth. I hadn't wanted to leave. I wanted to stay right here, in Repentance.

"Maybe Nadia felt all alone being in a new town and that was why she ran away."

"Her mama died when she was eight. And her daddy was busy fixing other towns and was hardly ever home."

"Nobody ever tells you how lonely it feels."

It was true. Trouble was, my loneliness was mixed up with other emotions.

"Being on your own all the time. Not part of a family. But how can you miss what you never had? Maybe that's better. I don't know." He shrugged. It was the saddest shrug I ever saw.

I wasn't sure what I would have said if Sheriff Kanady hadn't come back in then. "Go to the airport," he told Deputy Wood. "Check all afternoon and evening flights that connect to flights to LA. Someone's got to remember an underage kid. And hurry. She has almost half a day's head start." Then he took something out of a manila envelope.

It was a photo. I'd never seen a picture of Nadia, not even at her house. I looked down at my hands twisting in my lap. Anything not to see her face staring at me.

The sheriff gave the photo to the deputy. "We also need to check buses and trains going to the airport."

"She might have hitched a ride. She did the other time." I didn't know why I said that. Maybe because I knew they weren't going to find anyone who saw Nadia at any bus or train station.

Now they were both looking at me, the sheriff frowning like he remembered that time at the town limits. The deputy still had that strange look on his face as he turned to go. When he walked past me, he smiled, but it was sad, too.

"Just a few more questions, Mary Grace," Sheriff Kanady said. "You're doing great."

He couldn't have made me feel worse if he'd accused me of outright murder. My head was starting to pound. I wanted to ask for water but was afraid he'd see it as a sure sign of guilt.

"Do you know if Nadia had a boyfriend?"

I thought of Parnell. I could have told about Nadia and him kissing behind the Briggs High bleachers, but again the words refused to come out.

"Maybe a secret boyfriend? Someone she didn't want anyone to know about?"

I shook my head.

"It could be why she ran away. Did you ever see her with Hunter Fewell?"

Coach? That was a new one on me. Then I remembered him looking into my eyes in his office and wondered if he had a thing for sixth-grade girls. Did Nadia kiss him behind the bleachers, too?

"No," I said, and it was the truth talking again. "I never saw Nadia and Coach Fewell together."

Sheriff Kanady nodded. "We're almost finished, Mary Grace. When was the last time you saw Nadia?"

"When school let out yesterday." It was the same lie I'd told my aunt at supper.

"Did she tell you she was planning to leave for LA yesterday?"

I pictured Nadia outside school again acting so buddy-buddy with Madison. Not knowing it was an act until she showed up at our tree. "She didn't tell me because I wasn't talking to her."

"Why weren't you talking to her?"

I couldn't tell if he already knew that, too. But if Chloe Ann didn't tell him, some other kid probably would.

"My aunt and uncle were concerned about me keeping company with her." It was Miss Althea who said that, but how was he going to know? Besides, my uncle hadn't been any too fond of Nadia. If he knew she stole his money, he'd really have hated her.

"I see."

But he said it like he didn't see at all. "Thank you, Mary Grace. You've been really helpful."

I started to tell him my name was just plain Mary now. But then he'd want to know why, and I'd had my fill of his questions.

I jumped out of the chair and charged out of there as fast as I could.

TWENTY-SIX

The Devil Made Me Do It

After we were all back and accounted for, Miss Althea tried acting like everything was normal, but the minute her back was turned the whispering started up again. By the time lunchtime rolled around, we figured she'd let us out early. But no such luck.

The whole cafeteria was buzzing with what happened.

"Was Coach Fewell really sleeping with Nadia?"

"I thought he was having sex with Mrs. King."

"Did you hear he got into a fist fight over her?"

"Maybe the coach should drown himself in the creek like Bobby Simmons tried to do after Mrs. King dumped him last year."

"Or maybe Simmons should drown him," Nicholas Buck said. A few kids laughed, Dylan Bryant, Nicholas's partner in troublemaking, the loudest. But some of the fourth graders in Emily King's class looked like they believed it could happen.

"You've all got it wrong!" Timothy was practically shouting. "It's the Devil at work, I told you!"

"Which one's the Devil?" Austin Cooper asked. His voice squeaked like an old saw, probably because he hardly ever put two words together. "The coach or that Russian slut?"

Next to Austin, his constant shadow Brandon Cowan whispered something. But I doubted Austin could hear a single word Brandon said, what with his cleft palate.

"If Coach Fewell was fornicating with Nadia, he'll be charged with statutory rape. He'll go to jail." Wyatt Dake looked around to make sure everyone knew he was the smartest kid in school.

"I hear tell Coach is still in the hot seat!" Tyler Lee Hibbard yelled as he and a bunch of fourth graders ran over. His school blazer was missing a button and his white shirt looked as dirty as his gray coveralls.

That started everything going full steam again.

"He's been in there almost an hour!"

"Sheriff Kanady's going to put him in jail for sure."

"Wait till he finds out about the baby."

Everyone looked at Paige.

"What baby?" Dylan asked.

Paige's pretty blue eyes gleamed like gemstones. "I heard Nadia was pregnant."

Cadence Mills was the only one who didn't act shocked. "I tried to warn you all, but you wouldn't listen. That girl brought evil into this town and God is making her pay for her sins."

She'd been going on like that ever since Nadia moved here, so nobody paid her any mind. But my head was spinning. If Nadia was having a baby, wouldn't I have known? Or was I too busy being mad at her to notice? Then I remembered her telling me she went all the way once.

"If Nadia was pregnant, why'd she run away?" Olivia asked.

"Maybe she thought Coach Fewell was going with her," Paige said. "Maybe she thought they'd get married and live happily ever after."

Everyone laughed again.

"Then why's he still here?"

"Maybe Nadia didn't run away at all. Maybe she never left Repentance."

Now everyone looked at Skylar, who smiled like she knew something nobody else did. Did she? Or was she just jealous that Paige was getting all the attention?

"So where is she?" Wyatt asked.

"Maybe Coach didn't want to marry her," Nicholas said.

"You sayin' he did something to her?"

Nobody answered Tyler Lee's question. The cafeteria went silent as the grave. Everyone was staring at Skylar like they believed she spoke the gospel truth.

Nadia didn't run away.

But she was gone all the same.

❧

No one was surprised when the next day's big playoff game was cancelled. It was because Coach Fewell was in the hot seat again. Not at school this time, but in Sheriff Kanady's office. Wyatt said that meant he'd be arrested any second. But after he called everyone into the auditorium, Principal Sartin didn't say a word about Coach Fewell. He just said no extracurricular activities would go on while a sixth grader was missing. In the row behind me, Cadence whispered how no one cared about Nadia being gone because she was a sinful harlot and the town was well rid of her. Especially a harlot who got herself knocked up and stole her daddy's money, said Timothy in a voice loud enough for everyone to hear.

Nobody said it, but I thought about Nadia being a foreigner and not a practicing Baptist, which to some folks counted as a worse sin.

We were in the cafeteria when we heard the news. Someone saw torches in the woods.

That scared the younger kids, because no one had ever disappeared in our town before. It made the older kids try to top each other with stories of what happened.

The tales just got taller and taller.

Coach Fewell was keeping Nadia hostage in the woods until he figured out what to do about her and her unborn baby.

Coach Fewell murdered Nadia, but they'd never find her corpse because he cut her up in little pieces and buried her in different places in the woods. Or he burned up her body parts in the Boogeyman's chimney that was always fired up even though Wyatt said some of her would still be left because bones don't burn. That started some kids saying it was Meurice who killed her.

We were back in class after lunch when we heard Coach Fewell was out of the hot seat. Sheriff Kanady didn't arrest him, but PE class was cancelled. Then one of the kids heard from someone who heard it from someone else that Julia Allred saw Sheriff Kanady and Chief Deputy Wood heading into the woods, which she had a clear view of from her front porch. Which set off rumors that Nadia was hiding out there as part of her initiation into the popular girls' club that was so secret Skylar didn't tell Paige or Olivia.

It was all everyone talked about at recess when we piled into the schoolyard because it was unusually warm outside. Kids gathered around Skylar, asking if that was how she knew Nadia didn't leave Repentance and did she have to throw rocks at the Boogeyman's house like Olivia did? One of the fifth graders said Nadia was going to be in trouble if she was caught hiding in the woods where we were all forbidden to go. Someone else said she'd go to jail for stealing her daddy's money and would have been better off running away.

"Maybe Sheriff Kanady let Coach go because he isn't the baby's father."

Everyone stared at Chloe Ann.

"Then who is?"

Chloe Ann just smiled that stupid cat-that-swallowed-the-cream smile as kids crowded around her.

"She's just making it up. Come on, girls." Skylar started walking away. Paige and Olivia looked at each other, then probably decided it wasn't worth losing their places in the popular club even if they thought Skylar initiated Nadia behind their backs.

"I'm not making it up," Chloe Ann shouted after them.

Skylar stopped and put her hands on her hips. So did Paige and Olivia. "Yes, you are."

"No, I'm not."

"Are, too!"

"Am not!"

"Then tell us who it is."

Timothy gave a superior nod. "It's the Devil. Like I said all along."

"You are both so lame. Everyone knows there's no such thing. It's just something Pastor Mills says to scare us."

That would have been the only thing ever to come out of Skylar's mouth I agreed with. Until now.

Now I knew Satan really existed.

"You're dead wrong." Cadence fixed Skylar with her glare, probably because she didn't like her daddy being accused of lying to us. "True sin is here among us and God and his angels are no match for the unholy evil that's been unleashed in this town."

"Get away from me, you freak!" Skylar screamed.

"The Devil's among us," Timothy intoned.

Some of the younger kids took up the chant. "The Devil's here! The Devil's here!"

"With a soul as black as sin." Olivia's voice sounded strange, like someone else was making the words come out of her mouth.

"Did the Devil do something to Nadia?" a fourth grader asked.

"It's the Boogeyman! I told you! I told you!" Tyler Lee was so excited he was hopping up and down.

"What does the Devil look like?"

"He's got horns and a long tail, what do you think?"

"He carries a pitchfork the better to stab you with!"

"His eyes are red as a bloodsucker!"

"You are all so dumb," Wyatt said to Tyler Lee and the other fourth graders. "The Devil's too smart to go around breathing fire. He can change his appearance whenever he likes so he can fool us all."

"Is he Nadia's secret boyfriend?" another fourth grader asked.

"Oh, pul—lease." Skylar pulled one of her long-suffering looks. "Her secret boyfriend's handsomer than the Devil."

Everyone looked at Chloe Ann again. Was she talking about Parnell? Or making it up to impress the popular girls?

But if I saw Parnell kissing Nadia, she could have, too.

"He's right under our noses," Chloe Ann said. "And soon the whole town's going to know who it is."

"Shut up, you bitch! You don't know anything!"

Now it was me everyone stared at as I watched Chloe Ann cross the invisible line in the schoolyard that separated the outcasts and loners from everyone else. I wished I could take it back, but it was too late. I couldn't believe I was still protecting Parnell.

It was like everyone was holding their breath as Chloe Ann walked over to me. "You know more than you're telling," she whispered so no one would hear. "And I'm going to find out what it is."

"You shut your filthy mouth, you bitch!"

"Make me! Little Orphan Mary!"

"I told you not to call me that again!!"

"What are you going to do about it? You don't even have a best friend anymore. You're just a loser and always will be."

My head pounded so hard it felt like my brain was going to crash right through my skull. Before I knew it, Chloe Ann was on the ground and I was on top of her.

"Loser!" someone shouted. Suddenly the schoolyard was echoing with it.

Chloe Ann started flailing around and making choking noises. But I just squeezed her fat neck for all I was worth, trying to shut out the sound of kids chanting that awful word. Then I smelled a familiar perfume and strong arms were pulling me back.

I stumbled to my feet, at first not knowing where I was. Then I saw Miss Althea's face, which was white as a sheet, and it all came rushing back.

"She tried to kill me!" Chloe Ann said, clutching her throat as the other kids watched, their eyes huge. It was my fifth-grade fight with Alexis Hamilton all over again. "I'm telling my daddy and he'll have Sheriff Kanady come and arrest you."

"No one's arresting anyone," Miss Althea said, still holding on to me. "You girls should be ashamed, fighting at a time like this."

"She started it!"

"No, she did!"

"That's enough!!"

I'd never heard Miss Althea so mad. "We're going back inside now and I don't want to hear another word out of either of you." She finally let me go with a look like she was afraid I might attack Chloe Ann again. But all the fight had left me and I just felt dead tired. As I trailed them out of the schoolyard, the other kids gave me a wide berth.

In class, I stared at the back of Chloe Ann's neck where I could see the red marks from where my fingers had dug into her skin. And all I could think was how Timothy was wrong.

Nadia's secret boyfriend wasn't the Devil. Even if he fooled the world with his blue eyes and hair as golden as the sun.

Cadence was wrong about Nadia, too. She wasn't the Devil.

I was.

By suppertime, what happened in the schoolyard was all over town.

"Why did you have to fight? Haven't the Scriptures taught you that violence against another human being is a sin?"

My aunt looked pained as she asked it, like what I did was a personal affront to her and God. I wondered what she'd think if she knew what I didn't tell Sheriff Kanady. I kept sneaking looks out the window, any minute expecting to see the red lights of his cruiser. I was terrified that I'd end up in the hot seat again for trying to strangle Chloe Ann and instead of the lies I'd been telling, the truth would pop out. Then everyone would know how truly evil I was.

"Leave the girl be," my uncle was saying. "You can't blame Mary Grace for defending herself. It's the only way to handle a bully."

You could have knocked me over. Even my aunt looked shocked. It was something my daddy would have said.

"But Samuel, you know as well as I do. It's in the Psalms to seek peace and pursue it."

"That's all very well, but sometimes you have to teach somebody a lesson. Mary Grace can't let that girl go on tormenting her, no matter who her daddy is." It was no secret that my uncle didn't like Jackson Briggs. Him and half the town.

My aunt was quiet for a spell, probably wondering whether to cross my uncle when he had a few drinks in him.

"Do you think the Briggs girl knows something?"

My aunt's eyes were on the roll she was buttering, so I couldn't tell if she was putting the question to me. I looked at my cousin, who hadn't said one word since we'd sat down to supper.

"About what?" my uncle asked.

"What happened to the Doshenko girl."

"Why do you say that?"

"I heard around town the Briggs girl might know who her boyfriend is."

"She's a child," my uncle said, pouring himself more wine. "You know how they are. Making up stories all the time."

"But lying's a sin."

Which meant I was done for.

"Not if the liar has convinced herself it's the truth." I could have sworn my uncle was talking to me. Like he was waiting for me to come clean right here at the table.

My aunt didn't seem to notice. "Owen Kanady let Hunter Fewell go. I just wondered is all. Do you think the Doshenko girl was really in the family way?"

"Hester, I'm surprised at you. Listening to town gossip." My uncle's face was red. I wasn't sure if it was from the wine or all the talk of Nadia being pregnant and unmarried, an unforgivable sin in the eyes of God. A lot more unforgivable than two kids fighting in the schoolyard.

"Do you think she was lying with one of the boys from school?"

"That's enough! In this house, we don't spread tales like wicked children. What we should be doing is praying for her soul."

"Why, Samuel! You make it sound as if she were dead."

My heart nearly stopped beating. The only sound was the thumping of my cousin's leg under the table.

"Whether she is or she isn't, the Lord knows what she's done. The path to salvation is between her and her maker. All the more reason we should pray for her."

We closed our eyes and joined hands like we did when we said grace. Noah's hand felt as cold as the grave.

After supper, I started to clear away the dishes. When I leaned down to collect my cousin's, he whispered in my ear. What he said got me to shaking so hard, I nearly dropped his plate.

Later that night, I crept out of bed and climbed out my window like I'd done all those times I snuck off to meet Nadia. I stood in the field and looked up at the sky. It was inky black, and not one star winked at me. Even the moon was ashamed to show her face. Another sure sign I'd shut God out of my heart. I'd never felt so alone.

As I stared across the field at the place where my uncle's land sloped down to that thicket of pines, I could feel the evil rising up from my Devil's soul.

My uncle might think Nadia's soul could be saved.

But mine was damned for all eternity.

NOW

TWENTY-SEVEN

"Mom?"

She's floating, suspended somewhere between sleep and waking. Not yet ready to face the world.

"Mom?" The voice louder, the tone more insistent.

Mary Grace slits open one eye. Her head throbs like someone took a mallet to her skull. The light's blinding. She closes her eye. A mistake. A thousand knives stab behind her eyelid.

"Mom, wake up!"

The fear in the voice finally gets her moving. She's heard it before. When she was deathly sick with food poisoning and five-year-old Felicity found her on the bathroom floor covered in her own vomit. She'll never forget the raw panic in her little girl's face. She never wants to see that again.

Through a supreme effort of mind over body, Mary Grace opens her eyes—another round of skull-crushing pain—and lifts her head off the pillow. Felicity's face swims in and out of focus as she forces herself up on her elbows.

"Mom, you drank the whole bottle! That is so uncool!"

"Now just a minute," Mary Grace says. Except the words come out stuck together, a series of indecipherable sounds. Her mouth is so dry it feels like a hive of bees nesting on her tongue.

She turns her head. The pain behind her eyes recedes a millimeter, but now she's aware of a dull ache in her neck. There's an empty wine bottle on her night table, no glass in sight. She has no memory of guzzling like a heathen (although she has a dim recollection of rocking on the porch, the bottle in her lap), yet the evidence is right here in front of her.

"You have to get up. Now!"

"Could you please lower that blind?"

Felicity shakes her head as she goes to the window, as if she were the long-suffering parent and Mary Grace the recalcitrant child. As the room is plunged into blessed darkness, Mary Grace falls back onto her pillows.

"We're going to be late for church." Felicity's voice floats out of the void.

Shit. Church is the last place Mary Grace wants to be after the night she had. She's not sure which would be worse, being a no-show or for Repentance's sheriff to walk into the First Baptist Church bleary-eyed and hungover, which is sure to set tongues wagging. At least Cadence Mills isn't in the pulpit anymore thanks to Jackson Briggs, who has had it in for her these twenty-four years. Ever since Cadence went around town labeling Chloe Ann as evil as Nadia because of the circumstances surrounding her disappearance.

"Come on!"

Mary Grace has never known her daughter to be eager to go to church, which she suspects has less to do with faith than the chance to hang out with the Reeves twins.

A light goes on in her closet. Felicity pulls out a dress and hangs it on the closet door. In spite of her throbbing head, Mary Grace smiles. Her daughter loves picking out her clothes. "I'll go make coffee." And Felicity's gone, clattering down the stairs to work her magic on the temperamental coffeemaker. But Mary Grace has to admit she makes a mean cup of java. And truth to tell, she doesn't mind being coddled a little.

As the tantalizing aroma of coffee brewing wafts up the stairs, Mary Grace forces herself to get out of bed. In the bathroom, she splashes cold water on her face. As she meets her reflection in the mirror (shocked to see how pale and sunken her face looks), the dream that woke her in the dead of night rushes back.

She was standing in the spot where her uncle's land slopes down into that thicket of pines, a shovel in her hands. Except as she shoveled dirtful after dirtful of earth into the shallow graves, it wasn't the dead raccoon staring up at her.

It was Nadia and Chloe Ann.

"Mo—om!"

"Be down in five minutes!" Mary Grace yells through the open bathroom door, which sets her head pounding again. Then she dries her face and brushes her teeth, wondering how she'll quiet her unquiet mind long enough to get through the day.

An hour after church lets out, Mary Grace is once again pulling out of her driveway, she and her daughter having changed from their Sunday dresses into casual clothes—in Felicity's case, T-shirt and shorts. As they drive, a gentle breeze wafts in through the open windows of the car. It's another day of record-setting warmth, the temperature yesterday topping out at sixty-eight and today predicted to go even higher.

The last time they had a heat wave in November was back in '95 (which, together with Darryl Stokes's reappearance, has set rumblings around town that it's another sign, something Mary Grace is starting to agree with—one more nail in the coffin of her ever-present guilt and the source of her recent nightmares).

Felicity's texting on her phone as usual when Mary Grace turns into the familiar driveway.

"How many times do I have to tell you to put away that phone?" she says as she pulls the key from the ignition. "Out of the car. Now. They're waiting."

"Do I have to?"

"We made a deal, remember?"

The softball championship is this coming Saturday, and Mary Grace promised she'd practice with her later on the condition that Felicity play with her younger cousins first. Felicity tried to wriggle out of it, saying they were babies and couldn't pitch to save their lives. But Mary Grace refused to be swayed, her mind still on what Felicity and the Reeves twins did on Halloween.

As they climb the steps of the front porch, the door opens and out walks a tall man with white hair. He gives his great-niece a quick hug before she disappears into the house, the screen door slamming after her.

"I don't know where that girl gets her energy." Samuel Mathews shakes his head as if he hasn't repeated the same words since Felicity was a toddler.

"She's twelve," Mary Grace says as she greets her uncle with a peck on the cheek, taking note of the aftershave she bought him last Christmas. It's her stock answer; only the years change. He smiles, both of them no doubt remembering Felicity as a little girl. For her birthday this past April, he came back from the road with a birthday cake he swore was from the best bakery in Little Rock.

Mary Grace follows her uncle inside. Felicity and her second cousins are chattering upstairs. As she walks into the kitchen, Mary Grace automatically finds herself listening for something she knows she'll never hear again, its absence almost a sound itself: the squeak of her aunt's wheelchair across the now-worn linoleum. Ironic, how it was Aunt Hester who turned out to be her strongest ally.

It was after she passed that Noah moved back in with his family, taking over the upstairs bedrooms while Uncle Samuel moved into Mary Grace's old bedroom down here.

She watches her uncle walk to the refrigerator and take out a jug of apple cider. In the side door of the fridge, she can see several bottles of the red wine he still enjoys with supper. He moves slower than he used to, which she suspects has less to do with age than the loss of his wife. After he pours out two glasses, he brings them over to the round table where they had breakfast every day when she lived here. Supper was a more formal affair, taken in the dining room where it was her job to carry everything in and out.

"How's Pastor Mills?" she asks as she sips the cider. When she and Felicity left church, he and her uncle were engaged in discussion. Two

Bible men no doubt bemoaning the ills of today's secular world. Cadence was nowhere to be seen.

"He's failing."

"I'm sorry to hear it." It's all over town that Mills has a rare form of blood cancer. And if today's sermon was any indication, he isn't long for this world. It's probably what he and her uncle were discussing on the church steps: who'll take over the pulpit when Mills is gone. It's no secret that he doesn't hold with his daughter's Footwasher views. Neither does her uncle, as far as Mary Grace knows.

"Josiah's worried for our town. As am I. What with these extreme religious groups gaining a foothold in the south. They dare to call themselves Salvationists. What they preach has nothing to do with salvation."

"Amen to that." It seems like every day lately Mary Grace reads about some new evil the Salvationists are perpetrating in her state. It started in July, when a horse farm in Bentonville owned by Jews burned to the ground. In September, an Islamic mosque in Fayetteville was bombed. The latest atrocity happened just last week, when a lone gunman opened fire on a mall in De Queen, a town in Sevier County with a growing Hispanic population. Ten men and women were killed, seven wounded. Now rumors are circulating that the cult, led by a white supremacist named Silas Knight, has set its sights on Tontitown, home to a small faction of Mexican immigrants. Some worry that in spite of Repentance being a Baptist town, the Salvationists will find a reason to spread their hate here.

"And their numbers are growing," Uncle Samuel says. "Every day they're brainwashing others to take up their cause. The angry. The disenfranchised. They're just bullies, preying on the weak and vulnerable. Those who have lost their way, like Isaac Wood."

"Do you really think Knight's group could get to him?" The town was still talking about what happened at a custody hearing in family court a few weeks back. Wood threatened his wife, Adalynn, accusing her of turning their daughter Annabelle against him after the judge cut off his weekend visits unless he stopped drinking.

"If he's far gone enough. My fear is he may never find the path back. At least Josiah has his faith to sustain him."

Samuel Mathews's stock in trade. It's his faith in the Almighty that has kept him going these past three years. Mary Grace envies him. To have that kind of belief, you needed more than a clear conscience. You had to be pure in heart and soul.

Her uncle pushes back his chair and goes over to the oven. A tantalizing aroma fills the kitchen as he checks the thermometer on the roast cooking inside. Then he stirs the butternut squash soup simmering in a pot on the stovetop. With a fork, he tests the softness of the potatoes boiling in an adjacent pot.

Mary Grace can't help but smile as he takes a carton of milk from the fridge and adds it to the potatoes, the secret to their coming out soft. All that was her job back when she was an orphan living on the charity of her uncle and aunt.

Sunday dinner following church is a tradition here when the Mathews men aren't on the road, although Mary Grace has begged off on more than one occasion.

"Let me help." As if she hasn't been saying it every time she comes for dinner.

"Nothing to do."

"I'll set the table."

"Already done." Uncle Samuel puts the milk back in the fridge. "You just sit yourself back down. I daresay you have enough to do running this town and raising your daughter."

Less attuned ears might miss the underlying note of disapproval. Much as he adores Felicity, Mary Grace is after all a single (read: unwed) mother, a sin in the eyes of God.

As if on cue, three pairs of feet clatter noisily down the stairs. Seconds later, Felicity and Ashley and Lydia Mathews burst into the kitchen, mitt, bat, and softball in hand.

"Felicity's going to practice with us," six-year-old Ashley announces.

"All right," Uncle Samuel says, frowning. "Just remember, dinner is at two o'clock sharp. But first you have to tell me if this is up to snuff."

Ashley giggles as she stands on tiptoe to taste the gravy on the ladle he holds out to her. She gives it her seal of approval before racing her older sister out the back door, Felicity sending her mother one of her long-suffering looks, which Mary Grace ignores.

After Felicity follows the girls outside, Uncle Samuel leads the way into the sunroom, where he and her aunt used to share private time together before supper.

"Felicity's growing up to be a fine young lady," he says, gazing out the window where they have an unobstructed view of the girls playing in the backyard. Again Mary Grace hears the gentle censure in his voice as if it's in spite of there being no father in her daughter's life. "How's she getting on at school?"

"Straight As on her first report card." She can't help but compare Felicity to herself at that age.

Sixth grade was never the same after that tragic November, graduation from Vaughan Elementary a somber affair with what happened casting a long shadow over the town. Aunt Hester was also there for Mary Grace's graduation from Briggs High, seven years later because she had to repeat seventh grade. But it was after Mary Grace graduated from police academy, following years of wildness that would have unforeseen consequences, that her aunt showed what she was truly made of.

"Glad to hear it. Wouldn't want anything taking her away from her studies." Uncle Samuel's weathered face is unreadable as he watches the girls. But once again Mary Grace hears that note in his voice.

She knows it isn't the game of softball itself that her uncle disapproves of, being a big believer in keeping the body as fit as the mind. It's the idea of children competing against each other. When Mary Grace was Felicity's age, he and Josiah Mills lobbied unsuccessfully against sixth graders engaging in intramural sports when they could be studying the Bible. It's the one thing on which she and her uncle will never see eye to eye.

A scream followed by loud cries suddenly fills the backyard. Through the open window, Mary Grace sees Lydia Mathews at home plate leaning over her younger sister, who's holding her head and wailing.

"She did it on purpose!" Ashley Mathews yells when Mary Grace and her uncle rush outside, pointing an accusing finger at Felicity at the pitcher mound, the handsome red glove Mary Grace bought her daughter last Christmas covering her left hand.

"She's a liar!" Felicity yells back. "All I did was pitch to her. It's not my fault she got in the way of the ball."

That was what Mary Grace said, word for word, when she was in fifth grade and Alexis Hamilton accused her of deliberately hitting her with a softball.

"Let me take a look," Uncle Samuel says, Ashley's cries subsiding as he parts her hair to inspect her head. "You've got a little bump, but some ice will fix that up in no time." But Mary Grace can see the disapproval on his face as he takes his granddaughter by the hand. Lydia stands there for a minute looking at Felicity, who hasn't moved. Then she follows her sister and great-uncle inside, the screen door banging behind her.

"I told you I didn't want to play with them. Ashley's such a baby." Felicity walks over to her mother at home plate. "I didn't mean to hurt her."

Just like Mary Grace didn't mean to hurt Alexis Hamilton when she pitched that softball at her. Even though Alexis had scored more runs in their last game.

"Mom, I'm really sorry. Can you practice with me now?"

Mary Grace's first pitch is too high, but Felicity's ready. She raises her bat. The ball *thwacks* against the wood and goes flying over the outfield. It bounces off the grass at the edge of the field, then rolls downhill and disappears.

"Mom!" Felicity yells from across the field as she tags third base, then starts running for home. "Get the ball!"

Mary Grace stands rooted to the spot.

"Mom! Jesus!"

Mary Grace opens her mouth to remind her not to swear, but nothing comes out. She's staring down at the thicket of pines she hasn't gone near in twenty-four years and where no natural light ever finds its way in. Felicity runs over, giving her one of her looks. Then she clambers down the slope before she can stop her and vanishes into the pines.

If she squints, Mary Grace can just make out the tree where Nadia carved their initials. The one with the deep hollow where Nadia stashed pot and cigarettes and other things she didn't want anyone to find.

She can see her next to their tree, dark eyes glittering with secrets. Hearing that twig snap, Nadia yelling at Madison to get lost. Both of them expecting to see an overweight eleven-year-old girl emerge from the darkness.

"Cousin Noah! What were you doing back there?"

Mary Grace blinks. Felicity's standing there. Not Nadia. And there's no sign of a raccoon, like the one that scampered out of the brush that long-ago day. Just her mind playing tricks.

Noah's laughing as he comes out from behind a tall pine. "I scared you good, didn't I? Bet you thought I was a big black bear."

"I did not! And I'm not scared of any old bear."

"You should be."

Felicity stares at him, the softballs in her hands glowing in the dark. Trust her to find all those missing balls, Mary Grace thinks as her daughter tosses her long dark hair over her shoulder just like Nadia used to do. "I'm not scared of you, either," she tells Noah. "I'm not scared of anything." Then she scrambles up the slope and runs back across the field.

Noah shades his eyes from the sun as he looks up. "Well, if it isn't cousin Mary Grace. Been a while. You don't come around as often as you used to. Guess that happens when you're the law in town. You must be pretty busy keeping folks safe."

There's that undercurrent she always hears in his voice. As if beneath the words he's saying something else. He's part of the reason she hates coming here. "Don't you have anything better to do than frighten little girls?"

"Didn't you hear her? She's not scared of anything." Noah climbs up the slope, gangly as ever. "What about you, Mary Grace? Are you afraid?"

She takes a step back, heart hammering away. Hating herself for letting him get to her. "I have nothing to be afraid of."

"Don't you?" He stands a few feet away. The stringy, too-long hair now a fashionable buzz cut, pockmarks from his youthful acne barely visible. But the eyes are the same: cold and cruel. And there's dirt on his jean jacket and leaves in his hair. Just like the night he walked into the dining room twenty-four years ago. Her aunt didn't notice because Uncle Samuel had just gotten back from the road. Noah didn't even bother changing out of his mud-stained sneakers before sitting down to supper.

It was the Tuesday Nadia disappeared. Mary Grace can still hear her screaming.

"You saying Darryl Stokes showing his face here didn't rattle your cage just a little?" Her cousin's voice rises above the din in her head. "Didn't make you feel like you were seeing a ghost?"

He sidles closer to Mary Grace. This time she stands her ground in spite of her pounding heart. "Think it's a sign?" he whispers even though no one's around to hear him. "We both know God never does anything without a good reason."

He whispered to her back then, too. Two nights after Nadia vanished. As she was clearing away the supper dishes, his voice a slithering snake in her ear.

"You should have finished what you started in the schoolyard. Taught that Briggs cunt a lesson she'd never forget."

By the next night, Chloe Ann was gone, too.

"Daddy! Daddy!" Ashley and Lydia Mathews run toward them with loud whoops of delight, Ashley's altercation with her older cousin already forgotten.

Noah looks at Mary Grace over his shoulder as he walks away, his daughters clinging to him. The whole town may think he's a God-fearing family man and an emissary of the Lord himself, especially after he took up her uncle's salvation-selling business. But he can't fool her. Didn't fool his wife either, which is probably why she left. Even if her departure from Repentance set tongues wagging that a woman who could walk out on her baby girls wasn't worth the Lord's time.

Or maybe she was afraid.

Noah never did answer Felicity's question about what he was doing in the woods.

Mary Grace shivers in spite of the unusually warm early-November sun beating down on her.

❧

The fine weather continues through the next week, reaching an unheard-of seventy degrees on Saturday, the day of the big softball game. Mary Grace forgets everything else as she watches her daughter stride to the pitcher's mound. She's on her feet two hours later with Tyler Lee Hibbard and the other parents, cheering wildly as the Repentance Mockingbirds take the championship from the Highpoint Hawks.

The following week it turns cold, a bitter, bone-chilling cold that warns of worse to come. Despite the Farmers' Almanac of recent years predicting wild weather swings and heavier precipitation in the southern part of the Great Plains, Mary Grace can't help but view it as a sign: God giving with one hand and taking with the other. What else explains such temperature extremes? Or the torrential rains of this past summer? While global warming obviously plays a role, it's still unusual for this part of the country.

Mary Grace is now firmly in the camp of those who see omens in the weather.

And Darryl Stokes is still in Repentance.

That's why she isn't sleeping. Biting her nails until the cuticles are raw. Waiting for the other shoe to drop.

It happens on a Friday, six days before Thanksgiving. Today was a break in the cold snap, but a snowstorm is predicted overnight.

Just the idea is enough to spook the inhabitants of Repentance. Their state has seen its share of tornadoes and ice storms, but snow is a rarer phenomenon.

The last time northwest Arkansas saw a significant snowfall was a freak storm in May of 2013 that dropped almost half a foot on Decatur. Only two years earlier, on February 9, 2011, Siloam Springs hit a new record for the most snow in a single day—more than two feet.

Folks around here aren't taking any chances. They've already cleared out the local stores and are getting ready to hunker down.

Mary Grace has dispatched her deputy and assistant sheriff to help the Repentance maintenance supervisor get the town's snowplow and blowers ready. They were lucky to have even that, and only because Owen Kanady fought for the machinery after a nasty snow-and-ice storm that cost Arkansas damages in the multi-millions. What the town didn't budget for was a stockpile of road salt, which is one of the reasons Mary Grace has reached out to the county sheriff's office.

She just checked the generator that Kanady also fought for in the event of outages and finally got last winter.

Her cell phone *ping*s.

There's a text message from Felicity. *Where are you?!*

At work, Mary Grace texts back. Where else would she be?

Have you looked out the window?!

Mary Grace does and is stunned to see snow falling. It's only ten past six. It wasn't supposed to start for hours.

I'm starving!! Felicity texts.

I'll call Nick and order pizza, Mary Grace writes back.

Felicity texts back a smiley face. Mary Grace smiles in spite of herself. Then she swipes the screen for the phone icon, overwhelmed by a sudden need to hear her daughter's voice. She stops herself just in time, knowing how Felicity hates it when she babies her. She'd want to know why she's calling.

I just wanted to hear your voice.

A sharp knife edge of dread lodges itself under her left rib, making it hard to breathe. She closes her eyes, her mind forming the words. The prayer is always the same: Please keep my daughter safe.

But why on this green earth would He answer?

The phone on her desk rings, startling her. For a second she thinks it's Felicity, hearing her thoughts, attuned to her as always. But she'd call on her cell. Like everyone else. Calls rarely come through here anymore, especially after hours.

The phone continues to ring, echoing through the empty office.

She's tempted to let it roll over and pick up the message when she gets home.

It's probably someone worried about the storm. She's thinking about the town's elderly shut-ins, of which there are more than a few, as she reaches for the phone.

"Repentance sheriff's office. Mary Grace Dobbs speaking."

A voice shrills in her ear, hysterical and high-pitched.

"Slow down. I can't understand you."

More words fly at her. She finally recognizes who it is. And what he's saying.

It's Tyler Lee.

Cherie Leigh is missing.

PART II

TWENTY-EIGHT

It was gearing up to be a worse storm than the one in February of 2011.

Shortly after seven P.M., the snow that had started to fall more than six hours earlier than predicted covered most of the sidewalks in Repentance. As it started coming down heavier, the increasing winds and decreasing visibility sent most folks scurrying for safety inside the warmth of their homes. By eight, the forecast had been upgraded to a severe winter watch. Anyone fool enough to be out driving in this weather was warned to keep off the main roads, including the highway, where sometime after nine a deciduous tree that still had some late-autumn leaves clinging to its limbs snapped under the strain of the snow and split in half. All that remained was a jagged stump with the upper trunk and branches splayed out in the middle of the road.

Those looking for signs need look no further than their beleaguered town (though neighboring places weren't faring all that much better). Forecasters were now predicting a total of anywhere from twelve to sixteen inches.

One thing most were agreed on: there'd be no search parties heading out tonight.

Which set some wondering what His real intentions were. If this was God's way of rooting out the Devil in their midst (same as the mid-August rainstorm that blew him back in), there was no way they could do anything about it on a foul night like this. And if He truly wanted the missing girl found, He wouldn't have sent the white stuff hurling out of the heavens at such an alarming speed. Unless this was His way of making Repentance pay for not destroying the Devil when they had the chance.

By nine thirty, the weight of the rapidly falling snow had settled across power lines, which was when the first outages were reported. As the wind picked up, tree limbs crashed on those snow-blanketed lines, taking out more portions of the local grids.

Dealing with the twin crises of a surprise snow storm and a missing sixth grader was taking more resources than the Repentance sheriff's office currently possessed. By this time, everything had slowed to a virtual standstill. The snow was still falling and the roads were all but impassable. It was now predicted to taper off sometime after midnight, when temperatures were supposed to plummet into the single digits.

Which meant the snow that hadn't been plowed would turn to ice, creating even more dangerous conditions.

That didn't bode well for finding Cherie Leigh Hibbard. Dead or alive.

Earlier that evening, with the snow already falling hard and fast, Mary Grace drove to Tyler Lee's house. He took her up to Cherie Leigh's room, where nothing appeared out of the ordinary. The only things missing were her backpack and smartphone, eerily echoing Chloe Ann Briggs's disappearance (with the exception of the phone, which no Repentance sixth graders possessed back in '95, even wealthy ones like Chloe Ann). Tyler Lee insisting Cherie Leigh would never disobey him and sneak out of the house. Even for a secret boyfriend? Mary Grace asked, to which Tyler Lee responded that she was eleven years old, for Christ's sake! That didn't prove anything except that parents were often the last to know, and got Mary Grace wondering about her own daughter.

As she was getting ready to leave, thoughts swirling through her head as fast as the falling snow, Tyler Lee grabbed her arm. Begged her to find his baby as the tears rolled down his cheeks and onto the neatly pressed suit he hadn't changed out of after he got home from work and discovered his daughter gone. A far cry from the kid in dirty coveralls who followed her to her secret cave that hot August day. Now he was a single parent, terrified of losing his only child.

Something Mary Grace could relate to. Doubly guilty about the relief she'd felt when the missing child turned out to be someone else's, she did her best to reassure him. Told him chances were Cherie Leigh was waiting out the storm someplace where she couldn't get cell phone reception. Her own words ringing hollow in her ears.

Snow was coming down heavier by then and the wind had picked up. She told Tyler Lee to stay put, which meant not do something stupid like go out and look for his daughter himself. In spite of her own warning, along with the worsening visibility, Mary Grace drove slowly through town, making a pit stop at the bus station even though she knew (just as she knew with Nadia) that no one would remember having seen Cherie Leigh.

That was almost three hours ago. Now snow covers everything, even as it continues to fall. Outside the window it's a total whiteout, the wind howling as ghostly tree limbs crack against the glass. Power's out across most of the northwest corner of the state. Mary Grace sits back in her chair, massaging a crick in her neck as her phone lights up with a text. It's from Conner, telling her about another downed tree. She's waiting to hear back from the county sheriff, who already sent extra plows and road salt, and promised to send uniforms and dogs as soon as it's safe to start the search. Neither of them saying it'll include cadaver dogs because even if they find Cherie Leigh, it might be too late.

Just like twenty-four years ago.

The candles on her desk flicker as the door to the office blows open.

But it isn't the wind gusting through the room. It's Jackson Briggs, his face red with the cold, snow coating every inch of him. As he storms over to her desk, he looks like a deranged Father Christmas.

"Where is he?!"

"Who?"

"Stokes."

She should have known. What else would bring Briggs out on a night like this? "I have no idea. But he's probably inside, where you should be."

"No, he isn't. I was just there. Miss Lillian said he left the boarding house around four and hasn't been back since."

This isn't what Mary Grace wants to hear. Tyler Lee said his housekeeper told him she hadn't seen Cherie Leigh after she came home from school and went upstairs to do her homework. That was at three thirty. When the housekeeper called upstairs at five o'clock to say she was leaving, the only response was the music blasting from Cherie Leigh's bedroom. Cherie Leigh wasn't in her room—or anywhere in the house—when Tyler Lee got home at six.

"I wouldn't call Miss Lillian the most reliable witness of people's comings and goings," Mary Grace says. "And even if Stokes isn't there, that doesn't make him guilty of anything."

Briggs narrows his eyes. "That's funny, coming from you. You sure were ready to point the finger back then."

Mary Grace feels her hackles rise, but refuses to let him put her on the defensive. "How do you suppose Stokes pulled it off? Abducted Cherie Leigh out of her bedroom with the housekeeper downstairs? When Chloe Ann disappeared, your wife was in the kitchen, God rest her soul. You know as well as I do it was far more likely your daughter left the house on her own steam." With everything pointing in that direction, that had been the general consensus. No sign of forced entry. No evidence of anyone in her room other than Chloe Ann.

Now, with Cherie Leigh gone, Repentance faces a wave of déjà vu. And Stokes is unaccounted for.

Briggs pounds his fist on her desk, making Mary Grace jump. "How can you sit here doing nothing! Don't you care that another girl is missing?"

"I'll pretend I didn't hear that."

"You have to find him!"

She knows what he's thinking. Find Stokes, find Cherie Leigh. "Look," she says in her most reasonable voice. "We can't do anything until the snow lets up. Go home, Jackson. Let us do our job."

But Briggs isn't seeing reason, hasn't for twenty-four years. "If you'd been doing your job, he would have been run out of town back in August. Before he could hurt another girl."

Mary Grace sighs out a breath. It's going to be a long night. "We don't know that Stokes had anything to do with Cherie Leigh's disappearance. And have you forgotten he had an alibi for the time your daughter went missing?"

"That mechanic lied."

On the first Friday in November of '95, Darryl Stokes clocked into Parnell Vaughan's garage at eight a.m. Instead of leaving at four, he worked an extra half shift, filling in for another mechanic, Tyler Lee Sr., who was out sick. He didn't clock out until eight that evening. According to Jacob Weaver, the mechanic who alibied him and has since moved away, Stokes was under the hood of a Honda most of that day. Not even his half-hour lunch and dinner breaks gave him enough time to get from the garage to the Briggs mansion on the south side, abduct Chloe Ann, and spirit her into the northern part of the woods. All without being seen. And Stokes didn't own a car.

"You can bet your eye teeth if Tyler Lee Sr. hadn't been out on a drunken tear, that no-account drifter wouldn't have gotten away. And now his son's being punished for it, God help us all."

Mary Grace stares at him. Is that what everyone thinks? That Tyler Lee Jr. is paying for the sins of his father? "Why would Jacob Weaver do that? Risk his job? And you're not remembering it right. Even after Weaver came forward, Kanady didn't let Stokes go."

Because Stokes didn't have an alibi for Nadia. But he didn't need one after the call came in, leading them to the field behind that house. The evidence there for everyone to see. That was when Kanady finally cut him loose.

"It doesn't mean he was innocent, and you know it. Why do you keep defending him? I don't recall you having any love for that drifter when you told Kanady about the cabin."

"I just told him what I saw." She doesn't want to have this conversation, not with Jackson Briggs of all people.

"Why'd you take so long to tell about that place? Maybe if you had sooner, my baby girl would still be alive."

His voice catches. Mary Grace has to look away from the naked pain in his eyes. "There was no proof Chloe Ann was in that cabin."

"She was there! Same as the Russian girl."

No one ever knew that for certain. And they only knew about Nadia because of Mary Grace.

Briggs drops into the chair opposite her desk as if the effort of dredging it all up again has exhausted him.

"Do you really think Stokes would be stupid enough to do something like this when he knows he'd be the first one suspected? Go home," she says again.

"You never told Kanady how you knew about that cabin."

Because he never asked. He was too distracted by the discovery of their first solid lead.

"Why were you always hanging around this office?"

She has a flash of that unusually warm Saturday afternoon, the town abuzz after Madison Driver came forward that morning. Mary Grace with her ear to the wall next door to this very room, where Kanady and Isaac Wood were interrogating Stokes, who hadn't been arrested yet. Merely hauled in on the say-so, and secondhand at that, of an eleven-year-old girl.

Briggs leans across the desk. "I always thought you knew more than you were telling."

The exact words Chloe Ann whispered that day in the schoolyard.

"It's time for you to leave."

"Or what? You'll try to strangle me? You always had it in for Chloe Ann, didn't you?"

"That's not how it was." Does he really believe that? Or is it some kind of revisionist history he invented so he could live with the death of his only daughter?

"She wanted to have you arrested after you almost choked her to death. But she had to learn to defend herself against kids like you. Even if you were an orphan."

Mary Grace can still hear the schoolyard chorus of "Little Orphan Mary." Does Briggs know it was his daughter who started the horrible nickname? Twenty-four years later, and it still hurts.

"After my baby disappeared, I knew this wasn't just some schoolyard fight. That was when I told Kanady to bring you in."

Except Kanady never came for her that Friday, the last day anyone saw Chloe Ann alive. Maybe it was political, Kanady refusing to take orders from Briggs.

Or maybe he didn't believe Mary Grace had anything to do with what happened to Chloe Ann.

Or Nadia.

Briggs is still talking. "My little girl never got the chance to fight for herself. I told her she had to stand up to bullies."

Her uncle told her the same thing that night at supper, twenty-four hours before Chloe Ann disappeared.

"You've got it wrong. I wasn't the one calling kids losers."

"You calling my daughter a bully?"

Mary Grace says nothing, lets her silence speak for itself.

Briggs's face crumples and for a second she thinks he's going to cry. Then his eyes darken. "You're the bully."

"I was defending myself."

"From what? She never laid a hand on you!"

Maybe not, but Chloe Ann's words were crueler than any fist. Not that it's a justification. And yet. People have killed for less.

"You attacked Chloe Ann and the next day she was gone. It's like you put a curse on her."

Mary Grace's breath catches. Guilt rises up again, overwhelming her. For a crazy second, she thinks he knows what really happened. But how could he?

"You think I don't know about you?" Briggs hisses. "The whole town knows. A wild kid who couldn't hold on to her temper."

"Just what are you accusing me of?" Not sure how she manages to get the words out, but sure now that he's bluffing. Or he would have said something back then.

"You can't hide who you are behind that badge."

Rage overtakes the guilt. "Go home, Jackson. Before you can't get home."

"Are you threatening me?" He pushes back his chair and gets to his feet. "Don't you know who I am? You're only sheriff by default. Come next election, I can promise you someone else will be sitting behind that desk."

"Now who's threatening who?" Mary Grace is up like a shot. Might as well give him a taste of the hair-trigger temper she's so famous for. Even in flats, she's almost eyeball to eyeball with him. "Get out of my office."

He waggles a finger in her face, determined to get the last word. "You haven't heard the end of this!"

The candles on her desk flicker again as the door slams shut after him. Mary Grace listens to the wind battering the windows, her mind spinning back to another Friday night.

Chloe Ann's disappearance just a few hours old. The town in panic mode as search parties were organized and volunteer tables set up at Vaughan Elementary and Briggs High. Pastor Mills leading everyone in prayer at First Baptist Church, while candlelight vigils were held in backyards and on front lawns. Chloe Ann's pudgy face smiling out from posters tacked to every tree, side by side with Nadia's. Along with a $50,000 reward offered by Jackson Briggs for his daughter's return. Sightings of one or both girls in other towns overloading the tip line set up in the sheriff's office (at this very desk). Most of the calls cranks. No suspects.

That would change the next morning.

TWENTY-NINE

The snow tapers off just before midnight.

By the time the last flake has fallen from the sky, more than eighteen inches blanket the town, with downed trees and snow drifts along the shoulder topping out at four feet. If that weren't bad enough, the long, winding main artery that's the only way in and out of town is virtually a parking lot, with cars abandoned by unwitting drivers who didn't expect the storm to hit so soon and so fast and were forced to make their slow, treacherous way on foot.

The borrowed plows have been out since eleven p.m. Even with a shifting crew of volunteers, it could be hours before the main roads are clear. The back roads are another story. Without outside help, it could take days, maybe weeks, to dig out from under.

Cherie Leigh Hibbard is more than twelve hours missing when Mary Grace and Conner arrive back at the office just past seven Saturday morning after being out most of the night dealing with the worst of the storm.

"Damn, but it's cold out there!"

An understatement if ever Mary Grace heard one. It's nineteen degrees, but with the windchill it feels more like nine. Even with fleece-lined mittens and fur-lined boots, she can barely feel her fingers and toes. The mere act of unbuttoning her parka takes more dexterity than her frozen digits are currently capable of.

Conner stomps the snow off his boots and heads for the coffee machine. The power's back on but the phones are in and out, which is a blessing in disguise. The few citizens who've gotten through are worried that their daughters will be next, Lucas tells them. "They're afraid to go to sleep in case they're gone when they wake up."

"You kidding me?" Conner shakes his head as he starts a fresh brew. "How far they think their kid's gonna get in weather like this?"

The office goes quiet. Nobody wanting to be the first to say that even if Cherie Leigh was lucky enough to survive the storm, she could at this very moment be dying of hypothermia.

And Darryl Stokes is still unaccounted for.

Before heading back this morning, creeping along at a snail's pace after getting stuck in a drift that turned a ten-minute drive into a thirty-minute ordeal, Mary Grace and Conner made a pit stop at the boarding house. According to Miss Lillian, Stokes was paid up through the end of the month. When they checked his room, all his clothes appeared to be in the closet and drawers, along with a wad of cash under his socks that put Mary Grace in mind of another drawer full of cash and another missing girl. When they left, with one more item than they'd had when they arrived, Mary Grace told Miss Lillian to let her know the minute Stokes returned. Not if, but when. No one skipped town and left their stash behind.

Which set Mary Grace wondering where Stokes got the money. It wasn't like he had a job, leastways not here in Repentance. Parnell's daddy might have hired Stokes twenty-four years ago, but that was before Jacob Weaver alibied him for the Friday Chloe Ann disappeared. There'd likely have been a town mutiny if Parnell took him on again.

"Stokes has to be hiding out until the storm blows over," Lucas says into the silence. "Which could be our lucky break. He can't hide forever."

Mary Grace crouches in front of the space heater, trying to warm her frost-bitten hands. "You checked on Jackson Briggs like I asked?"

Lucas nods. "As of six a.m., he hadn't budged from his mansion. But the second the roads are clear, you can bet there'll be a lynch mob outside Miss Lillian's."

Mary Grace gives her assistant sheriff a sharp look as she goes to her desk. Does he know something she doesn't? "Briggs tries anything and he'll be arrested. Nobody takes the law into their own hands."

"Try telling that to him," Conner says. "Briggs thinks he's above the law."

"Not in my town."

Owen Kanady's exact words after he released Stokes from custody and Briggs organized a group of vigilantes to stop Stokes as he headed for the bus station. He ended up spending the night in lockup after Kanady arrested him. When Briggs later tried to have Kanady removed from office, he couldn't show he was guilty of malfeasance. So he started an election recall petition, claiming Kanady hadn't properly discharged his responsibilities by letting Stokes go. But he couldn't get enough votes. Those who voted against included Mary Grace's uncle and Pastor Mills, who quoted a passage from the Bible, about a man being innocent until proven guilty.

Decades later, after Mary Grace had been working for him a while, Kanady confided that he thought Stokes might have been telling the truth when he questioned him after his arrest. Yet he didn't let him go until he had irrefutable evidence. He thought it was also evidence of his own prejudice that he shared with those (Briggs among them) who needed Stokes to be guilty of something. It shamed him and caused him sleepless nights wondering if he might have been more disposed to believe Stokes had he been white.

"Stokes would have to be all kinds of a fool to take the Hibbard girl, knowing he'd be the first one suspected." Conner deposits a steaming mug on Mary Grace's desk, then ambles over to his own.

"Or he's just a lowlife black drifter who doesn't have much up here." Lucas taps his head. Mary Grace looks at him sharply. Of all people, she never took her sunny assistant sheriff for a racist.

"Whether he's got the brains God gave him or not, I have to admit it is a hell of a coincidence, another girl disappearing a few months after he shows up again." Conner puts his feet up on his desk and takes a long sip of coffee.

"It just proves what people have been saying for years," Lucas says. "He's guilty as sin."

"He wasn't the one who killed those girls."

"That not what half the town thinks. And now he's gone and done it again. Only this time he's acting alone."

"Or somebody's setting him up."

"Like who?"

Conner shrugs.

Lucas shakes his head. "It's Stokes. How much you want to bet he's the one who dug those graves back then, too?"

"That's enough! Aren't things bad enough without the two of you starting more rumors? Instead of spending time in idle gossip, why don't you make yourselves useful?" Mary Grace turns to Conner. "Keep texting the county sheriff's office. Find out how soon they can send uniforms. And a K-9 unit that's ready to go."

She doesn't expect a lot of cooperation. A missing girl, even one with striking similarities to the disappearances twenty-four years ago, isn't a priority in towns dealing with residents without heat and electricity, flooding caused by overflowing lakes and rivers, and a growing number of weather-related deaths.

Conner and Lucas get busy on their phones as Mary Grace goes over to the coffee machine. She keeps her back to them so they won't see how their conversation affected her. Her hand shakes as she pours coffee into her mug that's still half full. When Stokes showed up in Repentance again, she thought God was sending her a message. Then another sixth grader disappeared. And not just any sixth grader.

Jackson Briggs said Tyler Lee was paying for the sins of his father. He's wrong. Mary Grace is the sinner. She's the one who tried to strangle him after he followed her to her secret cave that hot summer day.

And now his only child has disappeared on her watch.

Is that her punishment? But if Conner's right and someone's framing Stokes (and she had her own reasons for believing he was telling the truth back then), who lured Cherie Leigh out of her house?

Back at her desk, she pulls out her phone. Felicity's last text came in a little after midnight, almost three hours past her usual bedtime. That was because she spent the night with the Reeves twins after Mary Grace called Paige and asked her to come get her daughter. Luckily she had the storm as an excuse.

That was then. Paige has texted several times since, just as frantic as other parents with daughters in their last year at Vaughan Elementary. In spite of the monster storm that guarantees no one's going anywhere, the weather creating its own form of lockdown.

Mary Grace is on her third cup of coffee when the door to the office bangs open. She braces for a return visit. But it isn't Jackson Briggs.

It's Madison Driver. And she isn't alone.

Conner's on his feet and moving toward the door before Madison even has her scarf off.

"What are you doing here?" Mary Grace asks. "No one's supposed to be outside. Or on the road."

"This couldn't wait."

"What couldn't wait?"

"Allison has something to tell you."

Madison's daughter stands next to her, her bulky coat making her appear heavier. She looks miserable.

"Can I get you something hot?" Conner asks.

"We're good, thanks."

Mary Grace leads the way to the interview room, where she turns up the thermostat against the chill. The room hasn't been used much in the past two decades, Repentance's most serious crimes mostly misdemeanors like petty theft or disorderly conduct. She motions Madison and Allison Driver to the two chairs Conner just placed on the other side of the table.

Once Mary Grace and Conner are settled across from them, Madison turns to her daughter. "Tell Sheriff Dobbs and Deputy Mitchell what you told me."

Bright red blotches appear on Allison Driver's face as she stares at the floor.

"It's okay," Conner says. "You won't get in trouble for talking to us."

"Allison." Madison's voice holds the warning tone every child knows. Her daughter looks up at her, then back down at the floor.

"Madison, how about going next door for a cup of coffee?" Mary Grace says. "Lucas can make a fresh pot."

"I said I didn't want any. And I'm not leaving my daughter!"

The girl's broad shoulders twitch at the anger in her mother's voice.

"Allison?" She looks up again. Mary Grace gives her a reassuring smile. "Is it a secret?" She shakes her head. "Is it about Cherie Leigh?" That earns a nervous nod. "It must be pretty important, for you to come out on a day like this. Maybe whatever you have to say will help us find her."

Allison closes her eyes. Her lips move like she's praying. When she opens her eyes, she lets out a breath as if she just made up her mind about something. She fixes at a point on the wall behind Mary Grace's head. "I saw him."

"Who?"

"The black drifter."

Mary Grace and Conner exchange glances.

"Where?"

"Outside the schoolyard."

"What was he doing?"

"He was behind a tree watching us."

"How do you know he was there if he was behind a tree?"

She shrugs.

"When did you see him?"

"Yesterday."

Friday. The day Cherie Leigh went missing. "What time?"

"Um." She twines a strand of long dark hair around her index finger. "It was recess."

"Did anyone else see him?" Mary Grace asks.

"I don't think so. I was all the way over by the chain-link fence and that's when I saw him."

"You could see him through the fence?" She nods. "Hiding behind a tree?"

"I told you that already!"

"Was Cherie Leigh in the schoolyard?"

"Uh huh. Can I go now?"

"Just a few more questions," Mary Grace says, hearing echoes of Owen Kanady the day after Nadia disappeared. "Was he watching Cherie Leigh? Did he try to talk to her?"

"Uh uh. The Devil's way too smart for that."

"You don't really believe in the Devil, do you? We both know he doesn't exist, right?"

Allison stares at Conner as if he'd committed a sacrilege. In a way, he had. They all grew up listening to the sermons every Sunday. Only by casting out Satan could you become good.

"He's the Devil! He killed those other girls!" Allison looks at her mother. "I want to go home now."

It's clear they're not going to get anything more out of her. As Madison pushes back her chair, Mary Grace stops her. "A minute, Madison." She turns to Allison. "Before you go, would you like a hot chocolate?"

Allison looks at her mother again. "Do you have anything that's low calorie or reduced sugar?" Madison asks. "She's on a diet." Allison's face gets red.

"I think we can rustle something up." Conner winks at Allison, who trails him out with one last glance at her mother.

"I'm guessing you didn't find him yet?"

"No," Mary Grace says, ignoring Madison's question in the form of an accusation. "And all we have is a story from an eleven-year-old that has yet to be corroborated."

"Are you calling my daughter a liar?"

"I'm just saying. And it's awfully coincidental that you point the finger twenty-four years ago and your daughter does the same thing now."

"I was telling the gospel truth and so is Allison!" Madison picks up her coat. "I didn't come here to be insulted!" She stalks to the door just as it opens, and almost gets knocked over by Conner. He grabs her to keep her from falling. Holds her a little too long for Mary Grace's liking.

"Jesus," Conner says, finally letting her go. "I leave for five minutes, and look what happens." He rolls his eyes, but both women ignore him.

"What were you doing in the diner with Darryl Stokes?"

Madison turns back to Mary Grace, thrown by the sudden change in subject. "That's my business."

"No, it isn't. See my problem here, Madison? Everywhere I look, you're in the middle of it."

"I resent your implication."

"And I resent you wasting my time."

"Just what are you accusing me of?"

"No one's accusing you of anything. Let's all chill out, okay?"

Mary Grace can barely contain her anger. How dare Conner undermine her! "You haven't answered my question."

"I don't have to."

"Why wouldn't you? If you have nothing to hide?"

"I'm not hiding anything." But Madison walks back to the table, where Conner immediately pulls out a chair.

"So why were you in the diner together?"

"I was apologizing, if you must know."

"For what?"

"For getting him in trouble back then. How was I supposed to know that mechanic would alibi him? And I was only repeating what Chloe Ann told me." She looks at Conner as she talks, as if Mary Grace weren't in the room.

Everyone knows the story. One afternoon a week before Chloe Ann disappeared, Jackson Briggs's driver picked up Chloe Ann and Madison from school, only to get a flat tire on the way home. When they stopped at Parnell Vaughan II's auto shop, the girls waited outside. Then Chloe Ann went into the shop because she had to use the bathroom. When she came out, she told Madison that the black drifter (who wasn't wearing a shirt!) stared at her like he wanted to do dirty things to her.

"You told Owen Kanady that Chloe Ann had a crush on Stokes."

It was what got him hauled in for questioning. Not much to go on, one young girl telling it to another, either or both of whom could be lying. But someone lured Chloe Ann out of her house, and Kanady was under pressure from Jackson Briggs.

Madison nods, still not looking at Mary Grace. "That's what she told me. She swore me to secrecy. Said I better not tell anyone."

"You sure you weren't the one with the crush?"

"No!" But Mary Grace didn't miss the beat before she answered.

"I hear you and Stokes were pretty cozy in the diner. Are you the reason he came back?"

Conner looks at Mary Grace in disbelief. It only ticks her off more. Isn't he the one who said a woman brought Stokes to Repentance? She'll lay odds it's the female sitting across the table.

"What? You're crazy." Madison's face changes. "I'm not the one you should be talking to."

"Who should we be talking to?"

"Who do you think? The town slut."

"You talking about Emily King?" Mary Grace asks.

Madison's the one who coined the name after King ran off with her husband. Not that the fourth-grade Vaughan Elementary teacher didn't have a reputation of cheating on her husband with Briggs High male students. And Hunter Fewell, although it was never proven. Then Nadia disappeared and rumors that she was sleeping with Fewell spread like wildfire. But it was more than whispers and innunendo that sent Fewell to prison, where he'll spend the rest of his life. Mary Grace alone knew that Hunter Fewell wasn't Nadia's only lover. Another secret she'd take to her grave.

She forces herself to stay focused. "You know for a fact that Stokes and King are seeing each other?" When Madison doesn't answer, she goes on, "I want to believe you. Just like I want to believe you were telling the truth back then. I'd hate to think Stokes got railroaded for no good reason."

"You're such a hypocrite, Mary Grace! Making it sound like it was all my fault. It wasn't because of me he was arrested!"

No. That honor went to Mary Grace.

"Here's my problem, Madison." She plants her elbows on the table the way Owen Kanady did when she was the one in the hot seat the day after Nadia disappeared. So she'd see the *Repentance Sheriff* insignia on his shirtsleeve and be clear who the law around here was. "Your daughter claims she saw Stokes outside the schoolyard yesterday. But so far she's the only one who's come forward. As for your story about why you were in the diner with Stokes, we have only your word for it."

"What else would I be doing there? I barely knew him!"

"So you say. Could be you were trying to seduce him. Sitting so close together in that booth."

"Why would I do that?"

"Maybe it's payback against Emily King for stealing your husband. While you spread rumors about her. Maybe Stokes rejected you and this was your way of getting back at him, too. Figured it worked twenty-four years ago, it'll work now."

"How dare you!"

"Ladies, please."

Neither woman pays Conner the slightest attention.

"Who says they're rumors?" Madison thrusts out her lower lip just like she used to do as a kid.

"You have proof about Stokes and King? Or we supposed to take your word for that, too? Are you starting to see a pattern here?" Mary Grace leans forward. "Stokes isn't here to confirm your story. And we can't very well ask Chloe Ann what she said back then, can we?"

Madison flinches as if she'd been struck. Even Conner looks shocked. It was a low blow, even if it's true. The eleven-year-old inside her wanting to get back at her old childhood nemesis for all the years of bullying.

As they meet each other stare for stare, it could be that Wednesday morning in 1995 all over again, gazes colliding across Nadia's empty desk.

Madison breaks eye contact first. She turns to Conner. "You know what? I think I'll have that coffee after all."

THIRTY

Madison stares at the door after Conner leaves.

Gathering ammunition against her? Getting ready to hurl her own accusations after Mary Grace's totally unprofessional behavior, not to mention her appalling lapse of judgment? She braces for an outburst, for an outpouring of the venom and malice that marked their relationship as kids. But Madison doesn't even look at her. Instead she casts her eyes fearfully around the room, then heavenward as if someone up there's listening.

"Does it feel like we're being punished?"

Mary Grace's heart hammers against her ribs. "I don't buy into that superstitious claptrap." A lie. She's believed every sign and portent since the June morning she bolted up in bed, heart in her throat. Then Darryl Stokes reappeared in Repentance and another girl went missing.

"Tell me you don't think about them."

She doesn't have to ask who Madison's talking about.

Only all the time. "Sometimes."

"I can't stop thinking about them. Especially now."

The door opens and Conner comes in with two steaming mugs. He looks surprised, as if he expected them to have come to blows by now. After he leaves, Madison goes on as if there'd been no interruption.

"Chloe Ann was my best friend since I was four years old. Hell, she was my only friend." She picks up her mug, puts it down again. "It's not like I didn't know what she was. She only picked me because I weighed more than she did. And I still felt guilty for telling her secret to Sheriff Kanady, can you believe it? She made me promise on my grandmama's grave. Said if I ever told, she'd spread it all over town that I was the one who had the crush on Stokes."

That sounded like Chloe Ann.

"All she ever wanted was to be popular. But it didn't matter how rich she was. She was never going to be one of them. Just like Allison won't." Anger flares in Madison's eyes, along with something Mary Grace never saw before. Shame. Because no matter how thin she gets, in her mind she'll always be the overweight, unattractive adolescent. Now forced to relive it with her daughter.

"But Chloe Ann never stopped hoping Skylar and Paige would choose her. When they didn't, she took it out on all of us."

"She sure did." Mary Grace is surprised to hear Madison own up to that.

"You probably won't believe this, but Chloe Ann was jealous of you." Miss Althea and her daddy had said the same thing, although Mary Grace found it hard to accept at the time. "You had something nobody could take away. You were an amazing softball player. And now your daughter's following in her mama's footsteps."

Chloe Ann wasn't the only jealous one, Mary Grace thinks. If she's reading Madison right.

"The rules sure have changed, haven't they? You don't just have to be skinny and wear the right clothes. You have to be a great athlete, too."

This time there's no mistaking the bitterness in Madison's voice.

"Remember how Skylar and Paige wouldn't be caught dead working up a sweat in case it ruined their perfect hair?" Madison's face changes again. "But those girls could be mean. I never forgot what Skylar said to you in the locker room after that first game."

The scene of the greatest triumph and greatest humiliation of Mary Grace's young life. "You laughed at me, too."

"I know. I'm sorry. And for calling you that horrible nickname. It must have been awful, losing both your parents."

You have no idea, Mary Grace thinks. Is that what this is about? Madison needing to clear her conscience? Twenty-four years too late.

"Chloe Ann started it. Not that I'm making excuses. I just want you to understand how it was for me back then. I wanted to be accepted so badly, more than anything in the world. Even if it meant going along with everything Chloe Ann did. But you let her have it, didn't you? That day in the schoolyard."

"You were pretty mad at her yourself that morning. I never heard that word come out of your mouth before."

"It felt so good calling her a bitch. Especially after she called us both losers. Chloe Ann was furious at me for dumping her for Nadia. My one act of rebellion. Looking back, I can't believe I did it. Chloe Ann *was* a bitch. But Nadia." Madison shakes her head. "I never understood how you could be friends with her."

Mary Grace wonders what she'd think if she knew that Nadia stole her uncle's money and tried to blackmail people for their secrets. "You could have fooled me." The words are out before she can stop them. "You acted like you couldn't wait to be her best friend. Especially that last day." When Nadia and Madison left Vaughan Elementary arm in arm.

"That was all for show. The minute you left, she dropped the whole act. I was so desperate to have a new bestie after throwing Chloe Ann under the bus. I was so excited! I invited Nadia to my house for cookies and milk. I figured she'd be impressed if she saw my mansion. How pathetic is that?"

Not pathetic at all. Money was Nadia's god.

"You know what she said? She looked at me like I was the lowest form of life and said, 'Why would I want to go anywhere with you, you fat fuck?' "

That was mean, even for Nadia.

"I couldn't believe it. I wanted to strike back, say something just as vicious. But it was like my brain shut down. I just wanted to sink into the ground and disappear."

Madison had finally gotten a taste of her own medicine. Kids could be cruel, sticks and stones be damned.

"She was pure evil."

Mary Grace can't disagree with that. It was the reason Nadia chose her out of all the sixth graders. Why Chloe Ann picked her to bully.

Evil recognizing evil?

So strong it swallowed up all the good.

So powerful it could make things happen.

"Do you think they deserved what happened to them?"

It's as if Madison were reading her mind. Their eyes lock on each other, the only sound the harsh rasp of their combined breathing.

"It isn't for us to judge." Mary Grace's voice is a whisper, her throat bone-dry. She feels like the worst kind of hypocrite.

"Who, then?" Madison casts her eyes upward. "Him?" When she turns back to Mary Grace, her face is filled with anguish. "They were our best friends!"

As if that explained everything.

In a way, it did.

Mary Grace pushes back her chair, indicating that the conversation (or whatever it is they're having) is over.

But Madison makes no move to get up. "You're going to the cabin, aren't you? Too bad he doesn't have someone to alibi him this time. But then most of the town thought that mechanic was lying, especially after Stokes admitted Nadia was there. How could he deny it after what you found?"

It was the reason he was arrested. But Stokes swore up and down he didn't hurt Nadia. That she left the cabin alive.

"One thing I always wondered about. If Stokes wasn't Nadia's secret boyfriend, who was? Hunter Fewell? He never confessed to that."

"Damned if I know."

Except she does know. And she is damned.

Madison's eyes bore into hers again.

This time Mary Grace is the first to look away.

She's still sitting there after Madison leaves, once again seeing herself on that long-ago Saturday. Sneaking into the station a few hours after Madison came forward, trying to listen to the interrogation taking place in this very room. Rushing away from the wall when the door opened and Chief Deputy Wood came out. When he saw Mary Grace, he gave her a conspiratorial wink.

Then Darryl Stokes came out.

It was only the second time she'd laid eyes on him.

"I wouldn't leave town if I were you," Sheriff Kanady said as he followed Stokes and Wood out of the interrogation room.

"Or what? You'll arrest me?" Stokes said in that deep drawl she remembered from their one conversation. "That'll never happen because I didn't do anything. I'm innocent, like I told you."

Stokes nodded at Mary Grace when he saw her, as if they shared a secret. Then he walked out of the station. That was when Kanady noticed her and told her she had no business being there and to run along home. By then she was at the window, watching Stokes walk down the street, her mind awhirl. For several seconds, she didn't move. When she finally turned back and said what she had to say, her voice sounded strange to her own ears. But Kanady must have heard her all right, because his whole demeanor changed. A few minutes later, he, Mary Grace, and Wood got into his cruiser.

"Mary Grace?"

Conner's in the doorway.

"They're ready for us."

THIRTY-ONE

"What were you two talking about?"

"Old times."

Conner shoots her a glance as he shifts into reverse and backs the SUV slowly out of the snow-covered lot. "Really? I didn't think you were ever friends."

They weren't. Certainly not at Vaughan Elementary or Briggs High. Most kids gave Mary Grace a wide berth after she attacked Chloe Ann in the schoolyard the day after Nadia disappeared. Including Madison.

Especially Madison.

They were our best friends.

"You listening to me, MG?"

She hates when he calls her that. "What?"

"I was saying I think I have it worked out."

"Have what worked out?"

"The Emily King angle. Maddie's right. King's got to be the woman Stokes came back for. And probably the woman he was sleeping with back then."

"How do you figure?" So it was Maddie now.

"Stokes was eighteen in '95. King was twenty-five, only seven years older. And she's married, which is why Stokes wouldn't tell Kanady who it was."

Mary Grace remembers. Her ear to the wall once again after Stokes was arrested, listening to Kanady and Wood question him. Stokes insisting Nadia surprised him at the cabin, refusing to say whom he was waiting for. Which just fueled speculation that it was Nadia he was meeting there all along.

"Stokes and Emily King could have been having this secret thing all these years."

"Even when she ran off with Madison's husband?"

Conner scowls, but on him it just looks hot. Mary Grace rolls down her window. The sun glancing off the snow piled along the side of the road is blinding, and the temperature has inexplicably begun to climb again. They can now add potential flooding from the rapidly melting snow to their list of concerns.

"Maybe he and King picked up after King came back and that's why he's here. It's not a perfect scenario, Stokes returning to the town that hates him. But I can't see King abandoning her kids again. Everyone knows it's only because of them she came back. How could anyone know another sixth grader would disappear?"

"Now you think he's innocent? So was Allison Driver lying about seeing him skulking around the schoolyard?"

"One thing I don't think is that her mother put her up to it." Conner levels another glance her way, his eyes accusing.

"You forget Emily King wasn't the one seen in the diner with Stokes. It was Mad-die." Drawing out the two syllables to let him know just what she thinks about that.

"To apologize, like she told us."

"Sitting in that booth practically in Stokes's lap?"

"It was an exaggeration. You know how things get twisted in this town."

"Why would she choose such a public place to tell him how sorry she was? She had to know it would get spread around." Throwing his words back in his face. "And Emily King would hear." Which was the whole point.

"You make her sound mean and spiteful. Maddie's not like that."

"So what is she like?" The Madison Driver she knew *was* mean and spiteful. And angry. Still is.

"What's up with you and her, anyway?" Mary Grace doesn't answer as they turn off the main highway. "You know what I think? You're jealous."

"No way!"

"You have no right to be, not with the way you make excuses every time I try to see you. What do you expect me to do, wait around for you forever? If it's not happening, at least have the decency to tell me."

She can hear the hurt in his voice. He's right, they can't go on like this.

Her mind as always circling back to Parnell.

"Maybe we—" The words die in her throat. They just turned onto the side road that winds around to the northern part of the woods. And once again she's thrown back twenty-four years, to that unusually warm Saturday in November. In the passenger seat of a cruiser just like she is now. Heading to the same destination, Sheriff Kanady's chief deputy relegated to the back seat. Keeping her eyes peeled as the cruiser's headlights sliced through the dark. It didn't matter that it was a bright and sunny afternoon. It was always night in the woods.

Conner slows to a stop.

Half a dozen official cars are parked at crazy angles along the path leading to the woods. Cops and handlers with their dogs stand there fiddling with their phones and talking among themselves. Conner parks behind the county sheriff's SUV.

As she gets out of the car, Mary Grace recognizes Sheriff Carson Mathis and his chief deputy, Ian Landers. Crime being low in Repentance, their paths haven't crossed much. There's also a woman and man with the K-9 unit and a pair of state troopers you can spot a mile away because of the wide-brim campaign hats dating back to the days when they were called Rangers. They brought out the big guns in case Stokes kidnapped Cherie Leigh, a state crime. Or spirited her out of Arkansas, which would make it a federal offense.

Conner slams his car door harder than necessary. He doesn't look at her as they make their way to the hub of activity. Their heart-to-heart will have to wait.

"Sheriff Dobbs!"

Jeremiah Jones, the longtime editor of the Repentance *Gazette*, steps out from behind one of the police vans. And he isn't alone.

"Any news about the Hibbard girl?"

"Think she's still alive?"

"Is Stokes behind it?"

"Why'd he wait twenty-four years?"

"You been in touch with the Death House?"

"Is he getting his orders from there?"

"You going to get justice for Tyler Lee?"

That last question didn't come from the reporters. Nicholas Buck stands apart from the others, arms folded across his chest. The church-going husband and father of four a world away from the prankster of Vaughan Elementary.

"Justice won't come until the day we stop breeding young whores."

A gasp goes up from the crowd behind Buck, which Mary Grace can see is at least thirty-strong. They've shifted their attention from her to Timothy Dickson, who stands apart from the others and whose eyes blaze with the religious fervor that has only grown stronger over the decades.

"You calling our daughters whores?" Wyatt Dake glares at Dickson, menace in his voice even if he's nearly a foot shorter. What he lacks in brawn, he makes up in brains. He always was the smartest kid in school.

"Our daughters are good," someone shouts. "Their souls are pure. They take the blessed sacraments of Christ!"

"They're sinners and must repent or they'll bring eternal evil on our town!" Dickson shouts back.

"The only sinners in this town are you freaks! Now get the hell out of here!" Dylan Bryant, still best buddies with Nicholas Buck, starts moving in on Dickson, fixing for a fight.

"That's enough! Everyone stand back." As she moves swiftly toward them, Mary Grace recognizes Austin Cooper and Brandon Cowan behind Dickson. She'd heard rumors about them allying themselves with the Footwashers.

"Who you calling freaks?" Cowan shouts, though it's hard to understand him because of his cleft palate that multiple surgeries couldn't correct.

"Those sluts got what they deserved!" Cooper shouts. The onetime loner of Vaughan Elementary became an outcast at Briggs High, along with Cowan and Dickson.

"That Russian whore had it coming!" Dickson's voice is the loudest.

"Hush your mouth! All of you. And Timothy! You should be ashamed."

All eyes turn to Cadence Mills. Dressed in her usual funereal black, she stands with the parents.

"I'm not saying anything you haven't." Dickson glares at her.

"I never called our children those terrible names. And I never said they deserved what happened to them. You're twisting my words. Maybe instead of changing religious ideologies to find the one that suits your latest mood, you should look to your Bible."

It's true. All through elementary school, Dickson was hyped up on doomsday scenarios. Until he discovered Mills's Footwasher group and found an outlet for his anger and rejection by Nadia.

"This isn't the time for divisiveness. We have to stick together if we're going to find Cherie Leigh Hibbard."

Mary Grace doesn't know if Mills's seeming change of heart is due to a falling-out with her followers or if she's embarrassed in front of her fellow Repentians. Or wants to get into the town's good graces to take over the pulpit despite Jackson Briggs's efforts to have her removed.

Or maybe the latest disappearance has her spooked, like everyone else.

"Pastor Mills is right," Sheriff Mathis says. "Instead of fighting amongst yourselves, you should be trying to help. We need volunteers to set up a table in the Briggs High gymnasium. Another group to hand out leaflets and put up posters. The rest of you should go home and be with your families."

"And do what?" Dylan Bryant practically spits at Mathis. "Wait for the next sixth grader to vanish?"

"How are we supposed to feel safe when she can't protect our children?" Nicholas Buck points at Mary Grace.

"We want to know what you're doing to find Stokes!"

"Isn't it bad enough the Salvationists are spreading their hate without all of us turning against each other?" Mathis says.

"Maybe they have it right."

"The Salvationists don't have anything right." Buck shakes his head at Cooper.

"Don't let them fool you," Bryant says. "They're not saving anyone. They're just trying to advance their supremacist cause."

"Isn't what you're doing just as bad? Would you be accusing Darryl Stokes if he were white?"

"Who the hell are you?"

A pretty Latina woman steps forward. "My name is Lucia Garcia. I'm a reporter with the Little Rock *Tribune.* You talk about justice, but so far all I hear is a lot of ignorance and superstition."

"Little Rock, huh?" Wyatt Dake says. "You dare to judge us? With your city the state home to the Ku Klux Klan and those new-alt groups?"

"Like the Salvationists? Believe me, I know. I'm trying to help get legislation passed to force Arkansas, Georgia, and South Carolina to put the hate-crime statute back on the books. But from what I can see, you people are railroading a man without a stitch of real proof."

No one has a response to that. Because it's true.

As the crowd finally disperses, Mary Grace remembers the fiery debates she used to have with Owen Kanady after he returned from law enforcement conferences in other states. He said sometimes he forgot it was a big world out there, that compared to other places, Repentance was still in the dark ages. Mary Grace would listen, but always end up defending her town. She grew up with most of these men and women and in her heart knows they're basically good, God-fearing people.

She forces her mind back to the task at hand as she and the rest of law enforcement start along the recently cleared path. Even the dogs are silent as they approach the entrance to the woods.

Although the snow blowing off the treetops hampers visibility, Mary Grace can see the perennial smoke billowing out of Meurice's chimney. It's become part of Repentance legend, how Owen Kanady tried to question him after Chloe Ann disappeared. That was when it became clear that she and Nadia weren't hiding out in the woods as part of a popular girl initiation. One sixth grader missing was one thing, but a second disappearance—this time one of their own—turned it into something else.

Kanady couldn't overcome the language barrier, confiding in Mary Grace that he suspected Meurice might have witnessed something but was too scared to say anything. Back then, all Mary Grace could think about was Wyatt Dake saying how bones couldn't burn. She knows now that isn't true; it only takes the right kind of fire to turn human remains to ash.

The dogs sniff and paw at the snow-blanketed ground as they pass Meurice's house, and the dilapidated front porch where Nadia ate some of the shepherd's pie that the town's Good Samaritan left there. To this day, no one knows the identity of Meurice's secret benefactor, although many still believe it's someone from the church.

Then Mary Grace forgets everything else as she sees it, rising out of the trees like a castle in some primeval forest.

She's eleven again, jumping out of Kanady's cruiser and running past the thicket of pines standing guard like silent sentinels. Racing inside the way she did back in August to get away from whomever was chasing her. Coming to a stop next to the musty-smelling sofa with the paisley slipcovers that were coming apart at the seams.

"It was right here," she said.

"You sure?" Sheriff Kanady asked.

She nodded. A few minutes later, she called him over again. His eyes got bigger when she opened her fist. His shaggy brows went all the way up as she told him what it was and to whom it belonged.

"Sheriff Dobbs? You okay?"

Mary Grace blinks. "Hibbard girl isn't here," Sheriff Mathis says. "No sign of Stokes, either. Dogs haven't picked up either of their scents. Doesn't look like anyone's been here in a long time."

She looks around. She's in the exact spot where she stood twenty-four years ago. The paisley slipcovers are more faded with age, more planks missing from the floor. Cobwebs hang from the ceiling's deteriorating rafters. Memories surface at the sight of the hutch against the back wall, with its dusty-looking china and dishes. In the far corner stands the wood-burning stove she also remembers. It looks like it hasn't been used in decades. And the window where she could swear she saw a face peering in, scaring her half to death. She gradually becomes aware of scurrying feet and the soft chittering of animals who must have sought shelter here from the recent storm.

"Didn't really expect to find him here," Mathis says. "I'm still trying to wrap my mind around him being back in town and another child vanishing. Unless someone's using it to frame him. But it doesn't tell us why he came back in the first place."

A woman? Mary Grace wonders. Was Madison lying about why she was in the diner with him?

"Stokes is no fool," Deputy Landers says when Mary Grace and Mathis have rejoined the others outside. "He has to know the cabin would be the first place we'd look."

"Maybe we're wasting our time," one of the troopers says. "We have no proof he's in the woods at all. Could everyone have been wrong about him?"

No one responds, all remembering the Little Rock reporter's words.

"He did have an alibi for the Briggs girl. And he isn't the one who confessed."

"Or led Owen Kanady to the bodies."

"Think that reporter's right?" the female K-9 handler asks. "It's being orchestrated from Death Row?"

"I've been wondering the same thing," Mathis says. "Easy enough to check the visitor logs."

Which is Mary Grace's job because it's happening in her town. Again. She can't use the power outages as an excuse because there's always her cell phone.

"Lots of folks thought they did it together," the other state trooper says.

"There was never any proof they were coconspirators."

"If they were both in on it," Landers says as if Mathis hadn't spoken, "makes sense that the Doshenko and Briggs girls were both killed in the cabin."

"No proof of that, either." Mathis gives his deputy a sharp look.

"Then the two of them buried their bodies in that field," the older state trooper says. "I remember thinking back then how warm it was for November. Easy to bury 'em, easy to dig 'em up."

"Which means this time Stokes had to change the m.o. There's no way he could dig a grave with the ground frozen over."

"So where is he? And where's the Hibbard girl?"

"That's what we need to find out. All this speculating isn't going to get us anywhere," Mathis says. "I say we keep going. Fair share of hunters' cabins out here, some stocked with supplies. Maybe they got stranded by the storm and we'll get lucky."

The snow from the trees blows harder as they head deeper into the woods, which lowers the odds of finding fresh tracks. As they walk, Mary Grace catches eyes with Conner. She sees the concern in his and feels the usual guilt. She doesn't deserve him. Doesn't deserve to be sheriff of a town she can't keep safe.

Her phone chirps. It's Lucas.

Darryl Stokes just walked into the station.

THIRTY-TWO

Except for the gray in his hair, he looks exactly the same.

She forgot how tall he was. Even perched on the edge of Lucas's desk (her assistant sheriff looking at him with open hostility), it's impossible not to notice his broad shoulders that seem to have filled out even more with age. And those unusual blue-green eyes that don't miss a thing. Full lips stretched into a smile that isn't really a smile, just a flash of white.

"Heard you were looking for me."

"Whole town's looking for you," Conner says. "Where've you been?"

"What kind of welcome is that after all this time? I didn't know I had to account for my movements. Isn't America still a free country?"

Mary Grace's own words to Lucas and Conner after he came back to town. "Cut the bullshit, Stokes. Tell us where you were since yesterday afternoon at four."

Eyes still on Lucas, Stokes pushes slowly to his feet. He walks over to Mary Grace and looks down at her with a half-grin that makes her feel eleven again, and powerless. As if reading her mind he says, "Last time we met, you were a kid listening at peepholes. Now you're the law around here. How does that happen?"

Anger bubbles up, but she refuses to let him bait her. "We'll be next door," she tells Lucas, then turns her back on Stokes. She walks to the door that leads to the interview room, Conner behind her. He holds it open so

Stokes can go in ahead of him. Stokes hesitates a fraction of a second, then shrugs and precedes Conner inside. When he's seated across the table from them, Mary Grace says (not offering him coffee because this isn't a friendly visit), "We're going to find out where you were, so you might as well get in front of it now."

"I don't have to get in front of anything."

"You're here, aren't you?" Conner says. "Why'd you come back to Repentance?"

"That's my business."

"No, it isn't. A sixth grader's missing, in case you didn't notice."

"You can't pin that on me."

"Really? You show up after twenty-four years and another girl disappears?"

"I was exonerated back then in case you didn't notice."

"You were alibied. It's not the same thing. And you didn't have one for the day Nadia Doshenko vanished."

"Last time I checked, someone else was sitting on Death Row."

"Paid any visits there lately? Don't bother lying because we'll find out."

Stokes's expression doesn't change. No muscle twitches, no tells. Nothing.

"Why would I lie? And I'm not the one who confessed."

"You know that confessions are meaningless without physical evidence," Mary Grace says.

No blood, hair, or trace evidence was ever found. No DNA under the fingernails of either victim. Folks figured that just meant they didn't put up a struggle, which was entirely possible given that the girls were only eleven.

Stokes gives Conner an incredulous look. "Why would someone confess to crimes they didn't commit?"

"You tell me."

"How the hell would I know?"

"So how do you explain another missing girl?"

"I can't."

"Think you're being set up? Do you have enemies?"

"Take your pick. I'm not exactly Mr. Popularity around here, in case you didn't notice."

"Why did you come back to Repentance?" Mary Grace asks. Stokes doesn't answer. "Where were you between four o'clock yesterday and today? We can't help you if you won't help yourself."

"You don't believe I'm innocent, give me a polygraph."

"Polygraphs can lie."

"So can deceitful little girls." Stokes leans forward. "It wasn't enough I got hauled in for questioning. You were going to make damn sure I got arrested. So you told Kanady about the cabin."

"That's not the way it happened."

"Why should I believe you? Bet you were hiding in the woods that Tuesday afternoon. That was the plan you and your Russian friend cooked up, wasn't it? To spy on us. Bet that was your idea too, having that tramp come on to me."

Except it wasn't. But Mary Grace knew her best friend better than anyone. She remembers Timothy Dickson's obsession with Nadia, how she had to seduce every male in Repentance. Then she realizes what Stokes just said. "Us? You told Kanady you were alone in the cabin when Nadia got there. Who were you waiting for?"

His face shutters.

"Emily King?" Conner asks.

"What? No!"

"Why were you in the diner with Madison Driver?" Mary Grace asks.

"She called me. She wanted to apologize. That's more than you or anyone else around here has done."

Mary Grace ignores his last comment. What he said dovetails with Madison's story. Doesn't mean she doesn't have an agenda. "Did she flirt with you?"

"Why would she do that?"

Instead of answering, Mary Grace asks another question. "Is Madison the woman you came back for?"

She hears Conner hitch in his breath as Stokes shakes his head. "You are so far off base. And you know what? We're done here." He pushes back his chair. "You can demonize me all you like and make me out to be a monster, but I'm innocent. And while you're passing around blame, you should look at yourself. Because the truth is, wearing a badge won't make you a good person."

Mary Grace flinches as if he'd struck her. As he gets to his feet, she struggles to regain control. "Where are you going?"

"I'm not under arrest, am I?"

"Not yet. And don't even think about skipping town."

As Conner walks him out, Mary Grace stares at the backpack on his shoulders. When she can think clearly again, she buzzes Lucas.

"I want you to sit on the boarding house. Stokes goes anywhere, I want to know."

THIRTY-THREE

Over the weekend, the power comes back, which starts the phone ringing off the hook, the station flooded with calls from terrified parents and cranks who swore they saw Cherie Leigh walking up Main Street. Floating down the river. On the front steps of First Baptist Church, where on Sunday a very subdued congregation once again looks for answers.

With Pastor Mills poorly and his daughter conspicuously absent—something Mary Grace was sure Jackson Briggs had a hand in—Samuel Mathews takes the podium to deliver the weekly sermon. His voice shakes with emotion as he begins to speak.

"We lift our eyes to you, merciful Father, creator of heaven and earth. You said whatever we ask for in prayer, we will receive once we believe and have faith. We ask you to forgive us our trespasses and bring peace to this child whose love and devotion to you is everlasting. Know this innocent angel as you know each one of us. You alone have the power to turn evil to good. Please give us the chance to repent our sins. Amen. Let us now pray together."

Sunday evening, everyone returns to church for a potluck dinner while the lights from hundreds of candles can be seen as vigils take place all across town. Praying continues through the night.

On Monday, it's back to worldly matters. Prayer can take you only so far, something Mary Grace knows her uncle would consider the worst kind of sacrilege.

Cherie Leigh is three days missing when Mary Grace and Conner pull into the Vaughan Elementary parking lot, where patches of melting snow are all that remains of Friday night's storm. And it's still unseasonably warm.

Most folks expected that school would be closed, given that a sixth grader is missing and Thanksgiving is three days away. But Mary Grace wants to keep things as normal as possible, with the exception of parents having to drive their children to and from school and the temporary suspension of all extracurricular activities.

And the curfew that has been in place since Saturday night.

It's 1995 all over again. And just like back then, Mary Grace is once again on her way to the principal's office. Only that morning it was Owen Kanady behind the desk and she was the one in the hot seat trying to keep all her lies and secrets straight as he questioned her about Nadia.

"That's the last one."

Conner kicks back in his chair. "What a waste of time. It was like they were all reading from the same script. Even down to calling Stokes the Devil. Think it's some kind of mass hysteria?"

"More like the power of suggestion." That was the other reason Mary Grace opened Vaughan Elementary today. She needed to know if anyone else saw Darryl Stokes outside the schoolyard the day Cherie Leigh disappeared. What she got was a group of hyped-up eleven- and twelve-year-olds who parroted what Allison Driver told her on Saturday. Even her own usually level-headed daughter seemed to have fallen prey to the same mysterious malady. "And we still don't know whether anyone actually saw Stokes. If it's a lie, somebody had to start it."

"It wasn't Allison Driver," Conner says. "She was too scared."

Or is he saying that because she's Madison's daughter? "We can't rule her out."

"Just because she's the one who told us doesn't mean she's the instigator."

Mary Grace remembers the wild rumors circulating after Nadia disappeared. Nobody ever found out who started those.

"What gets me is no one seemed worried about their missing classmate. You'd think Cherie Leigh didn't have any friends."

"Maybe she didn't." Mary Grace remembers the yearning on Cherie Leigh's face in the parking lot after the softball semifinal. Despite being a star athlete, she wasn't chosen by the Reeves twins. Which puts her just as low in the pecking order as Allison Driver who, like Madison at her age, will never be a popular girl.

"If she had a boyfriend," Conner says, "no one knows who he is."

And they're no closer to finding out why the sixth grader sneaked out of her house Friday afternoon.

Levi Tomberlin, the Vaughan Elementary principal, pokes his head in the doorway. "Everyone's back in class and accounted for."

"Good." Mary Grace pushes back her chair, suddenly anxious to be out of here. As she and Conner walk past the sixth-grade classroom, she sees someone in the doorway. It's Hannah McGowen, Felicity's teacher.

"Sheriff Dobbs, do you have a minute?"

Mary Grace looks past her to the empty classroom. Miss Hannah follows her glance. "I sent the students outside for a short recess." Something in her voice alerts Mary Grace. "Wait for me in the parking lot," she tells Conner, then follows Miss Hannah into the classroom.

She's hit by a powerful feeling of déjà vu as Miss Hannah places a chair on the opposite side of the desk. Althea Vale did the exact same thing the day she warned Mary Grace that her slipping grades could result in her losing her place on the softball team. All because of her friendship with Nadia. "Is this about Cherie Leigh?" she asks now.

Miss Hannah shakes her head. She's young and pretty, with wavy blond hair that reminds Mary Grace of Emily King. "I know this isn't a good time. But there never is a good time, is there? Not for something like this. And the next parent–teacher conference isn't until December so I thought I should speak to you now." She takes a breath. "There's no easy way to say this. But there have been complaints."

"What kinds of complaints?"

"About your daughter and her friends."

"Are you talking about Lauren and Haley Reeves?" The other woman nods. "I don't understand."

"Some of the younger children claim the girls have been bullying them."

"What?" Mary Grace feels like she's just been sucker-punched. It's the dreaded *B* word. The one that every parent fears hearing, and never more so than today. The laws protecting victims weren't around when Mary Grace was being mercilessly bullied by Chloe Ann Briggs. But this is different. Now her child is accused of being the bully.

"What exactly did these children claim Felicity and the Reeves twins did?"

"They said the popular girls ganged up on them at school. Called them names and used derogatory words about their ethnic and religious backgrounds."

"My daughter would never do that. There's obviously been some kind of misunderstanding."

"No, there hasn't. And I'm sure I don't have to tell you that at Vaughan Elementary we take these allegations very seriously."

There's a self-satisfied note in the teacher's voice, as if she alone is the keeper of the truth, that rubs Mary Grace the wrong way. "Do you have proof?"

"The children came to me."

Like that made it gospel. "Maybe they're lying."

"Why would they lie?"

"Children lie all the time."

"Why would they lie about something like this?"

"You'd have to ask them."

"I'm sorry. I know this is hard for a parent to hear."

"Why haven't I heard about it before? Why am I only learning about this now?"

"It wasn't easy for them to come forward. They're frightened of retaliation."

Mary Grace leans forward. "Maybe that isn't what they're frightened of. I just finished questioning a group of hysterical sixth graders who seemed pretty scared themselves. Don't you think that's understandable, with a classmate missing?"

"The bullying was going on before Cherie Leigh disappeared. I don't mean to pry, but is everything all right at home? What about Felicity's father? Is he part of her life?"

"That's none of your business."

"But it is my business to keep these children safe."

"And it's my job to protect my daughter from other children's lies."

"Why don't you talk to Felicity? Let her tell you her side of the story."

"I intend to do that. And I'm sure it's very different from what I just heard. Good afternoon, Miss Hannah."

Outside in the hall, Mary Grace stops to catch her breath. Her heart is thumping erratically in her chest. She knows she shouldn't have let her anger get the better of her. But how dare that woman call her child a bully! She's trying to calm down when she spies three girls coming out of the restroom, whispering as usual.

Felicity, Lauren, and Haley Reeves stop in their tracks when they see Mary Grace. Felicity glances toward the classroom, then back at her mother. "Is everything cool?"

Mary Grace studies her, but all she sees is the child she has always known. She couldn't have done what her teacher said she had. "I'll pick you up after school."

Felicity starts to frown. "Lauren and Haley invited me back to their house."

All three girls are looking at Mary Grace now. Gone is any trace of the hysteria that gripped them when they were being questioned. Lauren Reeves's pretty face, so much like her mother's, wears its usual guileless expression. "I think we've imposed on the twins and their family long enough."

"But we're going for pizza and then Mrs. Reeves is cooking my favorite dinner. She said I could stay over again." Felicity smiles at her mother. "You can get me in the morning, like you did last time."

They're all waiting for her answer, just like after the semifinal softball game when Felicity was still grounded for what she and her friends had done on Halloween. Mary Grace feeling outnumbered then, too, and finally relenting. Not this time. She and her daughter are going to have a talk that's probably long overdue. "I'll see you at three."

"Mom, that's so dumb. Why come all the way back here? And if I sleep over at the twins', you won't have to drive to their house later." Felicity's cajoling voice full of the unassailable logic that usually gets her what she wants.

"Be ready." The warning in Mary Grace's voice something her child also knows well: the tone that brooks no argument.

The three girls look at each other. Then Lauren Reeves whispers something to Felicity, who nods and glares at her mother.

How could Mary Grace have failed to notice how Felicity takes her cues from the other girl? Lauren threw the rock that broke Meurice's window. What else has she done? Made ethnic slurs and intimidated other children? Bullied Allison Driver into lying about Darryl Stokes?

Felicity crosses her arms over her chest. "I'm going home with Lauren and Haley."

Mary Grace can't believe how her daughter is challenging her, and in public. "Don't you disobey me, young lady."

"It's all Miss Hannah's fault. What did she tell you about me? You can't believe anything she says."

"Show some respect. She's your teacher."

"I don't care. She's a liar and everyone in town knows it."

Just like that Sunday morning in church when Felicity justified calling Isaac Wood a loser by saying that everyone knew he was. As if that made it right. "That's enough, Felicity. I'll see you later."

"You can't tell me what to do!"

"Yes, I can. And after school you're coming home." Mary Grace starts to leave but her daughter's angry voice stops her. "What did you just say?"

Felicity stands there with a defiant look on her face. Lauren and Haley Reeves move closer to her, closing ranks against Mary Grace. As if to protect their friend from her mother.

"This isn't over, young lady." Mary Grace turns and storms down the hall. She passes Miss Hannah standing in the doorway of the classroom, mortified that she was a witness to her daughter acting out.

As if proving her accusations right.

Mary Grace's phone buzzes as she walks out of Vaughan Elementary. Before she can slide it out of her pocket, she sees Conner coming toward her from the parking lot, his phone in his hand.

"That's me texting you. Adalynn Wood just called the station. Her daughter's gone."

THIRTY-FOUR

"We have to contain this."

"Fat chance."

What Adalynn Wood told them confirmed their worst fears. When she came up from the basement where she'd been doing laundry, her daughter wasn't in the house. She'd kept Annabelle home from school because she had a cold. She'd seen her in the kitchen half an hour earlier, making herself a cup of tea. Which gave them substantially more lead time than they'd had with Cherie Leigh. And there was no storm now to delay their search.

Like Cherie Leigh, Annabelle's smartphone and backpack were missing.

But Cherie Leigh didn't have two parents fighting over her.

Ten days ago, Mary Grace was called to Isaac Wood's ex-wife's house after he got in using his key and demanded to see his daughter. Mary Grace told him that he no longer lived there and if he didn't leave peaceably, she'd have to arrest him for breaking and entering.

"Maybe it's a false alarm," Mary Grace says as they pull out of Adalynn Wood's driveway. "And she went to see her father after all."

It was the first thing they asked when they got there, a hysterical Adalynn saying Isaac Wood's weekend visits had been cut off and Annabelle wasn't allowed to visit him. And she'd never go anywhere without texting her mother, especially now.

"It's worth a shot," Conner says as they head for the outskirts of town.

Mary Grace's phone chirps. It's Noah finally responding to her text, agreeing to pick up Felicity after school. He'd certainly taken his sweet time. She would have asked her uncle, but when she called the house Lydia said he wasn't home. Letting Felicity spend another night with the Reeves twins was out of the question. And no way was she letting her stay home alone. Not now.

"You okay?" Conner has been throwing her concerned glances ever since they left Vaughan Elementary.

"Yeah." But she's far from okay. Felicity's teacher called her a bully, then her daughter told her she hated her in front of her friends. And now a second child is missing.

Just like in '95.

Ten minutes later, Conner pulls into the parking lot of the Repentance Motel. The sorry-looking building with the peeling paint sits on a lonely stretch of road near the town limits. It's home to drifters and transients who aren't there to repent their sinful ways.

Every year the town hall votes to tear it down, and every year it ends up still standing. All because the original owner deeded it to the town with certain provisions that have kept things so mired in red tape some think it's the ultimate joke on the citizens of Repentance. As they walk to the office, Mary Grace's thoughts drift to Isaac Wood, and that the real sin is how far the former chief deputy has fallen.

The motel manager, an old-timer named Mason Nichols who's been here since before Mary Grace was born, says he hasn't seen Annabelle Wood. But all the rooms are accessed from the outside, so she could have gone to her daddy's room without his knowing. At Mary Grace's request, Adalynn Wood tried her ex's cell but the call went straight to voicemail. She said he was probably sleeping off a drunk.

But his car isn't in the lot. They enter Wood's room with the key Nichols gave them. The room is dark and narrow, with a low ceiling and a standing lamp missing its bulb. The bed is unmade and a pair of trousers and a shirt and belt lie across the room's only chair. The drawers in the tiny bedside table are empty save for a Bible gathering dust. Jackets, shirts, and several other pairs of trousers fill half of the small closet and a few sparse toiletries sit on the chipped bathroom counter. There's no sign of father or daughter. On the way out Mary Grace calls Adalynn Wood, asking if she has any idea where her ex-husband might have gone.

"To a bar. Where else? But I don't give a damn about him. Just find my daughter!"

In the car again, Mary Grace puts out an APB on Wood. Then she calls Lucas and tells him to leave his surveilling of the boarding house and help them look for Isaac and Annabelle Wood.

"Adalynn could be right and her husband's sleeping it off," Conner says as she starts the engine. "Or it's not as innocent as it looks." Mary Grace looks at him. "Lucas says Stokes hasn't set foot out of Miss Lillian's. So maybe it's like I said. Somebody's setting Stokes up."

"Isaac Wood?"

"I'm liking him more and more for this."

"He abducted his own daughter?" It makes an awful kind of sense, but Mary Grace isn't ready to believe it. "Then who was Cherie Leigh meeting? Stokes?"

"Or she's a smokescreen. His daughter was Wood's real target. With Stokes in town, he had the perfect straw man. Everyone thinks history's repeating itself. Two girls disappeared back then, and two disappear now."

"You saying Wood took Cherie Leigh, too?"

"To throw us off. Maybe she was supposed to be found by now, but the storm messed things up."

An hour later, they're no closer to finding Isaac Wood or his daughter. Out of the three bars they tried in nearby towns, only one bartender remembered seeing him. He served Wood several shots of whiskey at the bar and said he left sometime after midnight. They're back in the car with fresh coffee and discussing where to go next when Mary Grace's phone chirps.

"Dogs picked up Stokes's scent," Sheriff Mathis says. "Abandoned cabin a couple miles west of the first one. No one's inside, but there are clear signs of recent habitation. Stokes was definitely here."

"Cherie Leigh?"

"No sign of her. And the dogs haven't picked up her scent. Any news on the Wood girl?"

"No. Looks like it could be a domestic, but we're not sure. Heading back now. Keep me in the loop."

"Roger that."

"Wood probably is sleeping it off," Mary Grace says to Conner as she starts the car.

"I don't know. He could still have those girls hidden away somewhere."

"Why would he do that? If the point is to abduct his daughter, he and Annabelle would be miles away by now. You heard that bartender. Wood was by himself at the bar until after midnight."

They're driving back, approaching the town limits when Conner tells her to slow down. "Isn't that Wood's truck?"

Mary Grace sees the truck parked off the shoulder. "You're right. Jesus." She puts on the siren and flashing lights and pulls up behind the truck. Slides her revolver from its holster as they exit the cruiser.

"Get out of the vehicle!" she shouts as she and Conner approach.

The driver's door starts to open.

"Get out of the vehicle slowly." Mary Grace keeps her gun trained on the driver's door. A few seconds later, Isaac Wood staggers out.

"Put your hands where I can see them."

Wood raises his hands above his head. Conner goes around to the passenger side. After checking the rest of the truck, he turns on Wood. "Where is she?"

"Where's who?" Wood's voice is slurred. His legs in a pair of ripped jeans look as if they can barely hold up the rest of his body.

"How much did you have to drink? Needed some fire in your belly to kidnap your daughter?"

"What? Where's Annabelle?"

"That's what we'd like to know. Can you tell us where your daughter is, Isaac?"

Wood turns to Mary Grace, now fully roused from his stupor. "I have no idea! I didn't even know she was missing! Oh God!"

"Keep your hands where I can see them!"

"I'm not armed!"

Mary Grace isn't so sure. Wood turned in his weapon with his badge when Kanady fired him, but he could have another one stashed away. She nods to Conner, who goes over and pats him down. "He's clean."

"Where were you this afternoon?" she asks.

"I was out late last night. When I was driving back, I almost went off the road. I figured I'd better sober up before I hurt myself. Or someone else. Did you talk to Adalynn?"

"So Annabelle didn't sneak out of her house to meet you?"

"Meet me where? No! I told you, I was right here. In my car."

"What time did you drive back?"

"Around one."

"Anyone see you?"

"Who'd see me that time of night? And I was out of it. Please! Tell me what happened."

"Annabelle left the house around noon," Conner says. "While you claim to have been trying to sober up, your daughter walked out of her house and hasn't been seen since. What time did you leave the motel yesterday? Where'd you go? Don't try to lie because we're going to find out."

"I don't know. I left here around five."

"You sure it wasn't closer to four?"

"It could have been. Why you asking me that?"

"Cherie Leigh Hibbard's missing, too."

"What?"

"You didn't hear about it at your usual watering holes?" Conner shakes his head. "Oh, I forgot. You were too busy drowning your sorrows."

"I didn't do anything to Tyler Lee's girl. Or Annabelle. You've got to believe me!"

"Why should we? Why should we believe the word of a drunk?"

Conner's eyes blaze with anger. As a kid, Mary Grace heard the stories about his father's drinking and the rumors of abuse that were never substantiated. "We're going to need you to come to the station," she says to Wood. "Leave your truck here. You're not in any condition to drive."

Not that he'll be driving his truck for a while. Not until after it's examined for hair or fibers belonging to either girl that Mary Grace hopes they won't find. They walk Wood to the cruiser, Conner putting him none too gently into the back seat. And just like that, Mary Grace is thrown back twenty-four years. Kicking up a fuss when Kanady and Wood tried to get her into the cruiser after they caught up to her trying to hitch a ride out of town. Wood telling her as he walked her up to her uncle's front porch that running away never solved your troubles because you carried them with you wherever you went.

It was true then, and it's true now.

The call comes in when they're driving back to the station.

Annabelle Wood just came home.

THIRTY-FIVE

"You don't have to be scared."

Mary Grace smiles reassuringly at the fifth grader, who sits on the sofa between her parents looking as if she'd rather be anywhere but here. "Deputy Mitchell and I just want to ask you a few questions, okay?"

"Okay." Her eyes are huge behind her glasses.

"Did you really run away?" Annabelle looks guiltily at her mother, then shrinks deeper into the cushions. "You're not going to get in trouble if you tell us." Adalynn Wood opens her mouth as if to disagree, then thinks better of it. "Why did you go to the church? You sure you didn't escape from somewhere? The same place Cherie Leigh is?" Annabelle shakes her head. "You weren't meeting someone?"

"Uh uh."

"Annabelle," Adalynn says. "You have to tell the truth."

"I am. I swear!" She turns on her mother. "I was so sick of you and daddy fighting! This morning, I heard you yelling at him on the phone saying he couldn't see me on the weekends anymore. Or maybe ever again!"

"So you went to visit him." Conner looks at Isaac Wood, who shakes his head.

"No! I just wanted to get away. I couldn't stand it anymore! I thought if I could just find a place where it was peaceful and quiet. But I was scared because of Cherie Leigh. Then I remembered how the church doors are always open. There was nobody in the chapel and after praying a while I got tired. I knew Pastor Mills had a cot in the basement. I must have fallen asleep. I woke up when I heard voices upstairs. So I snuck out through the basement door. I'm sorry, Mama."

"It's all right," Adalynn says, drawing her into her arms and stroking her hair. "But you had us so worried."

"I'm sorry," Annabelle says again, tears forming in her eyes. "Are you going to punish me?" Her mother shakes her head.

"What were you praying for?" her father asks.

"That you'd get back together. Then you wouldn't have to fight over me anymore."

Over her head, Isaac and Adalynn Wood exchange glances. Mary Grace and Conner get to their feet. "Thank you for being honest," Mary Grace tells Annabelle. As the girls' parents walk Conner and her out of the living room, Mary Grace says, "You should have told us about the argument."

"I didn't think it was important," Adalynn replies. "Or anyone's business. But I never dreamed Annabelle would run away. She's never done that before."

"There's always a first time. She must have been really unhappy to run off with another girl missing. Anything could have happened to her."

"I know." At the door, Isaac Wood's face is grim. Mary Grace steps closer to him, pitches her voice low.

"Nobody tells you how lonely it is, do they? Not being part of a family." Wood looks at her. "You once said those words to me. Don't let your daughter feel the same way."

"Maybe it's too late. Maybe I already lost her."

"You're here, aren't you? Annabelle's lucky. She isn't an orphan like you and I were. Clean up your act and find a way to work it out with your wife. Be the family your daughter needs."

Adalynn Wood joins them. Wood starts to say something to his wife, but she's already opening the door. With one last glance at her, he leaves.

Annabelle comes into the hall. "Can I say goodbye to Daddy?"

Adalynn starts to shake her head, then relents. "Okay."

Mary Grace's phone starts *ping*ing as she and Conner leave.

There are at least a dozen texts. All from Felicity, each one angrier than the last. She's furious that her mother forced her to go to her cousins' house and vows never to speak to her again. Mary Grace can feel her daughter's rage through the torrent of words, all written in capital letters, punctuated by twice her usual exclamation points.

Something's obviously going on with Felicity. Something she can't ignore.

She sees Isaac Wood leaning against a lamppost watching his daughter as she heads back to the house.

"Give me a few minutes," Mary Grace says to Conner, then goes to meet Annabelle halfway down the path. "I just have a couple more questions, but this time it's just between you and me, okay?" Annabelle nods. She still looks nervous. "I'm sheriff, which of course you know. But I'm also Felicity's mom, right?" Annabelle gives another quick nod. "Have you noticed any of the kids being bullied at school?"

Behind her glasses, the fifth grader's eyes go wide. "I'm not sure."

"What do you mean?"

"I don't want to get them in trouble."

Mary Grace's breath quickens. "Who?"

Annabelle kicks away some dirt with her sneakers. "The popular girls."

"What did you see them do? It's okay. You won't get in trouble." Repeating what she said when she questioned the fifth grader in her house.

Annabelle looks at her to let her know she sees through her subterfuge: Mary Grace didn't say that the *popular girls* wouldn't get in trouble.

"Please, Annabelle. This is important."

"Because you're Felicity's mom."

"Right."

She kicks away more dirt. "It was like, a couple of weeks ago at recess. Everyone was in the schoolyard. I was hanging with the other fifth graders when the three of them came over. I mean, it's not like they ever pay attention to me. They don't even know I'm alive. But I wasn't the one they were picking on. It was a kid from my class. Yochi Chajon."

Yochi and his mother and father moved to town last winter. Some in Repentance looked askance when they celebrated the feast day of Santa Eulalia, the patron saint of a town by the same name in Huehuetenango where many of the Maya immigrants living in the South originally hail from. The irony is that it's a Catholic celebration, and notwithstanding the fact that the Chajons are Catholic, they weren't made to feel welcome in church, which was only exacerbated by the current political landscape. Until this summer's reappearance of Darryl Stokes overshadowed everything else.

"How was Yochi picked on?" Mary Grace asks.

"Lauren Reeves told him he should go back to Guatemala. She said nobody wanted him here and that was why our country was building a wall. To keep immigrants and border rats like him out."

"Lauren said that?"

Annabelle nodded. "Everyone heard it, too. She said it real loud. Then a few days later, she said something to Mei Ling while she was on the food voucher line in the cafeteria because her family can't afford the school lunches. I didn't hear what she said that time, but Mei Ling started crying."

Then she and Yochi told Felicity's teacher.

Something else just occurred to Mary Grace. Yochi Chajon is Latino. Mei Ling is Chinese. And Darryl Stokes is black. Is Lauren Reeves a budding racist? "You said it was three of them?"

Annabelle nods. "Lauren and Haley Reeves. Some kids thought maybe it was Haley who picked on those kids because some kids can't tell them apart. But I know it was Lauren. And Felicity was with them. They're always together."

"Did Felicity say anything to Yochi or Mei Ling?"

"No."

Mary Grace lets out a relieved sigh.

"Do you think it's worth it?" Annabelle asks.

"What?"

"Being popular. All my life, it was all I ever wanted."

Two days ago, Madison Driver said the same thing about Chloe Ann Briggs. But Madison could also have been talking about herself. And her daughter. In church, Allison Driver had the same envious look on her face as she watched Felicity and the Reeves twins whispering together. And Cherie Leigh Hibbard, when she watched the popular girls headed to Paige's car the day of the softball semifinal.

"But now I'm thinking maybe it's not such a great thing to want to be. Those girls can be mean." Annabelle pushes her glasses higher up on her nose. "Not that they'd ever choose me. I'll always be Four-Eyes to them."

Another cruel label. "Being popular isn't everything," Mary Grace says. Except that to most kids, it *is* everything. Wasn't she proud when Felicity was chosen, even though she herself never made the cut? But that was before she knew about Lauren Reeves, before her daughter started acting out. She wonders how Paige will feel when Miss Hannah tells her about her own daughter. Whatever else she and Skylar might have been, they weren't bullies.

Adalynn Wood comes out of the house. Annabelle looks up at Mary Grace. "Sheriff Dobbs, please don't tell anyone what I just told you. If the popular girls find out, they'll start picking on me next."

Mary Grace remembers how Felicity was willing to lie rather than rat out her best friend after Lauren broke Meurice's window. As she watches Annabelle go into the house, she knows it's a promise she won't be able to keep.

"Get anything more out of the Wood kid?"

They just dropped Isaac Wood off at his truck, which was still parked on the shoulder near the town limits, Conner sure he was going to hit the bottle the minute he got home.

Mary Grace shakes her head. Which isn't a lie because Annabelle didn't say anything about Cherie Leigh.

She sneaks a glance at her phone. No more texts from Felicity, thank God. But somehow her silence feels even worse. In her hand, her phone buzzes, startling her.

"What's going on, Lucas?" Mary Grace sent him back to resume surveillance of the boarding house after Annabelle Wood came home.

Except Stokes isn't there. "But we lucked out," Lucas says. "Miss Lillian doesn't think he's been gone more than half an hour."

"Stokes is AWOL," Mary Grace tells Conner. To Lucas she says, "Does Miss Lillian have any idea where he might have gone?"

"No, but I checked. His stuff's still here."

That was a relief. So he didn't skip town.

"He probably went to the diner," Conner says. "Man's gotta eat."

Stokes isn't at the diner. Gabriel Clark hasn't seen him at all today. But someone else has.

"I've been trying to reach you." Alma Allred's quavery voice is full of accusation.

"Sorry," Mary Grace says. "We had a situation."

"I know. The Wood girl should be ashamed. Running off and worrying her folks like that. And using the church. It's a sacrilege."

"What is it you wanted, Miss Alma?"

"I saw something I thought you should know about."

"What did you see?" Mary Grace has a flash of the town wag rocking on her porch at the top of the hill, knitting needles clacking away while she observes everyone's comings and goings.

Allred clears her throat, letting Mary Grace know she has something important to say beyond the usual gossip. "I saw that drifter."

Mary Grace's hand tightens on her phone. "You saw Darryl Stokes?"

"I just said that, didn't I?"

"Where?"

"Passing under the old railroad trestle."

That dead-ended at the abandoned tracks that divided the rich and poor sections of town. "What was he doing down there?"

"How should I know? But I don't think they had a day's outing in mind."

"Who?"

"Jackson Briggs and Tyler Lee Hibbard."

Dear God. They must have been staking out the boarding house. Then Mary Grace pulled Lucas off surveillance to help look for Isaac Wood and his daughter. When Stokes came out, Briggs and Hibbard seized their chance.

"Hello? Sheriff Dobbs? You still there?"

"Yes. Are you sure you saw Darryl Stokes with Jackson Briggs and Tyler Lee Hibbard?"

"My eyes may not be what they used to be, but I saw what I saw. You don't believe me, ask Miss Caroline. Her house isn't far from there. She's always on her porch tending those damn flowerpots, summer or winter. They're all dead now, of course. But then, everyone knows she isn't in her right mind."

"Thank you, Miss Alma. You've been very helpful."

"Let's pray the Hibbard girl is somewhere safe. If that drifter's guilty, the Lord will deliver a fitting punishment."

Caroline Womack's house is three blocks from the railroad trestle. The church organist isn't on her front porch, which is covered with large, cracked urns filled with damp earth and long-dead autumn blooms. When Womack opens the door, Mary Grace is shocked to see how unkempt she looks. In church, she's always flawlessly turned out in her high-necked dresses and wide-brimmed hats. Instead of her usual neat bun, her white hair hangs lankly down over a soiled nightgown.

At first she doesn't recognize Mary Grace and Conner, and Mary Grace fears they're wasting valuable time. But when she asks Womack if she saw the three men, the haze in the elderly woman's eyes suddenly clears.

"I was out here, getting the newspaper. I thought I was imagining it. I don't care what they say about that drifter, it's a shame what they're trying to do to him."

"Did you see them passing under the trestle?" Conner asks. Miss Caroline nods. "How long ago?"

"I'm not sure. I lose track of time." She gives him an apologetic look. "Do you think Mr. Briggs is planning to shoot him?"

Mary Grace's chest tightens. "Why? Did he have a gun?" Miss Caroline nods again. "You saw it?"

"I only wish I hadn't. At first I thought my eyes must be deceiving me. Mr. Briggs is a good Christian soul. Hasn't missed a Sunday in church as long as I've been organist there." She turns troubled eyes to Mary Grace. "He wouldn't kill a man, would he?"

"I don't know. Thank you, Miss Caroline." As Mary Grace turns to go, praying they're not too late, Womack grasps her arm with long-fingered hands made strong from years of playing the organ and giving piano lessons.

"It's a shame how Mr. Hibbard's girl got lost. Just like one of His lambs. You'll find her, won't you?"

"Yes." Mary Grace has to pry Womack's fingers off her jacket. She and Conner carefully sidestep the urns as they step off the porch.

"Don't trample my flowers, young man!" Womack suddenly shouts. "They are things of beauty. God's living creations that give untold pleasure. Planting them isn't a sin, I don't care what the Footwashers say."

Long after they've driven away, Mary Grace still sees her in her rear-view: a ghostly figure in her once-white nightgown.

THIRTY-SIX

"Over there."

They just passed under the old railroad trestle. The late-afternoon sun winks off the chrome of the other cruiser through the dense grove of trees that provides the perfect cover for the old tracks. No trains have run here for decades, not since long before Mary Grace was born. It has to be why Briggs chose this place.

She forgets everything else as she slams on the brakes and slides her gun from her holster for the second time today.

On the other side of the trees, Lucas's hand shakes as he aims his weapon at Jackson Briggs. A few feet away, Darryl Stokes is on his knees, Tyler Lee holding his arms behind his back.

"Drop your weapon, Briggs!"

"Get out of here, Dobbs. And take your troops with you. This isn't your business."

"Yes, it is. It's town business. Put down the gun."

"You're too late. I've waited twenty-four years. He's mine now."

"I didn't do it!" Stokes shouts. "I didn't kill your girl!"

"Everyone knows how you were staring at her in the garage. Only now you don't have a mechanic to lie for you. Or somebody else to confess. But you're not getting away this time. Where's Cherie Leigh, you son of a bitch?"

"Shooting him won't solve anything."

"Sure it will. Maybe one bullet will take out his kneecap. Another gores his shoulder. Or hits his chest just inches from what passes for his heart. What'll it be, Stokes?"

"Give it up, Briggs," Conner says. "You're outnumbered three to one." Not that that counts for much. Even five of them armed to the teeth would be no match for a lone gunman crazy with grief.

"Let Stokes go," Mary Grace says to Tyler Lee. "How will you raise your daughter from prison?"

"Don't listen to her! Cherie Leigh's dead just like my baby." Briggs cocks the gun.

"You're not a killer, Jackson. Don't let what happened turn you into one."

He clicks back the safety.

"Don't do this! It won't bring back Chloe Ann." Her own gun hand none too steady as Mary Grace says the name of her childhood tormentor.

Hearing his daughter's name also does something to Briggs. Mary Grace can see it in the way his shoulders start to sag.

"Make him tell us! What if she's right? Cherie Leigh could be alive . . ." Tyler Lee's voice trails off on a sob. Stokes suddenly rears back, elbowing him in the ribs. Tyler Lee stumbles back as Stokes leaps to his feet and turns to run. A shot rings out.

The blast sends him staggering back. He wobbles on his feet, then falls onto the tracks.

Next to Mary Grace, Lucas stares at the gun in his hand as if he can't believe he just fired. Then he runs.

Conner takes off after him, shouting at him to stop. Lucas disappears through the trees, shouts and gunshots filling the air. Mary Grace has her phone out and is calling for an ambulance as she rushes over to the tracks where Stokes lies unmoving.

She unzips his jacket. Blood's already soaking through his shirt. She removes her scarf and wraps it around his middle, then applies pressure to his abdomen with the heel of her hand. His eyes are closed. Only the shallow fall and rise of his chest tells her that he's still breathing.

A car door slams, followed by the screech of tires.

Conner comes running back, out of breath. "He got away. Never knew the son of a bitch could fire a gun."

Neither did Mary Grace. After being deputized, Lucas acquired his first firearm. But he hadn't yet begun practicing at the Repentance gun range, least as far as she knew. There's clearly a lot about her assistant sheriff she didn't know. "Arrest them," she tells Conner, indicating Tyler Lee and Jackson Briggs, whose unfired weapon has gone slack in his hand. Conner easily takes his gun away from him. As he reads Briggs his rights, Tyler Lee breaks away and runs for the tracks. "Tell me where she is!" he screams at Stokes.

"You're under arrest, Hibbard!" Conner trains his gun on Tyler Lee, who collapses into a sobbing heap. He's still hysterical as Conner hauls him to his feet. Mary Grace tells Conner to take them back to the station while she waits for the ambulance. Briggs puts up no resistance as Conner leads him and Tyler Lee away, staring blankly ahead as if he has no idea how he got here.

Stokes groans. Mary Grace presses down harder on the wound, blood seeping through her fingers. His eyes flutter open, then start to close again. "Come on. Stay with me."

His eyes open again. She might not get another chance. "We found the other cabin. We know you were there. Who was with you?"

She can tell from the way his gaze tracks her that he's listening. He gives an imperceptible shake of his head. His blood is soaking her hands now. "Are you protecting someone? Emily King? You have to see how bad this looks for you. Don't you want to save yourself?"

His mouth opens. He's trying to talk. ". . . those . . . girls . . ."

Mary Grace feels her own breathing go shallow. Is she about to hear a confession after all? One that would turn the past two decades into a lie? "What about them?"

It's a struggle for him to talk now. She leans closer.

". . . never touched . . . them . . . wrong then . . . wrong . . . now."

"Then who was in the cabin with you? Tell me!"

She wants to shake the truth out of him. His eyes are closing again, his breathing becoming more labored. In the distance, she hears the blaring siren of the ambulance.

He dies on the way to the hospital.

Three hours later, Mary Grace leaves the morgue after finally managing to shake the reporters who corner her outside. Drives home under a starless, pitch-black sky. The house is dark when she pulls into her driveway.

She keeps seeing Darryl Stokes lying on that table.

Another death she feels responsible for.

She can't shake the feeling that death is all around her.

She pulls out her phone. Still nothing from Felicity. Despite the lateness of the hour, she's tempted to go to her uncle's house and bring her daughter home. She hates how things ended between them today. One rule they've always lived by: they never go to bed mad at each other.

She sends Felicity a two-word text.

Love you.

She waits to see if she writes back. A text, a smiley face, *something.* But her daughter remains silent, as if she's punishing Mary Grace. And not just for refusing to let her sleep over at the twins'.

Miss Hannah's questions about Felicity's father blindsided her. It's not her daughter's fault that she has no male authority figure in her life. If she did, maybe she wouldn't be acting out and hanging around with bullies. Mary Grace realizes that she can't blame everything on Lauren. Just as she couldn't blame Nadia for what was already inside *her.*

But how could she not have known about Lauren? She chastises herself as she pulls the key from the ignition and gets out of the car. Or did she not want to know?

There is none so blind as those who will not see.

Blinded by her vicarious need for her daughter to be popular even though she told Annabelle Wood that being popular wasn't everything. That was what she used to tell herself as a kid, that it didn't matter if she wasn't chosen by Paige and Skylar.

Like Madison Driver and Chloe Ann Briggs back then.

And Allison Driver, Annabelle Wood, and Cherie Leigh Hibbard now.

Cherie Leigh Hibbard.

Was she missing something here?

She starts walking toward the house. A voice startles her.

"Wondered when you'd show your face."

THIRTY-SEVEN

The words are slurred, but she'd know his voice anywhere. "What are you doing here?" In the six years she has lived here, she can't recall his ever paying a visit. Not like back then when he'd show up regularly at her uncle's house.

She points her phone light at the shadow-filled porch. Parnell sits on the swing, his booted feet tapping the boards as he moves back and forth. "Planning to shoot me? Or better yet, why don't you put us both out of our misery?"

Mary Grace is surprised to see the gun in her other hand as she climbs the steps. "You're drunk," she says as she reholsters it.

"Why wouldn't I be?" His face changes as he leaps up and lunges at her. She moves away just in time, her mind spinning back to that unseasonably warm Sunday in November, the day after Madison came forward and Mary Grace led Owen Kanady and Isaac Wood to the cabin. Sneaking into the woods after church to see what else she could find there. Hearing footsteps, terrified it was the Boogeyman. Until she remembered her cousin coming in for supper the day Nadia disappeared, tracking mud on his sneakers. And the sound of Nadia screaming.

Only it wasn't Noah who grabbed her and spun her around.

"You fucking bitch! This is all your fault!" Parnell swipes at the air, stumbles, and grabs onto a column for support. They're almost the exact words he hurled at her that long-ago Sunday in the woods.

Parnell glares at her as if he knows what she's thinking. At least he's looking at her. It's better than acting like she doesn't exist. Shame and guilt and that terrible, wanting need rage through her, even now.

"You're just as evil as you ever were. And now because of you he's dead."

As if she needed reminding. "I was trying to save him. I didn't know what Lucas Smith was going to do, I swear." Hearing her voice rise as she went on the defensive, her go-to mode whenever she felt she was being attacked.

"Sure you didn't. Maybe you even put him up to it."

"That's cruel."

"No crueler than what you did in '95. You and your wicked lies."

"They weren't lies." She switches on the porch light. Parnell's leaning against the column as if it's the only thing holding him up. She goes over and sits on the swing that's still warm from his body heat. "I was at the station that Saturday when Stokes was being questioned." Less than an hour after Madison came forward with the story Chloe Ann told her about Stokes staring at her in the garage. That and Chloe Ann's crush on him was enough for Kanady to bring in Stokes, though not nearly enough for probable cause. "When he came out, I recognized his backpack."

Not the one Stokes was wearing when he left her office this afternoon—still alive—but a backpack with pretty scenes of mountains and lakes, with trees reflected in the water. It took a few minutes to remember where she'd seen it before. "When I told Kanady, he asked if I could pick out the cabin again. I said I'd try. I'd only been there once before." In August after the altercation with Tyler Lee when she took the shortcut through the woods and stumbled on the cabin by accident.

"When we got there, I showed Kanady the spot where I'd seen Stokes's backpack in August. On the floor next to a torn paisley sofa." Parnell shakes his head. "It's the truth."

That was when she saw something glittering behind one of the sofa legs. It was a charm from Nadia's bracelet that she never took off, not even for PE. When Kanady arrested him, Stokes said it must have happened when he rejected Nadia's advances.

"He wasn't lying," Parnell says. "He didn't hurt her."

"How do you know?" The words out before she can stop them, the same ones she asked in the woods that long-ago November Sunday. When she still thought it was Noah.

He opens his mouth to answer the question he never answered then. "Because he couldn't hurt anyone. He was so gentle. Never had an unkind word to say about a single soul. Even after the Briggs girl told her lies. Even after the town turned against him."

Because of Mary Grace.

"What does it matter now? He's gone." He starts to cry. "I loved him so much. From the first day I saw him at my daddy's garage."

Mary Grace feels like she just went into freefall. She stops the swing, the back-and-forth motion suddenly making her queasy.

Tears fall unheeded down his face. "At first he was afraid to get involved. I was the boss's son. And I was white. I told him I didn't care. I just wanted to be with him."

"You were lovers." A crazy-quilt of images pierces her shock. Her first year at Briggs High: Anna Mae showing off her senior class ring from her new boyfriend after breaking up with Parnell. Parnell always dating a new woman through the years; never marrying. How mad he got that day in her aunt's kitchen when she asked if it was true that Stokes was black as sin. The signs were there; how could she have missed them?

"It started right after the Fourth of July. It felt like the fireworks were our special celebration. After that, we were together every chance we got. We had to be careful, make sure we weren't seen by anyone in town."

"You met at the cabin in the woods." The pieces are starting to fall into place. "That's why Stokes wouldn't tell Kanady who he was meeting that Tuesday."

Parnell swipes at his eyes. "He and I had an arrangement. If I didn't show by a certain time, he'd go back to Miss Lillian's. That Tuesday I was with Anna Mae. I never made it there. But that little slut did."

Mary Grace has no doubt whom he's talking about. "How did Nadia know about the cabin? I never told her."

"She followed me."

"You said you didn't make it there that Tuesday."

"It was the day before. Monday."

"Where'd she follow you from?"

"She showed up after our track meet. Said she had something important to tell me. I should have known. It was deserted by the time we got there, which was part of her plan."

"What plan?" Is he making it up as he goes along?

"To seduce me. She was always hanging around Briggs High. That afternoon, she got me behind the bleachers and made her move."

Mary Grace can't believe what she's hearing. "Are you saying you didn't kiss her?"

"No way! She tell you that?"

"She didn't tell me anything." She can't look at him; she's too ashamed. "I was there."

"Then you saw me push her away." She shakes her head, remembering how she turned and ran, feeling betrayed by the two people she loved and trusted most. "It made her really mad. She cursed me and ran off. I thought she was gone and the coast was clear. But she must have followed me and saw us together in the cabin."

Mary Grace's mind is spinning. All these years, she believed that Parnell was Nadia's secret boyfriend.

I'm talking about big money. It's gonna be the biggest payout ever.

That was what Nadia said when she showed up at their tree the last day anyone saw her alive. It was only after Parnell accosted Mary Grace in the woods that she started to suspect Nadia was talking about him. Or maybe she didn't want to see it before. Easier to believe it was her cousin. Except Noah didn't have any money, especially when her uncle suspended his allowance after his money was stolen. And Parnell was the son of one of the town's richest men.

Nadia must have been planning to blackmail him. Maybe she threatened to tell Anna Mae. And Nadia was twelve; Parnell was four years older and could have gotten in a lot of trouble if anyone found out they were having sex.

Except the secret wasn't about Parnell and Nadia. It was about Parnell and Stokes.

Mary Grace flashes back to the first day she ever saw Darryl Stokes, as he emerged from the woods. Wondering what he was doing there. Now she knows. He was meeting his lover.

"I blamed you for years, hated you for what happened. But now I have to own up to my part in it. It might as well have been me who shot him."

Parnell pushes away from the column, starts to pace. "When Darryl came here twenty-four years ago, he couldn't believe a place like this still existed. People dominated by superstition and fear. He never wanted to come back. He kept begging me to leave. He would have gone anywhere, it didn't matter as long as we were together. But I wanted him vindicated. I was going to bring him into the business. Couldn't wait to see everyone's reactions when the temporary black help became a full-fledged partner. Only I was too much of a coward. Even with my homophobic daddy dead.

"It was too dangerous to meet in our old cabin. So we found a new one. And there we were, sneaking around just like in the old days. But yesterday, we got stranded by the storm. I heard what happened when I got back to town this morning. I knew what everyone would think. I called Darryl—we used disposable phones that couldn't be tracked—something we didn't have back then. He was still at the cabin. I told him to come see you, get in front of this. That it was okay if he outed us. Something I should have done months ago. I should never have let him leave the woods. When I find Smith, I'll tear the son of a bitch apart with my bare hands."

His fury spent, he sinks down onto a porch step. "What am I supposed to do now? How do I live in a world without him in it?"

"Parnell." She gets off the swing and goes to him, touches his shoulder. "He never told me about the two of you. He protected you to the end." Small comfort, she knows.

"What does it matter now? What does anything matter?"

"I know you're hurting—"

"You have no clue!" He lurches to his feet. "Wait until it happens to you. Wait until you lose someone you love."

She just did. And he's standing in front of her. The finality of it hits her, washing away the last vestiges of shock. Leaving only bleak reality. There was a part of her that still hoped they could make things right between them.

She watches him stumble down the steps and weave his way down the street, glad he wasn't foolish enough to drive. She hopes the walk home will clear his head. It won't slay his demons, though.

Or absolve her of the guilt that, for a brief moment, she believed they shared.

Her heart is heavy as he walks away. Just like he walked away twenty-four years ago, vanishing like an apparition through the trees as footsteps thundered through the woods.

THIRTY-EIGHT

The footsteps were getting closer.

She stood rooted to the spot, for once her shock stronger than her fear. Her arms hurt from where Parnell had grabbed her, his blue eyes almost black with rage. She'd thought he was going to kill her on the spot.

She remembered that terrifying encounter back in August when she took the shortcut through the woods after Tyler Lee followed her to her secret cave. Maybe this time the Boogeyman would finish her off for good. Then she wouldn't have to suffer anymore, wouldn't have to think that the boy she loved was a stone-cold killer. Not her cousin after all, who up until this moment she'd believed had graduated from murdering defenseless animals to murdering humans.

How else could Parnell be so sure that Darryl Stokes was innocent?

"He never laid a finger on those girls and we both know it. You're evil, Mary Grace, and if they string him up it'll be on your head."

That's when she started thinking about the things she hadn't wanted to think about. But she couldn't go on protecting the two of them anymore.

When the footsteps inexplicably died away and she saw the sun peeking through the pines where no natural light ever found its way in, she thought God was speaking to her.

That was when she made up her mind to confess. To everything, starting with the Thanksgiving night her folks died in the ice storm. It was the only way to stop being the sinful Mary Grace who had wicked thoughts, kept secrets, and told lies. The only way she could be saved.

She ran out of the woods and didn't stop until she reached the sheriff's office. When she threw open the door, barely able to catch a breath, she knew right away that something was going on.

Sheriff Kanady's back was to her; he was talking on the phone. Chief Deputy Wood didn't wink at her like he usually did. After the sheriff finished his call and saw her, he said they had important business to attend to and she should run along home. She asked what kind of business he was conducting on a Sunday, and he told her not to give him any sass. Then he put on his coat with the Repentance Sheriff insignia and the tall black hat he never wore unless somebody had died. He told her again to go home. She left, but didn't go home.

Outside, she watched them get into the cruiser. She knew where they were going because she heard Sheriff Kanady say the name on the phone. After they drove off, she ran for the back roads, winding behind houses and across backyards until she got there. The cruiser was parked in the driveway. Sheriff Kanady and Chief Deputy Wood were standing at the front door, partially blocking her view of the figure on the other side of the screen door.

She hid under the porch and listened. She heard Sheriff Kanady asking about Darryl Stokes. But she only caught bits and pieces of the reply—in a deep, raspy voice she'd never heard before—about Stokes doing odd jobs around the house. Then something about how he never hurt those girls and he shouldn't pay for crimes he didn't commit. Sheriff Kanady asked who committed the crimes, but Mary Grace couldn't hear the response. Then Chief Deputy Wood said something else she couldn't hear.

That was when Mary Grace poked out her head and saw her on the porch, her nightgown billowing in the breeze. She'd never seen her in anything but the pretty flowered dresses she always wore to school. And never without her glasses. She didn't seem to notice that she was standing in front of two men in little but her undergarments. Then she held out her hands, whether in prayer or surrender Mary Grace couldn't tell. Chief Deputy Woods said something too low to hear, snapping handcuffs on her wrists while Sheriff Kanady talked into his two-way radio.

When she raised her shackled hands and pointed to the field behind the house, Mary Grace raced around to the back, past a rosebush minus its roses and a barren vegetable garden, through tall grass squishy with mud from yesterday's rain, and hid behind a tall pine.

When the three of them walked into the field, she was in the middle between the sheriff and the chief deputy, who each had a firm hold of her like she might fall down otherwise. They walked to a spot not far from the tree Mary Grace was hiding behind. The ground was higher here, making it easy to see the two mounds.

She could hear cars pulling into the driveway. Then the field was ablaze with lights and people. Everyone stared at the ground as men with shovels approached the twin mounds. Everyone except Althea Vale, who stared at the tree as if she knew Mary Grace was concealed there. Her unblinking gaze never leaving that tree as they started digging . . .

THIRTY-NINE

The temperature is still climbing, drawing unsettling parallels to the record-breaking warmth back in early November of 1995, when two other girls vanished.

As if anyone needs reminding.

Some—the superstitious among them—are certain that the eerily similar weather pattern is an omen of worse to come. Though few could argue that the temperate climate makes it easier to continue the search, which has expanded beyond the woods. But dragging the no-longer frozen lakes of Repentance doesn't yield up a body, which is what most expect with Cherie Leigh now more than three days gone. Everyone knows that after the first forty-eight hours, the odds of her still being alive are greatly diminished.

Now prayers are going out to find Cherie Leigh so Tyler Lee can bury his only child the way Nadia Doshenko and Chloe Ann Briggs were given proper burials after their graves were unearthed in the field behind Althea Vale's house. Nadia's body was sent back to Russia to be laid in the plot next to her mama and Chloe Ann was buried in Repentance Cemetery, where generations of Briggses were interred.

As for Lucas Smith, he remains unapprehended.

And Althea Vale is on suicide watch.

⁂

Tuesday morning it's standing room only in the Repentance town hall, where a press conference is underway.

A reporter in the first row raises his hand. "Sheriff Dobbs, what can you tell us about what happened on Death Row yesterday morning?"

Mary Grace shifts the microphone on the table closer. "All I can say at this time is that Althea Vale is under observation at Mercy Hospital."

"Has she regained consciousness?"

"Yes."

Another hand goes up. "Is Vale's suicide attempt connected to Cherie Leigh Hibbard's disappearance?"

"We have no evidence to suggest that the two events are related."

"What about the newspaper found in Vale's cell?"

"According to our sources, the Repentance *Gazette* was delivered to the prisoner on a daily basis."

Jeremiah Jones, the longtime editor of the *Gazette*, raises his hand. "Is Vale behind Hibbard's disappearance?"

"There's no evidence to suggest that."

"Can you confirm that Vale hasn't had a single visitor in twenty-four years?" a reporter in the second row asks.

"Yes."

"What about letters and phone calls?"

"Any correspondences between prisoners and the outside world are carefully vetted by Death Row personnel. All calls are recorded and monitored. Inmates have no access to the Internet. If she were in communication with someone, we'd know."

"Is it true that Vale spends most of her free time in the prison chapel praying?" a reporter with the Fayetteville *Banner* asks.

"That is what we have been told."

"Is that why she chose rosary beads? And is there a connection to the rosaries Vale placed in the graves of Nadia Doshenko and Chloe Ann Briggs?"

"I can't answer that."

The next question comes from a reporter wearing a large gold cross. "When Vale confessed in '95, she said she buried the rosary beads with her victims to save their souls. Do you think she tried to swallow her rosary to save her own soul?"

Mary Grace takes a sip of water before answering. "We have no way of knowing what was in her mind."

"Are you going to find rosary beads buried with Hibbard's body?"

"How did Vale think she could save their souls by placing rosaries in the graves of victims who were Baptists?"

"Isn't that a sacrilege?"

"Althea Vale's religious leanings aren't pertinent here.'" Mary Grace remembers the rumors she'd heard as a child, of Vale attending a Lutheran church in the next town over. And, for the last twenty-four years, spending all her days on Death Row in prayer.

Because she has so much to feel guilty about.

"Do you think Hibbard was strangled like Doshenko and Briggs?"

"At this time there's no evidence to suggest that Cherie Leigh Hibbard is dead. The search for her is continuing. I'll take a few more questions." She acknowledges a reporter whose name tag identifies him as Christopher Bench.

"Was Darryl Stokes Althea Vale's accomplice?"

"There's no evidence to support that."

"Did he confess before he died?"

"No."

"Can you confirm that Darryl Stokes's DNA was found in the other cabin?"

"Yes."

"Is it true you've ruled out that the second set of DNA found in that cabin belongs to Cherie Leigh Hibbard?"

"Yes."

"Can you tell us whose DNA it is?"

"No. Next question."

"Why did Lucas Smith shoot Darryl Stokes?"

"You'd have to ask him."

"Was he trying to stop Stokes from getting away?"

"I can't answer that."

"Did Smith know Stokes was unarmed when he shot him?"

"Again, we have no way of knowing what was in his mind at the time."

"Is it true that the Salvationists are harboring Smith?"

"We don't know that for a fact."

"Is Smith the copycat?"

"That's part of an ongoing investigation."

"Was Smith trying to frame Stokes for his own crime?"

"Of course he was!" The question is answered before Mary Grace can respond. She recognizes Lucia Garcia, the Little Rock *Tribune* reporter. "It was all about promoting the Salvationist agenda," Garcia says. "When Stokes came back to Repentance, Smith saw his chance. Then he had to kill Stokes before anyone could find out he was innocent. That's why he shot an unarmed man. An unarmed black man."

"What's your proof that it wasn't Stokes?" a reporter with the Siloam Springs *Post* challenges Garcia.

"Blaming a dead man who can't defend himself is low, even from the media. Can't you leave us in peace?" Everyone stares at Cadence Mills. The black-garbed Footwasher stands at the back of the hall looking as if she were a disciple of Satan himself. "I haven't seen you in church lately, Jeremiah." The elderly reporter says nothing but doesn't meet her eyes. "Don't you know the only way to protect our children is to ask for His guidance? Instead of fighting for headlines, you should all be praying for Cherie Leigh."

"Is it true your father's dying of cancer?" someone asks.

"Will you be taking over his church?"

"Get out of here!" Mills shouts.

Mary Grace gets to her feet before things can escalate. "Thank you all for coming. As soon as we know something, you'll know. In the meantime, we could use volunteers to help with flyers and posters. Our tip line is open twenty-four-seven. Now if you'll excuse us. We have a missing girl to find."

Mary Grace leaves the dais, Conner beside her. Flashbulbs pop, momentarily blinding her, as someone thrusts a microphone in her face.

"If Cherie Leigh Hibbard's disappearance follows the same pattern as '95, do you anticipate another sixth grader being taken?"

The hall goes silent as everyone awaits Mary Grace's response.

"There's no evidence suggesting that Cherie Leigh was abducted."

"Are you saying she ran away?"

"We don't know that, either. That's why we've put safety measures in place."

"Is that why you've enforced a curfew like Owen Kanady did twenty-four years ago?"

"Yes. And until further notice, parents will continue to drive their children to school and pick them up. I hope you all have a safe and happy Thanksgiving."

That same morning, Jackson Briggs and Tyler Lee Hibbard are arraigned on kidnapping charges. Briggs is also charged with assault, threatening someone with a loaded firearm, and recklessly endangering another person.

An hour after Briggs and Hibbard plead out and are transported to a correctional facility in the next county, Parnell Vaughan III outs himself in the town square. The revelation that Vaughan was Darryl Stokes's lover, then and now, sets rumors flying that Vale, Vaughan, and Stokes were complicit in the '95 murders despite all the evidence pointing to Vale acting alone. At the very least, Stokes and Vaughan are the copycats in Cherie Leigh Hibbard's disappearance. Despite the absence of a motive or proof, some reason that if two men could lie together—a sin in the Baptist religion even if this is 2019—they could kill together, too.

Tuesday afternoon, Vaughan sparks further outrage by burying his lover in his family plot in Repentance Cemetery. That same day, as if God were punishing the town for its sins, a flu breaks out at Vaughan Elementary. Some see this as a pestilence, akin to one of the Seven Deadly Plagues, for failing to eradicate the Devil in their midst. Others fear it's happening because a man is dead by another man's hand, which ignites a furious debate:

Is the town being punished because Stokes was guilty?

Or because he was innocent?

FORTY

Thursday dawns cold and gray. Temperatures have been steadily dropping since Wednesday night, which, taken with the recent warming trend, is a disaster waiting to happen. Forecasters don't know exactly when it will hit, but nobody's taking any chances.

In homes all across northwest Arkansas, Thanksgiving dinner is pushed up several hours. When the sun peeks out at noon, some say it's God being bountiful, while others say it's because the holiday is really a celebration of Him. Still others say it's a time not to feast but to fast and pray. Another faction, Mary Grace's uncle among them, believing that Thanksgiving is a secular holiday having little to do with celebrating Christians' relationship with the Almighty.

But whatever thoughts Uncle Samuel shares with his Maker, he has never let them get in the way of the annual family gathering. And if his grand-niece isn't well enough to come to his house, as has been the custom since before Felicity was born, the Mathews family will come to her. Promptly at twelve-thirty they arrive at the Dobbs home with the twelve-pound turkey Uncle Samuel buys every year in Little Rock, always insisting it's the biggest bird they sell.

Mary Grace watches her daughter like a hawk all through dinner. When Felicity came down with the flu, she thought she was pretending in order to avoid the talk she knew they had to have. She'd been giving her mother the silent treatment ever since Mary Grace picked her up at her uncle's Tuesday morning to drive her to school. She never responded to the text Mary Grace sent the night before, when she told her daughter she loved her.

But Felicity couldn't fake a fever.

Today her temperature has returned to normal, but she's pale and listless. She picks at her food and barely talks to her cousins or uncle. Mary Grace can count on the fingers of one hand how many times she's been sick in her short lifetime and can't help seeing it as a sign.

By early evening, temperatures have dropped to below freezing, the ice storm now predicted to hit sometime this evening. God, as always, speaking through the weather.

Felicity's fever has inexplicably spiked again. Mary Grace can't call her pediatrician because a few minutes ago the power went out. Cell reception is spotty at best, and everyone has been ordered to stay indoors. Mary Grace sits at her daughter's bedside, holding cold compresses to her forehead that she fears will be of no avail because this is no ordinary flu. She remembers driving Felicity to school the first day of sixth grade, those terrifying few seconds when she couldn't see her in the rain. But her unease started before that, on the June morning she awoke to the unsettling sense of things starting up again.

She was right. And wrong. History is repeating itself, bringing everything full circle.

It's as if the last twenty-four years have been leading up to this, the clock ticking down to the hour almost a quarter of a century ago when she sealed her parents' fate. That was the night she allowed evil to take root in her soul. Compounding her sin the following November when two sixth graders disappeared, one the best friend she loved and hated, the other a bully who'd tormented her all her life.

When they unearthed the first grave, Chloe Ann was lying there in the navy blazer she wore the first day of sixth grade, the backpack with the yellow canaries next to her body. She was wearing her school uniform and backpack on Friday too, the day after Mary Grace almost strangled her to death in the schoolyard. So shocked to see her in class, thinking what was inside her wasn't so strong after all. Until Chloe Ann disappeared later that day.

When they dug up the second grave, she thought she'd jump out of her skin, even though she knew who was buried there. She looked so alive. Any minute she expected Nadia to leap up from the earth, point at the tree Mary Grace was hiding behind and tell everyone that it was her fault she was dead.

Not the person who'd just been arrested, the teacher Mary Grace adored. Althea Vale never gave a detailed statement, letting the corpses in her field speak for her. When later asked why she killed them, her response proved she wasn't in her right mind. Who else but a madwoman would call two innocent children evil? Request to be sentenced to Death Row instead of pleading not guilty by reason of insanity at trial? Reject the lesser sentence of life without the possibility of parole that the District Attorney offered in exchange for having confessed at her house and revealing the location of the graves?

Mary Grace was the only one who understood. What she didn't know was why Vale stopped with Nadia and Chloe Ann.

That's the question that has haunted her all these years.

If Althea Vale killed those girls because they were evil, why did she spare Mary Grace, whom they both knew was the most evil of all?

"Mama?"

"I'm right here, sweetheart." She tries to smile reassuringly as she smoothes Felicity's hair back from her damp forehead. All she cares about is making her well. Over the past twenty-four hours, she has tried to bargain with God: If He spares her daughter, she'll be a better person. She'll be the mother her child needs.

"Can you get under the covers with me?"

Felicity hasn't asked her that since she was a little girl. Mary Grace climbs into bed with her. As Felicity drifts off, she remembers when she came back to Repentance, her belly just starting to swell with life. After high school she'd left town, no longer able to live with the guilt and sorrow. She spent three wild years sleeping around, trying to rip Parnell from her mind and heart. She never knew who the father was, making up a story that he died when Felicity asked years later. Ready to kill the baby growing inside her, sure that she'd burn in hell.

But her aunt would have none of it. Abortion might be a sin, but that wasn't the only reason she was against it. Hester Mathews always wanted a daughter. It was why she stopped Mary Grace from putting her baby up for adoption when she was born, still with no name. She took care of that, too. She named her Felicity, for joy.

Mary Grace gazes at her daughter's face, so serene and innocent in sleep, and thinks how close she once came to losing her.

Parnell's last words on her porch float into her mind.

"Wait until it happens to you. Wait until you lose someone you love."

At the press conference, she was asked if she believed that another sixth grader would be taken. She thought (or tried to make herself think) that there would be no more victims. Cherie Leigh was personal, her punishment for almost strangling Tyler Lee twenty-four years ago.

She'd been deceiving herself.

Two then. Two now.

God's perfect symmetry.

But she never imagined that it would be by His hand, with no human intermediary.

Whatever mistakes Felicity has made can be laid at her door. She can't let her child pay for her sins.

She won't let Him take her without a fight.

Wind and ice rattle the windows as Mary Grace tucks the down comforter more snugly around her daughter's shivering body. Felicity's fever still hasn't broken, her downward spiral paralleling the track of the storm.

As the hands of the clock on Felicity's nightstand inch toward nine o'clock, Mary Grace leaves her vigil at her daughter's bedside and goes downstairs. Just like she did the night her parents called her into the living room to say they were sending her to Baptist Day. Racing from the room, throwing open the front door and running out into the ice storm.

She stumbles back as freezing rain hits her face, drenching her like she's being baptized anew as she shouts her sins to the heavens. But the wind keeps throwing back echoes of her voice just like it threw back her daddy's voice the night he went looking for her. It's as if something is stopping her from confessing, has always stopped her. Because of what's inside her.

But isn't God stronger than the Devil? Why won't He let her repent to save her child?

The wind slams the door shut and she has her answer.

"Mama!"

She races back through the entry hall, takes the stairs two at a time.

Felicity's thrashing about on the bed. She tries to talk, but her teeth chatter so hard Mary Grace can't make out the words. Felicity grasps her arm with icy fingers, her eyes full of fear as she whispers Cherie Leigh's name.

Mary Grace remembers Felicity telling Noah she wasn't scared of anything the day she found those lost softballs in the woods. But how could she not be afraid, with her classmate and fellow Mockingbird player missing? "I know you're scared, but don't worry sweetheart. I won't let anything happen to you."

Felicity's fingers dig into her skin. "Promise?"

"Promise."

Under the comforter, she's still trembling and Mary Grace fears it's a promise she won't be able to keep. Then she remembers her daughter's old security blanket. She gently disengages Felicity's fingers from her arm and goes to the closet. The blanket isn't in its usual spot on the middle shelf. Then she spies it at the back of the top shelf. She's reaching for it when Felicity screams, sending Mary Grace racing back to her bed.

"Don't leave me!"

"I won't."

She keeps that promise. She doesn't move from her daughter's side.

FORTY-ONE

Mary Grace startles awake, surprised to find herself sitting upright in the chair she now vaguely recalls bringing over after Felicity fell asleep.

Her daughter isn't in her bed. The sheets and comforter are tossed to the side as if she got out of bed in a hurry. Mary Grace goes into the hall. The bathroom's empty. Maybe Felicity's fever broke and she woke up hungry. She barely ate Thanksgiving dinner. Mary Grace goes to the top of the stairs, but there's no light coming from the kitchen. The house is completely dark. And silent. No tree branches battering the window. The wind appears to have died down.

She hears a noise and realizes that's what woke her. It's coming from the basement. In her bedroom, her hands shake as she removes her gun from its holster. She races down the stairs, tries to remember if she locked the outside basement door.

She's at the entrance to the basement when she hears it again: someone bumping against a piece of furniture. Lucas? Would he be brazen enough to steal into her house and abduct her sleeping daughter while her useless mother slept five feet away?

Her hand tightens on her gun. If it is Lucas, he'll be armed. She starts down the steps, trying to adjust to the dark. She can make out the outlines of familiar things.

The ping pong table Felicity begged her to buy one Christmas, then promptly lost interest in; the bicycle her daughter rarely rides anymore hanging on a wall; the ice skates she bought when Felicity turned ten. A lump rises in her throat as she stops at the bottom. And listens. Silence answers her. She moves across the basement with her weapon raised, eyes searching the gloom.

The outside door is bolted from the inside, the lock intact. The room's only two windows are also locked. There's no sign of forced entry, nothing to indicate that anyone broke in. Then she hears it: the uneven rasp of someone trying to hold their breath.

As she tiptoes across the concrete floor, shadows dance on the wall. Then one shadow detaches itself from the others. And disappears.

Footsteps sound behind her. She whirls around and starts to run, almost colliding with the chest of drawers she brought down here after her daughter asked for a new dresser. Someone's moving around behind it. Mary Grace creeps around the side, stops when she sees who it is.

"Felicity? What are you doing down here? Are you all right?"

She doesn't respond. She looks almost ethereal in her white nightgown, eyes huge in her face. Mary Grace pockets her gun and shines her phone light at the ceiling. When she pulls down the cord the overhead bulb goes on, illuminating what Felicity's holding. Her old security blanket that was on the top shelf of her closet.

Felicity's backing away, still cradling the blanket. Is she walking in her sleep? Fever making her delirious? "It's okay, honey. There's no reason to be afraid. I'm here now." She walks toward her, which only makes Felicity back up more. Then she turns and runs. She trips on one of her skates and drops the blanket, which clatters to the floor. She grabs for it, but Mary Grace gets there first. She picks up the blanket and pulls out the object that was concealed in its folds.

It's the MVP softball trophy she was so sure her daughter would win, especially after Felicity struck out the rival team's star hitter in the final inning of the championship game a few weeks back. Instead, she was named Top Pitcher and awarded a plaque Mary Grace has prominently displayed on the living room bookcase. Swallowing her own disappointment that Felicity didn't bring home the grand prize she herself was cheated of winning in '95 because the championship wasn't played that year.

But the Most Valuable Player is the athlete who makes the biggest contribution to the team's success, and it was decided that another Mockingbird met that requirement.

Mary Grace stares at the bronze statuette in shock. "Why do you have Cherie Leigh's trophy?" Still Felicity says nothing. "That's why you screamed when I went to get the blanket, isn't it?" She looks at the chest of drawers. "Were you going to hide it in your old dresser?"

"No!"

"Then why are you down here?"

"I thought you'd hear me if I used the front door."

"What are you talking about?"

Felicity looks at the trophy in her mother's hands, her eyes no longer clouded with fever. "I was going to try to sneak it back into Tyler Lee's house."

"Why? You still haven't told me what it's doing here in the first place. Did you steal it?"

"I'm not a thief!" Felicity's voice echoes through the basement.

"Then how'd it get here?"

"I can't tell. I promised."

"Promised who?"

"She's my best friend!"

"Are you talking about Lauren Reeves? What did you promise her?" Felicity stares down at the floor. "Did Lauren steal the trophy?"

"Nobody stole it!"

"Then how did it get here? I know about the bullying, Felicity. The terrible things Lauren said to Yochi Chajon. We'll talk about that later. Right now I want to know what Cherie Leigh's trophy is doing in our house and I want the truth, young lady." When her daughter remains silent she goes on. "Okay. I'm grounding you. Your internet and social media privileges are suspended."

"You can't do that!"

"And I'm calling Lauren's mother."

"No! She'll kill me!"

"You leave me no choice."

"Please, mom!" Felicity studies her mother, trying to figure out if she'll make good on her threat. Then she lets out a sigh. "It was Lauren's idea."

"What was Lauren's idea?"

"To initiate Cherie Leigh."

"Into the popular club?" Felicity nods. "What was the initiation?"

"I don't know. Lauren wouldn't tell me. But it was a total fake out. Like Cherie Leigh was really going to be a popular girl. Yeah, right. Lauren just told her that."

"Why?" Mary Grace once again sees the yearning look on Cherie Leigh's face after the Mockingbirds' semifinal game.

"To get her to meet us. Lauren kept texting me asking where I was. But she knew I wasn't allowed to go there. I must have told her like a hundred times. Plus I had a ton of homework. I wanted to make sure I got Straight As on my next report card." She smiles at her mother, who doesn't smile back.

"Not allowed to go where?"

"The woods. And I haven't disobeyed. Not once since Halloween, I swear."

"When was this?"

Felicity's gaze slides away. "After school last Friday."

The day Cherie Leigh disappeared. Mary Grace's heart has started beating against her ribs like something trying to get out. "What happened in the woods?"

"Nothing!"

"Don't lie to me."

"I'm not!"

"How do you know nothing happened if you weren't there?"

"Because when I didn't show, Lauren called and said she was changing up the plan. She told me to meet them at the cave."

"What cave?"

"The one you used to take me to when I was little, don't you remember? I brought the twins once and Lauren thought it was so cool that nobody knew about it."

"Did you go?"

"Promise you won't punish me."

"Tell me."

"I don't feel good. I think my fever's higher. You should take my temperature."

"We're not leaving here until you answer me!"

Felicity flinches at her tone. "I had to go! Lauren said if I didn't, I was out of the club. And I wasn't disobeying because you didn't say the cave was off limits." She looks at Mary Grace, who says nothing. "When I got there, Lauren told me to take a picture of Cherie Leigh holding her trophy to put on Instagram."

"Cherie Leigh brought the trophy?"

"Lauren told her to. She said it was part of the initiation. After I took the picture, Lauren told Cherie Leigh to take a picture with me holding the trophy."

"Why?"

Felicity's gaze slides to the statuette in Mary Grace's hands. "Lauren wanted to post both photos online and let everyone vote who they thought was the true championship winner. Cherie Leigh got mad and said she won the trophy fair and square. She looked at me like it was my fault! Lauren said if she didn't take the picture, she'd never be in the club. Finally Cherie Leigh gave me the trophy and took the picture. When she asked for the trophy back, Lauren grabbed it from me and told Cherie Leigh she'd have to wait and see how the kids voted. Cherie Leigh said she'd tell Coach Gould if Lauren didn't give it back. Lauren laughed and said she should try and get it."

Felicity's talking faster and faster, the words exploding out of her mouth. "Cherie Leigh tried to grab it from Lauren, but she tripped on one of those stalagmites sticking out of the floor. After she fell, she wasn't, like, moving or anything. I thought she was faking to get back at us. But Lauren kept screaming that she was dead and we better get out of there. Then Cherie Leigh woke up and said she was going to tell everyone we stole her trophy. Lauren told her to shut up. Then she pushed her, really hard. Cherie Leigh must have hit her head on the limestone ledge because this time she didn't get up."

As Felicity stops to catch her breath, Mary Grace feels her knees giving way. If the dresser hadn't been there, she would surely have fallen down.

"Lauren said we had to get rid of the body or we'd go to jail. I told her we should call you and you'd tell us what to do. She said I was stupid if I thought you'd do us special favors just because you're sheriff. She said she heard somewhere that water can wash away DNA so she made me and Haley drag Cherie Leigh's body into the rushing waters."

"You left her there? In the cave?" The room has started to spin. Mary Grace can't seem to get any air into her lungs.

"Lauren said no one would know what happened because no one would find her and even if they did they wouldn't be able to pin it on us."

"You didn't take her pulse to see if she was still alive?"

"Lauren said she was dead. I didn't know what to do." She starts to cry. "I was so scared."

But not scared enough to leave the trophy behind.

Mary Grace feels the weight of it in her hands. The trophy she never held before. The trophy she never got the chance to win.

"Lauren made me take the trophy," Felicity says as she swipes at her tears, with that uncanny knack for intuiting her mother's thoughts. "She said I was the true winner and it belonged to me."

Mary Grace remembers how the Reeves twins never missed a single one of Felicity's games. But that wasn't the reason Lauren made Felicity take the trophy. She wanted leverage in case Felicity ever told. Lauren could say the whole thing was Felicity's idea because Felicity was the one who lost first place to Cherie Leigh. Which would make her daughter a coconspirator in her death.

"I know I should have told you right away, but I was scared. Then you searched the lakes and I was afraid you'd get to the cave eventually. You'd find it and then I'd go to jail for sure!"

"Find what?"

"Cherie Leigh's phone! She must have dropped it when she fell. I forgot all about it until I went back to school Monday. I was going to go back to the cave and look for it. I had the whole thing planned out. I'd go home with the twins after school. They'd never say anything if I snuck out. But you made me go to Uncle Samuel's. I was so mad at you! Then I got sick."

For six days her daughter has been harboring this terrible secret. Mary Grace knows all about keeping secrets.

"Mom, you have to get it!"

"Why is it so important?"

"It's on her phone!"

"What is?"

"The picture Lauren made Cherie Leigh take of me!"

Then Mary Grace gets it. It's the photo of Felicity holding the trophy. The one that puts her daughter at the cave the day the other girl disappeared. "What about the photo you took of Cherie Leigh?"

"I already deleted it."

Of course she would have. Why isn't Mary Grace surprised?

"Mom?" Felicity looks about to burst into tears again. "I'm sorry."

The magical two words that bring forgiveness and absolution without having to actually confess your sins. If it were only that simple.

It can't change what happened.

It won't bring back Cherie Leigh.

FORTY-TWO

Mary Grace watches the sun rising in the east as she sits on the porch rocking, oblivious to the cold, her gaze fixed on the two objects on the table. One the three-pound statuette her daughter wanted so desperately to win. The other containing the proof of how far she'd go to keep it for herself.

When she parked at the foot of the mountain almost seven hours earlier, it was as if a hush had come over everything. No precipitation fell from the sky; not a single tree branch moved. Moonlight shone on a world that was almost preternaturally still. No sounds of life, no birdsong to lighten her way. Not at that hour, just past midnight the morning after Thanksgiving.

A thin coating of ice covered the ground as she got out of her car. The stars shining from the inky sky seemed to mock her. As she began to climb, slowly because it was slippery going and she was on the lookout for black ice, she felt like a thief in the night. Memories of the last time she was here assailed her. Not when she brought Felicity here as a child, but that long-ago August day with her heart still heavy with grief and guilt.

When she reached the mouth of the cave, she had to duck to avoid hitting her head; something she didn't have to do at eleven. It was just as she remembered: the stalactite hanging from the roof above the limestone ledge where she ate her peanut butter sandwich and started talking to her parents. Until Tyler Lee showed up.

Twenty-four years later, his daughter died here.

Dread lodged in her chest as she approached the ledge, where she could see traces of dried blood where Cherie Leigh had hit her head.

Then came the hard part.

She'd arrived prepared: thigh-high boots for wading into the deep waters. She heard it before she took a step: the roar that had almost drowned out her voice as she begged her parents to forgive her. The sound of the rushing water growing louder as she headed deeper inside, her flashlight illuminating the rivers of water that cascaded down the limestone walls and flooded the cave floor, reaching to the tops of her boots. She was halfway across the cave when she saw it: a backpack bobbing up and down in the churning waters. Then, a few minutes later: a young girl's sneaker.

Outside again she threw up, taking in heaving gulps of cold night air until she could breathe. She was back in her car and about to leave when she remembered the phone. She found it lodged behind the limestone ledge where she'd missed it before. Where Cherie Leigh must have dropped it when Lauren pushed her. She picked it up with the latex gloves she'd brought, knowing she was corrupting a crime scene. Tampering with evidence. The phone screen was black; the battery had run down. Six days in the elements would do that.

After she left the cave, she texted her daughter, who'd been texting nonstop asking if she found the phone. Then she got in her car and drove to a 7-Eleven that sold the charger that fit Cherie Leigh's smartphone. At an all-night bar, she ordered a Scotch straight up while the phone charged in an outlet behind the bar. When it came back to life, she tried a few combinations to get past the password-protected screen. She got in on her third attempt—the month and date of Cherie Leigh's birthday which she found on her Facebook page, followed by Cherie Leigh's Mockingbird team number—fourteen—that was emblazoned on the back of her uniform.

After tapping the camera icon at the top right-hand side of the screen, she swiped down to the photo gallery, to the last photo Cherie Leigh took. At first glance it looked exactly like the one next to it. She could see Felicity in both and figured Cherie Leigh took the picture twice in case the first one didn't come out. When she tapped the last one, there was her daughter looking flush with victory as she held up the MVP trophy. But in the middle of the image was a black arrow inside a white circle. She hesitated, then tapped the arrow, bringing the image to life. The whole thing lasted only a couple of seconds. A few minutes later, she paid her tab and left, ignoring the bartender who asked if she was all right. At the side of the road, she stopped and threw up again.

When she got home and played it, Felicity's eyes flashed with anger. "I can't believe it! She was recording me?"

The same anger Mary Grace saw on the video when Cherie Leigh said she was going to tell Coach Gould that Felicity stole her trophy if she didn't give it back. Felicity saying it was hers, that she was the true winner. Then Cherie Leigh's hand—the one not holding the phone on which she was secretly recording—moving into the video as she tried to grab for the trophy. Felicity raising it higher above her head.

For a heart-stopping moment, Mary Grace thought her daughter was going to strike the other girl with the statuette. Then Cherie Leigh grabbed for it again and there was a lot of yelling as the girls struggled for possession. That must have been when Cherie Leigh tripped on the stalagmite and lost her balance. Mary Grace could hear her screams as she fell. The thud as she hit the ground, the rushing water in the background a chilling counterpoint.

That was where the video stopped, after Cherie Leigh's phone must have slipped from her hands: on Felicity's horrified face.

After the video ended, it returned to the beginning of the loop: Felicity smiling as she posed with the trophy.

Dead silence followed, broken eventually by Felicity's plaintive voice. "I didn't know she'd hit her head, I swear."

"You lied to me." As if that were her worst crime. "You said Lauren grabbed the trophy from you."

"She did that after. When Cherie Leigh woke up and said she was going to tell everyone we stole it."

"When? I don't see or hear Lauren in this video. Were she and her sister even there?"

"Yes! You just couldn't see them in the video."

"I don't believe you."

"It's true! The whole thing was Lauren's idea. I've got proof." She pulled out her phone and started swiping the screen. "See? Lauren kept texting from the woods. Just like I said."

Mary Grace read the messages, all asking where Felicity was. "That doesn't prove anything."

"Cherie Leigh tripped! You saw it yourself!"

"Whose idea was it to go to the cave? To post the photos online? That was a lie too, wasn't it? Why would Lauren care if everyone voted for you or Cherie Leigh? She wasn't the one who lost first place. It was you. I saw it all on the video." And wished she hadn't. Wished she'd never found the phone.

Felicity didn't speak for so long Mary Grace feared she was trying to come up with another story. But when she looked at her mother, her face was as serious as she'd ever seen her. "You're right. I have to stop lying or I'll go to hell for sure. It's true. The twins weren't there."

Mary Grace didn't know whether that made her feel better or worse.

"I lied about that, too. After Cherie hit her head, she didn't wake up. I kept calling her name, but she didn't move. All I could think was she was dead and it was my fault. Then I panicked. I didn't know what to do. That's why I dragged her into the water." Felicity shook her head. "I know what I did was wrong. The Bible says it's a sin to covet what belongs to somebody else. But I wanted to be the one bringing home the trophy. I wanted you to be proud of me."

In spite of herself, Mary Grace felt her heart soften. "I was always proud of you."

Felicity looked at her as if she didn't believe her. "I couldn't stand keeping secrets from you. Having it all bottled up inside. I feel so awful for what I did. It made me sick."

And she'd carry that guilt for the rest of her life. Something Mary Grace was on intimate terms with. "You should have told me."

"I know. If I could take it back, I would. Please don't hate me. I couldn't stand it if you did. After—after Cherie Leigh was dead, I asked her to forgive me even though I knew it was too late. I felt so alone. Do you think God will forgive me?"

It was what Mary Grace has wondered for twenty-four years. "I don't know."

"Only He and I know what happened." Felicity looked at her mother. "And now you know."

That was three hours ago.

She was only able to get Felicity to bed by reassuring her that she wouldn't arrest her. As she sits rocking on the porch, Mary Grace thinks about things coming full circle. Her daughter asking Cherie Leigh to forgive her in the same place where, twenty-four years ago, Mary Grace asked her parents to forgive her.

The sins of the mother passed on to her child? But it was an accident. Cherie Leigh tripped; she saw it herself. Why should Felicity be punished for it?

And isn't Mary Grace partially to blame? She made softball such an important part of her life from the time her daughter could run, hoping she'd love it the way she had. And wasn't there a part of her that lived vicariously through her victories? That wanted her to win the trophy as badly as Felicity did?

Something that should have brought such joy.

Instead it resulted in another girl's death.

And no one knows except Mary Grace and her daughter.

And God.

She leans on the shovel and wipes the sweat from her face even though it's cold out here. It wasn't easy to find the right spot: beneath the enormous pine at the western edge of her property that, like all the houses on this side of town, abuts the woods. And then it took the hand-held auger that's been gathering dust in the garage to bore a hole in the still partially frozen ground. The shovel did the rest.

She looks down at her handiwork. She didn't need a deep hole. It didn't even have to be as big as the one Noah dug for the raccoon he butchered. Her eyes move to the trophy leaning against the tree. The moonlight has turned the brass to liquid gold. Inside the oblong circle dotted with stars is a girl swinging a bat the way Mary Grace taught Felicity. *Vaughan Elementary Sixth Grade MVP* engraved in bold black letters on the marble pedestal.

A cloud moves across the moon, turning the night dark as pitch. She shivers, sees the dead raccoon hanging by its tail. Hears her eleven-year-old self telling her cousin how the Bible said it was a sin to kill.

The shallow grave yawns before her, awaiting its two occupants. Once she buries Cherie Leigh's trophy and phone, she'll have betrayed the oath she took as sheriff. Broken the law she swore to uphold. But she also vowed to protect her child. She promised Felicity she wouldn't let anything happen to her.

The cloud moves, revealing the moon once more. And a sky agleam with dozens of stars. She can feel Him watching as she picks up the two objects and drops them into the freshly dug hole. Then, before she can change her mind, she shovels in dirt. After it's done, she gets the hose and washes off the shovel, just like Noah did after he made her bury the raccoon.

Back inside the house she climbs the stairs, her arms aching from the unaccustomed exertion. Felicity's fast asleep. She looks so small and defenseless in Mary Grace's bed, where she begged to sleep tonight. As if sensing her mother's presence, Felicity's eyes flutter open. Mary Grace goes over and sits on the bed. She smooths her hair back from her forehead. Her daughter sighs and goes back to sleep.

Guilt overwhelms her as she thinks about what she just did. But what parent wouldn't try to save her child? Even it it means she'll burn in hell. Is that why God wouldn't let her repent? Maybe it's another test. It isn't enough for her to confess her sins. She has to confess her daughter's as well.

She remembers that long-ago night at supper after she tried to strangle Chloe Ann in the schoolyard. Terrified that Owen Kanady was coming for her and instead of all the lies she'd been telling, the truth would pop out. Then everyone would know how evil she was even if God forgave her. Except Kanady never came and the next day Chloe Ann was gone and she went right on lying and keeping secrets.

Is this her chance to redeem herself at last? By sacrificing her only child?

Save her daughter or save her soul.

She already made her choice.

FORTY-THREE

The media is waiting when the sheriff's cruiser pulls up.

"Is Cherie Leigh Hibbard in that cave?"

"Who called in the tip?"

"Was it Lucas Smith?"

"Why'd he choose this place?"

"Did he think no one would find it?"

"Was he feeling remorse?"

"What about Althea Vale?"

"Is that why she tried to kill herself?"

"Have you been to see Vale since she was moved back to Death Row?"

"We can't comment at this time."

Mary Grace and Conner push past the microphones and cameras to join Sheriff Mathis and Chief Deputy Landers, who just parked nearby.

The reporters follow, still hurling questions, as law enforcement from three towns starts up the mountain Mary Grace trudged up less than half a day earlier. It's even colder today, but the sun bouncing off the peak is so bright it's blinding. She feels the weight of her guilt dragging her down as she climbs, grateful for the sunglasses that conceal the secrets in her eyes. Just like when she was a child and believed that everyone could see the evil glowing inside her like the Devil's light.

When she told Felicity where she was going, her daughter begged her to leave Cherie Leigh in her watery grave, to not reveal the secret only the two of them knew. And God, Mary Grace reminding her that she'd asked for His forgiveness. And wasn't Felicity the one who said she wanted to sneak the trophy back into Tyler Lee's house? So how could they deny him the chance to bury his only child?

That was what decided her. She had to think of a way to give Tyler Lee closure without implicating her daughter. After washing the damp earth from her hands, she got in her car and drove to a town over an hour away, where she bought a disposable phone.

Two hours later, she called Conner and told him about the anonymous tip. When he asked if she was able to trace the call, she said it didn't last long enough. The call woke her from a deep sleep, having rolled over from the office phone to her cell. The caller told her where Cherie Leigh's body was. She didn't think it was a crank.

They've reached the top, where everyone stops to catch their breath. As they duck down to enter the cave, the reporters start to follow them inside. Mathis holds up a hand. "You can't come in here."

"I don't see any crime scene tape," Jeremiah Jones says. "Which means it's not an official crime scene. We have as much right to be here as you do."

"No, you don't. You have a problem with that, take it up with your congressman." Mathis puts his hand on his holster. "Now get out of here, or I'll arrest you for obstructing justice."

The reporters don't leave; instead, they congregate outside the cave. Deputy Landers follows the sheriff inside. "If Smith's the copycat, he picked the perfect kill site. Don't know if we ever would have searched here."

"It's off the beaten track, that's for sure," Mathis says. "A lot of tourists don't even know about it."

"Good way to make sure she's never found."

"So what happened? He was suddenly overcome with guilt?" Conner looks skeptical.

"Could be." Mathis turns to Mary Grace. "You sure you didn't recognize his voice?"

Mary Grace shakes her head. She feels like the worst kind of hypocrite, betraying her badge and everything it stands for.

A few minutes later, Landers calls out. "Over here. I've got something. Looks like dried blood on the ledge."

"I think we found our crime scene," Mathis says, reaching for his walkie-talkie.

"So where's the body?"

The two men look at Conner. Then they all hear it: the sound of rushing water.

"ME's finishing up his exam," Conner says when Mary Grace walks into the office later than usual Monday morning. "Should be hearing any minute. How's Felicity?"

She takes her time hanging up her coat. "She still has the flu."

Felicity spent most of the weekend besieging her mother with questions, terrified she'd be caught. Her fear spreading to Mary Grace, who told herself that even on the remote chance they found DNA that didn't belong to Cherie Leigh, there was no way anyone would know it was Felicity's, who has never been arrested and isn't in any database.

"For the past three days I've been asking myself, could Lucas have done this? And why Cherie Leigh Hibbard?" Conner pushes away from his desk and heads for the coffee machine. "If the Salvationists really are behind it, why was she targeted? Or was she just collateral damage?" He shakes his head as he picks up the carafe and pours. "That's what gets me. The randomness of it all." He adds milk to one and two lumps to the other, then brings the steaming mugs over to Mary Grace's desk. "Althea Vale has to be the one pulling the strings. I called Death Row this morning. They're still not allowing any visitors." He sips his coffee, eyes her over the top of the mug. "You getting any sleep? You look like hell."

"Maybe I caught Felicity's flu."

He's still looking at her when the phone on her desk shrills. She jumps. It continues to ring. Conner reaches for it. She shoves his arm away and grabs the phone, almost knocking over her coffee.

"Repentance Sheriff's office," she says, feeling Conner's eyes on her.

"Morning, Sheriff Dobbs."

"Morning." She can barely get the word past her thick tongue. In the background, she hears the sound of shuffling papers. She pictures Parker Crook, Repentance's longtime medical examiner, at his desk next door to the morgue, surrounded by death but never personally touched by it. Because his conscience is clear.

"Got a cause of death on the Hibbard girl."

Conner just pulled up a chair; Mary Grace is sure he can hear her heart thundering against her ribs.

"It wasn't easy, what with her being in the water for near on a week."

Mary Grace almost lost it when the county sheriff's forensics unit pulled Cherie Leigh from the rushing waters, her blue, bloated corpse a world away from the graceful athlete who won the MVP trophy her daughter wanted so badly. She can still hear Tyler Lee's wails as he stood in the morgue surrounded by his police escort from prison, swearing that the body on the table wasn't his daughter.

". . . had one hell of a bruise on the back of her skull. I won't know for sure until I analyze the wound, but it's consistent with her hitting her head on that ledge."

"So it was an accident?" In her mind's eye seeing Cherie Leigh on the video as she grabbed for the trophy, then tripped on the stalagmite.

"Did you hear me say that? Don't put words in my mouth. Maybe it was. Or maybe she was pushed. Doesn't matter, though."

"Why not?"

"Trauma to her head wasn't what killed her. My first thought was she drowned."

"Drowned?" she repeats stupidly, aware of Conner's indrawn breath next to her.

"Because of the condition of the body. Near as I can figure, whoever killed her dragged her into the water, hoping her body'd be washed deeper inside. But if she drowned, there'd have been water in her lungs. And there was only air. Which means she was dead before she hit the water. If I wasn't so distracted about where she was found, I might have been on the lookout for it sooner."

"Lookout for what?"

"Petechial hemorrhaging. When I examined her eyes, I could see it. The bruises on her neck were harder to detect, but I have no doubt. Cherie Leigh Hibbard was strangled. Same as the other girls. Way I figure, she fell and hit her head. She tried to get away, but the killer was too quick. After she was dead, he dragged her body into the waters hoping the physical evidence would be washed away. I don't care if it's a blasphemy, I pray whoever did this rots in hell."

But Mary Grace is no longer listening, Crook's voice so much white noise in her head. She's dimly aware of him saying her name, then Conner taking the phone from her. Walking her outside to her car, saying she should go home and get some rest.

Mary Grace sits in her driveway, staring up at the second-story window.

A shadow moves across the curtains; then a face appears. A few minutes later, the front door opens and Felicity comes outside. It's a bright, sunny day, but the porch remains in shadow save for the white of her nightgown. The part of Mary Grace's mind that still works wants to tell her to go back inside before she catches her death. As if death were contagious, something passed from young girl to young girl.

Felicity runs down the porch steps. She sprints to the car, raps on the window. Mary Grace shrinks back in her seat as if the creature out there wasn't flesh born of her flesh, but something feral and dangerous.

Felicity's rapping harder now, mouthing words Mary Grace can't hear. Observing with that detached part of her mind how quickly her daughter's frustration turns to anger, something she never noticed before. As Felicity's eyes darken with fury—those hazel-specked-with-gold irises a mirror image of her own—she pulls the key from the ignition and opens the door. Taken unawares, Felicity stumbles back. Mary Grace pushes past her and heads for the house. She's approaching the porch when she hears her come up from behind.

She whirls around. "Get inside." For one crazy second, she thought her daughter was going to attack her.

"Crook told you, didn't he? He's old and makes mistakes all the time. Everyone says so."

"I said go into the house!"

Once inside she locks the door, Felicity watching her every move. "I'm sorry. Please don't be mad."

"Upstairs! Now!"

Felicity's expression turns mutinous, the way it did as a child when she didn't get her way. And at Vaughan Elementary, when Mary Grace wouldn't let her go home with the Reeves twins. That was when her daughter told her she hated her. Felicity looks at her mother as if she knows what she's thinking, then turns and runs up the steps. At the top, she races into her room and slams the door. When Mary Grace throws it open she's already in bed, cowering under the comforter.

"It wasn't my fault," she whines.

It never is, Mary Grace thinks.

"Are you going to arrest me?"

She follows Felicity's gaze, surprised to see her right hand resting on her gunbelt.

Once, when her daughter was five, newly appointed assistant sheriff Mary Grace arrived home and took off her gunbelt as usual. The landline rang and she spent the next half hour trying to calm a resident who swore he'd seen a black bear on his property. When she got off the phone, her heart nearly stopped. Felicity had taken her revolver out of the holster and was playing with it. Her heart didn't start back up again until she got the gun safely away from her. From then on, the first thing she did after taking off her gunbelt was to remove the bullets from her weapon. Today she did neither.

"What happened after Cherie Leigh tripped?"

Felicity's eyes are still on the gunbelt. "I didn't want to hurt her. But then she woke up and started screaming that she was going to tell everyone I stole her trophy!"

She sits up in bed. "You're not going to put me in jail, are you? I'm only twelve. Mom? Where are you going?" She jumps out of bed and races across the carpet. But Mary Grace is quicker. She runs out of the room, pulling the door closed behind her. Then she locks it, something she hasn't done since her daughter was a little girl.

"What are you going to do?" Felicity rattles the doorknob to no avail. She bangs on the door. "Let me out! Please! Mama! I love you!"

Lying in bed long after Felicity has tired herself out, Mary Grace can still hear echoes of her pounding on the door. She pictures her daughter's fists beating against the wood, the same hands that wielded a bat and curved around a softball. And strangled Cherie Leigh. Then she sees her eleven-year-old self that hot August day, hands around Tyler Lee's throat.

Did she pass on evil to her child like a thin or fat gene? Or the color of her eyes? Evil so powerful that Althea Vale finished what Mary Grace started in the schoolyard that long-ago Thursday. Strangling Chloe Ann three days after she strangled Nadia.

She must have dozed off. When she startles awake, her heart's racing. If she dreamed, she can't remember. When her mind finally clears, she realizes what's bothering her.

Felicity wasn't born when Nadia and Chloe Ann were killed. Yet twenty-four years later, she murdered a classmate in the exact same way. Then Mary Grace thinks about Althea Vale trying to swallow her rosary beads after Cherie Leigh disappeared.

What is she missing here?

The next morning, she makes her second call to Death Row. The first was when she learned about Althea Vale's suicide attempt. She explains that there have been developments in the Hibbard case and it's critical that she see Vale.

After leaving a breakfast tray for her daughter, who looks like an angel in sleep, she locks her bedroom door again and leaves the house. She stops for gas at a station just outside town and fills the tank for the three-hour drive to visit a woman she hasn't laid eyes on in twenty-four years.

PART III

FORTY-FOUR

In the visitors' room at the Arkansas Department of Correction, Mary Grace watches as Althea Vale is brought in.

The manacles around her ankles clank as she comes toward her; her wrists are shackled to a long chain at the waistband of her orange jumpsuit. The wavy brown hair she always wore parted in the middle has turned white, and what's left of it has been shorn off. Her skin is pale, her face gaunt. She has gotten so thin she looks almost spectral; a ghost of herself. Only her eyes—behind silver-rimmed glasses Mary Grace has never seen before—belong to the woman she remembers.

Eyes the color of grass after a hard rain.

That was what struck her the first day of school when Althea Vale turned from the blackboard to welcome her sixth-grade class. Eyes that radiated kindness and seemed to smile along with her mouth, lighting up her pretty face—a smile Mary Grace felt was meant for her alone. Eyes brimming with her own unshed tears as she held her in her arms after Mary Grace told her the partial truth about the night her parents died, saying there was good and evil in all of us.

The eyes of a killer.

Vale's gaze never leaves Mary Grace as she sits at the table, chains rattling again as she arranges her bound hands on top of the scarred wood. The sound of the heavy metal door closing echoes through the tiny, windowless room as the guard who escorted Vale stations himself outside.

Twenty-four years ago, everyone thought only someone insane would ask to be put on Death Row. Including the court psychologists, who said Vale couldn't understand the choice between life and death. Without the mental capacity to waive her right to appeal, lawyers filed appeals for her. While here she sat, waiting for the punishment that never came.

Is that what she prays for every day in the chapel next door? Not to repent or beg for His forgiveness, but for God to grant her the oblivion she'd been denied for so long?

"I knew you'd come."

Vale's tone is hushed, as if she isn't used to raising her voice. Or maybe she damaged her vocal cords when she tried to swallow her rosary beads.

"Why do you say that?"

Vale shakes her head. "It's a tragedy what happened to Darryl Stokes. He never hurt Cherie Leigh Hibbard. Town should be ashamed."

"How do you know he was innocent?"

"Lucas Smith wasn't responsible, either."

"How can you say that? What do you know about what happened?"

On top of the table, Vale's fingers flex and unflex. "They won't let me have my rosaries anymore. I miss holding them. They gave me such comfort. I always had them with me in church. It's next door to the prison, but it's a strangely peaceful place. I prayed for their souls every day. Never missed one, not in all these years. I don't seem to know what to do with my hands now."

Mary Grace forces her gaze away from Vale's hands. Hands that once comforted and held her. Hands that strangled two sixth graders.

"Why did you try to kill yourself after Cherie Leigh disappeared?"

"The answers are inside you, Mary Grace. They always have been."

"What are you talking about?" All the feelings of anger and betrayal that have been pent-up for twenty-four years come surging back. All these months spent looking back, searching the past for the signs she missed. And the guilt. Always the guilt.

"I know I have no right to ask for your forgiveness."

"For what? Stop talking in riddles and tell me the truth!"

"Are you sure you want to hear it? But that's why you've come. You found out. I can see it in your eyes. There was no anonymous tip, was there? I read about it in the paper."

"Why was the Repentance *Gazette* delivered to your cell every day for the past twenty-four years?"

"I was hungry for news. I used to scour the inside section for local gossip. Stories about families. School events. Sports. Unsolved crimes." Before Mary Grace can ask what she means, she goes on, "What happened when you confronted her? Did she lie? Try to deny it? I can't imagine she'd confess. Her instinct for self-preservation is too advanced even at her age."

She knows. How does she know?

"I've always known," Vale says as if Mary Grace had spoken the words aloud. "It was just a matter of time. But it won't end here. She's going to kill again."

"You're crazy."

"You know her. Know what she's capable of."

"She's a child!"

"So was she."

"Who?"

"I'm so sorry." A pained look crosses Vale's face. "I prayed it wouldn't come to this. Prayed you'd never have to know."

"Know what?" Were all the doctors right? Is Althea Vale stark raving mad?

"All I ever wanted was to protect you."

"From what?" Mary Grace has a vivid memory of herself at eleven, carrying the baby field mouse across her uncle's field. Watching it scamper off the dustpan into the woods, wondering whom she was really saving it from.

When Vale doesn't respond she goes on, "What did you mean when you said you've always known?"

Across from her, Vale rubs her shackled hands together as if she were holding rosaries. "I need to tell you a story."

"I don't want to hear a story!"

"Sit down, Mary Grace."

It's her teacher's voice, the one that brooks no resistance. Mary Grace does as she's told, sinking back into her chair.

"It's about a French girl who lived with her mother and grandmother on a farm in Kansas." Vale's gaze drifts to the wall behind Mary Grace, staring at a place only she can see. "The farm was the only home the girl had ever known. She felt safe there and loved. She never knew her father or grandfather and had no sisters and brothers. Late one summer night, her mother came into her room and said they were going to play hide-and-seek. But she had a suitcase and even in the dark the girl could see how frightened she was.

"Maman told her to be very quiet as they tiptoed downstairs. When they reached the front door, Grandmère was standing there. Maman told the girl to run. But she didn't want to leave her mother. Maman shouted again and this time the girl obeyed. As she ran, she heard her mother screaming and wanted to go back and help her. But the girl was frightened of what she saw inGrandmère's eyes. She ran out the back door and hid in the barn among the bales of hay. Soon she heard her outside, calling to her in the same voice that crooned French lullabies at night. Her eyes started to close as her grandmother sang softly outside the barn.

"'Where are you, my lost lamb? Come to me, little one. Come to me.'"

Mary Grace feels her own lids growing heavy, Vale's voice with its trace of a French accent washing over her the way it did when she was a child. As Vale talks, she can feel both the girl's terror and her love for her grandmother. She can smell the hay, and her grandmother's perfume as the door opened, Grandmère still singing to her in the language they both understood. She can hear the sirens outside, and her grandmother's footsteps as she ran from the barn.

She can picture the Kansas courtroom where the girl was deemed too young to attend or be a credible witness when Grandmère—Manon Lamb Robicheaux—stood trial for the murder of Maman. Robicheaux's original plan was to set fire to the house while her daughter and four-year-old granddaughter slept inside so she could collect the insurance money. She can feel the shock of the people in that farm town as more unsolved crimes were unearthed, some of them stretching back decades.

Robicheaux's husband and two sons who died under suspicious circumstances. The beating death of a boy who lived on a nearby farm. Robicheaux's younger brother, who drowned in a creek when he was five and she was seven. A girl in Robicheaux's fifth-grade class who vanished and whose body was never found.

She imagines the parade of witnesses, including the psychiatrist who testified that Robicheaux wasn't insane (as she wanted everyone to believe), but knew exactly what she was doing. The same man who adopted the girl shortly after the judge sentenced her grandmother to Death Row, where Robicheaux died in the electric chair the year before the method was changed to lethal injection.

"He changed my name to Althea, which means to heal. Ironic, isn't it?"

Mary Grace opens her eyes; the room swims back into focus.

"Alex Vale was a good man. He and his wife believed that love and the right environment could save me from what was inside me. When I was ten, we moved to Arkansas. My adoptive mother passed when I was fifteen. Dr. Vale died after I graduated from teaching college. I felt so alone in the world. That was when I decided to look for my birth father. I needed to find someone who wasn't tainted by the Lamb blood.

"But my father had died. He'd never married again or had any other children. His younger sister was also gone. But she left behind a son. Everyone in Repentance knew him although he lived like an outcast in the woods."

She could be talking about only one person. "You mean Meurice? He was your kin?"

Vale nods. "My first cousin. I made it my mission to see that he was properly clothed and fed."

Mary Grace remembers the covered dishes, the urns filled with fresh flowers. "You were the Good Samaritan who used to leave things on the porch."

"I wasn't the only one. I thank Him for that every day."

"There was someone else who brought him food? Someone from the church?"

"Yes. I saw her one afternoon in the woods as I was leaving. She had on that hat she always wore. The one with the wide brim."

"Caroline Womack?"

Vale nods. "After I was arrested, I could breathe easy knowing Meurice would be taken care of. I never knew exactly what was wrong with him. Today they'd call him mentally challenged. But I was his only living relative. I thought it was my penance for the terrible things my grandmother did. It seemed fitting that I came to this town."

"You were a child. You weren't responsible for her crimes."

"Maybe not. But her blood ran through my veins. I visited Meurice once a week. In the beginning, I tried to establish a relationship. Communicate with him in his native French. I knew he understood me as I talked to him through the screen door. He rarely came outside. One early November afternoon, I'd just dropped off some food when I saw Nadia Doshenko. She had rocks in her hands. I knew what she was going to do. Kids had been doing it for decades. She looked just as shocked to see me. Then her eyes turned mean. She asked what I was doing there. I told her to go home or I'd tell her father she was in the woods. She said he didn't care what she did and I'd be fired once everyone knew I was sleeping with the Boogeyman. She said if I didn't give her money, she'd tell everyone."

Vale shakes her head. "She was such a wicked girl. I told her she'd go to jail for trying to blackmail me. She said I didn't scare her, that she couldn't believe I was having sex with that retard. She must have seen it in my face because she turned and started to run. But I was too fast. I grabbed her and threw her to the ground. I could tell she was scared now, but she wasn't going to let me see her fear. She said I was the one who'd go to jail for trying to kill her. I told her she was corrupting you and to leave you alone. She laughed and said you did what she told you and I couldn't do anything about it. Suddenly my hands were around her throat. I didn't let go even after she stopped struggling. It was the sound of the rocks spilling out of her hands and hitting the ground that brought me back. Then I heard footsteps. Meurice was standing there with a shovel. But I knew the woods would be the first place they'd look. And he'd be the first one suspected. I had a better idea."

"The field behind your house."

"Meurice helped me get her body into the trunk of my car."

"What about Chloe Ann?"

"That was different. When I pulled you off of her that day in the schoolyard, I was afraid you were going to kill her. I couldn't let that happen. I knew how badly she wanted to be a popular girl. I left a note in her desk pretending it was from Skylar Hardisty. After that, it was like taking candy from a baby. She was already waiting in the basement of Vaughan Elementary when I got down there."

That was why Chloe Ann seemed so pent-up in school that Friday. She thought she was going to be initiated. The same bait Felicity used to lure Cherie Leigh out of her house.

"Those girls were evil."

"How can that be? Have you forgotten what you once told me?" Vale doesn't answer. "You said that no one is all evil. There was good in us, too. That Chloe Ann was able to bully me because she didn't try to fight the evil inside her. Why were you afraid I'd kill her?" Her voice has started to tremble. "Because you knew I'd lost the fight."

"No!"

"Yes! We both know what really happened to Nadia and Chloe Ann. But if you believed they were evil, why didn't you kill me, too?"

Vale's face changes, her eyes filling with anguish. "That was my greatest fear. I fought so hard against it."

"I don't understand."

"I haven't finished my story."

Mary Grace again feels that powerful urge to run.

Vale takes a deep breath, lets it out slowly. "When I arrived in Repentance all those years ago, there were practical things to consider. My small inheritance from my adoptive father wasn't going to last forever. I needed a job and a place to live. I saw an ad in the local paper for a substitute teacher at Vaughan Elementary and thought it was God's will . . ."

FORTY-FIVE

Later, in the woods, a part of her refuses to believe that this could be God's will.

Yet even as she ran from that room as if the Devil himself was nipping at her heels, refusing to accept Althea Vale's lies, she could feel her true self beginning to fade. What remained of Mary Grace Dobbs ebbing away as she fled the prison and sped back to Repentance. Driving through streets that no longer belonged to her just as she no longer belonged to them. Once again the child who didn't belong anywhere. A trespasser in her town, a ghost in her own life.

Surprised to feel her heart still beating as she ran into the house, taking the stairs two at a time. Stopping at the top of the landing, staring in horror at what was left of her daughter's bedroom door. Telling herself that this wasn't her child who wrought such destruction. The wood splintered and mauled open not by the overturned desk chair with the metal rollers that she begged her to buy her for her twelfth birthday, but by pure animal rage.

Thinking of Manon Lamb Robicheaux as she looked out the window and saw the figure in the field. Racing down the stairs and out the kitchen door. Her daughter whirling around as she ran toward her, mouth twisted up in a snarl, eyes black with fury.

"Where is it?"

"Where you'll never find it."

Felicity leaning on the shovel as she pushed her hair out of her eyes in an eerie imitation of her mother the night Mary Grace buried Cherie Leigh's trophy and phone. "I saw you out here Thanksgiving night. I'll dig up this whole field if I have to. Come on, Mom." Her face changing again, her voice wheedling. "Cherie Leigh won't miss the trophy. She's dead." Her hands tightening around the shovel. "Tell me!"

Backing up as Felicity wielded the shovel like a weapon, once again hearing Althea Vale's last words as she fled that room. Smelling her daughter's fear as her gaze flicked down to her gunbelt. Then she dropped the shovel and did what any cornered animal would.

She ran.

Taking off after her, across the field to the edge of her property where it became the woods. Catching sight of Felicity here and there, moving between the trees. Forgetting how fast she could run, shouting at her to come back. Stopping to catch her breath and get her bearings, the trees blocking out most of the light. Seeing the fat plumes of smoke curling out of the chimney that told her she was heading north. Ignoring the stitch in her side as she gave chase again. Seeing a flash of color up ahead, Felicity darting behind a pine like Mary Grace did the night Noah made her bury the raccoon.

"I know you're there." Repeating what her cousin said to her that night. "Come out, little one. Come to me, my lost lamb." Crooning in a sing-song voice as she crept toward the pine. "Don't be afraid, child. Come to your *maman*."

Felicity poking out her head, then emerging from behind the tree, eyes wide and trusting. The way she looked at her back when she thought her mother ruled the world.

"You won't arrest me?"

"No." That at least wasn't a lie.

"Promise?"

"Promise."

Felicity smiling as she ran into her arms.

Now Mary Grace feels the weight of the gunbelt on her hip as she holds her daughter close, the smell of her shampoo sending her back to when she was a baby. Inhaling the pure, clean scent of her, finally won over by this tiny creature whose life was in her hands.

Mary Grace thinks about Manon Robicheaux killing Vale's mother; Vale's fear that she'd kill Mary Grace. What she said as she came to the end of her story.

You always kill the thing you love.

How can she do it? How could this be His will? Knowing she won't be able to take just one life? Then she'll be damned forever, no possible hope of salvation.

As if sensing the terrible struggle raging within her, Felicity nestles against her, burrowing deeper into her chest. Mary Grace strokes her sweet-smelling hair, feeling that primal tug, a connection so strong it's like a physical pain. Then all at once she feels lighter, as if a weight were lifting off of her. It's Felicity pulling away, and she's already mourning the loss. Her right hand—the hand that just caressed her child's head—drops to her gunbelt.

It's empty.

Her daughter stands a few feet away, pointing her weapon at her.

But all Mary Grace can see is Manon. "Give it to me."

Felicity shakes her head. "I'm not going to jail."

"This isn't a game. Someone could get hurt."

"Cut me a break, Mom. It's self-defense. You were going to kill me."

Mary Grace flashes to that moment when her hand dropped to her gunbelt. Was she reaching for her weapon or did she already know it wasn't there? "You won't get away with it."

"Yes, I will. Because no one's going to find you. I Googled it. It's really hard to prove murder without a body. It's your own fault. If you hadn't gone snooping in my closet and found the blanket, I wouldn't have had to move the trophy to a safer hiding place. Cherie Leigh would still be in that cave. Everyone would think it was Lucas Smith or Darryl Stokes. Especially after Allison told you she saw him hanging around the schoolyard."

"Allison Driver never saw Stokes, did she?" Mary Grace remembers how frightened the sixth grader was, how she thought Lauren Reeves was behind it.

Felicity lets out a shrill peal of laughter. "It was so easy. All I had to do was start a chat on our anonymous school board saying someone heard that Allison saw him. You wouldn't believe all the posts that came in! Everyone telling her she should do the right thing and report it. Just like her mama did in back then. Wasn't that brilliant? Allison knew it was me, though. She knew she better tell you she saw him or she'd be sorry."

"What about Halloween? Whose idea was it to throw rocks at Meurice's house? Yours or Lauren's?"

"Seriously, mom? You think she has the brains to think of anything on her own? Lauren does what I tell her. She had to break the Boogeyman's window to prove her loyalty."

"Was bullying those children another test? Did Lauren have to prove her loyalty by tormenting Yochi Chajon and Mei Ling, too?"

Felicity's face darkens. "They don't belong here."

Mary Grace can't believe what she's hearing. Her daughter is a racist, no better than the Salvationists. "So it's you. *You're* the leader of the popular girls."

"Why? You don't think I'm smart enough?"

"Of course you are."

Felicity looks at her as if she doesn't believe her. "When Lauren and Haley ran the club, they thought throwing rocks at the Boogeyman's house was a big deal. That's such kid stuff. Once I was initiated, I said we needed to change things up. When I told them what they had to do, the twins were scared at first. But I knew what had to be done. I knew I could make things happen."

Evil so powerful it can make things happen.

The only difference is that Mary Grace recognized her own evil.

"My plan was so brilliant! Lauren kept bugging me about what I was doing after school that Friday. On the bus home, I told her and Haley to go to the woods and wait for me. They're not allowed there either, but they wouldn't dare disobey me. So while I was at the cave with Cherie Leigh, they were in the woods where no one would see them. And they couldn't tell anyone or they'd be punished. Which meant they didn't have an alibi for where they were when everything went down. It was my insurance, just in case. When I didn't answer Lauren's texts, she called. I told her to chill, I'd be there soon. I knew they'd go home before it got dark and their mother put supper on the table."

Mary Grace remembers Felicity's text that Friday evening as the snow started falling, saying she was starving. Texting her back that she'd order pizza, believing her daughter had been home all afternoon doing schoolwork.

Only now does she realize the true monstrousness of what Felicity has done. Forcing Lauren Reeves to do her dirty work so that no one could point the finger at her. "Lauren couldn't be part of your plan." She can barely get out the words. "Because Cherie Leigh was never leaving that cave alive. And you couldn't have any witnesses to your crime."

"If I told Lauren to go there, she would have done what I said."

"And if she had, you would have pinned Cherie Leigh's murder on her. Then you would have told me it was Lauren who strangled her." And she would have believed her, God help her. "But you didn't know Cherie Leigh was secretly recording you."

"I'm one step ahead of you, Mom. When you showed me the video that Hibbard bitch made, I had a better idea. I knew you were looking for a way to save me. So I told you the twins were never there, how you and I were the only ones who knew what happened."

Felicity waves the gun as she talks, as if she'd forgotten she was holding it. Mary Grace's only hope is to keep her talking. "That's why you chose the cave. You're the one who knew that water could wash away DNA. Not Lauren."

Felicity nods. "I remembered how you used to tell me to watch out for the rushing waters. I figured even if the body ever floated out, no one would know it was, her. It was like, so chill!"

Felicity beams, the way she does when she brings home a perfect report card. Or strikes out a batter. So proud of herself for her detailed planning of Cherie Leigh's murder.

A stone-cold killer. Just like her great-grandmother.

You know what you have to do.

Althea Vale's last words to her.

"Don't take another step."

She stops dead in her tracks, still too far away to get the gun. The look in her daughter's eyes enough to freeze her blood.

"I told you, there's no way I'm going to jail. Like I said, you and I are the only ones who know what happened."

"And God."

"Like I care what He thinks." Felicity cocks her head, as if she just heard something. A second later, her phone beeps. She slides it out of her back pocket, studies the screen. "It's Lauren. I'll text her later."

"Don't do this." One final, last-ditch attempt to appeal to whatever humanity is left inside her. In response, Felicity's hand tightens on the gun. "Wait! I'll show you where the trophy is."

Felicity considers that for a moment, then shakes her head. "I'll find it myself after I bury you."

Dooming Mary Grace to lie for eternity in unhallowed ground.

"After you're gone, everyone will think Lucas killed you because you were going to put him in jail for shooting Stokes."

"You think you have it all figured out. What do you think will happen to you after I'm gone? You'll have to go live with your cousins like I did."

Felicity shakes her head. "No, I won't. I'll get Mrs. Reeves to adopt me. She'll feel bad that I'm an orphan. That way I can keep an eye on the twins, make sure they don't get out of line. And I'll have a real father. Which is more than you ever gave me." Her eyes flash with anger. "Time to say your prayers, Mom." Only a few feet separate them as they stand together on the edge of the abyss. "I'm sorry." But Felicity doesn't look the slightest bit remorseful as she levels the gun at her mother's heart. Not that it matters now. Mary Grace knows how it has to end.

She makes her move just as Felicity pulls the trigger. The blast thunders through the woods, sending birds flapping off treetops and animals scurrying for safety. Her last thought that she mistimed it by mere seconds, underestimating her younger, faster daughter. A raccoon darting into the shadows of a pine the last thing she sees as she drops to the ground.

FORTY-SIX

The faithful and devout of Repentance make their way to the First Baptist Church dressed in their Sunday best even though it isn't Sunday.

Everyone bonded in their collective sorrow, brought together by another tragedy. Although the weather is fine, if a bit warm for December, no procession is planned down Main Street. Not like the pomp and circumstance five months earlier on that rainy July day when Parnell Vaughan II was laid to rest. And while some are divided as to where the true blame lies for what would be known ever after as the Tragic Shooting in the Woods, the church overflows with those who've come to pay their respects.

Among the congregants is Parnell Vaughan III. Some still give him the cold shoulder as he and his mother and sister head for their usual seats in the first pew on the left. As Miss Caroline starts up the organ, more familiar faces appear. Madison Driver and her daughter. Paige and Aiden Reeves and their twin girls. Isaac Wood and his ex-wife and daughter. Emily King with her husband and two sons.

While many still haven't forgiven King for running off with Madison's husband, most now believe her innocent of having had an illicit relationship with the former PE coach of Vaughan Elementary. It's because of what happened a few weeks ago in Little Rock, where Hunter Fewell was serving a consecutive sentence of forty years for the statutory rapes of two students eight years after he left Repentance under a cloud of scandal.

Allegations of his having sex with Nadia Doshenko and Skylar Hardisty, who moved away in the winter of '95, were never proven. Nor was Nadia found to be pregnant when the ME examined her body. That was a rumor Paige started, probably to one-up Skylar. At his parole hearing, Fewell said that his sinful addiction to underage girls was a sickness caused by allowing evil into his soul. But he had since found Jesus and, through daily prayer, had successfully cast out Satan. Parole was denied.

As the music crescendoes, Alma Allred hobbles in, accompanied by an aide. Murmurs go up at the sight of the town wag who, for the first time in years, has entered God's House without her knitting needles. Noticeably absent are Tyler Lee Hibbard and Jackson Briggs. That's why Briggs's mantle as head pallbearer has been passed to Samuel Mathews, which has particularly poignant resonance today.

The music begins to swell as Parnell Vaughan leaves his pew and disappears through a door at the back of the church. A few minutes later the door opens again and the pallbearers appear bearing the coffin. Samuel, his son Noah, and Parnell on one side. On the other longtime postmaster Matthew Chesbro, Landon Willcockson—Parnell Vaughan II's nephew on his sister's side—and recently anointed Repentance sheriff Conner Mitchell.

The music crescendoes as a door at the side of the church opens and Josiah Mills makes his slow, painful way to the podium. As he begins to speak the text that all know by heart, his voice rises out of his wasting body in sonorous passion.

"We are gathered here today in His merciful sight to pay homage to His greatness and glory and to celebrate the gift of eternal life. We are not here to question why the Almighty has seen fit to take another precious lamb from our fold but to give thanks for saving the soul of one of His devoted flock . . ."

Forty minutes later, a much smaller group stands before the open grave in Repentance Cemetery. Samuel Mathews delivers the final eulogy as the coffin begins its slow descent into the earth next to the graves where Sara and Parker Dobbs were laid to rest twenty-five years ago after their car was struck by a rig during that terrible ice storm.

And where, in a few minutes, another Dobbs will be buried before her time.

PART IV

I'm surrounded by ghosts.

Darryl Stokes.

Owen Kanady.

Cherie Leigh Hibbard.

Chloe Ann Briggs.

Nadia Doshenko, who isn't interred here but whose spirit lives on in me.

And my parents.

I haven't fully accepted the story Althea Vale told me. The part about my daddy really hurt. Would I ever be able to forgive him? Or my mama for her Devil's bargain with Vale?

It isn't a new story. Except for maybe the twist at the end. It's sordid and sad: a cliché. Until it happens to your family.

Two lonely people, in this case a married and a single teacher at Vaughan Elementary, who struck up a friendship that developed into a secret affair. Until the day his wife showed up at his lover's door.

His sterile wife who wanted a child more than anything. Who could tell instantly that her husband's mistress was in the early stages of pregnancy.

Vale torn between ending her unborn baby's life and giving her up for adoption to a couple she'd never meet. Knowing that her lover was a good man despite his temporary lapse; his wife a God-fearing woman. Hoping they could save her child from what was inside her.

She had one condition. After the child was born—in a different town because my mama supposedly suffered "complications"—Vale would return to Repentance, where she could go on teaching at Vaughan Elementary, a job she loved. She could not have any direct contact with the child, of course. Until the tragic chain of events that brought me into her sixth-grade class.

Try as I might to deny it, what Vale told me in the visitor's room on Death Row explained so many things.

Feeling that I never truly belonged, even though I was brought to Repentance when I was six weeks old.

My mama's coldness.

Why she never gave me a little brother or sister.

The immediate connection I felt to Vale the day I walked into her class.

Why my folks decided to send me to Baptist Day for my last year of elementary school.

It made sense now. My mama feared that if Vale were my teacher, I'd see the love she'd be unable to suppress. The same love I felt for my daughter, even at the end. She must have been terrified that we'd instantly know each other, even if ours was a connection that went far beyond the ordinary bond between parent and child.

Evil recognizing evil?

My uncle is concluding the eulogy. "Ashes to ashes, dust to dust," he intones. There's a catch in his voice because she was kin and he loved her and her death goes against the natural order of things.

"Mary Grace?"

My uncle's voice carries on the breeze, echoing in my head as I kneel beside the open grave. I don't tell him that Mary Grace is dead. She died in the woods.

I close my eyes and send up a silent prayer for His forgiveness even though I have no right to expect it. Then I throw dirt over the coffin that holds the body of my only child.

You know what you have to do.

Vale's final words to me were carried out after all. Felicity is gone. She was killed by a bullet from my gun.

But not at my hand.

The warbling of birdsongs and chittering of animals keep me company as I head into the woods on a fine early-spring day. Although three months have passed, my hearing hasn't come back completely. My head still reverberates with the sound of the gunshot, making me wonder if that's His way of forcing me to relive that horrific moment over and over. I'm told that will also ease up with time, and I should be thanking God I'm alive after the bullet slammed into the side of my head, missing my brain by inches.

The town felt nothing but sympathy for me; how could they not? Although some believed it was my fault, which was why I turned in my badge a few days before Felicity's body was placed in the plot that should have lain empty for decades. The natural order of things. While nobody disputed that I was suffering, how could I have been so irresponsible as to leave my loaded weapon lying around?

A child delirious with fever who believed she heard someone inside the house. Terrified she'd be the next sixth grader abducted when she grabbed the gun and ran outside. A mother crazy with worry when she discovered both missing. Finding her daughter in the woods where Felicity mistook her for the killer she believed was chasing her. It was the only explanation for firing at Mary Grace who, wounded and bleeding, knew that her only hope of survival was to get her weapon away from her daughter. A struggle ensued, and the gun went off again.

That was the cover story I told Conner when I called him and that he told everyone else. Except for the part where Felicity shot me (I had the head injury as proof) and she ended up dead. My plan had been to tackle her to the ground before she could get off that shot. I'd grab the gun, kill her, and then shoot myself.

It would have appeared to be a tragic accident followed by a suicide: A mother searching for her sick child, who'd gone missing. In the woods, unable to see very well or to think clearly in her panicked state, drawing her weapon. She was the one who fired first, mistaking her daughter for the killer. Turning the gun on herself when she realized what she'd done.

Of course that never happened, either.

After my daughter shot me, as I lay bleeding in the woods, the ground beneath me started to shake. At first I thought it was God, that He believed I was worthy of being saved after all. I figured I had to be hallucinating when I saw Meurice emerge from the brush. The woods echoed with the sound of Felicity's terror as she screamed "It's the Boogeyman!" I tried to warn him to stay back, but no sound came out. The part about the struggle was also true. But it was the struggle between Meurice and Felicity as he tried to get the gun away from her. That was when it went off for the second and final time.

I trudge deeper into the woods. As I head north, I see the smoke curling out of the chimney.

I remember the first time I ever saw him, that hot August day when I took the shortcut through the woods after Tyler Lee surprised me at my cave. The terror I felt when Meurice grabbed me, letting me go only after we heard those footsteps (probably belonging to my cousin) dying away. Remembering other footsteps, the day Parnell accosted me in the woods for telling Owen Kanady about the cabin. Parnell fleeing when he heard him coming.

He was always protecting me, even if I didn't know it. Right up to the day my daughter died.

When I reach the porch, I climb the steps and peer through the large front window. He has no idea that Paige Reeves and I paid to have it repaired after Lauren Reeves threw that rock at the instigation of my daughter. I remember how Nadia and I threw rocks the day she insisted I bring her here, my rock hitting him in the leg.

He's inside now, sitting at a table. He's wearing a heavy jacket even though the temperature topped seventy-five today; behind him a fire burns in the fireplace. I think of those plumes of smoke curling into the air no matter what the season and wonder for the first time if he has some kind of physical condition. Then I notice what's cradled in his hand. It's a small blackbird. No, not a bird. A baby bat. It looks like one of its wings is injured. For some reason, I feel as if I'm intruding. I start to back away, but it's too late. He saw me.

I wonder if he knows who I am, if Althea Vale told him that we're kin. His first instinct was to protect her, too. That's why he came out with the shovel after she strangled Nadia. But she also wanted to protect him by making sure nobody knew that Nadia died there and he was a witness to her murder.

In Felicity's case, he was more than a witness. I have no doubt she would have shot me again if he hadn't risked his life to get the gun away from her. After it went off, I must have passed out. When I awoke, he was tending my wound. Afterward, I thanked him for saving my life. Then I told him to go home. I thought he didn't understand me, but he finally did as I asked. As I watched him shamble away, he seemed smaller than I remembered, and older of course, with his white beard and gray hair. A long way from the Boogeyman of my childhood.

Meurice is still looking at me, the bat in his hand struggling to move its damaged wing. I smile. I could swear he nods, his long moon face moving imperceptibly up and down, before he returns his attention to the bat. I stand there a few moments longer, then place the covered casserole dish on the porch. A memory stirs, of Nadia sitting on the rocking chair that was now so decrepit I doubted if it rocked any more. Helping herself to some of the shepherd's pie that Althea Vale or Caroline Womack had left for him.

Nadia is still on my mind as I walk back through the woods. Only instead of continuing on to my house, I stop at the nest of pines that slopes down from my uncle's property.

I'm standing at our tree, thinking about what was recovered from the graves twenty-four years ago.

Along with the two sets of rosary beads, Althea Vale buried twin blankets with the bodies. The one to save their souls; the other to keep them warm. Which proved she felt remorse.

And Chloe Ann's backpack that she never went anywhere without.

None of us did.

That bothered me for a long time. Even after I thought I had it figured out, I couldn't bring myself to do it. Because of the guilt. But after Althea Vale told me what happened that Tuesday in the woods, I knew it was time to finally let Nadia go.

I feel the emotions of that long-ago afternoon as if it I were experiencing them now. Raging with hurt and anger at Nadia for her betrayal. Wishing she'd never moved to Repentance, telling myself she was dead to me. Running down here to look for the softball that had rolled down from the field. Seeing her standing there. Not realizing until later that she was just as surprised to see me. Surprised and annoyed. Because it interfered with her plan.

She lied when she said she came to tell me a secret. But when I ordered her to leave, she had no choice but to go. The scream I heard a few minutes later was Noah accosting her. I know he was in the woods that day when he came in for supper with mud on his sneakers; he admitted as much when I went to my uncle's house yesterday to say goodbye.

He admitted other things, too, like how angry he felt growing up, hating his father for being so strict and always believing the worst of him. How he used to go to the woods to be alone, only to end up taking out his anger on God's creatures who were weaker than he was. How jealous he was when his parents took me in. That surprised me.

Then he became a parent himself, raising two girls who adore him.

I thought about that November day when Felicity retrieved those lost softballs. Noah emerging from behind the pine, mean as ever and messing with my head. I wondered if my daughter's death changed him somehow. I was still trying to reconcile this Noah with the Noah who killed that raccoon. The boy I briefly suspected of murdering Nadia and Chloe Ann.

It was my cousin hiding behind the tree the day Nadia died, not Madison Driver, as Nadia thought. My cousin whose weight snapped the twig that sent the frightened raccoon scurrying out. He overheard our fight and waited his chance to confront Nadia about stealing his father's money. When she screamed, he was afraid someone might hear and took off. That was when she came back to our tree; the reason she'd showed up there in the first place.

Then she carried out the rest of her plan. She would have checked first to make sure Noah was gone, then continued on to the cabin where she hoped to catch the lovers together and make Parnell pay for her silence. But he never showed. Stokes had no money, but she figured she'd seduce him because she had to seduce every male in Repentance, straight or otherwise. That was when she lost the charm from the bracelet her mother had given her.

After she left the cabin, she knew she had to get home before her daddy did and discovered the cash missing from his sock drawer. Without the money from Parnell, she wouldn't have had enough to run away. Only instead of heading south, she decided to go a little farther north. I can picture it: Nadia frustrated and angry, figuring she'd blow off some steam by throwing rocks at Meurice's house. When she saw Althea Vale on the porch, she thought of another way to get the money. It cost her her life.

I find the place on the tree where she carved our initials. Then I inspect the hole in the side of the trunk. It's gotten bigger over time.

After Noah accosted her, Nadia would have been terrified that he'd get his hands on her daddy's cash and whatever was left of the money she stole from my uncle. She'd want to stash it where she knew it would be safe and come back for it after she got the payout from Parnell. Except she never made it back. That's why it wasn't buried with her body.

I reach in my hand. It's sticky with sap. I roll up my jacket sleeve and reach further inside. There's something wedged in there. I have to use both hands to get it free. Then I pull out the backpack I last saw Nadia wearing that day, standing almost exactly where I am now. Glancing over her shoulder as if daring me to follow her.

I lay the backpack on the ground. It's remarkably well preserved, as if the sap somehow protected it. The zipper's rusty though, and it takes a few tries to slide it open. Inside, it's packed to the brim with jeans, sweaters, training bras, underwear, a toothbrush, shampoo, make-up, nail polish, two packs of cigarettes, and the Swiss Army knife she used to carve our initials. After she made us swear our blood oath as best friends.

In a side pouch is a gold-framed photo of a smiling, dark-haired woman that's a twin to the photo on the charm that Nadia lost from her bracelet in the struggle in the cabin with Darryl Stokes. I remember her telling me that her daddy blamed her for her mama dying when she was eight because she ran away.

Althea Vale said Nadia was evil. Madison Driver said the same thing. And it's true she could be cruel. I thought it was because she was lonely. She missed her mama the way I missed my folks, not knowing then that my mother wasn't really my mother. But it was my father I missed so much. I still haven't decided if I can forgive him. Of all the betrayals, his hurts the most.

I search the rest of the backpack and find what I'm looking for in a zippered compartment on the inside flap: a fat white envelope filled with fives, tens, twenties, and a couple of fifties. I wonder how much of it is my uncle's.

I sit on the ground with the backpack in my lap, awash in memories. The first time we talked, on the Vaughan Elementary bleachers, when she told me about the times she ran away. Her plan for us to run away together. It was all she ever talked about. Once she had the money from Parnell, she would have come back to get this.

But would she have come back for me?

It isn't as easy to let her go as I thought. She was the only best friend I ever had. I remember how angry I was the last time we saw each other. I swore I'd never forgive her as long as I lived. That's a long time. I think of my daddy again. Althea Vale. Felicity.

I put the envelope with the cash back inside the backpack. After I zip it up, I slide it back into the hole where it rested undisturbed for decades. Then I leave our tree for the last time and move through the pines toward home.

REPENTANCE AT LAST?

Ghosts are still batting around my head as I come up from the field and around to the front of my house.

Parnell's sitting on the porch.

He moves back and forth on the swing, his shoes tapping the wood boards. It's déjà vu of what happened the night Darryl Stokes was killed except that he's sober.

And, in spite of everything, a sight for sore eyes.

"Is it true? You're really leaving?"

I nod as I climb the steps. He makes room for me. For a few minutes there's nothing but the creaking and groaning of the swing.

"I came to tell you how sorry I am."

"You already told me back in December."

"I'm not talking about the funeral. I'm talking about what happened to her. It was my fault." He turns to face me, those beautiful blue eyes as haunted as I'd ever seen them. "Remember the last time I was here? The terrible thing I said before I left?"

Wait until it happens to you. Wait until you lose someone you love.

I remember.

"You didn't mean it. You were crazy with grief."

"Don't make excuses for me. I meant every word. I wanted you to suffer the way I was suffering. It's like I made it happen."

I plant my feet; the swing stops. “Don’t say that. Don’t ever say that.”

He’s repeating the words I’ve been telling myself for twenty-four years. Except that he wasn’t the one who heard my wicked thoughts. It was the woman who shared my blood. But doesn’t my love for him make Parnell part of my blood, too?

“You okay?”

“Yeah.” How can I explain without giving away my deepest, darkest secret?

“How do you live with it? The guilt?”

For a minute, I think he knows. Then I realize he means the death of my daughter. The tragic accident that has already become a permanent part of our town lore.

I’m not sure how to answer him. I’ve been living with it so long it’s also become a part of me. And the pain that cuts deeper than anything else. I feel the loss every day I’m alive that my child isn’t. Even knowing what I know now.

“Gracie?”

He hasn’t called me that nickname in twenty-four years. My eyes fill and suddenly I’m crying the tears I couldn’t shed at my parents’ or daughter’s funerals. Then I’m in his arms where I’ve always longed to be and he holds me, murmuring comforting words into my hair.

“I’m sorry,” he says when I’m all cried out. “I didn’t mean to bring it all back. Though it doesn’t take much, does it?”

“No.” I look away as I swipe at my eyes, embarrassed to have a witness to my moment of weakness, even if it’s Parnell.

“Makes you wonder if it really is God’s will for us to suffer. To punish us for our sins.”

“What happened to Darryl wasn’t your fault.”

“And Felicity’s death wasn’t yours. Maybe one day we’ll both believe it.” He takes my hand in his. “I’ll miss you.”

“I’ll miss you, too.”

“You sure you have to go?”

"You sure you want to stay?"

"Maybe not." He smiles a sad smile. "I don't see Repentance letting go of its bigotries and prejudices any time soon."

"I'm not sure I agree," I say. He looks at me. "Our town is changing. Haven't you noticed? People are starting to become more forgiving. And accepting."

Although Parnell is still shunned by the homophobes among us, most have welcomed him back into the fold. Then, two weeks ago, Adalynn Wood agreed to share custody of their daughter Annabelle with Isaac Wood, who hasn't shown up drunk in church for months. And after the passing of Josiah Mills last month, there was no opposition to Cadence taking over as official pastor of First Baptist. She has pulled back from her rigid Footwasher views, although Timothy Dickson, Austin Cook, and Brandon Cowan still refuse to attend church.

Baby steps.

"I hope you're right." Parnell shakes his head. "As long as we can keep the Salvationists from our door. I'm trying to forgive Lucas Smith. He was obviously brainwashed. You think he'll ever be caught?"

"I don't know." Conner told me that apprehending Lucas for the murder of Darryl Stokes was his biggest priority. Even though he still has doubts about Lucas being the copycat who murdered another sixth grader. Most in town now believing that Stokes was innocent.

"I know one thing. I have to find a way to move on. I can't keep living with hate in my heart." He gets to his feet, setting the swing in motion. "Speaking of moving on, I'd better get back to the garage."

"Say goodbye to your mother and sister for me."

"I will." Something of the old Parnell surfaces as he winks at me. "You've still got the best pitching arm of anyone I know."

My heart twists at his words. How could he know that I'll never feel the same way about the sport I once loved? The trophy that I buried in my field is now interred with Cherie Leigh. When Tyler Lee was let out of prison for her funeral and discovered it missing, he went crazy. Said he couldn't put his daughter in the ground without it. That's when I dug it up and sneaked it back into his house. I gave the bat and catcher's mitt I bought Felicity last spring to her second cousins.

Cherie Leigh's smartphone remains under the earth.

"So long, Gracie. Don't be a stranger." Parnell leans over and kisses me on the cheek. Then he smiles the smile that used to feel like it was meant just for me and walks down the porch steps. I feel the loss I always feel when he leaves, as if something were being ripped out of me. But we're friends again. I have to hold on to that.

When he gets to his car—a moss-green convertible this year, the color of the trees in Repentance right now—he turns and waves. The sun bounces off his shades as he lowers his body into the driver's seat. I wave as he backs out of my driveway and eases down the street, the breeze stirring his blond hair.

Then he turns the corner and vanishes from view.

I drag the battered suitcase that holds most of my worldly possessions onto the porch. It's the same suitcase I brought with me to the house of my only remaining kin after my folks died. The one Tyler Lee swore he saw sitting on my uncle's porch because I was being packed off to the children's home in Fayetteville.

Everyone thinks I'm leaving because of what happened in the woods. Too much guilt, too many painful memories. That's only part of it. What about the lies I've been telling for decades? The secret that I swear one day will tear a hole right through my heart.

I know I should stop dwelling on the past and look toward the future. A place I once saw as a magic carpet that could take me anywhere and let me become anything. Someone good. Someone worthy of love.

All I did was bring about more death and destruction.

I torture myself with the what-ifs. The people who'd still be alive if it weren't for me. My parents. Nadia, whom I never would have met if I'd gone to Baptist Day. Chloe Ann. Darryl Stokes. Althea Vale, who succeeded the second time, hanging herself with her bedsheets a few months after I visited her. She died thinking that I'd done what she asked: killed my daughter before she could kill again.

If I hadn't found the trophy, Felicity would be alive, still breathing God's sweet air instead of lying in a place that will never see the sun. I would have continued along in blissful ignorance: the truth about why Althea Vale spared me and tried to kill herself when another sixth grader disappeared twenty-four years after she strangled Nadia and Chloe Ann secrets she'd carry to her grave.

I've asked myself whether it was also God's will that no DNA was ever recovered from Cherie Leigh's body. If it had been, people would have wondered how it was possible that a single strand found, perhaps, under her fingernails (from the struggle not with a middle-aged adult but with another sixth grader who was her athletic equal), could be a partial match to Althea Vale, who was on Death Row praying when Cherie Leigh was murdered.

A relative then. Except that Althea Vale had no kin that anyone knew about. Twenty-four years ago, reporters digging into her past came up empty. Vale's adoptive father made sure that no records could trace back to a four-year-old French girl who lived on a farm in Kansas with her *maman* and *grandmère*. There would have been no match found to Meurice either, even if he'd ever been a suspect and his DNA tested. He would have been ruled out because the DNA found on Cherie Leigh would have been mitochondrial, which meant the killer was related to Althea Vale on her maternal side.

Vale's granddaughter.

The same DNA runs through my blood.

At least I know now what I've felt inside me all these years. Call it evil. Devil. Lamb gene. Does it matter?

It's why I can't repent. Because I committed the most unforgivable sin. Not once. Not twice. Three times.

I was so angry at my parents for deciding to send me to Baptist Day. When I ran out into the ice storm, I wished with all my heart that they'd die. Then that rig collided with their car and I thought *I'd* die from the guilt.

I was furious at Nadia for kissing Parnell behind the bleachers. After she left our tree to go deeper into the woods, my curiosity almost got the better of me and I was tempted to follow her. Instead, I ran up into my uncle's field and prayed for God to strike her down dead. I took His name in vain, surely another transgression.

By the time I wished death on Chloe Ann, I knew I was beyond saving.

Althea Vale said that she was afraid I would have killed Chloe Ann if she hadn't pulled me off of her that afternoon in the schoolyard. Because she knew who I was. She had given her infant child to her lover and his wife, hoping they could save me from myself.

I spent my whole life waiting to be saved.

I know now that no one can do that for me. Not my parents. Not Althea Vale. Not Meurice, who saved my life (if not my soul). Not even God himself, though I can just see the sacrilege Pastor Mills would have viewed that as, perhaps the greatest sin of all.

Only I can save myself. And I finally have the answer to the question that has haunted me all these years.

Evil didn't choose me. I chose evil.

It's a choice, not a destiny. Again I hear Althea Vale saying there's good and evil in all of us and you have to fight the evil every day of your life.

She also said something else that day.

Your parents have forgiven you, Mary Grace. Now it's time to forgive yourself.

Is it that simple? I know that Parnell struggles with it every day, hoping one day he'll be able to forgive Lucas Smith. Is forgiveness the first step to salvation and eternal grace? I'm not ready to die, although I was prepared to sacrifice my life and part of me is buried with my daughter. Althea Vale must have wondered how I could go on living afterward.

I think a lot about that day in the woods. When Felicity ran into my arms, it was a calculated ploy to get my gun. But if I'd gotten to it first, would I have pulled the trigger?

And there's something else. Was I so consumed with guilt about my own wickedness that I failed to see it in my child?

The answers continue to elude me. Lately though, the nightmares that terrify me awake in the middle of the night have eased up some. I still dream about Felicity. Not the way she was at the end, but as a little girl; the way I want to remember her.

I think about Lauren Reeves. I wonder if she's relieved that she doesn't have to do Felicity's bidding anymore. After my daughter died, the popular girls' club disbanded, just like it did twenty-four years ago. I haven't heard about any more episodes of bullying, so I assume that also ended. I hope Lauren will grow up to be the woman Felicity never had the chance to become.

I carry my suitcase down the porch steps and set it in the trunk of the SUV. I'm not sure where I'm going. Maybe a pitstop in the town where Althea Vale gave birth to me even though it was my mama's name on the official documentation provided by my daddy. After that, I don't know. Perhaps Kansas, where the child who would become Althea Vale hid in a barn from the woman who planned to murder her for the insurance money.

Manon Robicheaux failed to kill her granddaughter, but Althea Vale ended up strangling two young girls. Then Vale's grandchild—my daughter—strangled another girl. As far as I know, Vale's mother never murdered anyone. Some of the research I've done indicates that the warrior gene often skips generations. Then I picture my hands around Tyler Lee and Chloe Ann's throats and wonder if that's true. Wonder what it takes to turn a carrier into a killer.

The one thing I'm sure of is that it's a cycle doomed to keep repeating itself unless I stop it. I won't have any more children. The Lamb line will end with me, as Vale had hoped.

I feel like an orphan again, all alone in the world. And now I'm leaving the only home I've ever known. I finally had that talk with Conner, who might have a future with Madison. He never had one with me.

I turn and look toward the woods, where a thin plume of smoke curls upward through the trees. I'm glad Miss Caroline is Meurice's other secret benefactor, although I worry about her worsening dementia. I'll try to send care packages from wherever I am. After all, he and I are blood, and kin takes care of kin. I make a mental note to find out where his mama—Althea Vale's aunt—is buried. Vale herself is interred with her adoptive parents. Just as one day I'll be laid in Repentance Cemetery in the empty plot between my daddy and my daughter.

The natural order of things.

A warm breeze stirs the leaves of the big elm in the front yard as I load the remaining bags into the car. In a few months, it will be summer again. There's no rain predicted, not like the floods of last summer when Darryl Stokes came back. Or the terrible drought during the summer twenty-four years ago. So far, this year's shaping up to be a perfect ten. When it's like that, the sun high in the sky, the grass laid out like a green carpet and the lakes and creeks shimmering with water so crystal clear you can drink from it, there's nowhere else you want to be.

I remember that summer when I was eleven, before the girls disappeared. Still grieving and guilt-stricken over my parents' deaths the previous November, yet still believing that this was the greatest place on earth. The only talk of evil was on Sunday when Pastor Mills railed about how we were born in sin and better repent or we'd go straight to hell.

I know now that it isn't how you come into the world, but what you do with the time you're here. We may be born in sin, but we sure as hell don't have to leave this sweet earth that way.

I look up. Not a cloud mars the endless expanse of blue. I open the driver's door, toss my shoulder bag onto the passenger seat. Then I turn back for one last look at the town I love. A place that's part of me for better or worse; no matter where I was born. A connection that runs deeper than blood.

Repentance never looked more beautiful.

THE END

ACKNOWLEDGMENTS

Writing a novel is a labor of love. But none of us can do it all on our own. I'm grateful to have had the love and support of so many people on this eye-opening odyssey from a voice in my head to the heady thrill of publication.

Mary Grace Dobbs and Repentance, Arkansas, might have lived forever in my imagination (and on my computer screen and recorder) if it weren't for my agent Doug Grad. He was instrumental in finding a home for *Saving Grace* at Scarlet, the new imprint of Penzler Publishers.

I feel fortunate to have an unbeatable team at the helm of Scarlet: Mysterious Press CEO Otto Penzler, proprietor of Manhattan's Mysterious Bookshop and the world's foremost authority on crime and suspense fiction; Publisher Charles Perry, who is also a whiz at social media and always has time to answer my questions; Editor-in-Chief Luisa Smith, who is every author's dream editor and delivers one heck of an audio introduction to my novel. I owe a debt of thanks to Jacob Shapiro, who is a tireless and enthusiastic promoter of *Saving Grace*. And kudos to Faceout Studio for designing a stunning cover that perfectly captures my story.

Patrick J. LoBrutto, award-winning editor and book doctor, has been a staunch champion of my work. His guidance has proved invaluable.

Katharine Sands, literary matchmaker, always believed that "the world would one day catch up to my astonishing talent" (her words, not mine).

A special shout-out to the authors and reviewers who took time from their busy schedules to read my debut novel. It's gratifying to know that you enjoyed discovering the world of *Saving Grace* as much I enjoyed writing it.

I'm honored to be a member of these wonderful organizations: International Thriller Writers, an incredibly supportive and welcoming community of authors; Sisters in Crime, whose members are always eager to discover new writers; my fellow authors in the 2021 Debut Group, who make each other feel we are all in this together.

Saving Grace is in memory of my mother Lila, who instilled in me an enduring love of mystery and suspense novels and predicted that I would be published. It happened, mom!

My sister-in-law Lydia is more like a sister to me. I admire her strength, empathy, and ability to triumph over adversity. She will always be one of my first readers.

My husband Ted has been my bastion of support, encouragement, and love. Not only does he have a brilliant legal mind, he knows how to hone in on the essence of a story. Here's to sharing many more fabulous dinners paired with your unerring selection of wine.